Tessa Barclay is a former publishing editor and journalist who has written many successful novels, among them the four-part Craigallan saga (*A Sower Went Forth*, *The Stony Places*, *Harvest of Thorns* and *The Good Ground*), the Wine Widow trilogy (*The Wine Widow*, *The Champagne Girls* and *The Last Heiress*) and the Corvill weaving saga (*A Web of Dreams*, *Broken Threads* and *The Final Pattern*), *A Professional Woman*, *A Gleam of Gold*, *A Hidden Beauty* and *Her Father's Child*. She lives in south-west London.

Praise for previous novels:

'A compelling novel of a life split between love and honour, work and home'   *Publishing News*

'Powerfully plotted and well-written'   *Daily Mirror*

'Takes up where Cookson left off'   *Glasgow Herald*

'Lots of intriguing detail'   *The Sunday Times*

'Filled with fascinating historical detail and teeming with human passions'   Marie Joseph

'[Tessa Barclay] always spins a fine yarn'
Wendy Craig

The Millionaire's Woman

Tessa Barclay

HEADLINE

First published in 1995
by HEADLINE BOOK PUBLISHING

First published in paperback in 1996
by HEADLINE BOOK PUBLISHING

10 9 8 7 6 5 4 3 2

ISBN 0 7472 5006 5

Typeset by
Letterpart Limited, Reigate, Surrey

Printed and bound in Great Britain by
BPC Paperbacks Ltd

HEADLINE BOOK PUBLISHING
A division of Hodder Headline PLC
338 Euston Road
London NW1 3BH

The Millionaire's Woman

Chapter One

The room crackled with tension. Ruth Barnett stood by the door, her shabby suitcase at her feet.

'Well, if you go, you needn't think you can come back any time you want,' her grandfather said, glaring at her through his wire-rimmed glasses. 'You leave this house now, you leave it for good.'

'Now, Granddad,' sighed his wife. Mrs Barnett sent a pleading glance at her granddaughter. 'It's only one of her notions – she doesn't really mean it. You don't, now do you, Ruthie?'

'Yes, I do.' Though the rounded chin trembled, the voice was firm. 'I've been offered a job and I'm going to take it.'

'You've *got* a job.'

'Oh, yes, eight shillings a week selling tape and safety pins, advising women who don't have the least idea about style which paper pattern will make them look like Mary Pickford.'

'That's no way to talk! Mr Colmer was very good to take you on, and he told me he often had to check you because you got impatient with customers.'

'Grandma, Mr Colmer was glad to have me because at least I could balance the till at the end of the day! How he

1

ever manages to stay in business I'll never know.'

'And now you're just leaving him in the lurch! Ruthie, is that any way to repay his kindness?'

Ruth Barnett shrugged. She'd known her decision to leave home was going to cause a row. Her grandparents were set in their ways, sure that the world began and ended at the boundaries of Freshton – well, no, perhaps they had to admit there were people living and working in Brooklands eight miles off, and perhaps even that a great town like Woking actually existed although they'd never had any wish to go there.

She had to leave. No matter how it hurt and shocked them, she had to leave home. Ever since she'd left school at fifteen she'd known that Freshton was a prison. She felt like a lark in a cage, fluttering its wings, longing to be free. Day after day at the silly, mind-numbing jobs that were all the village had to offer: tally girl on Mr Mellison's poultry farm, waitress at the Bull, and then – success, the pinnacle of employment in Freshton – a nice respectable job in a shop. There were few shops in Freshton, and since they were almost all family-run fewer paid jobs in them.

She let the immediate past flit through her mind as she stood, silent, by the door. A little over medium height, slender of wrist and ankle, her body was a little ill at ease in her Sunday-best clothes. Her grey-green eyes looked out from under the brim of her cloche hat, regret and pity deepening their colour. Her short light brown hair was tucked well into the hat with only two little waves spilling down on her cheeks. Her face was solemn: the vivacity and enthusiasm were missing, the liveliness that usually lifted it out of the merely pretty into the remarkable.

She was wearing her Sunday best for two good reasons. First, she was going to London – and everyone knew that

London was the centre of sophistication. Second, she had only this one old suitcase, dragged down from the loft. So to have room to pack the remainder of her clothes, she had to wear her home-made suit of dark blue barathea and her blouse with the embroidery on the collar.

The suitcase had belonged to her mother. Her mother – how long would it be before her grandfather dragged in her name? Norma Barnett, the shame of the Barnett family, the daughter whose wickedness could always be held up as a warning.

'I should never have allowed you to go to that racing track,' declared Granddad, hitting the parlour table with a gnarled hand. 'I should have put my foot down—'

'Granddad, there's nothing wrong with watching cars race—'

'Inventions of the devil!'

'Granddad, how can you say that! You know you rely on Pripitt's motor lorry to deliver your plants when it's too far for—'

'Pripitt drives at a reasonable speed. The Lord never intended men to whizz round a racetrack at seventy miles an hour—'

She didn't tell him that the drivers whizzed round at considerably more than seventy. 'Yes, he did, or how could it be happening?' she riposted. 'What makes you think you know what the Lord intended? You always start talking like that when you haven't got a proper argument—'

'Ruth!' Mrs Barnett threw up her hands. 'Ruth, child, that's no way to talk to your grandfather—'

'Then why does he go on at me like an Old Testament prophet? Good heavens, this is 1923 – the big towns are full of motorcars, even the post is delivered to our Post

3

Office in a van – more than that, liners are crossing the ocean in five days, aeroplanes are taking people to France—'

'France? What's France got to do with it?' Roger Barnett roared, so loud that the crystal pendants on the mantelpiece vases shivered. 'You hold your tongue, my girl, and don't talk nonsense! I'm telling you that all this uppity rubbish about needing a wider view of the world than just Freshton only started when you got bedazzled with all them silly cars whizzing round going nowhere at Brooklands, and what's more, that's where you met this *man!*'

'Yes, Ruthie,' his wife took it up. 'You can't deny you would never have met this man if you hadn't been hanging around Brooklands.'

'Stop calling him "this man"! He's got a name! His name's Ethan Coverton!'

'And he's old enough to be your father,' wailed Mrs Barnett. She began to cry, tears welling up in her faded blue eyes to trickle over cheeks wrinkled by too much exposure to wind and sun in their little nursery garden, by too much carbolic soap and hard water night and morning.

'Now, now, Grandma, don't cry,' Ruth said, hurrying to put an arm about her. She was a little taller than Mrs Barnett so that she was able to bring the moist cheek against her barathea jacket and pat the trembling shoulders.

'Cry she must and cry she will,' declared Granddad, 'unless you get the better of this silly notion and unpack that suitcase at once!'

'Yes, Ruthie, be sensible,' urged Grandma, drawing a little away and gazing up into her granddaughter's face.

Usually when Grandma resorted to tears, Ruth's efforts

4

at rebellion broke down. The row over her first pair of artificial silk stockings, the row over taking out a subscription to the *Autocar* – Grandma had won such tussles by crying a little. But today was different. Today Mrs Barnett could see from under her tear-rimmed lashes that the laughing, loving girl seemed to have a touch of steel in her.

'I *am* being sensible,' Ruth said. 'I've been offered a job in London and I'm going to take it. If I don't, I'll spend the rest of my life mouldering away in this cramped little hole—'

'Oh, so that's the way you speak of the house where we've given you shelter since you were a baby!' Granddad's red face grew even redder, his white moustache bristled. 'Not good enough for you after you've hob-nobbed with them rich madmen on the racing track.'

'Granddad, I didn't mean the house, I meant the village—'

'And what's wrong with Freshton, pray?'

'It's stultifying, that's what—'

'Stultifying? What the devil does that mean? Where d'you get these swanky words you keep coming out with? By the Harry, I should have knocked all that out of you while you were still a toddler! But no, you'd always have to come back with something else – always had to show you were a cut above, with your nose in a book and your thoughts in the clouds. I should have seen all this coming. You're going the way your mother went.'

Here it came. Your mother . . .

Grandma sat down, covered her face with her handkerchief and began to cry in earnest. She almost always cried when her daughter Norma was mentioned.

'A shame and a disgrace to us,' Mr Barnett stated. 'I've

told you a thousand times that you had to walk with care, because of the way your mother went.'

'Oh, yes,' agreed Ruth. And for the first time she allowed the full bitterness to flood into her voice. ' "You can't go into Woking, that's how your mother started. You can't have money for magazines, they put wrong ideas into your mother's head." I know it all by heart.'

'But do you *take* it to heart?' cried Granddad. 'Do you pay any heed? Selfish, wrong-headed—'

'Selfish? How dare you say I'm selfish? I'm nineteen years old and I've never had more than two shillings' pocket money—'

'You've always had food in your belly and clothes on your back! Don't forget we could have refused to take you in when your mother came creeping back here with you in her arms and no ring on her finger; we could have shut the door on her—'

'Maybe you should have,' cried Ruth, her eyes glinting with anger. 'Maybe if she'd been somewhere else she'd have got proper attention and lived to face you out. But no, she died and you've been able to name-call her ever since—'

'I wouldn't *put* a name to her,' shouted Granddad. 'Words like that never pass these lips. But she brought shame to this house and we've had to bear it—'

'*You've* had to bear it? *I've* had to bear it! Frosty looks from teachers at school, taunts from the other kids – if you wouldn't use the word, they weren't shy of it. Bastard, that's what they called me – and that's why I'm longing to get out of here,' Ruth ended, with a sudden gesture that took in the cluttered parlour, the starched lace curtains, the polished brass fender in front of the empty grate.

'Ruthie,' said her grandmother, 'Ruthie . . . I know,

dearie, I know . . . It's been hard sometimes . . . But you can't go to London, my love. You know what happened to your mother when she went there.'

'Oh, for goodness sake, that was different! Grandma, you know it was different. She went with a man because she'd fallen in love.'

'Huh!' grunted her grandfather. 'She certainly didn't have your brains or she'd have known he was a waster just by looking at him! A theatrical!'

'He probably seemed like a denizen of another world to her,' Ruth said.

'Denizen – denizen – why can't you talk English? He was a smarmy Sam who abandoned her the minute she got pregnant, as was only to be expected. And if you think this Arthur Coverton—'

'Ethan – Ethan Coverton,' she corrected. 'And it's nothing like that. He's simply offered me a job in his office—'

'That's what he says,' sobbed Mrs Barnett, 'but we all know he's got other ideas.'

Ruth didn't reply because the words that sprang to her mind were, 'I wouldn't mind if he had.' But, alas, she knew it wasn't so. Ethan Coverton – rich, brave, influential, a power in the land – such a man could have no romantic interest in a country girl like Ruth. He'd never seen her except in either a worn tweed skirt and a print blouse or in borrowed overalls. To him she was just another pair of hands to help roll the racing car to the grid, another voice to shout and cheer as the Coverton III took the lead at the Railway Straight.

Her grandparents were right. If she'd never become enthralled with the racing cars at Brooklands, she'd never have met Ethan Coverton. And if she'd never met him she wouldn't be leaving home now.

She met her grandmother's shrewd glance and flinched. Mrs Barnett shook her head.

'I don't understand you,' she said. 'If he were a dashing young man like that Oliver Whoever-he-was of your mother's, I could see a reason. But, Ruthie, he must be fifty if he's a day!'

Yes, fifty. Or rather, according to what she'd learned, fifty-one. Tall, still blond-headed although there was some silver among the Viking thatch, vigorous, vital – and brave, brave enough to drive his own racing cars whenever he got the chance. Pushing the speed up, past eighty, past ninety. Laughing with delight when the stopwatch showed he'd equalled the younger men who drove in the races. A real man, a fine man, whatever his age might be.

But that was simple hero worship. She knew nothing could ever come of it. He was who he was – Ethan Coverton, owner and managing director of the Coverton Electrical Company – and she was the granddaughter of a nursery gardener in a small village in Surrey.

But not after today. After today she'd be a London office girl with a life of her own and freedom to pursue it. She'd always known she wasn't meant to spend her life in Freshton and settle down with some farm labourer or roofer or house decorator. She'd always been 'different' – not only because she was born the wrong side of the blanket. No, because she was clever, ten times as clever as any child in her class. Too clever for her own good, the schoolmistress had warned her, vexed that the child could outthink her on almost any subject.

Scholarships – at one time there had been talk of scholarships. But Granddad had recoiled in horror from the idea. It would have meant letting her go to board at a school twenty miles away – over his horizon, in unknown territory. No, no, not after what happened to Norma. Norma's illegitimate child must be stay-at-home where he could keep an eye on her.

To no avail. He looked at her now, starry-eyed at the mere thought of this rich Londoner and the job he'd offered. It was hopeless. He could drag her upstairs and lock her in her room, but she'd only climb out the window on to the outhouse roof and be off down the road. And what a scandal that would cause.

No, if she was bound and determined to go, let her. Straight to the bad, like her mother.

'Very well,' he said on a harsh, heavy note. 'Go if you must, you silly, wicked girl. But don't ever think we'll take you back—'

'I wouldn't want to come back!' she flashed. 'D'you think it's enticing? D'you think I've loved every minute of my life here? The women and their snooty looks, the men with their knowing winks? A bunch of narrow-minded blockheads, that's what they are, and I've had my fill of their sneers and jeers! I'm glad to leave and if I never see the place again that'll be too soon!'

'Ruth Barnett, you should be ashamed of yourself,' wept her grandmother. 'After all we've done for you . . .'

To Ruth's own surprise, her anger died suddenly. She felt a qualm. Poor Grandma, poor kind old woman. 'I'm sorry, Grandma. Maybe I didn't mean all that. But I'm going.'

Marion Barnett sighed and nodded. 'You've always been a handful,' she murmured. 'But you're making a mistake, Ruthie – no good can come of this.'

'I'll take that chance.' She glanced at the old clock on

the parlour mantelpiece. 'I'll have to go if I'm to catch that train.'

'Well, go, nobody's stopping you,' her grandfather said and walked past her out of the room.

With a shrug she picked up her suitcase and followed him out into the little hall. But there, instead of turning as he did, towards the back of the cottage and the nursery ground beyond, she opened the heavy front door. No one ever used the front door, everyone always walked round to the back of the cottage so as to come in through the kitchen. The front door was for ceremonial occasions – weddings, funerals.

And in a way this was like a funeral – the ending of a life.

As she stepped out onto the main street of the village, Marion Barnett caught her elbow. 'Take care, Ruthie.'

'I've left my new address on my dressing shelf.'

'I don't know whether I ought to write.' Her grandmother twisted her hands in the skirt of the big apron she always wore on weekdays.

For a moment Ruth was about to beg. But then her anger took over again. 'Please yourself,' she said.

From the back of the house came Roger Barnett's voice as he leaned in at the kitchen door. 'Are you going to get me my tea, woman, or am I to starve?'

'I've got to go, Ruth. Goodbye, dear, and good luck.'

'Goodbye, Grandma.'

The oak door closed. Curtains twitched in the house across the village street. Hefting her suitcase, Ruth Barnett set off for the little station.

Because for some reason railway builders had decided that stations mustn't be close to villages, it was a two-mile walk to Freshton Halt. There was a stopping train only three times a day – at five in the morning for the milk and the newspapers, at one in the afternoon for shoppers wishing to go to Woking, and at six in the evening to pick up the mail. It was the six o'clock train that Ruth would catch.

It would get her into London before nine. She was to take the Underground to Earl's Court and there present herself at the Euphemia Grey Hostel for Business Girls, where accommodation had been reserved for her. It was all in the letter she'd received from the Coverton Electrical Company when, at the suggestion of Ethan Coverton, she'd written to the personnel manager applying for a job.

She knew Ethan had given her the chance out of casual interest. There she was, a reasonably pretty girl who'd shown herself to be his greatest fan during the racing season of the past summer. Not a bit like the other women who came to the track. These divided into two categories – wives and sisters who came to cheer on their menfolk, and society or theatre girls who were caught up in the thrill and the glamour of motor racing.

By contrast, Ruth had, no doubt, seemed different. Ruth had no objections to getting her hands dirty. She didn't rush for shelter if it came on to rain. Nor did she scream and faint if a car came to grief. No, Ruth Barnett was someone you could depend on.

In the first place she'd got into Brooklands by accident. Mr Pripitt had had some catering supplies to deliver in his ex-Army lorry to the restaurant at the track and had offered Ruth a lift just for the ride. Extra food was required because a big crowd would come for the first meeting of the spring. She'd helped carry in the trays of locally made cakes and buns.

Then, since Alf Pripitt had accepted a cup of tea and

she was left to her own devices, she sauntered along to the 'paddock'. Visitors weren't allowed, yet no one thought to stop her because somehow she looked as if she belonged.

There were cars being readied in front of the workshops in the paddock. She stood quietly by as they were pushed out to the starting grid. Someone said, 'My goggles?' and she saw them lying on a pile of tyres. She fetched them, handed them to the driver. With a smile he accepted them, put them on, then gave her his cigarette case. 'Hold that for me, lovey, it's digging into me when I change down.'

From that moment she was accepted. Pripitt couldn't drag her away when it was time for him to leave. 'It's all right, I'll give her a lift,' someone said casually, and that was that.

From the very first, it was magic to her. The throb of the engines as they started and idled, the roar as they took the track, the exotic names of the makers – Hispano-Suiza, Alvis, Bugatti, the pale blue Crossley with its big rigid steering wheel and massive levers, the strange shape of the Torpedo Renault—

And the men, the drivers and mechanics – intent on their work, devoted, quick to laugh and just as quick to kick the car when something unexplained spoiled a record attempt – they seemed at once to be her friends, as if she had always been meant to meet them.

She was given the promised lift back to Freshton and a pass that would enable her to get through the gates the following weekend. Her benefactor then was called Jack, just one of many drivers whom she came to know on first-name terms.

It was some weeks later that she met Ethan.

She'd heard him spoken of. He was rich, owner of a big

electrical engineering firm who spent money on financing the building of racing cars. In time past he'd driven in races himself but now, it was said, he'd decided to leave it to the younger men. 'Reflexes not fast enough,' he'd said.

Yet he still loved to take out the Coverton III when he had the chance. On that Saturday morning he had the car on the grid, mechanics standing by grinning, stopwatches in hand.

'All right, Ethan, twice around while the rain keeps off, because I'm not polishing again this morning.'

'Oh, Peter won't mind a speck or two.'

'Yes, I will,' declared Peter Stokes, the official race driver. 'You bring her back as shiny as she goes out.'

'Whose car is this, anyhow?' laughed Ethan.

'You be careful of that gear change,' ordered David Epps, the Coverton mechanic.

'I'll treat the gear change like filigree,' promised Ethan. He dragged his soft leather helmet over his wiry fair hair, gave the bystanders a wink, pulled down his goggles and drove out onto the track.

Ruth loved to watch him drive. She had one or two special favourites among the regulars – some for the delicacy of their touch on the gears, some for the courage of their attack, some for the nicety of their tactics. Ethan Coverton she admired for his panache. A big man himself, he took big chances.

'What's he after today?' she asked the mechanic.

'Somewhere up in the nineties, I think. Nothing much.'

The official starter came wandering up. He wasn't yet on duty. 'Want me to send you out?' he asked Ethan.

'Oh, we're going to get bureaucratic, are we?' called Ethan over the engine's rumble.

'Might as well time it properly.'

'Right. I'm going to do ninety-five, so mind you keep your fingers ready to stop the watch at the mark.'

'If you get spots on that new blue paint I'll throw the watch at you,' shouted the mechanic.

With a grin and a wave, Ethan turned his gaze on Mr Ebblewhite the starter. Ruth realized that it was a tribute to Ethan's importance that Mr Ebblewhite was giving up his time to this unofficial record attempt.

The Coverton III was a version of the Delage straight-eight, a single-seater with no room for a mechanic although many racers still carried one. It was a low-slung chassis, painted a duck-egg blue with the racing number 8 on the sides.

The car was going to take a special circuit comprising the old Finishing Straight and Members' Banking, then the bend under Members' Bridge. The first round, the car zipped past in a haze of blue and a wave from the driver. The second time round it was clear as he approached that Ethan wasn't wasting any thoughts on waving – he was driving for his own personal record.

'By God, that's quick!' cried Peter Stokes. 'He's coming up at damn near a ninety-eight, surely!'

'Nah,' said the mechanic.

Ruth found she was holding her breath. She wanted Ethan to make the beat. She'd heard that in this car he'd so far attained ninety-four point three in good conditions but today, with a faint drizzle coming down and the visibility imperfect, he probably wouldn't make it.

The Coverton III went roaring past. David Epps threw his hand up in the air to click the stopwatch. By some mischance the watch went sailing out of his fingers and into the bushes on the bank.

Everyone gave a shout of dismay. The airstream of the

Coverton was still disturbing the grass, the smell of the Castrol R lingered in the drizzle.

Epps ran off the bridge and onto the bank, scrabbling to find the watch. 'I've got it, I've got it,' he called.

'Fat lot of good that'll do,' grunted Stokes, and walked away in disgust, shrugging his shoulders in his tweed jacket.

Ruth could hear the Coverton growling its way more slowly round the circuit to return to the Old Finishing Straight. Mr Ebblewhite was examining one of the several watches he always carried. 'Did you get it, Mr Ebblewhite?' asked Epps as he regained the vantage point.

'We-ell, yes, but it's not proper time-keeping,' said Ebblewhite. 'What's yours show?'

'Can't tell, the glass got broken.'

The racing car came sweetly up the track and turned into the Old Finishing Straight. Ethan was waving his fist in the air as if he expected a good result.

'Oh, Lor',' muttered Epps.

The long lean legs came out of the cockpit. Ethan shoved his goggles up. 'Well?'

'I'm sorry, sir. I didn't get it.'

'Didn't get it!'

'I dropped the stopwatch – or least it flew out of my hand, sir.'

No camaraderie, no friendly use of his employer's first name. Ruth could tell David Epps was anxious.

'You mean you haven't a figure?'

'I checked it as ninety-four even,' said Ebblewhite.

'Ninety-four!'

'But I didn't line up the markers with any accuracy, Ethan. I just started the watch from force of habit.'

15

'I saw the watch, Mr Coverton,' Ruth volunteered.

'What?'

'I saw it, Mr Coverton.'

'Saw what? Mr Ebblewhite's?'

'No, sir, the mechanic's. Just before he threw it up in triumph to click it. It read ninety-four point eight.'

'Ninety-four point eight?'

'Yes, Mr Coverton.'

'You sure?'

'Yes, Mr Coverton.'

'Davie?'

'I thought it was near that, sir.'

'We wouldn't be just "thinking" it if you'd keep your hands clasped round the watch. What the devil did you think you were doing, throwing it up in the air?'

'Sorry, sir, it just happened.'

'It really did read ninety-four point eight, Mr Coverton.'

'You often do time-keeping?'

'Over somebody else's shoulder – yes, often.'

'So you're by way of being an expert?' he asked with a twinkle in the hazel eyes.

Ruth heard the mechanic give a sigh of relief. No heads were going to roll, it seemed.

'Well, let's take it as ninety-four point eight then. Nothing official in it, anyhow. Good for you, young lady – Miss—?'

'Barnett, sir. Ruth Barnett.'

And that, really, was how their friendship began. And how it came about that he offered her the chance of a job with his firm in London.

Chapter Two

A good thing Ruth was too tired to care about anything when she reached the hostel. She introduced herself to the warden, signed a register, paid and was given a receipt for ten shillings, the cost of a week's board.

Then she was shown upstairs – bathroom, communal kitchenette, bedrooms. A door with a number affixed. She had a vague view of beds but her attention was centred on the one to which she was ushered. Within five minutes she'd washed the surface grime off her face, brushed her teeth, pulled off her clothes and fallen into the deep sleep of exhaustion.

When she woke she couldn't think where she was. The ceiling above her wasn't the low cracked surface of her bedroom. It was high, and had fancy plastering round a central hanging electric light. Below that there were pipes.

Pipes?

She closed her eyes and opened them again. Yes, indeed, pipes, but used to hold curtain rings from which hung print cotton curtains. Round the bed.

I'm in hospital! she thought. I'm ill! I'm dying! – for the curtains were closed.

Oh, God!

She sat up. She felt perfectly well. From beyond the

curtains came a murmur of voices and the sound of a teacup against a saucer.

Definitely a hospital, but she wasn't dying. She got out of bed, pulled open the curtain and looked out.

Three girls in various stages of getting dressed turned at the sound of the curtain rings moving. One was sitting on another bed drinking a cup of tea.

'Morning,' said the tea-drinker. 'How're you?'

Ruth was on the brink of saying, Where am I? But aware that it would make her look a fool, she said instead. 'I'm all right. Who are you?'

'We're your roommates,' said another girl, pausing hairbrush in hand to give her a grin. 'When we came upstairs last night from the common room, we found you spark out in bed with your curtains wide open. So we closed 'em for you, put your suitcase under the bed and your handbag in your locker, and Bob's your uncle.'

'Oh . . .' It began to come back to her. This was the Euphemia Grey Hostel for Business Girls in Earl's Court and today she had an interview with the personnel manager of the Coverton Electrical Company.

She sat on the bed. She was aware that the others were viewing her with interest – not unkind but not committed to liking her. Her nightdress, home-made without a pattern from cotton at sixpence a yard, hung loosely on her body. Her short hair stuck up in spikes. Her mouth felt dry, there was sleep grit in her eyes.

One of her roommates had on a nightgown and matching negligée of artificial silk, very slinky. One was in her underwear – sturdy interlock and bemberg stockings. One was already dressed in a black dress with white collar and cuffs.

Their ages ranged from about twenty to about thirty. It

was the one in the slinky night attire who looked thirty. 'I'm Rosalind,' she said, 'this is Evie and this is Benita. We saw your name added to the door card – Ruth, isn't it?'

'Yes,' said Ruth faintly. She felt unfocused, adrift. Never in her life had she woken up with anyone else in her room, let alone three others. She was sharing a room with three girls? Could it be true?

But what else could you expect for only ten shillings a week?

'Like a cup of tea?'

'Oh, I'd *love* one.'

'Ha'penny,' said Benita, the girl who had been drinking tea when Ruth looked out. 'We share the expense of an early morning cup – make a pot, everybody gets a cup every morning, puts a ha'penny in the jar to pay for the makings.'

Ruth fumbled in her handbag for her purse. Meanwhile Benita poured her tea. It went down her parched throat like nectar.

'Now,' Benita went on, 'the house rules for the mornings. There's two bathrooms on this floor, no one allowed to use them before six a.m. unless they've got a train to catch or something like that – the plumbing makes a terrible row. From six onwards you queue up outside and get ten minutes to make yourself decent. Baths have to be taken at night. Understand?'

'Yes.'

'Breakfast's from seven thirty to eight thirty weekdays, eight to nine on Sundays. Prayers fifteen minutes before breakfast every morning and it stands you in good stead with the warden to turn up two or three times a week. That's enough for now, it's nearly eight o'clock so you'd better get a wiggle on if you're going to queue up and get washed and down to breakfast before the tables are cleared.'

Ruth sought for her watch. It was on the top of the locker. She'd forgotten to wind it. The other girls, having performed introductions and set her on the right path, went about their own affairs.

She queued fifteen minutes for the bathroom. She dressed in a room that had suddenly emptied. She ran downstairs, following the sound of voice until she found the dining room, a big room on the ground floor that had clearly once been a splendid drawing room. Girls sat at long tables. A serving table with a maid behind it offered porridge with syrup, scrambled eggs on toast, pats of margarine, a big jar of marmalade from which you had to lever a spoonful, and tea from an urn.

She found a place between two girls who were just about to leave. The room emptied as she began on the porridge. A big clock showed the hour. She'd have to hurry if she were to make her appointment in Holborn at ten.

'Holborn,' she said to the girl opposite just as she was about to go, 'where's Holborn, please?'

The girl gave her a half-smile. 'New? Where you from?'

'Freshton in Surrey.'

'First time in London?'

First time in a city, thought Ruth in panic. 'Holborn?'

'Take the Underground. The station's five minutes away.'

'Yes, I came from there last night. But it was dark—'

'Out the door, turn right, five minutes' walk. There's a map on the station wall, or ask the ticket man how to get to Holborn.'

'Thank you.'

'Eat up. If you don't, Sadie will come and clear your scrambled eggs from under your nose at eight thirty sharp.' With a nod and a wave, the other hurried out.

Ruth didn't quite believe her but it proved to be true. Just as she was finishing the scrambled eggs and about to turn to the toast and marmalade, a wrinkled maidservant whipped them away with all the other crockery left on the table.

Well, it didn't matter. She was too nervous to eat more anyway.

By nine o'clock she was on her way to Earl's Court station. She was once again wearing the dark blue barathea suit but with a fresh blouse – what happened about doing personal laundry, she wondered? She'd find that out this evening together with all the other information she needed for hostel living. Laundry would be important because she only had a small supply of clothes.

She only got lost twice in the Underground system. She came out at Holborn into a noisy, busy traffic junction. She looked at the address on the letter: 185 High Holborn. Inspection of the name boards showed she had to turn right. She did so, and walked for a long time past shops and office buildings and the openings to lawyers' chambers. There were more shops and offices in this one street than in the whole of Woking, the only town she'd ever been in.

It was a fine October day, but to Ruth the air seemed heavy and without vigour. She was to find she got used to it quite soon, but at first it seemed so different from the breezes blowing through Freshton that it made her feel almost listless. The dirt surprised her. She'd thought that in a city, with paved roads and cement pavements, there would be no dust and grit. But on the ledge of every shop window, in the folds of the togas of the statues, on the brackets of the streetlamps, on every handrail and handle, there was sticky grit. Litter blew along the gutters, the noise was unceasing, and she had a headache.

In the end she found the address. By that time she'd passed another Underground station and realized she should have got out at Chancery Lane instead of Holborn. The head office of Covelco, the Coverton Electrical Company, was an Edwardian building of grey stone, well kept, imposing. The doorman in a black uniform piped with blue sent her to the reception desk. There a forbidding lady with her hair in a bun checked by means of a sort of voice box before giving her a chit: 'Interview with Mr Daniels, Room 114, ten a.m.'

She took the lift to the first floor as instructed, turned left, counted along to Room 114, knocked and went in. Mr Daniels's secretary nodded at her to go in. She walked across the outer office to the farther door.

There she stopped. Her head was pounding. She'd never been in a building this size before, never gone up in a lift, never seen a secretary let alone a personnel manager.

I don't want to do this, she thought. I want to go home!

She must have knocked on the door for a voice called 'Come in.' Too dazed and confused to disobey, she entered.

She could never remember the interview afterwards. She must have handed over her school certificates because later the manageress of the filing office mentioned something about the school prizes she'd won.

It appeared she was qualified to be a filing clerk. She found herself in the lift going up to the third floor.

Someone else in the lift got out when she did and pointed her in the right direction. This door said 'Filing Department: Enter and Ring.'

The bell brought a young man to a window. He slid back the glass. 'Yes?'

She looked at the new chit she held in her hand. She couldn't read it, everything was a blur. She handed it to the young man. He stretched out an arm protected by a glazed cotton sleeve guard. 'Huh? Oh, yes, to see Miss O'Keefe. Just a minute.'

He disappeared. A moment later a door opened in the wooden partition. He gestured her to follow him. She went with him down avenues of filing cabinets and plan cupboards. At a large desk to one side, he paused. 'Miss O'Keefe, a new arrival.' He handed her the chit which he'd taken from Ruth before leaving.

'Ah? Let me see.' Miss O'Keefe examined the chit. 'Ah . . . Ruth Barnett . . . age nineteen . . . no qualifications . . . This is your first job?'

Ruth could see something was expected of her. But her tongue seemed to have stuck to the roof of her mouth.

'Miss Barnett? Pay attention.'

Ruth nodded. She gathered herself together. She must speak, she must respond. No matter that the blacksmith pounding the anvil inside her head made concentration difficult, no matter that the scrambled egg breakfast seemed to be on the verge of leaving her.

'Your hours here are from nine to five thirty Monday to Friday, nine to one on Saturdays. There is a one-hour break for lunch which can be taken any time between twelve and two but there is a rota which you must abide by. There is a ten-minute break for afternoon tea at four o'clock. Your salary will be eighteen shillings and sixpence a week, paid on Fridays. You must sign a guarantee of confidentiality, because the documents that come to this department can be very important. Do you understand?'

'Yes, Miss O'Keefe.'

'Overalls are supplied by the company. It also supplies subsidized meals in the canteen in the basement and free medical attention by a nurse on the fourth floor. There is a rest room for the female staff also on the fourth floor. There is a shopping scheme whereby, if you subscribe, you can achieve considerable savings at certain stores such as Swan and Edgar, Gamages, and so on. Here is a leaflet which gives details of that and other benefits. Is that clear?'

'Yes, Miss O'Keefe.'

Instructions and information followed one after the other. She said she understood whenever she was asked although much of it passed her by. She was asked to sign the declaration, which she did. She was given a key for a personal locker.

Miss O'Keefe then surveyed her with her head a little on one side. 'Is something wrong?'

'I . . . I have a headache. It's the . . . the noise. I'm not used to it.'

Miss O'Keefe dropped her eyes to Ruth's employment sheet. 'Freshton, Surrey,' she murmured to herself. A faint softening might have been observed in the line of her mouth. She too had once been new in London, straight off the boat from Ireland.

'Well,' she said, 'let's see, it's Friday, and just past eleven. I'll let you be going up to Nurse for something for the headache and then perhaps you'd like to go home and take it easy for the rest of the day. It would be quite a good thing to start with a half-day to get yourself run in, so you'll present yourself tomorrow, Saturday, at nine sharp.'

'Yes, Miss O'Keefe.'

The nurse, formidable in a stiffly starched cap and a blue dress the colour of the piping on the doorman's uniform, gave Ruth something to drink from a tiny glass. It tasted vile. She lay down, as instructed, for half-an-hour. She fell into a light doze. When she awoke she felt better.

'All right, now?' asked Nurse Linley when she sat up. 'Good. Now off you go, and you should be just in time to get lunch in the canteen before the crowd gets there.'

'Thank you.'

In the canteen there was a strong smell of lentil soup. Alternatively the menu offered stew, fish cakes, a choice of vegetables, date pudding and custard or jelly with cream. Ruth didn't feel up to any of it. The plump lady serving behind the counter advised a roll and butter and a cup of coffee. The roll was crisp, the butter was real butter, but the coffee was poor. Ruth had never had coffee before so she didn't know the difference.

She spent the rest of the day wandering around Holborn and then Oxford Street, trying to get her bearings. Nothing she had read had prepared her for the sheer size of London. She was sure she'd walked most of the way back to Earl's Court when she got to Marble Arch but not so, the journey back on the Underground took just as long.

It was just after five when she got to the hostel. The house was already filling up with girls home from work. She went up to the room she shared with Benita, Evie and Rosalind. She unpacked her clothes, hung them in the narrow compartment of the communal wardrobe that was allotted to her. She ran a bath – oh, marvel, a stream of piping hot water gushed into the tub when she turned on the tap, quite unlike the rusty trickle that emerged from the tap at home.

The house rules were tacked up on the inside of the dormitory door. No smoking, cooking must only be undertaken on the gas ring in the kitchenettes, the meter for the gas ring must not be clogged up with tokens or other inappropriate items but was for pennies only, the laundry room was open from six thirty to eight a.m. and from six p.m. until lights out in the evening. Lights out was at ten thirty except on Saturdays when it was extended to eleven. The fire exit on each floor must be kept clear. Sanitary towels must be put in the bins provided and not flushed down the lavatory. The nearest Anglican church was St Barnabas, the nearest Catholic church was Queen of Heaven.

A long list, but she knew she'd become familiar with it in a day or two.

She no longer wanted to go home. It was all so interesting, so challenging. And once she started work at Coverton Electrical, she'd see Ethan.

Not at all. Though she eagerly looked out for him next day there was never a sight of him. Nor on the following Monday – and it dawned on her that he was never going to cross her path. The building was much bigger than anything she'd envisaged, and, moreover, the executive offices were in a separate wing reached by a separate entrance. She wouldn't even have a glimpse of him in the entrance hall.

Even if he had used the same entrance as Ruth, she still

26

wouldn't have seen him. For Ethan Coverton was at his desk in his office at Covelco by seven thirty most mornings, and seldom left before eight at night.

There were two things in his life that made it worth living. One was the business – inherited but built up by him to a powerful enterprise. The other – the other was not, as interviewers always seemed to expect, his family, a wife and three grown children. In interviews he always avoided talking about his family. The second great interest in his life was racing cars.

Whenever he was absent from his office for a day or two, whenever he went abroad, it was to watch racing cars. There had been a time when he himself had driven the Coverton cars – he'd raced the first one and then the Coverton II. But after a couple of spills, one of them quite bad and due to his own misjudgment, he felt it best to leave the races to the young lions. Old lions like himself could find their excitement in practice runs.

The Berlin Circuit, the Targa Florio Road Race, the Grand Prix at Rheims – he went to support his drivers, to cheer his winners and console his losers. Brooklands saw him most often. Easy to get to, informal yet efficient.

It was at Brooklands he'd met Ruth. Nice kid, a lot more sense to her than his own daughter Lorette, who didn't know a brake pedal from a wheel disc. Not even his sons showed any interest. Antony thought car racing was a distraction from the serious matter of making money. Martin, God help him, wanted to be a playwright. As to his wife Diana— Well, the less said about Diana the better.

Ethan hadn't exactly forgotten that he'd offered Ruth Barnett a job. On a day early in October it had crossed his

27

mind that that eager child from Brooklands might have taken up his offer.

'Ring Personnel, Miss Krett, and see if they've heard from a Miss Ruth Barnett,' he said.

With a set to her lips intimating that she disapproved, she put through the call. 'Daniels,' said the personnel manager.

'Have you had a letter from Miss Barnett?' Miss Krett inquired.

'Barnett, Barnett— Lizzie, have we had a letter from Miss Barnett?' A pause and an exchange of words off-line. 'No, Miss Krett, is it someone in particular you were expecting?'

'Not at all,' said Miss Krett. Managing directors should not take a personal interest in members of the junior staff. She went into her employer's office. 'Nothing from Miss Barnett, sir,' she reported.

He shrugged. Too big a step for her, he supposed. He'd thought that she was wasted in her poky little village, and that she deserved a chance. But it seemed he'd misjudged her.

He'd felt a kindly interest. Or was it something more? Just as well she'd let the offer go. She was young enough to be his daughter. There were plenty of women he could turn to for consolation – no need to get involved with an innocent country girl.

Three days later Ruth's letter arrived. By that time Mr Daniels, who wasn't the most efficient man in the world, had forgotten Miss Krett's inquiry.

Ruth soon got the measure of her job in the Filing Department. In her grey overall piped with Coverton blue, she trotted between the lines of cabinets and the plan cupboards.

She pushed a trolley with blueprints and copies of patents from one end of the long room to the other, pausing en route to stack them where they belonged. She went to the same cupboards and cabinets to unearth papers needed in the design offices or the legal department.

It was as dull as watching grass grow.

Within two weeks she'd realized she must do something to get out of the Filing Department. Her colleagues seemed for the most part content to stay there: sedate, finicky, unambitious. But Ruth found herself thinking: if I'm ever going to see Ethan, it won't be from Filing. In chats over the canteen lunch she'd learned that the executive suite was in a separate wing, that Mr Coverton only appeared in the main building at retirement parties or Christmas celebrations.

Walking in Holland Park on a Sunday at the end of October, she came to a decision. She'd been a fool to imagine she would be in daily contact with Ethan Coverton. She'd had no idea of the size of his organization. Now she knew, and she must give up all the girlish dreams of being in contact.

She would moulder away to paper dust in the Filing Department. She had to get out. And the only way to do that was to acquire some qualifications.

She went back to the hostel to borrow Saturday's evening paper from Rosalind. There she found advertisements for secretarial classes in the evening. They were expensive – thirty shillings for a course of twenty lessons. But she had some money saved from her Freshton days, and it was worth it.

She began classes on the Wednesday. Wednesday evening was shorthand, Friday was typing, Monday was book-keeping.

She'd always been good with her hands. Typing was no problem. Nor was book-keeping, because once you'd grasped that for every entry there had to be a counterbalancing entry, it was simply a matter of organization and accuracy. Shorthand was more trouble. For weeks she kept putting the wrong hooks in the wrong positions. And then one day it suddenly happened – she found herself making outlines without hesitation as the teacher droned out dictation at the rate of about forty words a minute. It was perhaps what it would be like to learn a foreign language – you had to stop translating it in your head before you wrote it down, you had to *think* in shorthand.

Christmas came. There was a concert in the office canteen presented by talent drawn from the staff. The standard was surprisingly high, the costumes bought and paid for by Covelco's Social Fund. There was a Christmas party, with balloons and cake and fruit punch and one of the sales staff as Father Christmas. A present for everyone – Ruth got a pretty scarf of artificial silk. Covelco liked to look after its workers.

Most of the other girls in the hostel went home or to friends for Christmas. Ruth and five other girls were left to celebrate on their own. But the warden and assistant warden of the Euphemia Grey put on a decent show – stems of holly in vases on the dining-room table, wellbrowned capon served with all the trimmings, Christmas pudding and mince pies.

Ruth had sent a Christmas card to her grandparents. Very late – well after the beginning of 1924 – a card arrived from Freshton, signed only by her grandmother. Sighing, Ruth put it in her bedside locker.

'Boyfriend trouble?' asked Rosalind kindly, looking up from manicuring her nails.

'No, nothing like that.'

'He's not worth looking sad over,' Rosalind said, disbelieving her. Rosalind was the kind who thought the only trouble in life came from men.

But he is, thought Ruth, her mind wandering to Ethan Coverton. There had been a little piece about him in the papers yesterday: he'd been in South America to attend some race meeting in Buenos Aires. The Coverton III had put up an unofficial record for the track, '. . . but not much should be read into this,' said the reporter, 'since the track is not ready to run Grand Prix events as yet. Coverton is quoted as saying his design team are doing preliminary research for a Coverton IV.'

It must be wonderful to be part of his team, thought Ruth. Always forward-looking, always planning improvements. Not settling down in a pile of old documents.

But she hoped soon to escape the Filing Department. Seven weeks after she began her secretarial course she had passed the exams that gave her certificates to offer employers: shorthand at a hundred words a minute, copy-typing at sixty words a minute, book-keeping up to School Leaving Certificate Lower Level. She was the only one in her evening class who'd worked hard enough on her own to reach this standard – most of the others were signing on for a second course. Ruth couldn't afford to do that. She'd got at least something: not much, but a springboard.

She took her new certificates to the personnel office. 'Thank you,' said Mr Daniels's assistant, 'those will be most useful. Mr Daniels is doing the annual regrading of staff, he has to do it every spring.'

Innocent that she was, Ruth expected to be transferred to some more interesting job by next day, or by the following week at latest. But nothing happened. She was about to go and ask for the return of her certificates so that she could apply elsewhere, when she was sent for.

'Mr Daniels has completed his review of junior staff and wishes me to offer you a job as a typist,' said his assistant, pulling distractedly at a stray lock of hair. 'Here are the conditions of employment. Please read them through and let me know tomorrow whether you wish to take up the offer.'

Ruth read them as she went up to the Filing Department in the lift. Junior copy typist, five shillings more per week, at the same hours and with the same benefits as she now enjoyed.

Somehow she'd imagined herself being upgraded straight into the executive wing. But at least it would get her out of the Filing Department.

So it did. Into the typing pool.

Chapter Three

The typing pool was as big as the Filing Department but had fewer cabinets and more people. Typists were allotted work by the department manageress. A few specialists worked from Dictaphone recordings, popular after it became known that the detective writer Edgar Wallace used the machine. Some girls with good qualifications were sent to fill in for secretaries of executives when they were on holiday or sick.

Most worked from pencilled notes sent down by junior executives, stock controllers, experimental engineers or salesmen from the main offices. There were also formats used as examples for run-of-the-mill letters.

It was dull, but not as dull as the Filing Department. Ruth set herself to earn approval so that she could rise from the lowest levels (replies to letters of general inquiry) to something better.

Miss Myland, the manageress, took note of the perfectly typed letters efficiently produced. A little boost in status was appropriate. Ruth was allowed to type from hand-written notes and then, a big step up, was sent to take dictation from some of the junior executives. No increase in pay came with these responsibilities; but Ruth didn't mind.

There were interests outside the office. With other girls she went to the cinema to see *Robin Hood* with Douglas Fairbanks and Wallace Beery, to the sixpenny gallery of theatres to see musical stars such as Phyllis Dare and Binne Hale. She spent a lot of time walking around department stores looking at fashion, letting the mode of the moment sink into her consciousness – the level of the hemline, the detail of collars and trimmings, the dark glow of colour. Colour wasn't allowed on business days: a black dress with white collar and cuffs or a black skirt and a white blouse – these were *de rigueur*.

At the hostel there was an invited speaker after the evening meal every Wednesday. Sometimes it was a traveller with a projector and slides of African warriors, sometimes a nurse with instructions on how to lead a healthy life (sometimes with veiled hints about birth control). Sometimes a poet would read his verses. Ruth never missed one of the lectures. If a subject interested her she followed it up at the local library. If not, she filed it in the back of her mind. She felt that, after the narrow life of Freshton, she mustn't miss or discard anything until she'd tested its worth.

From time to time there were reliability trials for cars at venues on the outskirts of London. Whenever it was possible to get there by public transport, Ruth went to them. She stood in a howling gale on Croydon Airport to see Windsors, Fiats, Calthorpes and Sunbeams roaring round the perimeter. She went on a *concours d'élégance* near Hampton Court to admire the Hotchkiss limousine, the Delaunay-Belleville saloon, the Rolls-Royce tourer. She gloried in the gleam of the polished brass, the throb of the engines, the smell of petrol and motor oil.

34

And once she glimpsed Ethan Coverton getting out of a Hispano-Suiza.

One day in late June the typing pool was working away at its steady pace. The rattle of the typewriters and the *ching* of the carriage-return was momentarily vanquished by the ring of the telephone on Miss Myland's desk.

She listened for a moment then said, 'Of course, sir. Immediately, sir.'

Everybody was steadily typing on, yet every mind was concentrating on Miss Myland. A request had come through for a temporary secretary. Each of the girls hoped she'd be chosen because it meant a break in routine.

But there were a few particular girls who were usually summoned out of the ranks to meet these requests. And everyone sighed a little when Miss Myland could be seen beckoning to the most senior typist, Doris Dooley.

A colloquy followed at Miss Myland's desk. Out of the corner of an eye, everyone watched. To the general astonishment it could be seen that Doris was shaking her head.

Miss Myland was frowning and insisting.

'No!' exclaimed Doris in a high, scared voice. 'Last time I went he shouted at me and called me an idiot!'

'Miss Dooley,' reproved Miss Myland, 'that's no way to speak—'

'It's true! He marches round and round and up and down behind you so you can't see him and when you query what he's said he loses his temper.'

'Miss Dooley, this is an emergency. Mr Coverton's secretary has fallen and broken her wrist. An immediate replacement—'

'I'm not going!' cried Doris Dooley, retreating to her desk and her typewriter. 'It's not fair to send me!'

In her agitation Miss Myland followed her. 'Now, now, my dear,' she said in a soothing tone, 'you're just having an attack of nerves.'

'So I am, and if you make me go I'll only make a mess of it. I can't *work* if people shout at me.'

'I'll go,' said Ruth.

There was a startled silence.

Miss Myland turned slowly from Doris's desk to frown at the speaker. A girl sitting four desks back – Ruth Barnett. Almost six months in the department – reasonably good certificates to begin with and she'd improved since then.

But not senior enough. She cast her glance around. Miss Olliver – but then she had the whole of that scientific summary to finish. Miss Ewbank – but she was a Dictaphone specialist and would be needed.

Ruth was already rising from her chair. She knew this was the moment of decision. Once let Miss Myland's eye light on someone more suitable and the chance would be gone. She gathered up notebook, pencils, handbag and looked expectantly at the department manageress.

'Mr Coverton is a demanding man,' Miss Myland said. 'I think perhaps Miss Netty would be—'

'I'm typing up Miss Moore's letters from yesterday's dictation,' confessed Alice Netty with a shrug. 'I don't think anyone else could read my shorthand.'

Miss Myland stifled a sigh. She would go herself, but who would control the department? She knew that the moment she left the room the girls would start to gossip and waste time.

'Very well,' she said to Ruth. 'You can go for the time being. As soon as Miss Netty's finished I'll send her through to take your place.'

'Very well, Miss Myland.' Ruth kept her head bent as she walked between the rows of desks to the door. A smile was pulling at her lips. She was going to see him. No matter if he shouted at her or treated her like a nincompoop, she'd be in the same room with him, perhaps for as long as half-an-hour.

Before she went down in the lift to walk through to the executive wing, she went to the cloakroom. Her dress was the required black, made on the hostel sewing machine from a McCall's pattern – slender, coming to just below the knees. It was trimmed with collar and cuffs of machine-made lace, less severe than the plain linen or piqué favoured by others for ease of laundering. She was wearing artificial silk stockings and black shoes with a button-strap, the most expensive shoes she'd ever owned, ten shillings and sixpence in Barker's sale.

As for the body within these trappings, it was thinner than when she'd lived in the country. Hard work, constant activity and hostel food had fined her down. Her hair was better cut than formerly: London hairdressers were a lot better than the barber shop in the village. As to make-up, she still hadn't confidence enough to use it except for the faintest brush of powder.

She knew she fell a long way short of the smart girls she saw each morning in the hall hurrying to their secretarial jobs on the lower floors. But she didn't suppose for a minute that her appearance would matter. If Ethan even remembered her, she'd be surprised.

She made her way to the other wing of Covelco's building. In its reception area a clerk manning a switchboard checked that she was expected upstairs. She was directed to the first floor. At the door bearing the sign Managing Director, she knocked and entered.

This was clearly the secretary's office, the outer guard-post to keep the unwanted from bothering the boss. A young woman was seated at the secretary's desk anxiously scanning a telephone book.

'Hello, are you the temp? Thank heaven!' She sprang up, thrusting the telephone book at her. 'You sort it out. Miss Krett's got him down for a lunch at some place in town but had her accident before she got round to booking the table. Too late now; they say they're booked up for today.'

'Yes, Miss—?'

'Giles, I'm Mr Antony's secretary from next door. I've got work of my own waiting for me. And someone's rung from Dartford saying they must see Mr Coverton and he says – Mr Coverton says – he's got to be fitted in somewhere this afternoon.'

As she spoke, the other woman was retreating from the room. One of the phones on the secretary's desk rang. Ruth jumped. Mr Antony's secretary said, 'It's all yours,' and disappeared.

Ruth picked up the phone. She was still rather afraid of telephones. She swallowed hard. 'Mr Coverton's office,' she said.

'Maisie, is that you? Put me through to Mr Coverton, there's a dear.'

'Miss Krett is not here,' said Ruth. 'Who is this speaking?'

'Who's *that?*' said the voice.

'I'm just filling in for Miss Krett. Who is speaking, please?'

'Oh, well, whoever you are, put me through at once. I've got something urgent to say to Mr Coverton.'

Should she? Should she not? The ease of manner seemed to imply that this was someone on very friendly terms with Mr Coverton and his secretary. On the other hand, it might be someone who regularly made a nuisance of himself. And he still hadn't said who he was.

'Who's calling, please?' she asked in a very firm voice.

'Sinclair Adams of Adams Components. Now look here, girlie—'

'I'm sorry, sir,' Ruth said in immediate response to the patronizing tone, 'the office is in some disorder due to Miss Krett being taken ill and I'm afraid this isn't the time to put your call through. I'll let Mr Coverton know you rang. Do we have your number?'

'Now just a minute—'

'I'm afraid I have something urgent to attend to, Mr Adams. I'll tell Mr Coverton you rang.' She put the phone down.

And then suddenly she felt weak at the knees and had to sit down. What had she done? Antagonized a business colleague?

Well, if she had, it was done now. And she must find a restaurant for the lunch. She picked up the phone book and then had a thought. In a drawer she found Miss Krett's personal phone directory. Under 'Restaurants' she saw the name of the one on the scribbled note from which Miss Giles had been working. She dialled the number of the next down. No, alas, said the maître d'hôtel, at this late hour it was useless to hope for a lunchtime table at his fine restaurant. She went on, and at the fourth on the list, to her relief, they had a cancellation and would be glad to fit Mr Coverton in.

'How many covers?' asked the head waiter.

Covers? What were covers? 'Er – four.' She'd no idea how many but if it meant places at table, better have a safety margin.

That done, she had to tell the lunchtime guests. Who were they? In Miss Krett's daybook she found them, two of them as it happened, and their telephone numbers in the telephone list. She rang to tell the secretaries where their employers should go. Now she had to tell Mr Coverton.

With trembling fingers she switched on the intercom.

'Yes?'

'Mr Coverton . . . I'm the replacement secretary . . . I rebooked the lunchtime engagement; it's at La Diadema now.'

'Right, Ring my chauffeur and tell him.' The intercom was switched off.

Chauffeur, chauffeur. Once again it was in the personal telephone directory. The number for the basement garage, the chauffeur's name Bignall. He accepted his instructions without question.

Now what? Someone from Dartford must see Mr Coverton this afternoon. She opened the appointments book. There was something pencilled in every half-hour except for lunchtime, all afternoon until five thirty. Five thirty was the end of the office day for everyone else but it was well known that Mr Coverton and the senior executives often stayed longer. She wrote in at five thirty, 'Dartford visitor.' The man presumably had a name which she could get later from Miss Giles.

The phone rang. She picked it up, announced herself. A rush of hissing sound came and then a voice said, '*Hier spricht Meistbein von Wussterlach AG. Möcht' ich mit Herrn Coverton sprechen?*'

'What?' said Ruth faintly.

The caller patiently repeated the request.

'I'm . . . I'm sorry . . . I can't understand you.'

'This is not Miss Krett speaking?' said the voice in English.

'No, Miss Krett has had a slight accident.'

'Oh, I am so sorry. Please convey to her my kind regards. This is Meistbein of Wussterlach AG in Zürich. May I please speak to Mr Coverton?'

'Kindly hold the line,' said Ruth. She switched on the intercom.

'Yes?'

'Mr Mice-vine of . . . of Voostaly Aggie in Zürich is on the line, sir. Shall I put him through?'

There was a pause. 'Who's that speaking?' asked Ethan Coverton sharply.

'I'm filling in for Miss Krett, sir.'

'Do I know you?'

'I . . . We have met, sir. Ruth Barnett.'

'Barnett? Barnett?' A pause. 'From Brooklands?'

'Yes, sir.'

'What the devil are you doing in my outer office?'

'Filling in for Miss Krett, sir.'

'I suppose you think you are. The name of the caller is Meistbein, not Mice-vine.'

'Yes, sir. He's still holding on, sir. Shall I put him through?'

'Of course put him through, you fool!' The intercom went off.

But how? Ruth looked at the phone. There was a button to press, clearly transferring the call to the desk of the inner office. But should you press the button and replace the receiver, or replace the receiver and press the button? Closing her eyes in something like prayer, she pressed the button while she still held the receiver.

The phone rang in the inner office. She waited for it to

be picked up and, thankfully, heard the men greet each other in German. She replaced the receiver.

The intercom buzzed.

'This is Ellen Giles from next door. Did you solve that restaurant problem?'

'Yes, thank you. What's the name of the Dartford man?'

'Heaven knows, you'd better ring back and find out. Letts, Winckley and Co., wire manufacturers. There was something I forgot to tell you, something about a pass for something. You have to get one – for a car race on Saturday, is it?'

'Oh, yes. That's all right, that's Brooklands, I can deal with that.'

The second phone on the desk rang.

Clearly being a substitute for Miss Krett was no rest cure. The influx of calls and inter-office queries went on until a quarter to one. At that moment the door of the inner office opened and Ethan came out.

Ruth stood up to greet him. She tried not to stare at him, but she wanted to fill her eyes with this view of him. For it might not come again, this chance to see him so close. Miss Netty would probably be here after lunch, shooing her out of the office.

'Well,' he said. 'So you took up that job offer?'

'Yes, sir. Thank you.'

'But you're not a secretary? I thought you told me you had no training.'

'Oh, no, sir. I'm just from the typing pool to fill the gap for the moment.'

'I see. Do you like the typing pool?'

'It's all right, sir. Better than Freshton.'

'Glad to hear it.' He went to the outer door. 'I'll be

back from lunch at two thirty. You'll find some notes on my desk; they're what I want to hand out at the planning meeting this afternoon. Type them up and leave them in the boardroom – there'll only be six people but be sure to make two spares – people draw diagrams on their information sheets and minutes.'

'Yes, sir.'

'Well. Glad to have you in the firm, Miss Barnett.'

'Thank you, sir.'

He smiled, nodded, and strolled out. One o'clock and he was off to lunch. For his secretary there was no such possibility if the notes were to be typed up and taken to the boardroom in time. Presumably there was someone who took phone calls when Miss Krett was out of the office, but who? Having no idea, Ruth could only stay where she was.

The two telephones rang constantly until one thirty, at which hour, it seemed, the rest of the world went to lunch. She went into Ethan's office. The notes were on his desk, scrawled in thin drawing-pen ink. She picked them up and then, greatly daring, went round to the side where Ethan sat.

His chair was buttoned leather with a high back. She touched it, and it swivelled to and fro. She stopped it, set it to face the desk, and then sat in it.

This was where he worked. This was his view of his office – desk somewhat cluttered with rolls of blueprints, an expanse of carpet in the Coverton colours of dark grey and duck-egg blue. Two chairs for visitors, shelves of reference books on engineering. On the walls, photographs of racing cars. Behind her – she swivelled to see – two tall windows with a view on to a garden she hadn't even known existed.

'Who the devil are you?' demanded a voice.

She swung round. A young man in a dark grey worsted suit and a college tie was glaring at her. She sprang to her feet. 'I— I'm the typist filling in for Miss Krett,' she stammered. 'I'm sorry, sir— Did you want something?'

'My father's gone to lunch?'

'Yes, sir.'

There was a faint resemblance – the same fair hair and sharp hazel eyes, but he was less tall and didn't have that attractive outdoors look.

'I'd get back out to Miss Krett's desk and be about your business, if I were you,' he said coldly.

'I'm sorry, sir, I just came in to get some notes Mr Coverton wants typed up—'

'For the meeting?' He nodded to himself. 'Bring a copy next door as soon as you finish them.'

'Excuse me, sir, Mr Coverton told me to put them in the boardroom—'

'Don't be impertinent! You can tell my father when he comes back that I asked for an extra copy.'

'Yes, Mr Coverton.'

'You address me as Mr Antony.' He walked out as suddenly as he'd walked in.

Shaken, Ruth collected up the notes. Mr Antony had been quite right to rebuke her. She had to remember that there was a strict hierarchy in office life and one thing must never happen – office girls must never answer back to their superiors.

Especially not to the boss's son.

He looked to be about twenty-four, young to have earned an office in the executive suite. Well, perhaps not, not if he was the boss's son.

Ruth sighed to herself. There had never been any

mention of his family when Ethan was at Brooklands, nor did the sports pages report their existence when they spoke of the Coverton III's owner. Was Antony his only child? There must, of course, be a Mrs Coverton—

With some interruptions she worked at the notes. No indication was given of how they were to be presented. She drew a deep breath and decided to follow the rules of the typing pool concerning scientific reports – double spacing, wide margins for anyone who wanted to scribble notes, engineering terms underlined and all scientific calculations given special blocks to themselves.

Then she had to find the boardroom. She put her head in next door to ask Miss Giles and to leave the extra copy for Mr Antony. But the office was empty. Yet the boardroom must surely be on the same floor as the managing director's office. She went on along the passage, found it, set out the typed copies by the chairs close to the top of the table.

Then she bethought herself that Miss Krett would probably make other preparations for a meeting. She glanced about, saw a carafe and some glasses. She filled the carafe with fresh water at a cloakroom tap, put it on its tray in the centre of the table. She found pencils in a cupboard. She laid a pencil by every report.

Anything else? Ashtrays – men always wanted to smoke in meetings. She found ashtrays on another shelf in the cupboard together with a handsome cigarette lighter and a box of cigarettes from a Mayfair supplier.

She returned to Miss Krett's office to find both phones ringing. It was after two: the general lunchtime was over. Certainly the canteen in the basement would be closed, yet she hadn't had a bite to eat herself.

No, Miss Krett clearly didn't have an easy life, thought

Ruth. But to be in daily contact with Ethan Coverton – that was compensation enough for anything.

He returned almost exactly at two thirty. As he walked through the outer office he said, 'I ought to have told you, you have to put things out in the boardroom.'

'Yes, sir, I did that, at least I hope I've done everything.'

'You did? Good for you. Now I'm going to the meeting and I hope it'll be over by three. I have an appointment at three so if I'm not back, you'll look after Mr Patterson.'

'Yes, sir. And may I say, sir – there was a Mr Jollife of Letts Winckley and Co. who had to be fitted in   ?'

'Yes?'

'As there was no vacancy I told him you'd see him at five thirty. Was that all right, sir?'

He gave her his brief smile. 'Quite right.'

No one came to relieve Ruth of her secretarial duties. The afternoon wound its way to the tea break. The tea trolley appeared. Ruth, starving from having had nothing to eat since seven thirty, bought two bath buns and a cup of tea.

She was just about to start on them when Miss Myland of the typing pool appeared, greatly agitated. 'May I just have a word with Mr Coverton?'

Ruth looked at the appointment book. 'Someone's just gone but he's got someone else coming in ten minutes. I'll buzz and ask him if it's all right for you to go in.' She felt strange speaking in this way to the manageress of the typing pool but after all she was acting as watchdog to the boss.

'Miss Myland would like a word, sir, if you could spare the time.'

'Who's Miss Myland?' said the voice from the intercom

box. 'Oh, yes, the typing manageress. All right, send her in.'

Miss Myland went in. Ruth was greatly tempted to keep the intercom switched on, but resisted. Miss Myland was certainly here to apologize for not having sent anyone better qualified to replace Ruth, and to say who would come in her stead next day.

In a moment or two Miss Myland opened the inner door and emerged. Behind her came Ethan Coverton, waving her out.

'No, no,' he was saying, 'she's doing all right. I think I'll keep her.'

'Yes, of course, sir, if you wish it,' Miss Myland agreed in a fluster. She nodded at Ruth as she walked to the outer door. 'You'll report directly here tomorrow morning, Miss Barnett.'

'Yes, Miss Myland.'

In a moment she was gone.

Ethan was standing at the door of the inner office. He gave Ruth a grin.

And Ruth, with bath bun crumbs all over her chin, smiled back.

Chapter Four

If Ethan Coverton had an ulterior motive in keeping the Barnett girl in his outer office, he wasn't admitting it to himself.

From time to time her fresh young face had flashed into his mind like some image on a cinema screen, but he'd shrugged it off. He'd done what he could to help her escape from the cage of village life by recommending her for a job: the rest had been up to her.

She'd done well after having been thrown in very much at the deep end. Why not let her enjoy her triumph for a day or so more? he thought. Miss Krett was sure to be back by Friday, if he knew that redoubtable lady.

Sure enough, there she was on Friday, but somewhat later than usual due to problems getting dressed with one wrist in plaster.

'Good morning, Miss Krett,' he greeted her when she buzzed through on the intercom to say she had arrived. 'Please come in.'

She presented herself at once. She was carrying a notebook and pencil in her left hand, expecting to deal with correspondence as usual.

He surveyed her. 'Can you write with your left hand?' he asked.

49

'I've been practising,' she replied with a glint of her steely blue eyes.

'I suppose you have,' was his reply. He should have expected it of her. 'Well, if you feel up to it, let's give it a try.'

He picked up the first of the morning's post. 'This is to Tower Housings Company, see their letter for address etc. Dear Mr Tanvers, Thank you for your letter of 25th June. You are perhaps correct in saying that industrial conferences are not effective, comma, but there seems to be no other way—'

There was a clatter as Miss Krett's notebook slipped off her bony knee to the floor. The effort of holding it steady with her plaster-wrapped right hand while pressing more heavily than usual in an attempt to write left-handed, had ended in the notebook's getting away from her.

Ethan waited until she'd picked it up. 'Perhaps you'd better put your notebook on the desk while you write,' he suggested.

'Thank you, sir.' This she did, but it was a posture she wasn't accustomed to. She'd always written with her notebook on her knee so as to be able to glance up and catch an expression on her employer's face – an important clue as to how he intended his words to be written up. Trying to write left-handed at a different level meant that her speed was drastically reduced. She lost the gist of what he was saying.

'Would you repeat that, sir?'

He broke off. Then he said, 'Read back what I've said.'

'Tower Housing Company, address as letter. Dr Mr Tanvers, Thank you for your letter of 25 June. You are perhaps collected for savings that industry . . . ineffective, comma, but they seem to know their way . . .'

'Well, that doesn't make much sense, does it?' he said, not unkindly.

'I'll get it back all right, sir,' she said. 'My outlines are a bit wobbly.'

'Not only your outlines, I'd say. Now, come on, admit it, Miss Krett, you're not feeling a hundred per cent.'

'I'm quite all right, sir—'

'Not from where I'm sitting.' He got up, came round the desk, and gave a kindly pat to her black-clad shoulder. 'Now be a sensible secretary and get back that kid who was here yesterday and the day before. She can do the chores like dictation and typing, and you can deal with the phone and my engagement book.'

'I'm quite able to—'

'Miss Krett,' Ethan said, in a tone she'd come to know well in her twelve years as secretary, 'get back the girl from the typing pool and divide up the work between you to the best advantage. Is that clear?'

'Yes, sir.'

'And don't sulk about it, Miss Krett. If you do I'll send you home to sit about and annoy your mother.'

Miss Krett, who was the middle-aged and only daughter of a demanding widowed mother, admitted defeat.

Ruth was truly astonished to be summoned up to Miss Myland's desk. She thought for a minute she was going to get a lecture about her work but couldn't think of anything she'd done wrong so far this morning.

'Mr Coverton's secretary has rung through to say she requires an assistant while her wrist mends, and since you apparently acquitted yourself reasonably well yesterday and the day before, she's suggested taking you on for a week or two,' Miss Myland told her.

'A week or two!'

'You'd better hand over those sales tallies to Miss Royce.'

'Yes, Miss Myland.'

'Well, don't just stand there, child – hurry along!'

She didn't need a second prompting. She gathered her belongings, made a hasty visit to the cloakroom to make sure she was tidy and practically ran all the way to the executive wing.

Miss Krett greeted her with muted enthusiasm. 'You can't share this office, there isn't a second desk. Further along the passage there's a desk available in the Advertising Department – I've inquired, and you can have that. But at the moment you'd better go straight in to Mr Coverton; he has letters waiting and I can't take them.'

'Of course, Miss Krett. I hope you're not in too much pain from your wrist?'

Miss Krett, who was in considerable pain, snapped, 'No, not at all, I'm fine.'

'And I'd like to thank you for giving me this chance.'

'Don't thank me yet,' returned Miss Krett. 'You might get by while Mr Coverton was making allowances for your inexperience, but *I* have a different outlook.'

'I'll do my best,' Ruth said humbly. In the office hierarchy, Miss Krett came only second to the male executives. Miss Krett was the power behind the throne of the managing director.

At a nod from her, Ruth tapped on the inner door and went in. Ethan was reading through his correspondence. He looked up and she thought there was the faintest hint of conspiracy in the way he greeted her – a mere glance and a lift of the eyebrow, but it seemed to her to have a message.

'Are you ready?' he said. 'Tower Housings Company,

and that's housings, not housing, Miss Barnett. Address as letter. Dear Mr Tanvers, Thank you for your letter of 25 June . . .'

It became an established routine, and went on beyond the expected two weeks because Miss Krett's wrist didn't mend readily. Every morning first thing there was dictation. Then she retired to her desk in the Advertising Department to type the letters. They were on Ethan's desk by after lunch for signing. Occasionally he asked for a retype – he'd thought of something to add or she'd made a mistake. The first two mistakes he handed back with the word struck through and the command, 'Do it again.' The third mistake, he said, 'What's wrong with you, are you deaf and blind?'

'I'm sorry, Mr Coverton.'

'Do it again. It has to go out by the four o'clock post to get there before the Bank Holiday.'

'Yes, sir.'

'Miss Krett never has to retype anything.'

'No, sir, I know she's a wonderful secretary.'

'Well, get along and do it, then.'

She scurried off.

Rolling fresh paper and carbon into her machine, she told herself she had to expect reproofs. She wasn't in the same class as Miss Krett.

Despite these sensible conclusions, she was blinking back tears as she began on the retype.

When it was finished she read it. Perfect. And the typing was perfect, too – crisp and clean, beautifully formatted. She hurried along to Ethan's office to get his signature.

He leaned back in his chair, swinging himself a little from side to side as he read it. 'Good,' he said. 'Why couldn't you do that the first time?'

'I misread an outline, sir.'

'Do you know what happens to a machine if you make a mistake in a component? It seizes up or goes out of control.' But the tone was kinder than when he'd handed back the first version.

'Yes, I see that, sir.'

'Talking of machines . . .'

'Yes?'

'You know there's an August Bank Holiday meeting at Brooklands?'

'Of course, Mr Coverton.'

'The Coverton III is racing.'

'Yes, sir, I know.'

'You know? Still taking an interest, eh?'

'Oh, yes. I go to every event I can, sir.'

'Like to go to Brooklands on Bank Holiday Monday?'

It was so unexpected she felt as if he had dashed cold water in her face. 'What?' she gasped. And then thought, Fool, he just means he'll get you a pass to get in.

'You'd like to see Stokes win with the Coverton?'

'Oh, I'd love to.' There was no doubt of her sincerity. Her eyes glowed as she spoke.

What a girl, thought Ethan. 'Right, I'll pick you up at eight thirty. Where the devil is it you live?'

'The – the Euphemia Grey Hostel for Business Girls, Earl's Court Road.'

If he flinched at the address, he hid it well. 'That's a date then.'

'Yes,' she said faintly.

That was Thursday 31 July. August 1 was a full working day: she didn't see Ethan at all on that day even for dictation, for he had gone to a business meeting in

Blackburn. Saturday morning had been awarded to the staff as part of the Bank Holiday weekend. She spent it going up and down Kensington High Street trying to find something she could afford to buy but all the summer dresses were beyond her purse.

In the end she bought a well-made beige linen skirt reduced to ten shillings as a tag-end of the July sales. The theory was that she would thereby transform her four blouses into summer dresses. On Sunday she ironed them all then tried them with the skirt. True enough, the effect was quite good – what the fashion magazines called *sportif*. She shampooed her hair, experimented with a sixpenny lipstick bought in Woolworth.

'What's all this in aid of?' her roommates inquired.

'It's love,' said Rosalind. 'What else?'

'Nothing of the kind,' protested Ruth. 'It's just that I'm going to Brooklands tomorrow and I don't want to look a fright.'

'Aha! But who're you going with, that's the question?'

It was a question Ruth had no intention of answering, and since few of the hostel dwellers got up early on the holiday morning, she was able to slip out unnoticed to wait on the doorstep for Ethan. When his Rolls-Royce Phantom II slid to the kerb she was pleased to see that he had dispensed with his chauffeur and was driving himself.

'Good morning,' he said, leaning across to open the passenger seat door for her.

'Good morning, Mr Coverton.'

'Looks like fine weather for a bit. Thunder storms forecast, though.'

'I hope not.'

She got in beside him. Every fibre of her body seemed aware of him. He was wearing grey flannel trousers and a coarse brown linen shirt with the collar open and the sleeves rolled up. The morning sun glinted on the blond hairs on his forearms. The gaze of the hazel eyes was on the street where the traffic was streaming by. 'Busy roads out of London today,' he observed. 'We'd better get a move on before the day-trippers start out. You ready?'

'Yes, sir.'

'For heaven's sake don't call me sir. This isn't the office.'

'No, s—' She broke off, laughing.

'Look here, for today, it's first names, eh? I'm Ethan and you're Ruth.'

'Oh, Mr Coverton, do you think that's . . .'

'We're not in the office. We can forget protocol.'

'I don't know. It seems . . .'

'What? Daring? Unseemly?'

What she might have said was, It's dangerous. But that was taking too much for granted. So she said with meekness, 'You know best, Ethan.' And at that he laughed.

As they wended their way out of London into Surrey she asked how things had gone in Blackburn. 'Bunch of thickheads,' he grunted. 'I've got a bit of a design for a new kind of battery for use in a radio. You know, until most of Britain gets linked up to the electricity supply there are still going to be thousands of people buying a radio set that uses a battery. Great big things, they are.'

She nodded. 'My grandparents have a battery set. The battery has to be taken to the local garage to be recharged once a week.'

'Did you carry it? Weighs a ton, I bet! My idea is to make it more compact. But could I get those numbskulls in Blackburn to see it?'

'So what will you do?'

'Oh, I'll tinker around with it and keep trying to find a manufacturer who'll give it a trial. Patterwick made a prototype for me – have you met Patterwick?'

'No, Mr— Ethan.'

'He's the manager of our experimental division. A decent sort but he spends more time in the lab than in the executive wing. Who have you met so far?'

'Well, of course, when I first arrived, I met the personnel manager. And then I met Miss O'Keefe of the Filing Department and Miss Myland of the typing pool—'

'No, I meant in the west wing.'

'Mr Welland of the Advertising Department and Mr Glynn of Sales and his assistant Mr Shoesmith. And Mr Antony.'

'Ah, Antony. His title's "Personal Assistant" but what it really means is "understudy".'

'Understudy?'

'Yes, he's waiting in the wings for me to pop off so he can step into my part. You might say he was in training from the minute he left Harrow. He read economics and modern history at university but all he really thought about was the economics of Covelco and the day when its current managing director would be history.'

'Ethan!' exclaimed Ruth, shocked to the marrow of her bones.

'Oh, it's true,' he said, turning his head to give her a grin. 'If you were to ask him, he'd admit it. He thinks I'm a fool, wasting money and time on racing cars. He doesn't mind so much about the time – he's quite happy, really, if I'm out of the office so that he can get in a bit of practice at being the boss. But he hates to see money being spent on anything except building up Covelco to No. 1 in electrical engineering. A great empire-builder, is Antony.'

She was silent, troubled by the throw-away manner. She knew, from her own experience, that it was possible to have mixed feelings about one's relatives. Yet she couldn't ever have spoken about Grandma or Granddad with so much indifference.

'Sorry if I've shocked you,' Ethan remarked as she said nothing. 'I'm afraid there's no love lost between me and my family. I'm used to the idea by now – it's been that way for about fifteen years. Just one of those things – we don't see eye to eye about anything. Luckily I've got enough money so we don't have to live in each other's pockets but can go our own ways.'

She'd heard at the racetrack that no one from Ethan's private world ever came to cheer on the Coverton III. His friends there seemed to be racing drivers, mechanics, designers, race organizers, all kinds of enthusiasts from that special group. What she'd been able to glean in the office was much the same. Mrs Coverton never appeared at the Christmas and New Year events, almost never telephoned. Miss Krett said that sometimes she received a call from Mrs Coverton's social secretary, whatever that might mean.

There were two other children besides Antony: a son Martin, whose efforts as a playwright got occasional mentions in the gossip columns, and a daughter Lorette who'd just had her coming-out season. Neither of these ever came near the office. Only Antony seemed to take an interest and on that point he seemed almost obsessive, staying as long as or longer than his father, sometimes coming in on Sundays.

'What does he do when he comes in on Sundays?' Ruth

had wondered aloud when she heard of it.

'Thinks up extra work for me to do on Monday,' said his secretary Miss Giles in a long-suffering tone.

It could well be that while Ruth Barnett was travelling with Antony's father towards the freedom and excitement of Brooklands, the son was poring over ledgers in Holborn on Bank Holiday Monday.

Smiling to herself at the picture, Ruth watched the countryside unfold around her. It was all familiar to her – the meadows with the willows marking the edges of the brook, the pastures with cattle lazily swishing flies away with their tails, the grain turning golden in the August sun.

'Miss it?' Ethan inquired.

'The countryside? Oh, no! London's so marvellous – always something to see, something to do. We had a lecture last Wednesday at the hostel by a man who's got the most complete collection of Egyptian scarabs in Britain. Imagine that! Little carvings taken from Egyptian tombs! I'd read about them while I was in Freshton but I never ever imagined I'd see one!'

'And now that you've seen one, what d'you think?'

'How do you mean?'

'Going to start a collection?'

'No, but I wouldn't mind going to Egypt to see where they're found. Have you ever been to Egypt?'

'During the war. The government sent me. There was a problem over wireless communication. Didn't have time to look for scarabs.'

'I suppose not.' The reminder of his importance subdued her. Her spirits didn't revive until he'd talked for a while about his travels – Germany, France, Italy, America – sometimes on business but mostly for car racing.

'I'm going to Montlhery for their opening events,' he said.

'It sounds wonderful.'

'Perhaps you'll go abroad some day.'

'Perhaps.'

When they reached Brooklands, a good crowd had already arrived. Ethan parked the Rolls on the sandy area to the right of the pavilion, almost in among the gorse. They walked together back along the road to the sheds. Peter Stokes and David Epps were in a fierce argument as they approached.

'One thing you can always be sure of,' Ethan said to Ruth but loudly enough to be heard by the two men, 'the driver and the mechanic will be at odds with one another.'

'And with good reason,' said Stokes. 'This nincompoop's managed to lose the new gaskets from Thompson and Taylor.'

'I didn't mislay them, they never arrived—'

'That's your story. Look here, Ethan, we agreed the cylinder heads needed—'

'We know all that, Peter, for heaven's sake! If they'd come I'd have put them in and adjusted—'

Ruth let the talk fizz and sparkle around her. It was like coming home, to hear the men arguing and trading amiable insults, to feel the heat reflected from the great expanse of concrete that formed the track, to smell the strange mixture of pines and trodden grass and petrol.

'So what kind of practice times have you clocked up?' Ethan said, breaking into the thrust and parry of the other two.

'Not bad, not bad. Ninety without too much effort. But we'd be doing better if we'd got the car fine-tuned.'

'Pete, you say that every time I ask you. *I* can get

ninety-four out of her. You've got to do better than that. You're driving against Campbell today.'

Pete Stokes shrugged as if he thought the champion racing driver were negligible competition. Ruth stifled a laugh. Ethan met her eye and smiled. 'They're all the same, racing drivers,' he said. 'That's why I gave it up – my head was getting too big for my driving helmet.'

'You gave it up because your hair was beginning to fall out,' Pete retorted.

This was so demonstrably untrue when you looked at Ethan's thick wiry mane that they all laughed. 'Nice to see you again, Ruthie,' said David Epps. 'Haven't been around for quite a while, have you?'

'No, I'm working in London these days, David.'

'Too bad. Nobody keeps my tool shelves in order any more.'

This was a hint to her to take the job in hand. She was about to go into the mechanics' area but Ethan kept her at his side by putting a hand on her elbow. A surge of pleasure went through her – he wanted her to stay with him.

All the same, his attention didn't remain with her once race time began to draw near. Everyone took part in getting the Coverton III ready, checking and listening for a fault, tightening the bonnet strap, polishing the pale blue paint and the aluminium trim.

Starting time. A cinema cameraman on a truck was driven out to the best vantage point. The cars were pushed out on the old Finishing Straight which ironically enough was the starting area. Push-starting was general, yet there were some that had to be primed with the handle. The motley assemblage lined up – Crossleys, the Napier-Campbell, the inimitable Type 35 Bugatti, a Sunbeam or two, the Coverton III, all the models and modifications of a new and developing sport. Mr Ebblewhite studied his watch, gave the signal, and they were off.

The torpedo shape of the Coverton was among the first four on the Railway Straight on the first circuit. Epps was holding the big watch with its mph markings round the dial edge. He shook his head as the cars flashed by. 'Eighty-nine,' he groaned.

'What's he waiting for – Christmas?' Ethan was impatient.

'You know he always takes his time to get into his best position,' Ruth protested.

'Ruth, he knows the car's not at its best, it's no good hanging about expecting to make it up in the last two laps . . .'

'Get on, man!' shouted David to the fading roar of the engines.

A few minutes later they were charging down again along the straight. The air was full of the shrill scream of gear-trains, the spitting of the superchargers. The spectators were buffeted by the powerful airstream as the cars sped past.

'What's he doing?'

'Ninety point one this time.'

'Not good enough. David, *why* didn't you chase up that order with Thomson and Taylor?' Ethan asked.

'I did, boss! What d'you think! But it was no use . . .'

His attention was back with the cars as they came tearing up to them again. One of the Sunbeams had to go into the pits for a tyre change. Another had run its big end and was being pushed off the course into a bulwark bearing the legend *Dunlop*. A Speed Six was belching out black smoke as it whirled past.

As the race progressed, thunder clouds came towering

up from the south. 'Oh, marvellous,' groaned Ethan. 'A nice slippery surface, that's all we need.'

'The clouds are passing over,' Ruth said.

'Don't be a Pollyanna about it; if we're not going to win, we're not—'

'Ninety point seven,' reported the mechanic.

The storm broke, the rain poured down, the 2.75 miles of track became a skating rink and two cars skidded off in quick succession. The competition against which Peter Stokes was driving had considerably thinned out. 'He'll do it yet,' Ethan crowed.

But, no, in the end he came in second to Malcolm Campbell in his Napier. The average speed of the winner had been ninety-two point two with the Coverton only decimal points behind. In the conditions in which the race ended, and considering the Coverton wasn't at its peak of performance, it wasn't a bad result.

But Ethan didn't think it good, either. He grumbled at the mechanic, argued every detail with the driver, and finally stamped back to join Ruth with his hands thrust into his trouser pockets and his shoulders hunched.

'Money down the drain,' he mourned.

'There'll be other races.'

'I've a good mind to find another driver.'

'Don't do that; Stokes is good and you know it.'

'I was sure we could do it today. Do you realize this damned car hasn't won a single worthwhile race yet?'

'Well, then, give it all up and take up stamp-collecting,' Ruth suggested lightly.

Ethan stopped in his gloomy march to swing round and glare at her. Then the corners of his mouth twitched and he began to laugh.

'You watch your tongue, young lady,' he warned, 'or

you won't get any of the champagne I'm planning to open and get drunk with.'

The champagne was in a picnic hamper in the boot of the Rolls. They'd been too busy and too excited to think about food, but now discovered they were starving. The rain having stopped, they brought out the picnic. There was cold chicken, little patties of salmon, salad in a japanned box, and even forks and knives to eat with. Ruth had never seen anything so elegant.

Nor had she had champagne, although she'd read about it. It made her nose tickle and her head spin. As the sun came out to form a rainbow against the receding thunder clouds, she sat in the back of the Rolls-Royce with Ethan Coverton and felt herself to be living like a princess.

The other, more important races were held. Sheltering under big umbrellas from the intermittent showers, the Coverton team cheered on their friends. The Coverton III was rolled into the mechanics' shed, the bonnet was opened, the engine was mused over.

'Well, I'll strip it down tomorrow . . .'

'Ring me and tell me what you find, Dave.'

'All right, boss. Where'll you be?'

'At the office. Some importers from France are coming to discuss terms for handling the new radios we're going to launch in the autumn.'

'Those you showed the designs for last May? With the walnut cabinets?'

Ethan nodded, his attention on the car engine. Ruth had seen the advertising leaflets for the new radios, big affairs with legs, looking almost like china cabinets.

'You'd have to have a big room for one of those,' she commented.

'One of what?'

64

'Those cabinet radios. For most people, they'd be too big – when are Covelco going to bring out a set that will fit into an ordinary kitchen?'

'Nobody wants a radio set in their kitchen,' Ethan said. 'They want to settle down of an evening and listen to a programme from 2LO.'

'But most people settle down of an evening in their kitchen,' objected Ruth. The champagne had made her argumentative.

'Nonsense. Families settle down in their living rooms.'

'For most people, it's the same thing. Kitchen and living room – same thing.'

'You know, you may have a point there,' said Ethan. 'Not everybody wants a piece of burl walnut with five valves inside. Perhaps I should give it some thought . . .'

'Never mind about radios, hand me a spanner and let's see if we can get this lug off,' protested the mechanic, who tended to have a one-track mind.

Ruth found a spanner and then set about tidying the jumble of tools on David's bench. The men tinkered about and chatted in low voices over the car. By and by the truck and trailer arrived to transport the Coverton III back to the main workshop in Croydon for extensive examination. Ruth helped push it on board and tether it in place. Epps and Stokes got into the truck to go with it to Croydon, to spend the evening and perhaps most of the night trying to work out where the flaw had arisen.

The crowd was slowly making its way to cars and motorbikes to head for home. 'Time to go,' Ethan said.

'I suppose so.'

'You've got a smudge of oil on your blouse, Ruth.'

'Oh, no! Where?'

'Back of your sleeve.' He took hold of the hem of the

half-sleeve to twitch it forward so she could see it, but it was beyond her gaze.

'Oh, bother,' she mourned. 'It's so difficult to clean up heavy oil once it's soaked in.' It was a good blouse, of shantung silk.

'There's some solvent in the mechanics' washroom,' Ethan suggested.

'May I?'

'Of course.'

The washroom was nothing more than a partitioned section of the mechanics' shed, with a sink and a tap and a roll towel and a cupboard containing a few necessities. She found the tin of grease solvent, fetched it down and took off her blouse. There it was, a long smear going down the back of the left sleeve from shoulder to hem.

She laid the blouse on the draining board, poured the chemical on to a washrag and rubbed at the stain. Five minutes' work had diluted it enough to let her think that a wash with warm water and Lux soapflakes might lift it entirely. She hung the blouse on the open cupboard door to let it dry.

The door to the main shed opened. Ethan came in.

Ruth turned in surprise. Reflexively she crossed her arms over her thinly clad torso and clutched her shoulders as if in defence.

He stood staring down at her. Then he took her hands one by one and held them away from her body. Slowly he bent his head to kiss the soft hollow between her breasts.

'Ethan,' she breathed.

Next moment they were body to body, arms entwined, in an embrace of passion and desire.

Chapter Five

As at last they drew apart, Ruth's head was swimming. Her heart was beating fast. A luxurious warmth seemed to suffuse her entire being.

Ethan said in a hoarse voice, 'I'd better take you home.'

'No!' She grasped at the front of his shirt, holding him close as he made as if to turn away. She glanced about at the untidy washroom: packets of tea and blue bags of sugar on the cupboard shelves, enamel mugs on the draining board. Nothing could have been less romantic.

'No, Ethan, we'll go – but not home.'

His brows came together. 'Look here, you're just a child—'

She put her palm across his lips. 'S-sh. Why do you think I left Freshton? Why did I move to London? Just to be with you – that was the reason.'

He gave a little laugh of delight, bent his head and kissed her again. This time the passion was controlled, and there was joy, exuberance. Then he sobered and let her go.

'Do you know what you're doing?' he asked gravely.

She coloured up under his gaze. 'I know – something – a little – enough to know that what comes next must be with you. no one else.'

'Ruth!'

A faltering, hesitant smile. 'Am I doing this all wrong?'

'Nothing could sound more right to me, my darling,' he said.

She twitched the still-damp blouse off the cupboard door, shook it out and tried to put it on. The damp silk clung to her.

'Can't we find you something else?' he said, looking about. But there was nothing except mechanics' overalls and a grease-stained tweed jacket.

'It doesn't matter,' she said. 'Look, it's raining again – I'd get as wet as this in a rainstorm.'

They ran for the car under the shelter of one of the big umbrellas, but even so feet and legs were splashed with the sandy mud of the banking. Laughing, they fell into the Rolls.

As they drove out, a few late stayers nodded farewell. Once they were on the road towards London, Ruth let her head rest against Ethan's shoulder. He had one arm about her most of the time. They scarcely spoke; they had no need of words.

The rain increased, lashing against the windscreen so that it was almost impossible to see the road. Although it was only about eight, the heavy clouds had brought a darkness almost like night. But Ruth felt no concern. She had utter confidence in Ethan. Her future, now and henceforth, lay in his hands.

They had passed signposts, scarcely visible, signalling Surrey towns which Ethan avoided. At a triangular junction marked by a little green, he turned off to the left between tall trees whose arching branches blotted out the night sky and to some extent sheltered from the rain. Then they turned yet again, into a lane with high hedges.

There was a glimpse of a signboard, then a long wall and pillars topped with heraldic beasts leading to a gravel drive.

Lights were visible. As they drew nearer Ruth could discern that they were grouped to display a painted sign: Manley Grange Hotel. Light spilled from windows and door. Ethan drove past the main building to a stabling area at the back as if it were well known to him. As he parked the Rolls, a doorman in a brass-buttoned uniform was coming with an umbrella to shelter them on their walk to the porch.

'Evening, Mr Coverton. Been to Brooklands?'

'Yes, came in second. Many people here, Simpson?'

'No, sir. August, you know, they're abroad mostly, won't be back until the shooting starts.'

Ethan urged Ruth forward through the doors into a handsome foyer. At the desk the receptionist looked up. The doorman said, 'Here's Mr Coverton got caught out by the weather, Miss Dodds.' He added in a low voice to Ethan, 'New on the job, I have to give her a hint now and again.'

Miss Dodds clearly recognized the name. 'Good evening, sir. A dreadful evening.' Her hand hovered over the hotel register: she was asking herself, had they come to stay or for a meal? And if to stay, should she offer a double room? This could hardly be Mrs Coverton, she felt: not turned out well enough, no wedding ring on her left hand.

'What we want is two single rooms and some hot food sent up with a pot of coffee.'

'Yes, sir. With bath?'

'Of course, with bath,' grunted Ethan, with a gesture that took in his mud-splashed trousers and shoes.

'Certainly, sir.' She glanced at the room plan on her side of the reception desk. She hesitated. She was new to the Manley Grove but not new to hotel work. She could see out of the corner of her eye Mr Coverton's hand protectively resting on the girl's elbow.

'Rooms 108 and 109,' she suggested. 'A view over the grounds to the lake, but hardly visible in this weather.' She moved the register forward, offered a pen. Mr Coverton signed in a wide, masterful scrawl. The girl wrote 'R. Barnett' in a neat, almost clerkly hand. Miss Dodds rang a bell. 'Tommy, show Mr Coverton and Miss Barnett to 108 and 109.' She handed the keys to the bellboy.

'Luggage, sir?' he asked.

'No luggage, we're caught in the rain, that's all.'

'Yes, sir,' said Tommy impassively.

Room 108 was beyond anything Ruth had ever seen, even in Harrods Department Store. It had a bed canopied in pale green cotton-satin, with a matching spread. The upholstery of the chairs and dressing stool was the same. The furniture was of cream-painted wood with mouldings and edgings of pale green. The curtains, which the bellboy quickly closed, were of pale green-and-cream-striped silk. Ruth's rain-soaked feet sank into a carpet like deep green velvet.

Tommy threw open a door. To her astonishment, a bathroom was revealed – a sparkling display of cream tiles and pale wood surrounds, with thick towels folded on the towel rails and an array of bottles and jars on the shelf.

'Is there anything you require, miss?' Tommy inquired.

Speechless, Ruth shook her head. Smiling to himself, he pointed out the bathrobe folded on the bathroom shelf and remarked that the housekeeper could have her clothes dried and pressed by the morning if she so desired.

'Yes . . . Thank you . . .'

Tommy ushered Mr Coverton to Room 109, which was just such another only in maroon and cream. There was no need to display the bathroom to Mr Coverton who knew where to find it for himself. Nor was there any need, Tommy felt, to point out the intercommunicating door between the two rooms.

'Anything else, sir?'

'Send the waiter.' Ethan picked up the menu from the bureau. 'And someone for these wet things – in about fifteen minutes.'

Tommy pocketed the tip and was gone. Ruth, still standing transfixed in Room 108, heard him go whistling down the passage.

Next moment she heard a sound at the door between the two rooms. It was the click of a bolt sliding back. Then a tap on the door panels. She hurried to slip the bolt on her side, and at once the door opened.

There stood Ethan. And next moment she was in his arms.

They kissed as if they had been parted for years instead of only a few moments. Then Ethan said, 'Poor little drowned kitten! You'd better get out of those wet things and have a hot bath. There'll be some food by and by. Are you hungry?'

She shook her head.

He smiled, kissed her lightly on top of her head and, turning her, sent her towards her bathroom. 'The maid will come for your clothes. Leave them on a chair for her.'

'Yes, Ethan.'

Hot water gushed from the shining taps. She put in some pink bath crystals, and soon the bathroom was full of rose-scented steam. The bath towels seemed enormous when she stepped out of the tub. She dusted herself with talcum powder, rubbed her damp short hair and combed it with a comb she found in a tissue wrapping and put on the bathrobe of thick white towelling. She avoided looking at herself in the cheval mirror; she was sure she looked a fright. But the mirror would have shown a slender neck emerging from the thick collar of the robe, a rounded chin, lips that trembled into a smile, grey-green eyes aglow with expectation.

When she came out into the room, the maid as foretold had taken her wet clothes. The door to the adjoining room stood open. She went across the thick carpet, silent on bare feet.

Ethan was standing by the bed, a towel tied round his waist, his torso bare. She drew in a breath. He was spare, muscular. His damp fair hair was clinging to his skull like a cap. He made her think of a Roman gladiator such as she'd seen in book illustrations.

She ran to him. He took her in his arms, held her close. 'Darling, this is your last chance to change your mind,' he warned.

For answer she merely clung closer to him. She knew that when first he kissed her, a door had opened for her, beyond which was the entire and perfect love she longed for. She was his from that moment. Perhaps always had been his since first she saw him among the smoke and fumes of the racetrack.

Gently he untied the sash of the robe. It fell away, revealing creamy skin, rounded curves, the treasure trove for which he longed. Ruth shrugged the folds away so that the robe fell to her ankles. She pressed herself against him, and for the first time felt the contact of skin against skin. She shivered with delight.

They fell together on the bed, arms about each other, mouth seeking mouth. In kisses and caresses they made the first encounter last until passion began to move them on to deeper needs.

Ruth was innocent but not ignorant – no country child could remain unaware of the facts of life. She gave herself eagerly to her lover, learning from him what must be done to bring that ecstasy she sensed just beyond the barrier of her inexperience.

He was tender, leading her by gentle steps along the road. He made her aware of her body so that she was ready for his next demand and, more than that, eager to meet it. He would whisper to her as she yielded to his touch: my angel, my darling, my treasure. And she would reply just as softly: my own one, my love.

But at last words were forgotten in the race towards uttermost bliss. Her breath was snatched away in an exultant cry. They lay spent for a time, still clasped together, pulses gradually dying to normal pace, hearts quieting after the turmoil of desire.

He kissed her cheek and her hair, murmuring that he adored her, that she was wonderful, that he couldn't believe she loved him.

'It's more wonderful from my point of view,' she said as she nestled yet closer into his arms. 'Who would ever have thought you'd bother about someone like me?'

'You're just fishing for compliments.' There was a smile in his voice.

'I suppose I am. But you must meet so many beautiful women . . .'

He silenced her comparisons with kisses. Later he said, 'I suppose I decided you were meant for me when you knew the time on that stopwatch.'

'That was almost a year ago, Ethan. Think of the time we've wasted.'

'But, Ruthie, how could I possibly imagine you'd – I mean, you're so much younger than I am. I thought you'd want some smart young lad.'

'Don't be silly.'

'But most girls . . .'

'I don't know about most girls. I only know about me. And I knew I belonged to you from the first.'

She felt him nod. 'It's serious, then,' he said.

She hesitated. 'Only if you want it to be, darling. I wouldn't ever want to be a nuisance.'

'Now you're talking nonsense.'

They let words slip away for a time while they kissed and embraced almost negligently in the aftermath of passion. Then he acknowledged, 'It may be unromantic of me, but I'm getting hungry. I ordered the food for nine thirty.' He leaned on an elbow to look at the bedside clock. 'Nearly that now.'

'Will a waiter come in?' she asked, a little at a loss.

'Yes, but you can hop next door for a minute while he brings the trolley in.'

So it was. To Ruth it was like a delightful game of hide-and-seek. She felt no guilt, no shame. She was too inexperienced to think that the hotel staff might be gossiping, nor would she have cared if she had known. She was Ethan's lover: nothing else mattered.

Her still-damp hair was in spikes about her head. She tidied it in the mirror, decided the bathrobe made her look like a teddy bear and substituted one of the bath-towels. Tucked in around her breasts, it was like a sarong.

When Ethan opened the communicating door to say

that supper was served, he smiled in approval at her new attire. 'This way, Maharani,' he said, bowing her in. He was wearing a bathrobe: by slipping his hands in the sleeves, he looked vaguely oriental as he spoke.

'Maharani means princess, doesn't it?'

'Yes, it's Indian. I've actually met a maharani.'

'You know such a lot, Ethan,' she sighed. 'You make me feel an ignoramus.'

'Fishing for compliments again. You want me to say I think you're perfect.'

'Well, yes, I do.'

'You're perfect. *Perfect*.' He set her in a chair by the wheeled trolley and kissed the top of her head. 'What will you have, Your Highness? I can offer quail in aspic, lobster salad, olive and chicken cocktail, Parma ham, all kinds of greenery to go with them, and a rather fine Bernkastel Kabinet Auslese.'

'I don't know what any of those would be like except the chicken and olive cocktail.'

'Then you ought to sample everything.' He picked up a plate and began to load food on it.

'No, no, Ethan, you're the one that's hungry, not me.'

'All right, I'll eat and you can watch me. Thirsty?'

'Yes.'

He picked up a bottle, its side misted with moisture. 'To improve your store of general knowledge, this is the Bernkastel.' He poured wine into a glass. It was a clear pale gold, like captured winter sunlight. 'Try it.'

She tasted the wine. It wasn't like the champagne she'd had earlier, yet it had a piquancy, a tingle. 'It's delicious,' she said.

'Now I know why I love you,' he said. 'You can appreciate German wine.'

He set a chair alongside, sat down, and began to eat from the plate of food he'd prepared. At every second bite, he offered her a taste. By and by they were eating from the same dish and sharing the same glass of wine. And as one hunger was sated, another was aroused.

He put a hand under her elbow to help her up from the table. He guided her to the bed. There he untucked the bath towel and pulled it aside. 'You're so beautiful,' he breathed.

'Do you really think so, Ethan?'

'Of course, you're beautiful. You must know that.'

She shook her head.

'Hasn't anyone ever told you so?'

'No, never. And I'm glad you're the first to say it, because you're the one that matters.'

'Oh, God, I can't believe you feel like that. It's a dream; I'm afraid I'll wake up and you won't be there.'

'I'll always be here, Ethan, always, always.' She put her arms about his neck to pull him down to her.

At some point around midnight she woke to find he had risen to pull back the curtains. The sky was clearing, stars were peeping out. She sat up. He brought the wine to the bedside, poured her a glass.

'It won't taste so good this time. It should be chilled.'

'It's still delicious.' She leaned back on the pillows, smiling at him over the rim of the glass in the dimness. 'Bernkastel?'

'That's it. One day I'll take you to the area where it's made.'

'In Germany?'

'Yes. Of course.' He added, with a half-hidden grin, 'There's a motor race not far off.'

She laughed and shrugged, then shivered.

'Ah, you're cold!' He found his bathrobe, draped it over her shoulders. 'Is that better?'

'I'd be warmer still if you'd put your arms around me.'

'Yes, Your Highness.' He got in beside her, hugged her close. 'I love you, Ruth.'

'I love you, Ethan.'

'There are some things we ought to say to each other besides that, though.' He sighed. 'You know, of course, that I'm married.'

'Yes, of course.'

'I've got a wife and three children.'

'Yes.'

'Ruth, two of my children are older than you are.'

'What does that matter?'

'Are you sure . . .? I'm not too old for you?'

She put the wine glass down on the bedside table. 'Never say that,' she said angrily. 'I don't want you ever to say that. I love you. The only thing that means anything to me is that you love me in return.'

'Heaven help me, I do. I never thought I'd ever know what it felt like to be in love.'

'But Ethan – your wife – surely you must have been in love when you married her?'

He was shaking his head before she ended the question. 'It's difficult to make it seem sensible now. You have to understand, I inherited the business when I was just out of university. I spent five or six years putting into effect all the good ideas I'd had while I was studying engineering – building it up to what it is now. Then my mother . . .'

'I've never heard anyone mention her?'

'No, she died about eight years ago. She took up good works after my father died and served on a couple of committees with Diana's mother. So when she started saying things about wishing she could have grandchildren around her, and wasn't it time I settled down, she had a bride already lined up.'

'In other words, Diana.'

'Yes.' He looked back into the past. 'Diana had had her London season and I think some fellow had let her down. Of course, we never talked about it but I think she wanted someone with a title. I was very much a second-best choice.'

'Oh, that can't be true!'

'I think you're a little biased,' he said ruefully. 'I don't blame Diana – her mother was pushing her just as mine was pushing me. So we got married, and within a few months I realized it wasn't going to work. We had nothing in common. She was only interested in making and holding a place in society, and I was only interested in my work.'

'But surely she took an interest in that?'

'Are you serious? I soon realized she thought there was something almost "common" about electrical development. She always tries to give people the impression I'm in engineering – the kind that produces dams and bridges – big-scale stuff – it seems more prestigious somehow than electrical engineering which in my case means making wireless sets and things like that.'

'That's absurd!' Ruth exclaimed.

'Oh, you don't know how absurd a marriage can be when the two people have nothing in common. Well, that's not true, of course, first of all we had a son, Antony. But she was determined to bring him up to have more class than his father and I somehow got blocked off from getting to know him. We had a tremendous row over it and I walked out. My mother talked me into going back and we had a reconciliation – resulting in Martin. And then several other rows, one of which was patched up with a peace pact that resulted in Lorette. That was eighteen years ago. After that we just agreed to go our separate ways.'

Ruth said nothing at first. Then she murmured, 'It's awfully sad, Ethan.'

'Do you think so? I've got so used to it, it seems quite ordinary to me.'

'But – weren't you awfully lonely?'

'I've had lots of friends in business and, of course, you know, in motor racing. There's a great camaraderie in that. And if you mean, lonely for women . . . Well, there have been women, Ruth. You mustn't imagine I've been celibate.' He watched her as he said it, and when she flinched he said quickly: 'But never like this, darling. I realize now I've never been in love with anyone but you.'

She laid her head against his shoulder. 'Same here,' she said.

'Hah! Little that can mean, considering how short a time you've had to try falling in love. But as for me, I speak from long experience. I've had years of it – and never felt like this before, ever.'

'Aren't we lucky?' she mused. 'Out of anybody in the world we might have met, we met each other.'

'Guardian angels. I never believed in them before tonight.'

'Oh, yes, we've got good fairies looking after us, and influential gods and goddesses planning our future.'

He laughed, but let a moment go by before saying: 'Our future – we've got to give that some thought. It's all so new and strange, I don't know what to say to you. I want you to understand how things are: Diana doesn't care about me except as an escort when we go to big events like dinner at the Mansion House or the opening day at the Royal Academy. So you're not breaking up a marriage or anything like that. But on the other hand, the marriage does exist.'

'Don't worry about it, my dearest. Let's just treasure what we've got.'

'Yes, but what *have* you got? A man who's no young Romeo and married to boot—'

'Will you stop talking like that? It hurts me to hear you belittling yourself. There's no one like you in the whole world, Ethan. You're all I want.'

'Truly?'

'Truly.' And as proof she turned to put her arms about him and ask for his kisses.

From the first long night of love she woke to find morning light streaming in at the window. She sat up to look at the time. Her moving roused Ethan, who said drowsily, 'Good morning. What time is it?'

'Just after six thirty.'

He yawned mightily, then started up. 'My God, I've got people coming to the office this morning!'

'Yes, and if I don't get back to the hostel in time for breakfast, they'll know I never came in last night!'

'Right, quick as you can, get washed and dressed.'

'My clothes?'

'I think you'll find them outside your door.'

True enough, the garments were on a hanger covered with tissue paper on the outside doorknob. Her shoes had been cleaned and polished and were in a little basket on the floor. She was washed and dressed in fifteen minutes.

She went back to Ethan's room. He was shaving with a safety razor presumably provided by the hotel just as her bath salts and comb had been provided. He called from the bathroom: 'Soon as you like, go out to the car. I'll be there as soon as I've paid the bill. We'll get breakfast at a roadside stall on the way – quicker than hanging about in the hotel dining room.'

Ruth was thankful to hear it, because she had a feeling she would look out of place in the dining room, despite the freshly pressed skirt and blouse. She went downstairs and out to the yard where the Rolls was waiting. In five minutes Ethan joined her and they were on their way.

'It'll be simplest if I drop you at the office, Ruth. Then I can go on to my club – I keep some clothes there.'

'But I can't go to the office in these!' she protested. 'My black dress is at the hostel.'

'That damned black dress. All right, I'll drop you at the hostel.' But he was frowning at the thought.

They reached Earl's Court just as the milk cart was leaving. Ruth knew that the milk would be taken in at the area door at any moment, which meant that the area door would be unlocked. She kissed Ethan goodbye and waved him away. He was still frowning in angry disapproval as he drove off.

As she'd foreseen, Sadie the maid opened the area door and took the milk in off the doorstep. Ruth waited five minutes then tiptoed down. The door opened easily onto a stone-paved passage. She went quietly in. She could hear the kitchen staff talking loudly in the big kitchen and clattering saucepans. She stole past the door, up the stone steps to the ground floor, across the hall and up the back staircase.

Rosalind was sitting on her bed drinking her early morning tea. 'Hello, where have you sprung from?' she asked in surprise. 'Didn't you come in last night?'

'No, the weather was so awful I stayed overnight.'

'But I thought you were going to a motor race?'

'Yes, at Brooklands. My grandparents live in a village a few miles off.'

'I see,' said Rosalind without interest.

And so, without actually lying, Ruth got away with an absence which would certainly have caused the hostel warden to give her at least a lecture, if not her notice.

She took off her clothes, put on her dressing gown, and went with her toothbrush and soap to queue for the bathroom. As she waited, it occurred to her to think that not only the warden, but her grandparents, would disapprove of her conduct.

She could imagine Grandma and Granddad glaring at her as they stood in the front parlour. 'Straight to the bad,' they were saying. 'We always knew you were a wicked girl.'

But she didn't feel wicked. She felt treasured, favoured, triumphant.

Ethan Coverton loved her. Nothing else in the world mattered.

Chapter Six

Ruth was rather late getting to the office. Her status as an assistant to Miss Krett prevented any adverse remarks, however. Miss Krett had routine tasks to give her which occupied the morning. Not until almost lunchtime was she summoned to Ethan's office.

'Mr Coverton says there are five or six letters, Miss Barnett,' said Miss Krett. 'I think two have very important schedules to go with them. You will be careful, won't you – they must be accurate.'

'Yes, Miss Krett.' She was trembling so much at the thought of seeing Ethan that she could scarcely hold her notebook.

'Good morning, Miss Barnett,' he greeted her as she came in.

'Good morning, sir.' She closed the door, moving to the chair she usually occupied.

He got up to stand behind her. He put his palm against her cheek. She turned her face so as to kiss it. He pressed his hand against her mouth for a moment then moved away.

Both understood that moments like this couldn't be allowed. Miss Krett might walk in at any moment with some urgent inquiry. She was his private secretary; it was accepted that she wouldn't knock unless he'd told her he didn't wish to be disturbed.

The letters took a long time. As they were finishing he said, 'I'll see you this evening?'

'Of course.' Whenever you want, she might have added.

'I have people coming here, they'll keep me till after seven. Shall I pick you up outside the hostel?'

'Better not, Ethan. A Silver Ghost is such a noticeable car.'

'I shan't be using it, it's in the garage at my club.' He sighed. 'All the same, perhaps it's better not to bowl up to collect you in a taxi. Can you come to the Chertfold Hotel in Park Street? The restaurant there isn't bad. About seven thirty?'

'I'll be there.'

She skipped the evening meal at the hostel so as to be in good time. The hotel staff at the Chertfold looked somewhat askance at her as she sat in the hotel lounge. She knew her clothes weren't up to the standard they expected.

A waiter approached, looking a query. 'I'm waiting for someone,' she said.

'A hotel guest?'

'No.'

'Ahem.'

She understood that he expected her to spend some money to pay for waiting in comfort in his lounge. She ordered coffee. She would have preferred tea but knew it would be unsmart to ask for it at this hour.

The coffee came in an elegant white china pot with matching cream jug and sugar bowl. The sugar was an unaccustomed jumble of big coloured crystals. The cup and saucer were also elegant, the cup shaped like a tulip.

She was nervous about pouring the coffee but all went well. Time went by. She finished the coffee in the pot and was reduced to nibbling on the sugar crystals. The waiter approached with something on a silver plate.

'The bill, miss.'

She looked at it and went cold. 'What? For two cups of coffee?' she gasped.

He gave her a glance of disdain. 'I knew you were out of your class here,' he said in a low, angry tone. 'Why don't you go and ply your trade somewhere where you fit in?'

'What?'

'Pay up and clear off.'

Intimidated, embarrassed, confused, she opened her handbag. It was Tuesday, and she still had a fair sum left from last Friday's pay. But if she gave this dreadful man enough to cover the bill, she'd have to go without lunch by the end of the week.

There was no help for it. She took out a pound note. He accepted it on his silver plate, went off, came back with the change. She picked it up. As she was about to pick up the final shilling, his fingers closed over it.

'Listen, girlie, if you're going to come into first-class hotels you'll have to learn to give decent tips.'

'Hello, darling. Sorry I'm so late.'

She sprang up, practically falling on Ethan's chest. 'Oh, Ethan, I'm so glad you're here!'

'What's wrong? Why are you so flushed?' He turned on the waiter. 'What's been going on?'

'Nothing, sir. Nothing at all, sir. Are you here for dinner? I'll fetch the menu.'

'No, Ethan, let's go!' Ruth cried.

'But I booked a table—'

'Please, let's go!'

Kicking himself for having made a bad guess and lost a good customer, the waiter pocketed the tip. He watched them go out, the man's arm around the girl. It seemed he'd been quite wrong about her.

Ethan took her to a quiet restaurant in St James's Street where he was clearly known. Waiters scurried about, a table was offered in an alcove. By this time she'd managed to talk her way out of the embarrassment she'd been in when he arrived. But he guessed something unpleasant had happened and was protective towards her.

Both were hungry, they had a good meal then sat long over the remains of the wine, talking sometimes, sometimes holding hands and saying nothing.

'Ethan, I've got to get back to the hostel,' she said unwillingly, catching sight of the time on his wristwatch.

'What, now? But we've only just got here.'

'No, we've been here two hours and it's after ten.'

'So what?'

'The hostel locks its doors at ten thirty.'

'My God,' groaned Ethan, 'where are you living, Holloway Prison?'

'I'm sorry, Ethan. It's the rules.'

'All right.' He beckoned for the bill, and they left. In the taxi he took her hand and said, 'We could go to a hotel.'

She looked up at him with distress. 'I can't – not twice – nobody noticed this morning but I'd never get away with it a second time.'

'It's too ridiculous!'

'I know. I'm sorry. If I'd known, I could have made up some story for the warden – said I was going to stay

86

overnight with a friend – but we hadn't planned anything. I'm sorry.'

'Stop saying you're sorry,' he commanded. 'I'm to blame, I should have thought ahead.'

'Oh, darling, I feel it's all my fault.'

'It's not, it's mine.'

They kissed to make up after what might have been called their first quarrel. At her request the driver stopped some way from the hostel so that she could walk the last few yards without being seen getting out of a taxi by anyone at the drawing-room window.

'Tomorrow night?' Ethan said.

'Of course. Shall I tell Miss Ledder that I'll be staying over with a friend?'

He nodded, kissed her goodnight, and then she was walking along the pavement to the hostel steps. He sat back, cursing himself for having been so inadequate. He seemed to be all at sea, like some boy in his first love affair.

But in fact this *was* his first love affair. He'd gone to bed with other women, but they'd been women who knew what to expect, who were free to come and go as they pleased. Some of them had had comfortable flats to which they could invite him. Some had accepted invitations to spend a weekend in Paris or Ostend.

But Ruth was so utterly different. He was at a loss how to deal with the situation. He didn't want to hurt her by being too businesslike about the affair; he would have liked it to be all roses and champagne for her. Yet there were difficulties that had to be overcome if they were to be together in the sense that each of them wanted.

Next evening he drove her out to a little hotel on the edge of Richmond Park. The parting – or what had seemed like a parting, the forty-eight hours since they left Brooklands – seemed only to make their night together more wonderful.

For the following weekend he borrowed a cottage in Hampshire from a fisherman friend. She told the hostel warden she was going home to her grandparents and packed her best clothes, uncertain whether he would take her to fashionable places for meals. But they spent most of the time alone together in the cottage, too much engrossed in each other to want to go out into the world.

They talked about themselves, explaining, enlightening. She heard about his children: Antony was a money-man with a degree in economics. He wanted to take Covelco into the sphere of government contracts, into undertakings overseas.

'I try to tell him that it's not as easy as he imagines. I had enough of it during the war, always getting bound up in red tape and having to kowtow to Army top brass. And then, abroad, there's always bribes to add to the costs. But he won't see it. He thinks I say these things because I'm a stupid unadventurous old dolt.'

That made her laugh.

'No, I mean it,' he insisted. 'His mother has taught him to despise me to some extent.'

'But surely, when he sees how successful you are – not only in business . . . A stupid unadventurous old dolt wouldn't be a respected figure in motor racing.'

'Oh, that! That's just a way of pouring good money down the drain according to Antony. Besides, you get your hands dirty messing about with car engines.'

'Do the others feel like that?'

He shrugged. 'Martin's in the clouds most of the time. As far as he's concerned, my chief attribute is that I've got money that could be spent on producing one of his plays.'

'Have you ever done that? Backed a play for him?'

'I backed a thing he contributed to – a sort of review with lots of songs and sketches, supposed to be satirical.'

'Was it any good?'

'Well, I never laughed,' he sighed. 'And the critics slated it. It closed in ten days. So when he came back for more money for the next one, I told him to rob someone else's pocket.'

'What about your daughter?'

His gaze softened. 'She's still just a kid. She was away at boarding school most of the time so I didn't see much of her but we seemed to get on together. Until all this hoo-ha about being launched into society. Most of last year her head was full of court procedure and learning how to manage a train and curtsey without falling over, and then this year after the presentation it's been parties and balls and a new dress for every one of them. Diana's thrilled with her so I suppose it's all working out all right . . .'

She held him closer. She would love him to make up for what he couldn't find with his family. She couldn't understand how they could fail to appreciate him as she did. They must be blind, or stupid, or both.

'Well, that's enough about me, any road,' he said. 'What about you? Born and brought up in Freshton, parents run – what is it – a nursery garden?'

'It's my grandparents. Actually . . .'

'What?'

'Actually . . .' She was trembling. It would change everything when she told him. People sneered at bastards.

'What is it?' he asked in anxiety, holding her away so as to look down at the tears that sparkled on her lashes. 'What's wrong? Tell me, sweetheart.'

'My grandparents brought me up. My mother died of an infection soon after I was born; she didn't get proper hospital treatment and she just didn't recover. And as to my father . . . Well, I never had a father.'

'How d'you mean? Did he—' He broke off. 'You mean you're illegitimate?'

The tears welled over and ran down her cheeks, no matter what she did to restrain them. 'Now you'll despise me,' she whispered on a sob.

'Good Lord, Ruthie, you didn't really think that would make any difference?' He was holding her close, rocking her to and fro, smoothing her hair to comfort her.

'It makes a difference to other people when they hear it,' she murmured, burrowing in against him for the warmth of his body.

'Nothing could ever make me think less of you, Ruth. I love you. You've changed my life.'

She had told him her awful secret. Her conscience had been worrying her about it because she was only too well aware of the difference it made in the attitude of other people. She'd been sure he'd think less of her and begin to wish he'd never got involved with her.

No, she hadn't thought that. She'd been sure he loved her just as she loved him.

It had swayed her mind to and fro for days, this awful secret. And now it was out. And he truly didn't care. She could see it in his smiling face as she looked up at him through her tears. He was actually laughing.

'You little idiot,' he teased, and kissed her.

As the weekend was coming to a close he told her he had to be away on business in the north – 'my homeland,' he called it – for a few days during the coming week. 'But on Friday I'll be back, and I thought of taking you with me on Friday night to Lyons for the Grand Prix.'

'Lyons? In France?'

'Yes, would you like that?'

'Oh, Ethan, that would be wonderful!'

So they thought, and lived on the pleasure of expectation until, on the Friday morning, he discovered she had no passport and therefore couldn't travel.

Not even Ethan Coverton could produce a passport for her in ten hours. She couldn't go.

'Then I won't go either.'

'But you must go, Ethan – your car is racing.'

'The devil with my car!'

'Don't say that. You know you're dying to see it race again after that disappointment at Brooklands.'

'No, I'm not.'

'Now don't tell lies, Ethan. You *must* go. Peter Stokes and Dave Epps would think you were losing interest if you didn't turn up.'

They argued off and on throughout the office day. Other members of staff thought that the boss was in a foul temper, and pitied poor Miss Barnett who had to keep going back into his room to take dictation from a man who seemed to hate the entire world.

In the end, he went without Ruth to Lyons. The Coverton III came in second again. He left as soon as the race was over but was delayed at the ferry by bad weather. He didn't get back until mid-morning on Monday.

When in the afternoon he'd got into the swing of routine enough to be able to call for his dictation secretary, he had made up his mind. But he didn't say anything to Ruth about his plan. Instead he said, 'I must see you tonight.'

'Yes, Ethan, I hoped for that.'

'I've something I want to say to you.'

She nodded. 'We'd better get these letters done. It's very late in the day to be starting them.'

He muttered, 'To hell with the letters,' but all the same he dictated brief replies. As she got up to leave he came round his desk, grabbed her, and kissed her hard. She had to stand for a moment to get her breath back and to stop blushing before she went out to meet Miss Krett's eye.

They met at the Rosaire restaurant. Their table was in a quiet corner where the shade on the lamp prevented other diners from seeing much. When the waiter had taken their order and gone away, Ethan said: 'Don't say no when I tell you what I have in mind. Take time to think.'

'What is it, darling?'

'I want you to leave the hostel and move into a flat.'

After a long moment, she said. 'You mean a flat you would pay for?'

'Yes.' He hesitated then hurried on: 'I can't keep delivering you back to that stupid hostel. I can't part from you at ten thirty in the evening. I want to be with you as much as possible. Snatched hours and weekends aren't enough. I want to be able to come home to you at night, I want you to be there, waiting for me. I want to share every possible hour I can with you.'

She was silent. He thought, I've said it all wrong. She's going to turn me down. Why couldn't I make it sound more romantic, less like a business proposition?

When she spoke, she surprised him. 'Should I still be acting as assistant secretary? It's going to be difficult not to give ourselves away. And while I'm not ashamed of our being in love, I don't want people gossiping and giggling about it. And Antony might get to hear of it.'

Ethan was staggered. 'You mean, you will? You'll leave the hostel?'

'Of course. It *is* terribly inconvenient, isn't it? And it would only be a matter of time before someone there began to ask questions about all the nights I spend away from it. Oh, I do agree with you, Ethan – life would be much easier if we had somewhere to be together without having to scheme and contrive.'

'Darling! Angel! I was so afraid you'd turn me down. I mean, it's a big step for you.'

She gave him a hesitant smile. 'I don't mind any step, so long as I take it with you, my dearest.'

'You'll never regret it, Ruth. I promise you, I'll do everything in the world to make you happy. You'll never have to hang about waiting for me in some hotel where the waiter is rude to you. We won't have to try to live all our lives in a few snatched hours together. We'll have time, we'll have room to breathe.' He took her hand, bore it to his lips.

She turned her hand so that her fingers could touch his mouth before they drew apart. Then she said, 'You didn't answer about my being in your office. Don't you think I'd better find a job elsewhere?'

'No!'

'But, Ethan, I don't see how we could manage to be completely businesslike—'

'No! I don't want you to go elsewhere and be bullied by some rotten employer—'

'Well, you'd better have me transferred to some other department.'

'And have people saying you weren't up to the job and had to be moved out? Hanged if I will.'

'Ethan, you're not making sense. Unless we want to take very big risks, I really think I ought to get another job—'

He drew in a breath. 'I don't want you working at all,' he said.

'What?'

'I don't want you drudging away in an office doing dull chores all day long. I agree we ought not to be seeing each other at work – I can scarcely keep my hands off you, I admit. But I don't want to think of you somewhere else, taking orders, running about – you're my girl, Ruth. I want you to have everything you need without having to slave away at a typewriter—'

'But, darling—'

'You'll have a flat to look after. You'll have meals to plan, all that kind of thing. And I want you to spend time buying clothes, get some shoes made, go to Bond Street for perfume and face powder and all the rest of it.'

'No, listen, really – I don't need all that.'

'It's not what you need, it's what I want you to have. You're mine, Ruth, I want you to have everything.'

'But think what it would cost.'

'Good God, Ruthie, I'm a millionaire! I can buy you half of London if you want it!'

She stared at him. 'Really?'

'What?'

'You're really a millionaire?'

'Last time I looked at the balance sheet.' He gave a burst of laughter. 'Didn't you know?'

'Well . . . I suppose . . . yes . . . no . . . I never thought of it.'

He looked at her embarrassed face and his heart melted in love for her. What other woman on earth would have given herself so entirely to a man without once thinking that he was very, very rich?

'Well, then,' he said softly, 'I'm a millionaire, and I can buy you anything you want. So there's no need to make life difficult for yourself by spending nine hours a day in a stuffy office.'

'But are you sure you want to do all this for me?' she asked. 'I said to you once I didn't want it to be serious between us unless you wanted it too.'

'I want it to be serious. I want to make you happy. Let me do this, Ruth. It means we can be with each other almost any time we want – no scheming and contriving, as you put it. If I take time off to go to a race meeting, you can be there with me, no one to notice you're not at your desk, no asking permission or inventing excuses, no one beginning to have suspicions and dropping hints. We'll only have to answer to ourselves. What do you say?'

'Yes, Ethan.'

They spent the rest of dinner making plans. Ruth could contribute little. She'd no idea how to look for a flat in London nor what kind of rent would be expected. Ethan told her she wasn't to worry about it, he had friends in the property market. 'It'll be a furnished place, that'd be easiest, but if you don't like the furniture you only have to say so and I'll have it replaced.'

'No, no,' she demurred. The idea of arguing against anything Ethan approved was to her absurd. She fell in with all his suggestions.

'I should imagine that by the end of the week I'll have got it all fixed up. You'd best go to Personnel in the morning and hand in your notice.'

'What reason shall I give?'

'Why should you give any reason? Just say you're leaving.'

'But Mr Daniels is sure to ask.'

He shrugged. 'I believe you're right. He keeps graphs about the flow of job applications and staff movement. All right then, if he asks, tell him you've had a better offer!' They laughed at the aptness of this reply.

Mr Daniels showed minimal interest. Miss Krett, on the other hand, was quite offended. 'After all the trouble I've taken, starting you on the road to promotion! Is this the thanks I get?'

'I'm sorry, Miss Krett.'

'You're making a big mistake. You could have had a secretarial post almost equal to mine. Mr Antony was asking only the other day if I thought you'd fit his requirements.'

The idea of being asked to take on the role of secretary to Mr Antony was enough to make Ruth shudder. She said hastily, 'I'm leaving office work, Miss Krett. I don't think I'm cut out for it.'

'You realize that by giving such short notice you'll lose two days' pay?'

'I hadn't thought of that.'

'You'd better go back to Personnel and say you want your notice to start from Friday, and leave Friday week.'

'No, I'd rather leave this Friday.'

'Oh, well, do as you like.' You silly girl, was the unspoken corollary.

Ruth gave notice at the hostel. Miss Ledder was surprised. 'But you've only been such a short time in London! Are you going back to Surrey? Something wrong at home?'

'No, I'm moving to a flat.'

Miss Ledder, small and grey-haired and aware of her responsibilities, shook her head. 'You'll find living on your own in a flat isn't all it's cracked up to be.'

'It's all right, I'm going to share with someone.'

The warden took it for granted she was going to share with another secretary. 'Be careful about money,' she advised. 'Make sure your flatmate puts in her share every payday.'

'Yes, Miss Ledder, I'll remember that.'

On Friday Ruth was packed and waiting when the taxi drew up outside. The other girls had had a whip round to give her a goodbye present – a pretty tablecloth for the table in the furnished rooms they imagined her inhabiting. They hugged her in farewell. 'Give us a ring some time,' they urged. 'We'll come to tea.'

'Yes, of course,' lied Ruth. She couldn't quite see herself inviting them to her new flat. She liked them, but she'd never shared her secrets with them.

The flat to which Ethan took her was in Knightsbridge, in a handsome block near Montpelier Square. She knew at once – from the straight-backed hall porter, the expanse of dark red carpet, the marble hall tables – that this was an expensive address. They went up in a lift to the second floor. Ethan produced a key, opened a door. The taxi man carried in Ruth's suitcase. He accepted a handsome tip, touched his cap and left.

Ethan picked Ruth up and carried her over the threshold. 'Welcome to your new home, my dear one,' he said softly as he set her down.

Arm in arm they went through the flat. There was a living room, a dining room, a bedroom and a room that could be either a spare bedroom or a study. The furnishings were reproduction antique in dark oak, the curtains and chair covers were chintz. The kitchen and bathroom on the other hand were very modern, gleaming with chrome and glass.

'Good heavens, it'll take me weeks to get used to an electric cooker,' exclaimed Ruth. 'I never used one in my life!'

'Good lord, Ruth, you're not going to do the cooking!'

'I'm not?'

'Of course not – there's a daily coming in in the morning who'll do all that sort of thing for you.'

'A daily?'

'A daily maid, Mrs Monash. The house agent hired her – she used to work for the last occupant, she's very reliable, I'm told.'

'Mrs Monash.'

'See how she suits. If you'd rather have someone else by and by, that's easily arranged.'

'I'm sure she'll be fine,' murmured Ruth.

'What's the matter?'

'Ethan, I've never had a servant before! What do I say to her?'

'You say, "Do this", and she does it,' he laughed.

'But how do I know what's to be done?'

'You'll manage,' he said. He pulled off her hat and ran his hand through her short brown hair. 'Come on now, stop standing there all in a dither. This is the beginning of a new life for both of us.'

'Oh, yes!' She threw her arms about him in sudden realization. 'We're here, together, alone – it's like heaven.'

'Come and see what I've done.' He urged her into the bedroom. On a bedside table a huge vase of roses stood side by side with a silver bucket in which nestled a bottle of champagne. Two downturned glasses were waiting. 'It's for our house-warming,' he explained, as he popped the cork. 'Moet et Chandon, you'll like it.'

The wine foamed over. Ruth caught the sparkling upsurge in the first glass. He poured the second and picked it up.

'Here's to us,' he said, holding up the glass in a toast.

'To us.'

Smiling, they drank. Then they set down the wine and went into each other's arms.

Much later, Ruth unpacked and put away her belongings. They seemed unsuited to this fine room. But then, she thought, soon I'll have other clothes – Ethan had already opened accounts for her at expensive establishments.

She had put on her cotton dressing gown. She looked at herself in the wardrobe mirror. In her mind's eye she saw her grandparents, shocked and disapproving.

'What are you shaking your head about?' Ethan asked, coming out of the bathroom as she turned away from the mirror.

'I was thinking about Grandma and Granddad. They're very strict, you know. They told me when I left home that I'd go straight to the bad – and I have, haven't I?'

He laughed outright. 'It depends what you mean by bad,' he remarked. 'I'd say what we have here is something very good.'

'All the same, I'm what Grandma would call "A Kept Woman".'

'That's all right. As long as you're "kept" by me.'

The first two or three weeks flowed by like a swift river, carrying her with its current. Mrs Monash did all the work, shopped for the food, prepared it according to Ruth's requirements and tactfully withdrew each evening at five thirty. Ethan would arrive as soon thereafter as he could manage. Sometimes he telephoned to say he'd be late, and on two occasions he had to go for a few days to Lancashire. She found the nights lonely when he was away.

She bought new clothes. It was surprising how much time you could spend looking at a mannequin showing a dress, choosing lingerie, being measured for shoes. She let a *parfumier* in Bond Street devise a scent for her exclusive use – light, flowery, with overtones of honey. It was all strange and new, exciting, enlivening.

But not engrossing.

By the end of the fourth week she was beginning to wonder how she would fill her days. She could, like the late Mrs Coverton, take up good works, she supposed. Yet she didn't know how to go about it, and wondered what the other ladies of the committee would say when she had to admit she was living with a man to whom she wasn't married.

The problem was solved almost accidentally and before it could really become a problem. Ethan came home one evening in some annoyance. He threw himself into an armchair, sprawled there looking cross. 'You know Stokes is going on ahead to Spa with the Coverton III? Well, there's been a mix-up over the trailer. The overseer at the repair shop let someone else borrow it and it's vanished – only for the time being, I imagine, but we can't get hold of it to take the car to France.'

They were both going over to Spa Francorchamps for a racing event. It would be Ruth's first trip abroad, and this time she had a passport. She was looking forward to it enormously.

She asked the obvious question. 'Dave Epps must know

100

someone who's got a trailer?'

'It's got to be the right size. Most of the folk who've got trailers that'll take a racing car are using them to go to Spa themselves.'

'It probably just needs a few phone calls, Ethan.'

'I haven't got time to mess about with it – I've got some Norwegian agents coming over this week; I have to look after them. But I know if I give it to Miss Krett to see to, she'll make a mess of it. Last time she hired a trailer it was fourteen inches too short to take the car.'

'I'll see to it for you, Ethan,' Ruth said.

'What?'

'I'll do it. I know all about racing cars, after all.'

'Well, that's true.' He gave her a smile and pulled her down towards him so that he could give her a kiss.

'I'd like to do it, Ethan,' she said, leaning over him as he sprawled in the armchair, 'Let me.'

'But I want you to go out and about and enjoy yourself.'

'Huh! It's only possible to stay enthusiastic over shoes and dresses up to a point! I'd much rather be dealing with something sensible like arranging transport for Cov III.'

'You would? Really?'

'Really.'

That was how Ruth Barnett took up the role of manager of Ethan Coverton's racing projects.

Chapter Seven

Spa Francorchamps was a good launching ground for Ruth's new career. A small town in Belgium, it was just far enough away to involve her in train and ferry time-tables, road maps, hotel bookings.

She used the telephone when she could, sent telegrams otherwise. Always in English, although some of the Belgians with whom she was dealing could speak only French or Walloon. By persistence, she always found someone who could translate for her. But she was left with a strong notion that she ought to learn at least some French.

This race meeting was to try out the course for next year. Next year the first Belgian Grand Prix was to be held here, and it was necessary to find out well in advance whether the stretch of country road was suitable – difficult without being absurdly dangerous, yet providing enough problems to make the drivers use their brains. In a word, it had to prove itself of Grand Prix calibre.

Eleven drivers turned up with thirteen cars between them. This was considered unlucky so the owner of the pair of cars was induced to withdraw one.

'Even so, twelve fast cars on this bumpy stretch . . .' grumbled Ethan, staring down the flat expanse sheltered by tall lime trees. 'They haven't done a thing to the surface.'

'Well, that's what this meeting's for, boss,' said Peter Stokes, 'to find out how much they need to do. The town elders aren't going to waste money putting down a special surface where it isn't needed.'

'They ought to brighten up their ideas,' said Ethan. 'A Grand Prix will bring a big influx of business – can't they understand that?'

'I hope they do something to the hotels,' murmured Ruth. She'd had a hard time finding rooms that were anything like the standard Ethan was used to.

'A few decent bathrooms wouldn't be a bad idea,' sighed David Epps. He had had to be accommodated in a little *auberge* on the edge of the town. He had referred to it as a fleabag after the first night's sleep there, and had the pink spots on his wrists to prove it.

'Never mind, love,' Ethan said to Ruth. 'We can rough it for a couple of days. You ought to see some of the places in Italy.'

'That inn outside Naples,' suggested Peter. 'The bed was too short even for me.' He looked down his short wiry frame with amusement. 'You might have fitted it better, though, Ruth. But mind you, there was nowhere to hang a dress – we had to drape our clothes on nails in the wall and the landlady nearly went for us with a knife because we got oil on her new whitewash.'

There were always plenty of reminiscences when racing men got together. What pleased Ruth was that they included her without a second thought. Perhaps they cleaned up their language a little when she was around, but on the whole they just accepted her. She knew quite a bit about racing cars and she was Ethan's girl – that was enough for them. There were one or two other girls who hung around with the motor-racing crowd but they were mostly showgirls or so-called flappers, in love with the thrilling ambience. Ruth was different; she knew what she was talking about.

Peter Stokes brought the Coverton III in first in both the morning and afternoon races on Saturday. The afternoon event was the more important, resulting in a small silver cup the size of a large thimble. Ethan and his team were delighted.

On Sunday afternoon, when the locals brought their family cars to take part in an informal race, Ethan himself took the wheel of the Silver Ghost and went gliding off to demonstrate the superiority of British cars. Unfortunately he finished third behind a Peugeot and a Renault.

'Well, who'd have thought it!' he said as he rejoined Ruth at the finishing line. 'Tricky lot! They boxed me in between them.'

'The car's too big for these roads, that's what it is,' she soothed.

'That's right, tell me it wasn't my fault, that's what I want to hear.'

'Also you tend to forget the Rolls is a limousine, not a racing car – the shape's entirely different, there's more wind resistance.'

'Oh, so now you're an expert!' He kissed her on the nose. 'Come on, let's go and get cleaned up and see the Cov loaded for transport.'

When this was done they packed, paid the bill at their dark little hotel and started off in the Rolls for the ferry. But en route Ethan decided to give Ruth the chance of seeing Brussels. They spent the night in a hotel utterly different from their little place in Spa Francorchamps, found it so pleasant they lingered another day, and returned to London late on Tuesday evening.

'Is Miss Krett holding the fort while you swan about enjoying yourself like this?' Ruth inquired, for they had been due back in the early hours of Monday morning.

'She's used to it. But I bet Antony's hopping mad – we were supposed to meet and discuss some money-making plan of his yesterday afternoon.'

'Ethan, that's wicked of you.'

'Oh, fiddlesticks! It's always the same. He spends half-an-hour talking hard at me, showing me columns of figures, and then I have to point out that it's going to cost us six hundred pounds a week over four years before we begin to make the expected profit.'

'But maybe in the end the profit would be worth the investment.'

Ethan was shaking his head. 'Ruth, radio communications is one of the fastest developing areas in business. Pushing money around isn't how to help it grow. We have to concentrate on research and development, that's where our spare funds have got to go. But Antony seems to imagine we can just keep on producing the sets we're making now for the next ten years, while we invest in taking over other firms so as to mop up the opposition. That's daft. Opposition, competition – that's what keeps us on our toes.'

'But then you enjoy competing. Perhaps Antony wants to achieve the same result some other way.'

'It's nice of you to try to stick up for him. But I've had two years of his "expansion plans" and other such schemes. It's just no go, love, he doesn't understand science, and that's what electrical engineering is, a branch of science. I spend a lot of time at our factories in the north, I know what's being done and what people are *trying* to do. That's where the money has to go. At the moment I don't see the sense in taking over, for example, a valve manufacturer. Let the manufacturer run his own experiments, come to me with any improvements he achieves. That's better sense than having him as part of my own firm and paying for his experiments myself.'

'Oh, very crafty!'

'Don't you laugh at me, you minx!'

Yet, though she laughed, she loved to have him tell her his thoughts on business and research. She herself had no scientific training; the village school at Freshton had taken her no further than anecdotes about James Watts and a boiling kettle. But she understood that there was a great new world of communication coming into being through the marvel of wireless telegraphy. In the flat in Knightsbridge there was a wireless set – or radio, as smart people were now beginning to call it – on which not only London broadcasts could be heard, but those from Paris, Lisbon, Amsterdam . . . The whole world seemed to lie before them.

She could take no part in the workings of the Coverton Electrical Company except to listen and discuss. But in the development and racing of the Coverton III she could be active, useful.

From finding it difficult to fill her days, she now discovered they were too packed with activity. She found a French teacher who was willing to start at the very first stages and took lessons three times a week. Every morning from nine until lunchtime she spent either planning for future race meetings or ensuring that the car was being properly serviced between races.

She spent a lot of time with David Epps although Ethan

sometimes growled at her about it. 'You keep away from that Handsome Harry,' he would say, only half joking. Dave had something of a reputation with the ladies.

But, despite these grumblings from Ethan, all she ever talked about to Dave was motor racing. As team mechanic he had care of the Coverton III but most of the actual work was done by a firm in Croydon under his supervision. He grumbled continually about the inefficiency of this. 'If I had my own proper workshop, with a couple of assistants—'

'Think of what it would cost, Dave.'

'But, Ruth, the boss spends an awful lot on bills to the repair shop, I know I could do it cheaper.'

'Not if you had to pay two assistants!'

'No— well— perhaps that was a bit of a daydream. But if I had, say, a lad and Peter Stokes to help me— I mean, Peter's a good mechanic, and as driver he's already on the payroll. And the two of us, we've got some ideas for a new version of the Cov . . .'

'What, you mean a Coverton IV?'

'Why not?'

'Look, Dave, we'd have to be doing a lot better with the Cov III before Ethan would want to start thinking of a Cov IV.'

'But don't you see, that's the whole point. The Cov III isn't going to get much further. We've got to develop that double overhead camshaft. We're not giving enough attention to the cam wheel.'

'You don't have to build a whole new car to have a better camshaft, Dave.'

He gave up. But only for the moment. Dave Epps felt his whole life depended on improving the racing car, and in the end he knew he'd persuade the boss to finance the building of something better than the Coverton III. One way to help matters along was to interest Ruth in the plan. Ruth had a lot of influence with the boss.

Ruth was likely to be less easily persuaded than he thought. She kept the books of the racing project and calculated the profit and loss. Mostly it was loss. The Coverton III wasn't yet winning many prizes and when it did, the prizes were silver cups of no great value. The spin-off from motor racing was supposed to be in the development of more sophisticated machines for the ordinary car owner – better steering, easier gears, more reliable tyres. But these advantages would benefit motor manufacturers first, although electrics played a great part in the efficiency of the internal combustion engine.

Ethan might claim that his motor racing was to some extent a research project, to find better sparking plugs and headlamps. The truth was, he did it for pleasure. Ruth sympathized with him entirely: it was his money, he was entitled to 'waste' it if he wanted to. And there would in the end be improvements in the electrics of the family car, although this couldn't be written into the profit and loss account as yet.

Winter came. Car racing almost ceased in Europe except in the Mediterranean areas where there were no specially built circuits and precious few roads up to motor-racing requirements. Drivers still went abroad but it was for reliability trials mostly.

Ethan and his team knew the Coverton III was reliable. What they wanted was to increase its speed.

So it was to the United States that they went.

'America?' gasped Ruth.

'Yes, of course. I thought you knew. I go to the States

at least once every year with the Cov.'

Of course she had known it. She'd seen mentions and occasional photographs on the sports pages. But the records of the Coverton Racing Team were sketchy in the extreme before she took over, so it somehow hadn't impinged on her consciousness as a matter for her to organize.

Now, it seemed, she was faced with the transport of the team to Daytona Beach in Florida.

There was no racetrack at Daytona. Cars raced on the hard-packed sand. There was no actual race programme either. The beach was used mainly for attempts on the land speed record.

'This year the Cov ought to come up over the hundred. We've ironed out all the wrinkles, I think. Of course, that won't be anything like a record – Campbell will be there, he'll outshine anything we put up, but my chief interest is getting the Cov's electrics absolutely foolproof under extreme testing. You'd better arrange for plenty of tyres, Ruth – the sand friction plays the devil with tyres.'

'Is there a list of Daytona dealers?'

'Er . . . No . . . There's an American Automobile Industry reference book at the office. I'll bring it home. No, I'll buy a new copy because you might need one while we're there.'

'You mean, I'm going?' Ruth cried in surprise.

'Of course, you're going.' He stared at her. 'Why ever not?'

'But, Ethan!'

'You've been to every other race meeting. Why wouldn't you go to Daytona?'

'I don't know. It just seems . . . I don't know,' she confessed.

He hooked a finger in the belt of her winter dress to bring her close. 'Wherever I go, you go,' he said. 'Hasn't that sunk in yet?'

Daytona received quite a lot of coverage in the British press. Sometimes the events had sufficient drama to move an item from the sports page to the general news. That year, an inexperienced British driver turned his car over on the beach, emerging alive though shaken from a wreck that seemed unsurvivable.

'Among the British contingent,' reported the motor-racing correspondent of the *Daily Telegraph*, 'it was felt that Harrison had a miraculous escape. Ethan Coverton, the millionaire car owner and driver, said he thought Harrison's goggles might not have been close-fitting enough. "One grain of sand would do it," he remarked. His companion, Miss Barnett, said she thought Harrison had had to borrow goggles from another driver.'

This was enough to cause interest to the gossip columnists. There had been many previous references to Ruth, but only on the sports pages. Now they took notice. 'Ethan Coverton and his racing companion, Miss Barnett.' 'Miss Barnett, seen here watching the Coverton III being shipped aboard the SS *Alicia*.' 'The British contingent arriving home from Daytona: left to right, Mr Leslie Loudon, Mr Malcolm Campbell, Mr Ethan Coverton and his driver Peter Stokes, Miss Ruth Barnett, Mr Winders . . .'

Ruth and Ethan were unaware of it or, if they were aware, paid no heed. But there were others who took note and were appalled.

Diana Coverton had been able to ignore her husband's recent behaviour until now. True, he had been spending very little time at home, but that wasn't by any means unusual: he went regularly to Lancashire to inspect his factories and talk to his research teams, he stayed many nights at his club, and, of course, he was always wasting time on motor racing.

There had been rumours of a girl. That was nothing unusual either. Diana, who had closed down the intimate side of her marriage after the birth of Lorette, shrugged off the occasional mistress. Men were like that, she knew. A succession of short-term liaisons meant nothing.

But this girl, whoever she was, seemed to have lasted much longer than the others.

The first hint had come toward the end of August. A friend of a friend had remarked that Ethan had taken the lease on an expensive flat in Knightsbridge.

'A lease?' That was rather alarming. That implied some sort of permanence.

But Diana decided not to be worried about it. Men were like that, she told herself yet again. So long as the affair was conducted with a decent reticence, she wouldn't let it bother her. In a way it was one side of a bargain she seemed to have with Ethan: she would look after his house and bring up his children if he would cause her no embarrassment.

But now . . . Now the newspapers were talking about his 'companion'. Whoever she was, this Miss Barnett, she'd lasted from August until January – six months, much longer than any of her predecessors. What was more, he was taking her motor racing.

Somehow that alarmed Diana. It meant she was different from the pretty, empty-headed women he'd chosen hitherto. She knew of three – an actress, a society woman married to a boring lawyer and an expensive lady of leisure who claimed to be a Spanish countess.

Diana studied the photograph of the group disembarking from the *Alicia*. The only girl in the group: small, slender, undistinguished so far as one could tell in this grainy black-and-white photo: certainly nothing to get frightened about!

And yet . . . she'd lasted six months. And she was going with him on his motor-racing jaunts. What did that mean? That there was something important holding them together?

In the past, thought Diana Coverton, I knew the situation. Ethan was in it for sex, the woman was in it for money. And probably that's still the case: after all, why would a young chit like this take on a man old enough to be her father? Of course she's in it for the money.

And yet – Ethan wasn't taking any trouble to be discreet. It was almost as if he didn't care. And that seemed to mean something more compelling than casual sex.

Could it be that the poor fool had fallen in love?

Chapter Eight

Antony Coverton had been his mother's confidant and adviser since he reached his twenties. His advice about money had been advantageous: a legacy from Diana's parents had, by his management, been invested very well even in these years of post-war depression.

She summoned him to the family home in Hertfordshire from his pied-à-terre in Belgravia. Her other children were there for dinner, but Martin was off immediately afterwards to a theatre first night and Lorette was going to a dance.

When they were alone over coffee in the drawing room, Diana broached the subject that was gnawing at her.

'I suppose you saw those items in the gossip columns the other day?' She knew the answer would be no. Antony only ever read the financial pages.

'What items?'

'About your father and some girl.'

Antony frowned, his narrow high-cheeked face flushing darker. He never enjoyed discussing his father. He always felt at a loss because he simply didn't understand Ethan Coverton. How could a man who held the reins of a hugely successful business be so deaf to the idea of taking it into the world of international finance?

'I didn't see it,' he mumbled, stirring sugar into his coffee.

'Ring the bell, will you, dear?' When he'd done so she said, 'I told Pollard to keep the papers. I knew you'd miss it. There are two items in yesterday's and one in the day before's linking him with a girl called Barrett or Barnes or something.'

'In the papers?' That was a little surprising. Antony was well aware there had been other girls but never, so far as he knew, any mention in the newspapers.

'That's why I'm telling you about it.' The butler came in. 'Oh, Pollard, those newspapers I told you to keep? Bring them here.'

'Yes, madam.'

'Why were the newspapers mentioning this girl?' Antony asked when the door closed behind Pollard.

'Because she's going to those motor-racing things with him, it seems.'

Antony considered this. 'Perhaps she's one of those ladies who've got money invested in racing cars? I believe there are a couple who—'

'That's not what the news items were implying. They were hinting that this Barnes or Bennett is his new light of love.'

'Bennett?'

'Something like that. Barnett, I think.'

'The name seems familiar. There was a girl in our office . . .' He paused, trying to summon up her face. Slightly suntanned skin, grey eyes – no, green, perhaps – soft brown hair in a short bob. Not unattractive although, of course, her black office dress masked any charms.

She'd been working in his father's outer office. He'd

thought he himself might take her over once Miss Krett finished training her, to replace the impertinent Miss Giles. But then she vanished. When Miss Giles received her inevitable marching orders, he had to ask Personnel to find him someone else.

'Someone in your office?' Diana took it up. 'A secretary?'

'No, just a typist, working under Miss Krett.'

'Who's Miss Krett – oh, your father's personal assistant. And this person, Barrett or Barnsley, she was just an office girl?'

'Yes. But could it be the same girl?'

Pollard came in with the newspapers. At a nod from Diana he handed them to Antony, who set to work paging through them.

'The gossip columns,' his mother directed. 'There's a photograph in one of them, a group.'

'Yes, I've found it. "The British contingent arriving home".' He stared at the grainy picture. He said slowly, 'I do believe it's the girl from the office.'

Diana set down her demitasse with a clatter. 'Oh, really, it's too bad! Until now I've been prepared to turn a blind eye to that sort of thing, but really, Antony, to be talked about in the *newspapers*! And the girl's such a *nobody*! I shall be a laughing stock.'

'Now, now, Mother, don't get upset.' Thrusting aside the newspapers, he leaned over the coffee table to take her hand. 'It's all right. These things never last long.'

'I don't know so much!' She allowed herself a sniffle or two. 'He's hardly been in this house for more than twenty-four hours together since last August. You remember Lorette's birthday party – he only showed up for long enough to give her her pearl necklace and then he was gone. And he wouldn't come to Gstaad with us for Christmas.'

Her son patted her hand. 'Shall I get you a brandy?'

She shook her head then nodded. 'The Armagnac, dear. I feel so *stricken*.' Her handsome dark head was bowed, her brown eyes hooded. She looked at her clasped hands on which sparkled the diamond engagement hoop, the wedding ring of platinum. Some little chit from the office! It was so humiliating.

After a sip or two of the Armagnac she let herself be coaxed into looking up. Antony was always receptive to her trusting glances. 'I feel so – exposed, Antony. We've got to do something about her.'

'But what, Mother?'

'Buy her off. It shouldn't be difficult. There can't be any deep feeling on her side. What do the Americans call it – he's her sugar daddy. But that's only on a sort of day-to-day, week-to-week basis, I imagine she gets what he feels like giving her, presents and money for expenses, things like that. If we offer her a considerable lump sum, that ought to attract her. After all, she can't really want to stay with him for anything other than his money.'

'I suppose not. But how do we go about it?' He wasn't keen on the idea. He never liked parting with money. His mother, on the other hand, thought you could solve every problem by throwing five-pound notes at it.

'Well, she was in your office, you must have an address for her.'

'I can't just ask for her address!'

'Why not?'

'Think how odd it would look.'

'Nonsense. Just ask your secretary to find it for you.

This Miss Krett who works for your father – she must have it. Your girl has only got to ask for it; these girls chatter together all the time,' said Diana, who had never worked in an office in her life.

Next day Antony Coverton told his secretary to get the address of Miss Barnett from Miss Krett. Miss Clifford duly went down the corridor to Miss Krett's office. Miss Krett said in surprise, 'Why ever would he want that?'

'No idea,' said Miss Clifford. And couldn't care less, her tone implied.

'I don't have it, there was no reason why I should,' said Miss Krett sniffily. 'Ring Personnel.'

Personnel supplied the information. Miss Clifford typed it up to put on Antony's desk with other items. When he came to it he stared at it, aghast. The Euphemia Grey Hostel for Business Girls? There was no way he was going to telephone or write to anyone living there.

But his mother's requests were best attended to. Once she took hold of a thing, she never let go until she had her own way. He was about to tell Miss Clifford to put through a call when he thought better of it. No reason why Miss Clifford should know he was personally interested in Ruth Barnett. He asked for an outside line and put through the call himself.

'Miss Barnett?' repeated the warden. 'There's no one of that name living here.'

'This is her former employer. That is the address we have on our files.'

'Barnett?'

'Miss Ruth Barnett, employed by us until August 1924.'

'Ah, yes, one moment. Ruth Barnett.' Miss Ledder

was flipping through her card index. 'Yes, you're right, she was resident here for some months but left last August.'

'Left?'

'Yes.'

'What is her forwarding address?'

'We – er – we don't seem to have one,' said Miss Ledder. 'Let me see— I seem to recall— So many girls come and go here, you must understand it's difficult to keep track. I seem to recall she was moving out to private digs. But I think she couldn't give us a forwarding address because she was going to move again almost at once to share with someone.'

'But what happened to her letters? Haven't you been sending them on?'

'So far as I can remember, there never were any letters,' said Miss Ledder. This persistence made her uneasy. 'May I ask the reason for this inquiry?'

'We have some uncollected salary we'd like to send on,' lied Antony, and said goodbye.

His mother came up to town for lunch in order to hear his news. When he reported his lack of success, she was displeased. 'Really, Antony, you should have been more insistent.'

'It was no use insisting, the hostel had no information to give.'

'You must find out where this girl is living now.'

'But how?'

'You've got inquiry officers on your staff, haven't you? Didn't you say you'd had them investigate the leak of some industrial information last year?'

'Mother, I can't ask a member of our staff to find Ruth Barnett!'

'Why not?'

'Because Father would be almost sure to hear about it, that's why! Is that what you want?'

Diana toyed with her chartreuse of fruits. 'You must hire a private detective, that's all.'

'A private detective? But— but— I wouldn't know where to find one.'

'Ask one of your inquiry officers. These people must know one another, surely.'

It was good reasoning, but no more attractive for that. However, he knew he must do as he was instructed. His mother was determined to get rid of the girl his father had taken up with, so the sooner he got on with it the better.

The Investigation Department was a two-man team. Without quibble they supplied him with the names of two reliable firms, and if they thought the request strange they kept the thought to themselves.

He used a private line to arrange an appointment later that afternoon with the first name on the paper. He left the Holborn office and walked the short distance to the firm's premises in Kingsway. A very discreet setup. An outer office with a middle-aged receptionist, another office with two or three desks. At one of the desks sat a big, relaxed man.

'Well, now, sir, what is it that's troubling you?' said ex-Sergeant Twyford of the Hammersmith police.

Antony was irritable now. He was angry. Angry with his mother for making him talk to this man, angry with his father for being the cause.

'I want you to find a girl who used to work for us,' he said.

'A servant, sir?'

'No, in the firm's office.'

'Could I have the name and address of the firm?'

'Is that necessary?'

Twyford's lips folded together in an expression that was half a smile, half a grimace. One of those, was he – ashamed to be consulting a private detective but anxious to use him for work he couldn't do himself.

'I need to know what I'm taking on, sir. Your name is Coverton. The firm isn't by any chance the Coverton Electrical Company?'

Antony was taken aback.

'Oh, yes, sir, after your call I looked you up in the phone book and there right next door to your private number was the firm and its office numbers. Still, it was just a guess. So, this girl used to work for Coverton Electrical. Is she suspected of some crime or misdemeanour? Pilferage, perhaps?'

'No, nothing like that.'

'Why don't you just tell me what it's about, sir,' urged Twyford, stifling a sigh. 'It doesn't really make any difference to me why you want her found, you know. But I do need to have the real facts so that I don't blunder about.'

Cornered, Antony told him the truth. Twyford took it without comment. So the wife and son wanted to find out something about the father's mistress – quite commonplace.

'That shouldn't take long, sir,' he remarked. 'You say your father returned from the States the day before yesterday. And this young lady was a member of the party?'

'Yes.'

'Is he back at his desk in the office today?'

'Yes, of course, he has a lot of catching up to do.'

'I gather he doesn't often go to the family home in Hertfordshire. Are you expecting him there this evening?'

'Not that I know of,' Antony said.

'In that case, sir, I don't think there will be much of a problem. I should have the information you want by tomorrow or the next day.'

'So soon?'

'I expect so, sir.'

And Twyford got Ruth Barnett's address that evening by the simple expedient of following Ethan Coverton home.

Since there was no point in being too efficient, and pay for two days' work was better than pay for one, Twyford went back the next morning to watch outside Crecy Court. Early though he was, he was too late to see Ethan leave. Soon after nine o'clock, the girl came out.

Younger than he expected, nice-looking, fresh and eager. Clad in a blue tweed coat with a big fur collar that framed her gold-skinned face. Neatly shod in brown brogues, gloves to match, blue felt hat hiding most of her hair.

She walked off briskly. Twyford followed. She went to an address in Kensington near the museums. It was her French teacher, although Twyford couldn't know that. About eleven she reappeared. She spent some time going to travel agents in the area. She lunched in a restaurant in Basil Street. By two thirty she was indoors again.

Twyford went to chat to the hall porter. 'John Roding?' the porter said. 'Nobody of that name lives here.'

'You sure?' Twyford produced a scrap of paper, studied it. 'That's the address I've got here. Or – wait a bit – could the flat be in the name of his cousin? Miss Barnett?'

'Oh, Miss Barnett! Oh yes, in Flat 22. Shall I ring through and tell her?'

'Her cousin's not living with her?'

The porter smiled a knowing smile. '*Oh,* no,' he said.

'In that case, I'll try the other address I've got for Roding,' sighed Twyford. 'Who'd be a bill collector!'

Flat 22, Crecy Court, Knightsbridge. Easy as kiss your hand. If his client wanted to know whether the lease was in her name, he could find that out from the letting agent. He had the address she went to in the morning: that might prove of interest, but it seemed innocuous, as did her flitting about among travel agents. On the whole, an innocent-seeming little thing.

All the same, you had to have some trickery in your nature to land a millionaire as your protector.

He rang Antony at his Belgravia flat early next morning to report success.

'How on earth did you find out so quickly?' cried Antony, astounded.

'We have our ways, sir,' replied Twyford. Followed him home, you could have done it yourself and saved the fee, he was thinking. 'I've seen the young lady, checked on her activities for just one day. Do you want a report on that?'

'No— well, I suppose so.'

He gave a quick resumé of Ruth's morning activities. 'She lunched with a gentleman in a restaurant in Basil Street. From what I could observe through the window, they seemed to be conferring over a catalogue which the gentleman was showing her. I could only glimpse its cover but it had an illustration of a car. She did some shopping in Brompton Road. She arrived home at about four p.m. She came downstairs to the hall with a woman I take to be the domestic – that would be about five thirty. The domestic and Miss Barnett had a short conversation with the hall porter. From the gestures I noted and the fact that they went outside to point upwards, I gather the conversation was about the cleaning of the windows. The domestic left and Miss Barnett went upstairs. At about seven p.m. your father arrived. At about eight they went out together, to Wyndham's theatre, sir. They returned to Crecy Court at about eleven p.m. at which time I ended the surveillance, sir. Is that satisfactory?'

Antony was more impressed than he would admit. 'That's fine, thank you.'

'Do you wish to close the investigation at this point, sir?'

'Ye-es. Yes, let me have your account. Send it here to my flat.'

'Naturally, sir.'

Diana Coverton was not surprised at the speed with which the detective had supplied the necessary information. You paid people to work and they did what they were expected to do.

'So what next?' her son inquired.

'Well, now you must go to see her and pay her off.'

'Me?'

'Well, good heavens, Antony, you can scarcely expect me to do it surely?'

'But— I've never done a thing like that before.'

'Neither have I. But it's got to be done. We must put a stop to this public notoriety before it makes us look ridiculous.'

'Wouldn't it be better to let it die a natural death?'

'And how long would that be? It's lasted six months, at a guess. I *certainly* don't want it going on for six more. Just imagine how the society gossips would carry on if Lorette's engagement were announced – "Lorette Coverton, daughter of Ethan Coverton, pictured here with his friend Ruth Barnsley".'

'But is Lorette likely to get engaged soon? I got the impression she hadn't—'

'Don't argue, Antony. I want this thing put a stop to, and the way to do it is to send the girl packing. If it costs us some money to get her to go, it's worth it. And since I can't go and haggle with her, you must.'

He could see it was no use to object. 'How much should I offer, do you imagine?'

'I don't know. A thousand? Two?'

'Two thousand! That's an awful lot of money!'

'Darling, we mustn't scrimp on this. We're talking about the family reputation. We have our position in society to think about. Two thousand – you could start lower and go up to that, couldn't you?'

He didn't want to do anything of the kind. He felt they ought to send someone else to represent them, but couldn't think who. Not the family lawyer – Romstock represented the whole family, Ethan as well as Diana and the children. Not the detective, Twyford – although the man was efficient. This was too delicate a matter to entrust to him.

No, as his mother said, he'd have to go himself.

He rang Twyford next day to tell him to resume surveillance on Miss Barnett. Twyford said he was busy on something else but would send an associate. 'Is there any special information you require, sir?'

'I want to know when Miss Barnett is at home. Tell your

colleague to ring me at the office when he knows she's there.'

'Certainly, sir.'

The first time he got the information, he couldn't take the opportunity because there was a board meeting he couldn't skip. The second time, his father was out of the building and, for all he knew, might be heading for Crecy Court himself. But the third time, Ethan was in Lancashire and Antony himself had no office engagements.

Third time lucky, he told himself grimly as he took a taxi to Knightsbridge.

At the building, the detective from Twyford's touched his hat in greeting as he got out. 'She's been indoors now nearly an hour, sir. Went to a bookshop, came out with a couple of books – I'd think she's settled down for a nice read.'

The February day was just the kind on which it would be nice to settle down with a good book. Squaring his shoulders, Antony went into the foyer.

'Yes, sir?' said the hall porter.

'I'm visiting Miss Barnett in Flat 22,' Antony said.

'Oh, yes, sir. You know your way up?'

'Yes, thank you.'

The lift bore him to the second floor. He walked down the carpeted corridor, rang the bell at Number 22. The door opened. A middle-aged woman in a blue wrap-around apron looked at him inquiringly.

'Yes, sir?'

'Miss Barnett, please?'

'Yes, sir. Who shall I say is calling?'

'Mr Coverton.'

'I beg your pardon, sir?' The daily maid knew Mr

Coverton, had glimpsed him from time to time over the last six or seven months. This wasn't he.

'Mr Coverton. Just tell her, will you?'

The voice of authority carried the day. The maid closed the door without fastening it. Antony waited in the corridor, annoyed, ashamed, resentful at having to be here at all.

The door reopened. Ruth Barnett stood there, a book in one hand. She stared at him, dropped the book.

'Antony!'

Startled at hearing her use his first name as if she knew him, he brushed past her into the flat.

The maid was hovering in the vestibule. He gave her a glare but she stood her ground.

'That's all right, Mrs Monash,' Ruth faltered, with a little gesture that told her to go back to her dinner preparations. To Antony she said. 'You'd better come in.' She showed him into the living room.

He glanced about. Quite good taste, if she was responsible for the furnishings. A comfortable fire glowed in the grate. An armchair with an exercise book balanced on an arm showed how she'd been engaged when he rang the bell. She came in behind him, placed the book she'd dropped on a table. He glanced at it. French Revision Exercises – how extraordinary.

'What are you doing here?' she asked, her voice gaining strength as her first astonishment left her.

'Paying you a visit, obviously.'

'But how did you know where to come?'

'Oh, it wasn't difficult to find your little love nest.'

She gave a little gasp at the gratuitous rudeness. 'Why are you here?' She had drawn near the table as if to support herself against it.

'To buy you off.'

'*Buy me off?*'

'Oh, don't bother with the bewildered look, Miss Barnett. If we could skip all the protestations of innocence and so forth, we could get down to business.'

She seemed to him to straighten, to become more alert. The triumph he'd felt at taking her so much by surprise began to leave him. Despite her femininity there was strength there.

She had certainly changed since he used to see her trotting to and fro in the corridor outside his office. She was wearing a dress of soft moss-green wool that brought out the colour of her eyes which were, he now saw, grey-green. Her soft hair was held back from her cheeks by a big clasp of tortoiseshell. Her only adornment was a pair of earrings that looked like real jade.

You could have put her side by side with his debutante sister and no one could have told the difference in their background.

It angered him. Who was she to dare to look as pretty, as well turned-out, as Lorette? This trollop from nowhere who'd somehow managed to entrap his father?

'The only question to ask,' he said with a cold briskness, 'is how much?'

'How much for what?'

'To pack up and go.'

'Go where?' She was looking at him as if he were insane.

'Wherever you like. I imagine you have plans for your eventual future – I mean, you couldn't expect to live off my father for ever.'

Her brows came together in a frown of astonishment. 'This is my home, Mr Coverton,' she said. 'If you can't be polite, I must ask you to leave.'

'Polite? All right, let's play the game that way if we must. Miss Barnett, I want to ensure that you have a decent sum to hand when you leave here so that you need have no financial worries. Would you like to give me some idea of the amount you'd need?'

'I don't need any money. I'm not going anywhere.'

'You certainly are. It's quite outside the bounds of decency to have you and my father talked about in the newspapers—'

'So that's what this is about!' Her tone expressed something he'd never expected – contempt. 'You don't like to see Ethan's name linked with mine, is that it?'

'You'd hardly expect my mother to enjoy such a thing. She . . .'

'She never bothered her head about it before. She must have known something had changed for Ethan but she's never made the slightest move, taken the slightest interest until the journalists put it under her nose.' Ruth's chin came up. 'So now you're here to put a stop to it, not because any of you care about him but because you've been made to feel uncomfortable.'

'Miss Barnett, I'm not here to make an extended study of my father's silly behaviour. All I want to know is, how much will you take to move out?'

'Please leave.'

'Let's say a thousand. How does that strike you? A thousand pounds to make a start somewhere else.'

She made a sound that was almost a laugh. 'Are you offering me a thousand pounds to leave Ethan?'

'I have my chequebook here.' He took it out, offered it to her. 'A thousand clear and free.'

'Mr Coverton, you're beneath contempt. Go away.'

Her disdain was so damaging to him that he found himself almost dropping the chequebook. 'Don't you take that tone with me!' he cried. 'What are you, after all? A pick-up, a tart—'

She took a step towards him, her eyes glinting. 'Get out of my home,' she whispered.

'Your home! Paid for with my father's money!'

'Get out! We have nothing to say to each other!' Her voice was strong and clear now.

He made a huge effort, controlled his temper. 'I'm prepared to offer two thousand—'

'Stop it!' she said. 'It's revolting to hear you speak like this about someone your father loves.'

'Love? Is that what you call it? A man as old as my father buys a pretty young thing and throws money away on her—'

'Money! Money is all you think about, isn't it? Spy out where I live, rush here to offer me money – does it never occur to you that there could be something good and valuable between us, something you can't put a price on?'

'That would be a lot more convincing if I didn't know you'd set out to trap him from the beginning. Don't forget I saw you working your way into his good books at the office—'

There was enough truth in this to make her falter. 'That wasn't how it was.'

'No? How was it, then? He made all the running, was that it? Besieged you until you couldn't resist any more? Or battered your door down when you were alone and helpless? Go on, tell me how it was you went to bed together the first time – dragged you there, did he?'

'Stop it, stop it, you're making it seem horrible – you don't understand!' She put her hands over her ears.

He seized one wrist to pull her hand away. 'You're going to hear what I'm saying. And it's what everybody else will be saying. No fool like an old fool, isn't that it? Soak him for every penny you can get?'

'Let me go!'

'Not until we sort this out. How much will you take to clear off?'

'You're hurting me!'

Recalled to himself, he let her go but stayed close, using his height to dominate her. He flourished the chequebook. 'Come on, how much?' he shouted.

She took him by surprise. She stepped to the telephone, picked up the receiver, dialled.

'What are you doing?' he exclaimed, alarmed.

Behind him the door opened and Mrs Monash put her head in. 'Is everything all right, miss?' she asked in a frightened voice.

Ruth was speaking into the telephone. 'Johnson, there's a man in my flat who refuses to leave. Would you come up and—'

'Wait a minute!' Antony flared.

She turned her eyes to him. 'You're going?' she asked.

'I . . . I . . .'

'Please come up, Johnson,' she said into the phone.

'All right, I'm going,' he said, shoving the chequebook into his pocket. 'But you haven't heard the last of this!'

She ignored him. With Mrs Monash at his elbow, he went into the vestibule. Behind him he heard Ruth say into the phone, 'It's all right, Johnson, he's going. Please make sure he leaves the building.'

Furious, baffled, defeated, Antony Coverton went to the lift while the maid stood in the doorway. She stayed until it had come and borne him downwards. In the hall the porter was awaiting him, tall and military, full of disapproval.

'This way, sir,' he said haughtily, and walked with him to the glass doors.

Outside on the pavement Antony stood for a moment, trying to understand what had happened. The porter took up a position inside the doors, regarding him with a steady eye. A taxi cruised by. Antony threw himself into it.

What a disaster, what a fiasco . . .

And what was he going to say to his mother?

Chapter Nine

When Mrs Monash returned to the living room she found Miss Barnett sitting on the sofa, as white as rag paper.

'I'll make you a nice cup of tea, shall I, miss?'

'No . . . thank you . . .'

'Come on now, Miss Barnett, you need something. A spot of brandy?'

Ruth had allowed Mrs Monash a little more familiarity than Ethan would have approved. The truth was, she'd no idea how to treat servants. Mrs Monash had not taken advantage, but a warmth had developed between the two that wasn't precisely usual for mistress and servant. So the maid advanced into the room, determined to be comforting.

'All right, then, tea, Mrs Monash, thank you.'

Instead of using the Earl Grey (considered suitable for afternoon tea), Mrs Monash put three spoonfuls of Breakfast Blend into the teapot for a reviving brew. She didn't take in the usual paraphernalia of silver pot and cream jug, but poured the tea, added a good tablespoon of brandy, and brought that to Ruth. She was pleased to see her young employer swallow it down without even noticing it had been strengthened with spirits.

It clearly made her feel better. Colour flowed back

under the suntan on her cheeks. Satisfied that her first-aid methods had succeeded, Mrs Monash retired to the kitchen to render the same treatment to herself. Mrs Monash was pleased she herself had not been found wanting. Men shouting at the poor girl – whatever next!

Ruth's first instinct was to ring Ethan in Blackburn to tell him what had occurred. Then she realized it would bring him hotfoot back to London from an important research meeting. Better not. Better not to mention it to him at all.

But during the twenty-four hours that passed before he returned late on the Wednesday evening, she'd had second thoughts. It couldn't be kept quiet. This was surely not the only attempt that would be made to separate them. Ethan had to be warned.

She unpacked his travel bag while he poured himself a whisky and soda. He'd had dinner on the train, needed nothing more than a nightcap.

'I've got something to tell you, Ethan,' she said when he set down his glass.

Her tone was so serious that for a moment he wondered if she was going to tell him she was expecting a child. But that was most unlikely. Ever since that night when, weeping in his arms, she'd confessed her illegitimacy, they'd agreed that they shouldn't risk a pregnancy. Ruth didn't want to burden a child – even Ethan's child – with the nicknames she had suffered.

'All right,' he said, preparing to listen, although he was dying with fatigue.

She came to sit beside him on the sofa. She took one of his hands in both of hers. Merely to recall Antony's words engulfed her in a wave of distress and uncertainty. But she must speak, and she must do it in a way that wouldn't make matters worse.

'Don't be angry,' she began.

'With you? Of course not!'

'Not with me. With Antony.'

'Antony?' His light-blue eyes suddenly snapped with interest. Antony was a thorn in his side at all times. What now?

'He came here.'

'Antony?'

'Yesterday afternoon. He rang the doorbell.'

'How the devil could he—'

'He said it wasn't difficult to find out where I live.'

'But why on earth should he want to?'

'To offer me money.'

A long, frightening silence ensued. At its end Ethan drew a deep breath then said, with grim humour, 'And how much was it worth to get rid of you?'

'Two thousand.'

'Only two! That's just like Anthony – he never wants to part with money unless it's some grandiose investment.' He gave Ruth a gentle kiss on the cheek. 'And what did you say, sweetheart?'

At his tenderness her composure broke. Tears brimmed over. She bent her head to hide them but he tilted her chin up. 'Damn him,' he said softly. 'I'll cut him in little pieces and feed him to vultures.'

'You p-promised not to b-be angry, darling,' she sobbed.

'I'm not angry,' he said, although he was – he was enraged. At his son, his own son. If Antony had walked in at that moment, his life wouldn't have been worth a farthing. 'All right, now, love, all right, don't cry. He's not worth it. Come on now, Ruthie, it doesn't matter what he did.'

'B-but you've got to realize, Ethan, that was p-probably just the first shot.'

He thought that over. She might be right. Antony wouldn't have come here offering to give away money without prompting from his mother.

'Diana probably put him up to it,' he muttered, putting an arm round Ruth and resting his chin on her hair. 'But why the hell has she suddenly got interested enough to do a thing like this?'

'Because of the picture in the papers and the mentions in the gossip columns,' she said, recovering and wiping away her tears with her fingers. 'He said as much. He said it was "outside the bounds of decency".'

'Decency! What does he know about decency, if he could come here and treat you like a mercenary one-nighter!'

'Be fair, Ethan. He doesn't know me at all. He's just going by what other people might expect.'

'I'll knock his teeth in!'

'No, please, darling – please, you promised – don't stir things up. I sent him away, but I know that can't be the end of it. You have to see him at the office every day. It would only make things impossible there if you had a fight with him.'

'I'll give him his marching orders.'

'He's resentful enough. That would only make things worse.'

Well, that was true. Diana would take it very hard if Antony were to be dismissed. She was in full agreement with her son's plans to enlarge and augment Covelco so that it became an international company to be mentioned with pride to her society friends.

Antony himself set a lot of store by his position at Covelco. He liked being the heir apparent, the tycoon-in-waiting. To be honest, he did his job well enough – took on some of the routine paperwork that Ethan himself found so tedious. This wasn't to say that Antony was indispensable: Ethan had managed quite well without him before his elder son left university to join the firm.

All the same, his first furious instinct – to have Antony thrown out of the office – should be curbed. It would cause talk at work, which was never a good thing. Some bright spark might even work out the reason for his dismissal and that would lead to gossip and sniggering.

Then there was his wife to consider. Diana would take it as a mortal insult if he dismissed the son to punish him for speaking to the mistress. Long experience had taught him that Diana could be vindictive.

Better to cool things down, as Ruth was advising.

He kept his word. He was early as usual in the office next day, so that when Antony arrived at nine there was a message on his desk requiring him to go at once to the office of the managing director.

Antony knew it could only be as a result of his visit to Ruth two days ago. He'd expected the girl to drag Ethan back from Blackburn to take up the cudgels. For some reason, she'd waited until he returned in the usual run of things. But, of course, she'd have wept all over him and built up a case against him.

He was ready for a fight. He had talked it over with his mother and had been primed with some telling phrases: family honour, flagrant behaviour, a man of your age should know better, grasping little minx . . .

His father didn't ask him to sit down. He himself was standing, and managed as always to dominate the room by so doing.

Antony stood in front of his father's desk, already beginning to feel like a schoolboy hauled before the head.

'I have something to say to you, Antony, and I'm going to say it without raising my voice,' Ethan said in a very level tone. 'I've left instructions with the hall porter that if you ever turn up again at Crecy Court, he's to throw you out at once. If you approach Miss Barnett in any way, I'll dismiss you from the firm.'

Antony was startled. Startled, horrified. 'You can't do that! My shares entitle me—'

'Oh, yes, I can. It's true you were given shares on your twenty-first birthday that allow you a seat on the board, but it doesn't guarantee you a job here. As managing director I have control of hiring and firing, and I will fire you, Antony, if you ever say another uncivil word to Ruth.'

Stung, Antony riposted with a sneer. 'I suppose she worked on your feelings to get you to make this cheap threat.'

'Quite the contrary. She asked me not to get angry, and I'm trying very hard to remember her advice.' His father shrugged a little. 'People working together in a company don't have to be on loving terms, it's true, so I can despise you as much as I like so long as we manage to get the work done.'

'Despise *me*!' How dare he? His father was the one who was acting despicably, flaunting his kept woman in the face of his wife and children.

'What did you think I'd feel? Pride? You went sneaking

behind my back to see the woman I love, and tried to bribe her . . .'

'Don't talk as if she were something special! She's got her hooks into you for the money. The truth is, I didn't get the price up high enough.'

Ethan took a deep breath. This was as difficult as he'd thought it would be. 'Antony, we are not going to discuss Miss Barnett. I got you in here to tell you the way things are going to work in future. You are still my assistant. I want you to go on learning the business because in the fullness of time you'll take charge here and I want you to have got over your daft ideas about expansion, and to handle things sensibly. But you're on probation from now on. Do you understand?'

'You can't expect me not to support Mother in her reaction to what's going on.'

'What your mother does is her own affair. Don't let her make you a cat's-paw. If you and I can just be polite to each other in business hours, that's all I ask – that, and some respect for Miss Barnett.'

'Respect for your mistress? Do you really imagine I can *respect* her?'

'Very well, if that's too much, just steer clear. Is that understood?'

'You do realize you're making us all a laughing stock?'

'I don't care, Antony,' Ethan said, with a sudden wide smile. 'For the first time in my life I'm in love, and if people laugh, let them.'

Antony went out almost staggering under the realization that hit him at that moment. His father really meant it. He was *in love*.

'I tell you he was in earnest,' he told his mother that evening. 'He's serious. Even if the girl were willing to take money, he wouldn't let her go.'

'You're being absurd, Antony. I can't believe your father's lost his head to that extent. She's just another in the succession of grabby girls, only she seems to have more intelligence than the others because she knows how to hang on to him.'

Diana went on the assumption that everyone else held the same view of society as herself. The daughter of a country squire, she'd been brought up to expect forelock-tugging from inferiors, agreement from equals and patronage from superiors. Her great aim in life was to climb the social ladder so as to be able to bestow patronage rather than receive it. If, as she'd intended, she'd married a member of the landed aristocracy, no such efforts would have been needed.

But on the whole she'd done well with the husband material fate had sent her. With his money and his tolerance she'd made a life that suited her and which, until now, she'd felt could only get better.

Now her stupid husband was going to reduce all her success to nothing. People would talk about her behind her back, people would think her a fool for letting it happen. Yet it could only be a temporary insanity. He couldn't *really* want the world to know he was living with some little slut of a girl from nowhere.

However, although Diana had no intention of letting the matter rest, Antony's future mustn't be endangered. She must give the situation some thought.

Her two other children, of course, became aware of what was going on. Martin, lean and languorous, affected to be Bohemian, and shrugged at the idea of a mistress. Lorette, still young and easily hurt, took it much harder.

'Everybody's *talking* about it,' she wept to her mother.

'Last night at Ciro's, someone actually asked me what she's like – as if I was likely to have *met* her!'

'Well, these days, you know,' mused Martin, 'conventions don't really tie people down in the way they used to.'

'They do in this family,' his mother retorted sharply. 'Don't bring your theatrical morals home, Martin, I won't have it.'

The interest aroused by his father's indiscretion moved Martin to creativity. He wrote a piece for a nightclub entertainer of his acquaintance, a parody of a song enjoying popularity at the moment because it was part of the repertoire of the comedienne Gracie Fields.

His friend Edith Quatrell couldn't pay him much, but money wasn't the important thing. If the parody were successful, some theatrical producer might take note and ask him to write something for a review.

Ethan Coverton noticed the name of his younger son in the entertainment column of his evening paper. 'Edith Quatrell's programme at the Oyster Shell Club is varied and amusing. At her opening last night the piece by Martin Coverton caused many a smile, and her satirical rendering of the torch song "Who's Sorry Now?" was full of unexpected fun . . .'

'We could drop in to hear her,' suggested Ruth when Ethan, rather proud that Martin had done something worth while, pointed out the item.

'Would you like that?'

'I'd like to hear the kind of thing Martin's good at.' Anything to do with the Covertons interested her. Antony had proved to be awful but Martin, being as she supposed less obsessed with money, might turn out to be more friendly.

Nightclubs were a new thing for Ruth. So far Ethan had taken her to two: one with a negro band playing New Orleans jazz, the other with a South American group playing tangos and rumbas. The dance steps learned at local hops in Freshton were adequate for the jazz tunes, but she'd been totally at a loss over the Brazilian rhythms.

The Oyster Shell, however, had a four-piece combination playing only popular songs. The noise level was bearable and the decor – pearly glass and pink silk to illustrate the oyster-shell motif – pleasant enough, though hard to distinguish in the dim lighting and cigarette smoke. She danced with Ethan, letting him lead her in a slow foxtrot to 'It Had To Be You'.

The floor show came on. It consisted of a male tap-dancing pair in white tuxedos, and 'our pretty, witty chanteuse, Edith Quatrell'. Miss Quatrell came on in a slim knee-length dress of scarlet satin to a scattering of applause. She sang, in a clear though slight voice, a song by Noël Coward, an ironic version of Jack Yellen's 'Glad Rag Doll', and then announced her new piece. 'The words were written for me by my friend Martin Coverton. I hope you like it, folks.'

She launched into the Gracie Fields song.

> 'I'm just nineteen and oh so sweet!
> This tycoon's swept me off my feet.
> It's love – or electricitee –
> Or cash – it's all the same to me!
> Yet there's a chap I'm pretty keen on
> A younger shoulder for me to lean on.
> Shall I be an old man's da-arling?
> Or shall I be a young man's slave?'

The audience laughed knowingly as the piano accompaniment tinkled on to lead into the next verse.

> 'Covelco calls with all its charms,
> But Johnny's got such big strong arms.
> And though he's interested in cars,
> He's not among the racing stars
> Because he'd rather be with me
> Than win the stupid Manx TT.
> Shall I be an old man's da-arling,
> Or shall I be a young man's slave?'

Ruth felt her face go hot. The words were about Ethan!

The singer had launched into her third verse, which told her audience that though she was young and liked young men, she had the sense to know that it was the old men who had the money. In the merciful dimness Ruth turned to look at Ethan. His face was like stone.

She leaned across the table. 'Shall we go?' she whispered.

'Not until she's finished,' he replied. 'Just think what a gossip item it would make. "Coverton walks out on son's masterpiece".'

Ruth felt almost sick with anger and revulsion. Ethan's own son had done this. How could anyone be so heartless?

In stoic silence they sat through the remaining two verses. They even applauded at the end, though with less enthusiasm than the rest of the audience. Edith Quatrell sang one more number, adapted from 'Who's Sorry Now?' After that, mercifully, they were able to make their escape.

Neither spoke as the taxi carried them away from the nightclub. After a while Ethan put out his hand and Ruth took it.

They were home and indoors within a quarter of an hour. Ethan walked angrily to the drinks table and poured himself a whisky he didn't want. Ruth went to put her evening wrap in the bedroom.

As she came back into the living room, Ethan said, 'I apologize for my family, Ruth.'

'Oh, darling!' She ran to him, threw her arms around him. Although she knew nothing in the world would ever have made him admit it, he was hurt. Not by the public ridicule, although that was bad enough, but by the fact that his son Martin had been so cheap and thoughtless.

'Never mind,' she whispered, 'never mind. We know the real story, never mind what they say about it.'

He held her close and buried his face in her hair. If Martin had thought by his parody to please his mother and drive some sort of wedge between them, he had miscalculated. His cruel words only brought them closer together. Their lovemaking that night was intense and demanding, giving and taking comfort in their physical rapport.

In the morning they decided that the best course to take over the insulting song was to ignore it. 'But I shan't forget it,' Ethan said, and his tone was unforgiving.

Easter was approaching, and the activities of British car enthusiasts revived. The first major event was a *concours d'élégance* in the grounds of a baronial mansion in Dorset. 'What d'you say, Ruthie? Let's go,' suggested Ethan.

She was surprised. 'You can't call the Cov III a *voiture d'élégance!*' she laughed.

'Oh, clever clogs! I'm talking about the Rolls. Bignall would like a chance to show it off.'

Bignall was Ethan's chauffeur who collected the Silver Ghost from the garage at Ethan's club each morning and drove him from Knightsbridge to Holborn, then back in the evening. Sometimes he was summoned to drive them on evening occasions, sometimes he took them for a weekend in the country if Ethan himself didn't feel like driving. He didn't go abroad with the Rolls. But the machine was his pride and joy. There was no doubt he'd simply love the chance to show it off.

'But you have to dress up like anything for a *concours d'élégance*, don't you?' Ruth asked doubtfully.

'Absolutely. The "Easter Parade" – you must at least have a new hat, but better still you should go out on the spree and get something really special.'

'Oh, no, Ethan.'

'Oh, yes, Ruthie! Come on, it's been a long winter and we've had some nasty knocks recently. Let's go out and enjoy ourselves.'

She could see he was filled with an almost boyish enthusiasm. Since she never felt she could deny him anything he really wanted, because there were so few ways in which she could show him how much she loved him, she fell in with his plan.

The couturier who had become a favourite showed her the costumes being prepared for the spring list. She settled on a knee-length primrose-yellow dress of georgette over wool marocain with a matching loose coat of wool trimmed with velvet. The hat to go with this had to be specially made – a primrose velvet cloche with a big rose of velvet to rest over her left ear.

Ethan whistled when she gave him a preview of this splendour on the Friday evening before the event. 'My word! I'd better get out my top hat and morning suit! I generally only wear them at Ascot but I don't want to be totally outshone.'

'Do you like it?' she asked, almost hugging herself with delight at his admiration.

'Do I like it!' He engulfed her in an embrace.

She said, 'You'll crush the voile!' and he said, 'Take it off then,' and one thing led to another until they were far too late to go out to the play they'd selected.

As promised, Ethan sent Bignall to get his formal clothes. He in his morning suit, Ruth in her haute couture, they entered the Rolls on Sunday morning in all their splendour. It was a cool, bright April day, ideal for driving into the country. After a late spring, the trees were in young leaf. Lambs frisked in the fields. Bignall sent the car coasting along, pride and dignity in every line of his back view.

Lord Pemberley had spared no pains to make the event a success. He'd had his groundsmen lay out a great circular track for the cars to enter the rally field where they were to line up in rows all facing the same way. There was a huge marquee for lunch, offering a fine cold buffet and champagne.

Insignificant money prizes were presented for meritorious efforts. There were flowers for the ladies, cigars for the men. The two main prizes were the *prix de luxe* for the car with the most elegant and comfortable fittings, and the *grand prix d'élégance* for the most splendid turnout.

'We'll win that,' Ethan remarked hopefully. 'The Ghost is looking her best and you're an absolute eyeful.'

Not so, however. The *grand prix d'élégance* went to another Rolls-Royce owner who'd brought along an actress friend in almost the equivalent of the Crown Jewels.

'It's a fiddle!' Ethan laughed, and charged off to tell the winner so. Once with him and his actress friend, a certain

148

amount of back-slapping went on.

Ruth would have been quite glad to take off her wool marocain coat and exchange it for a thick knitted cardigan. The breeze was decidedly cool. Should she get in the car where it was warmer? She looked about for Ethan, but he had gone to the marquee with David Epps who, having heard on the grapevine that the boss was taking part, had come to see the fun.

A voice behind her said, 'You're Ruth Barnett, aren't you?'

Ruth turned. A girl of about her own age was standing a few feet away. She was pretty in a soft, unformed way, her pale face and big blue eyes almost hidden in the great fox collar of her coat.

'Yes, I'm Ruth Barnett. Who are you?'

'I'm Lorette Coverton and I just wanted to tell you I think you have no shame! Flaunting yourself here in a Leduc dress, letting all the world see how much money you can trick my father out of—'

'Lorette?'

'If I'd known you were to be here, I'd never have come! You've wrecked the day for me.'

'Well, I didn't know you were going to be here either.'

'Don't pretend it makes any difference to you! You don't care what you do!'

'Lorette, keep your voice down! People are staring.'

'Are you claiming you care about what people think?' cried Lorette, paying no heed to the warning. 'You don't care about anybody except yourself.'

'That's not true.'

'Now you're going to tell me you love my father! Oh ha ha, a likely story.'

'I'm not going to discuss anything of the sort.'

'Have you any idea the damage you've done? My mother's prostrated with misery, my brother Antony says Father is impossible to him—'

'And your brother Martin writes cruel lampoons about him and has them sung in nightclubs!'

Lorette drew back, startled by the anger in the other girl's voice. But in a moment she rallied. 'Well, whose fault is that? If he weren't making a fool of himself over you—'

'No matter what Ethan is doing, his son has no right to hold him up to—'

'You've got a nerve to lecture me about rights! You've turned my life into a nightmare. Last year was my London season and you ruined everything, everything!' Tears gushed out of the blue eyes and the girl pushed at them angrily with a gloved hand. 'I hate you!'

There was something so schoolgirlish about the outburst that Ruth's heart melted. 'Come on, now, don't be silly. You don't even know me.'

'No, and if I'd never had to hear of you I'd be a lot happier,' raged Lorette. 'Everybody is laughing at me! When I walk out of a room people start to snigger at me behind my back—'

'Then why don't you walk back in again and have it out with them?'

'Because they're right! They're saying my father's making a poppy-show of himself over a girl young enough to be my sister!'

'Lorette,' said Ruth, 'Lorette, it doesn't matter what people say about you.'

'You can say that because you're hard, you're heartless—'

'I say it because I know it's true. It only matters if you

150

let it matter. I grew up in a village where everybody called me names—'

'Because you're a bad woman.'

'Lorette, I had unkind things said to me from the age of three or four – far too young to have had any reputation to lose! It hurts – of course it hurts! But people who knowingly hurt other people aren't worth bothering about. People who laugh at you because your father's in love with me are shallow and silly.'

'But I have to live among them! And Mummy is so bitter and it makes me so unhappy.'

'I'm sorry if that's so,' Ruth said. 'But she should have enough concern for you *not* to make you unhappy.'

'Don't you dare criticize my mother.'

'No, I'm sorry, I shouldn't do that. The way everyone else sees it, I'm doing her a great wrong, I suppose. But if you could only see it from your father's point of view—'

'He's awful, I hate him! He's besotted, that's all it is – it's so undignified!'

'Are you saying looking dignified is more important than being happy?'

'Happy?' The word seemed to astound Ethan's daughter.

'Happy, yes, he's happy. I think he's had very little happiness in his life for quite a long time.'

'But he's always enjoyed himself all the time! His business, his racing cars—'

'A business or a racing car can't love you back, Lorette.'

'What?'

'Nobody has loved him.'

'That's nonsense! Mummy loves him – I love him—'

David Epps walked up from the far side of the Rolls. 'Ruth, the boss says—' He broke off. 'Oh, hello—'

'Go away!' shouted Lorette in rage and desperation. Then, with tears streaming down her cheeks, she turned and ran over the turf and out of sight among the other cars.

Dave stared after her. 'Who was that?' he asked in amazement.

'That was the boss's daughter, Lorette.'

'Oh,' he said, nodding in comprehension. 'Reading you the riot act, was she?'

Ruth blinked and sighed. 'What did you come to tell me?' she asked.

'Oh, yes. The boss says the Grand Parade is about to start, so if you want to powder your nose or anything, now's the time.'

'Where is he?'

'Knocking back the bubbly with Lord Pemberley. Thank heavens Bignall's driving.' But Dave wasn't paying proper attention. 'So that was Lorette,' he said. 'Quite a looker, so far as I could tell among all that fox fur.'

'David, behave!' Ruth said with more sharpness than was quite reasonable. David Epps was well known for gathering lady friends among the girls who came to admire the racing drivers, but it was silly to think he'd try anything with Ethan's daughter.

'Be easy, I only meant she was a credit to her dad,' he said. 'Who'd she come with? He has a Buick Opera coupé.'

'I've no idea and it's no business of yours.'

'Cars are my business, Ruth, and I like to know who owns them,' he said with a smile as he sauntered away.

After the Grand Parade, which took them all round the grounds and out through the village of Pemberlake, it was time to head for home. Ethan sprawled in the back seat with Ruth in a state of high good humour. He'd shown off his car and his woman, had a chat about business with Chiddington the winner of the *grand prix*, and now they were to have a good dinner in Dorchester.

They had brought evening things in the car. As they changed, Ethan sobered up. 'You're quiet,' he remarked.

'I'm sorry.'

'I wasn't complaining.' He was struggling with the studs in the front of his stiff shirt. She came to put them in for him. He bent his head to look at her. 'I saw you chatting with Dave.'

'Yes?'

'What were you talking about?' When she spent any time with David Epps, it always made him uneasy. He knew his mechanic's reputation.

'As a matter of fact, we were talking about Lorette.'

'Lorette?' He jerked back. 'My Lorette?'

'Yes.'

'What on earth for?'

'She was at the rally.'

'No, she wasn't – she's not interested in cars.'

'She's got a boyfriend who's interested. He drives a Buick Opera coupé, Dave tells me.'

'That thing? The cream and green affair?' Ethan was frowning and shaking his head. 'She wasn't with him . . .'

'She was – the girl in the dark blue coat with the big fur collar.'

'Didn't notice *her*.'

'No, when she realized you were there she took pains to stay out of your sight, I think.'

'So how did Epps come to find out about her?'

'He walked up while she was talking to me.'

Ethan opened his mouth to deny the possibility, then at

the look on her face closed it again. After a moment he said, 'What happened?'

'She sought me out to tell me she hates me.'

'Oh, God,' he said, and sat down on the dressing stool.

Ruth busied herself with putting on her evening shoes. When she looked up, he was watching her. 'Did she say anything awful to you?'

'Never mind about that. What worries me is that she's so unhappy, darling.'

'Unhappy?'

'She minds terribly about being laughed at.'

'Good heavens, she's supposed to be grown up.'

'She's not as grown up as all that, Ethan. She's led a sheltered life. Nothing prepared her for having to face ridicule and disapproval.'

'No-o.'

Now that both were ready, they ought to have gone down to dinner. Instead they stayed where they were, he on the dressing stool, Ruth on the chair by the bureau.

'I don't see there's anything to be done about it,' she said, 'but I hate to think she's having such a bad time.'

'You can bet Diana isn't making it any easier for her.'

'No, she said something about her mother growing bitter and unhappy.'

'And taking it out on whoever happens to be around, I bet.'

'She *is* unhappy, Ethan. I would be, in Diana's position.'

'She never was before . . .'

'But it didn't become public knowledge before, my love.'

'That's true. It's having it talked about that she can't stand.' He gave a groan of regret. 'I should have been more discreet,' he admitted. 'I just didn't think. I was too happy to care.'

'It seems so – unfair. That our happiness has to be gained by the unhappiness of others.'

'Ruth, I'm sure I don't have to tell you that life is often unfair.'

'Yes.'

They talked for a long time until the phone rang and the maître d'hôtel reminded them they had a table reserved for dinner. They went down and ate a meal for which they had little appetite.

In the morning as they were driven back to London, Ethan took Ruth's hand in both of his.

'I've come to a decision,' he said.

'About us?'

'Yes. It's clear my family don't know how to cope with the situation as it is. So it seems to me the best thing to do is regularize it.'

'Regularize the situation? How?'

'I'm going to ask Diana for a divorce.'

Chapter Ten

A whole week would have to go by before Ethan could ask the important question. Diana always went to the South of France for Easter: she wouldn't be back until probably the following Sunday.

The interim was spent by Ethan and Ruth in daydreaming about what their life might be like.

'You're sure it's what you really want to do?' Ruth asked.

'I was never more certain about anything.' He gave her a hesitant smile. 'As soon as the decree's granted, you buy a wedding dress. Yes?'

'Oh, sweetheart, that's looking awfully far ahead.'

'True.' He sighed. 'I think it takes about a year for the machinery to grind out the divorce. I'm the "guilty party", of course. I'll see Romstock in a day or two.'

She was shaking her head.

'Why not?'

'Romstock's the family lawyer. He'll be acting for Diana, surely?'

'Oh, lord, I never thought of that. Oh, well, then . . . I'll go to Tadsley – he's handled some of the firm's work – you've heard me speak of Keswick Tadsley?'

'I think so. But if he does commercial cases, will he want to handle divorce?'

'Oh, there'll be someone in his office who takes on family law. Bound to be. Or if not, he'll recommend someone.' He gave a little shrug. 'The nuts and bolts of this kind of thing are always a bit wearisome. But I don't want you to bother your head about it. You won't be brought into it, I'll fix up to supply "grounds" in the usual way.'

'The usual way? What does that mean?'

'Oh, well, you know . . .' He coloured. 'I go to a hotel with a girl, a detective hired by Diana's lawyer hangs about outside till morning and swears in court that we spent the night together. It's how these things are done.'

'But that's not necessary!' she cried, distressed. 'Diana has all the grounds she needs already, surely! She knows you and I are living together – "living in sin", as the saying goes—'

'I'm not having your name dragged into this.'

'But Ethan, don't be silly, everyone *knows* we're lovers.'

'That's an entirely different thing from having your name put on the court records.'

'Darling, what does it matter? You want a divorce from Diana so that we can get married and we ought to have enough courage to stand up and say so.'

'I won't have it, Ruth.'

In the end she had to agree that Ethan would supply 'grounds' in the usual way.

In order to obtain a divorce for adultery, there had to be an innocent party and a guilty party. The innocent party had to bring the case against the erring spouse. It was part of the accepted chivalrous convention that a man wouldn't let his lover's name be used in the proceedings: detective agencies could supply young women who, for a fee, were perfectly happy to spend an innocent and boring night in a hotel room with a man so that the detective could give evidence of 'adultery'.

This was what Ethan was determined to do. Ruth sighed at the idiocy but, seeing that it was important to him, gave in.

That having been settled, the next thing they began to imagine was their marriage. It would be a register office wedding, of course – no Church of England priest would marry a divorcé. Ethan urged Ruth to order a dress from Leduc: 'Something as gorgeous as that outfit you wore for the *concours d'élégance*. You'd like that, wouldn't you?'

'All right. A lot depends on the time of year, of course.'

'Might be around Easter next year.'

'Yes.' Her thoughts had wandered ahead.

'What?' Ethan prompted as she fell silent.

'I was thinking . . . Once we're married, I would like it if . . . but only if you would . . .'

'What, my angel? What are you thinking?'

'Could we start a family?'

'You'd like that?'

'Oh, Ethan, it's the one thing that would make our life together perfect! If you knew how often I've thought about it, dreamt about it . . .' She broke off, suddenly alarmed at her own flood of words. 'But only if you want it, Ethan. I'd never expect you to settle down with a second family if you didn't want . . .'

'Oh, Ruthie, Ruthie.' He gathered her to him, dropping little kisses on her eyes and cheeks. 'A baby girl, just like you— I'd love that.'

'You would? Really?'

'Yes, and we'd better get on with it, hadn't we, because I'm not getting any younger!'

'Oh, you! You'll never be old!'

'I'll be old by the time this baby girl wants to be presented at court!'

She laughed and hugged him. Neither of them said that this dream baby could never be presented at court, because with one parent a divorcé, she would be *persona non grata*.

During that week they were sometimes ecstatically happy at the dreams of their future, and sometimes apprehensive about how society would treat them. Divorce, although not so unheard of as before the Great War, still had its penalties.

Finally Bignall conveyed the news to his master, heard through the servants' grapevine, that Mrs Coverton had returned from Cannes. Ethan gave her another twenty-four hours to settle down at home. Then, having ascertained that she had no evening engagement and would be dining at home, he went to the big house in Hertfordshire.

The family had had dinner and dispersed for their evening activities. Lorette and Martin had gone to the cinema to see Harold Lloyd in *The Freshman*, Antony was at a lecture on European Business Trends. Diana was going through her wardrobe with her maid, deciding which of last season's dresses to give to charity.

She was startled when the butler came to announce that the master was downstairs in the drawing room. Not likely to be a plea for yet another reconciliation. He hadn't bothered with anything like that after the last two or three liaisons – but then he'd never lived away from home with any of those.

More likely he was going to lay down the law to her. Perhaps he'd heard some of the unkind things she'd said about his butterfly girl? One or two of her friends had quipped about her; Diana's replies had been somewhat waspish, and no doubt the friends had been quite eager to repeat them.

She accorded him a frigid greeting. 'To the best of my recollection, this is the first time in over four months that you've set foot in this house.'

'Quite right, Diana. It seemed best.'

'I won't inquire where you've been spending your nights. Do I take it you've come home to stay, or is this just a flying visit?'

'Neither. I've come because I have something very important to say to you.'

'Indeed.' She sat down, smoothing the skirt of her ruby silk dress over her knees. She didn't want him to see that she was holding her breath. She'd been right. It could only be something to do with that woman.

'Diana, you know that Ruth Barnett and I are living together. I realize I should have tried to explain how serious it was long before this, but we've never been good at speaking about serious things to each other. I've come to tell you that it's not a frivolous affair. We want to get married. So I've come to ask you for a divorce . . .'

All the strength seemed to leave her body. For a moment she could neither see nor hear. Her husband's voice faded. The sense of his words ebbed away. His tall figure on the hearthrug was swathed in mist. She was in a void, lost and without guidance.

Then her strength returned, borne on a wave of fury. She felt the blood rush into her cheeks, knew that her dark eyes had come alight with a glance of fire. A divorce? How dare he! Here, in her own house, to broach a subject that was an insult!

'. . . And as you would probably consult Romstock,

I've been to see Tadsley.' Ethan wasn't even looking at her. He was studying the pattern on the carpet.

She stuttered as she tried to form the words. 'You – you've already been to see him?' It was an insult, an added insult: to have consulted a solicitor already, as if it were cut and dried.

'Yes, last week.'

'You took it for granted, did you? That because you want us to break up, I would agree?'

'Listen, Diana, I know it's the kind of thing you've never imagined happening, but I promise you won't suffer financially.'

'Won't suffer? Do you really imagine you can put an end to my marriage and there will be no suffering?'

'Well, of course, it will be unpleasant, I understand that. But these days there's a growing tolerance, and after a few months people will forget.'

'Oh, they will? And will I forget?'

'You have such a busy social life, Diana. In six months I'm sure you'll have come to terms . . .'

'You know nothing about it! You don't know how other women sneer. These last four months, when I've had to ask Antony to escort me – do you think I haven't heard the whispers? If you imagine I'm going to subject myself to more of that just so that you and your – your *doxy* can settle down in wedded bliss, you'd better think again.'

'Diana, I know this has come as a surprise to you, but when you think about it calmly you'll see it's for the best. It's years since we lived together as man and wife. There's nothing holding us together any more—'

'Three children,' she broke in, 'that's what's holding us together. I'm the mother of your three children.'

'But, good lord, they're grown up and out in the world.

162

They don't need me – they never have, it seems to me—'

'And if they needed you, where were you?' she flashed. 'At the office, at the works, at the machine shop, at the motor-racing track – you were never here!'

'You made it clear I wasn't needed,' he replied, taken aback by her vehemence. 'You put up a barrier between me and the children—'

'That's right, turn it against me, that I was a devoted mother—'

'I'm not trying to turn anything against you, for heaven's sake,' he said, alarmed at the dark emotions that flooded across that autocratic face. He'd never seen her like this before. He tried for a tone of absolute reason. 'Be honest, Diana, we've only just managed to rub along together for the last twenty years, and before that we had what's called a "civilized marriage", held together more by habit and convention than by affection.'

'Don't sneer at habit and convention! It ensures our place in society—'

'Society? You know I'm not interested in society—'

'But I am, and if you think you're going to demolish all that I've built up over the years you're wildly mistaken!'

'There's no question of my "demolishing" anything. You can stay on here in the house – I know it's important to you, this place. And you'll have the same income as always, so you needn't curtail any of your activities—'

'And who do you think is going to invite me anywhere? Who's going to want me at her dinner table? My charity work – you have to have an unblemished reputation to serve on charity committees.'

'But *your* reputation won't suffer! You'll be the innocent party in the divorce.'

'No, I won't!'

'But you will, Diana—'

'No, I won't, because there isn't going to be any divorce!'

That took him totally aback. He'd expected to have to haggle with her over money, for instance, to promise to buy the house in the South of France she'd always wanted, and perhaps to settle something more on the children, particularly her favourite, Antony. But that she'd refuse totally and with so much passion – that hadn't entered his head.

'That doesn't make sense, Diana. We don't mean anything to each other, you can't pretend you would be heartbroken if we split up. And as for this nonsense about how society would react – all you have to do is live abroad for a season – by the time you got back everybody would have something else to gossip about.'

'Not if you were still making a fool of yourself over that little whore!'

'Diana!'

'Oh, that shocks you? You tell me not to bother about what society might say, yet when I use the word that describes her, you go white to the lips and look sick. What's sauce for the goose, my good man! I'm not going to be a laughing stock to all my friends.'

'What kind of friends are they if they laugh at you? They're not worth bothering about—'

'They are to me! It's taken me years to get close to the people that matter and you've spoiled it all with your stupid fling with this little trollop—'

'It isn't a fling, Diana. It's serious. We want to get married.'

'You can just forget it! I'm not going to clear the way

for you to settle down with someone else, even if it were someone decent, someone acceptable – but *her*! Never!'

'You talk about her as if she were evil, but you don't even know her,' he said, unwisely. 'She's a good, sweet girl—'

'You fool! You silly, brainsick fool! She's only after a rich husband, anyone can see that! But she won't get you, you can rely on that! I'll never set you free to marry her, and when – if there's a God in heaven I hope it's soon – when you die and she's left alone, I'll hunt that little bitch back into the gutter where she belongs!'

Her tirade left him dazed. He stared at her out of stricken eyes.

She felt an enormous triumph. She could hurt him! For the first time in their life together she saw that he was vulnerable. He, who had always been so quick to parry her thrusts when they rowed, he could be wounded.

'Go back and tell her,' Diana raged. 'Tell her she's not going to hear wedding bells. You'll see! She won't hang around very long after that. She'll be off after some other old dupe with money in the bank, somebody she can drag to church. Then you'll be left trying to pull your life together again, but don't come running to me, because I won't raise a finger for you, ever, ever!'

'You speak as if – as if you hate me, Diana.'

'Does it surprise you?' She laughed with harsh bitterness. 'Life's hard for a woman, Ethan,' she explained. 'If the man she wants doesn't propose, there's nothing she can do except take what she can get. Well, you were what I could get, and I made the best of it. When we went to bed together on our wedding night, did you think it was married bliss for me? When I had to sit at the dinner table with your boring business friends, did you think I enjoyed it? When we had a row and then you came back prattling about reconciliation, did you think I forgave you? I've had a score to settle with you for a long time, and now you've shown me how to do it. No divorce, Ethan. And when your good sweet little mistress finds a better prospect, I'll laugh in your face.'

She stopped, breathless from her own emotion. Her husband stood silent, looking at her in dismay.

Then, over a moment or two, his expression hardened. She'd forgotten, in the joy of hurting him, what a formidable opponent he could be.

'Very well,' he said, thin-lipped. 'Now we understand each other. No divorce. But as for Ruth ever leaving me, you can put that idea out of your mind. She and I are going to live together and be happy.'

'But not as man and wife, my friend!'

'No, I see that you intend to make that impossible. All right. I can't have the marriage I want so I shall turn my back on the marriage I don't want. From now on I shall never enter this house again. I'll have Bignall pack up my belongings and bring them to me—'

'If you think you can get me to bring an action for desertion it'll be a long wait, my friend.'

'You can do what you like. I don't care what you do. Oh, don't be alarmed, I won't cut off the money supply – you won't lack for anything. But from now on anyone who cares to ask will know that I don't regard myself as your husband any longer. Don't come to me with any of your problems, don't try to communicate with me except through Romstock. From now on we're strangers.'

'And the children?' she challenged. 'You're cutting yourself off from them too?'

'That's up to them. If they have the moral courage to

treat Ruth as she deserves to be treated, we can be on good terms. But no one – no one, Diana – who speaks ill of Ruth can expect anything but coldness from me.'

'You'll soon see!' she cried. 'You can't make a life that depends on only one person! You'll soon find it restricting, boring, you'll see her for what she is, a shallow, mercenary little tramp . . .'

But she had lost her power to hold him in thrall with her hatred. He turned and walked out.

When Ruth heard his key in the lock at almost midnight, she ran to the vestibule of the flat. The questions died on her lips at sight of his face.

'Don't ask me what happened, because I won't ever tell you,' Ethan said.

She followed him into the living room. She had never seen him so angry. At the office there had been temper displays over inefficiency, business mix-ups. But those had been like summer tempests. This was different – as cold and unforgiving as an arctic ice-storm.

'Do you want anything to eat?' she ventured.

'No, nothing.'

'A drink?'

'Stop fussing at me, Ruth. I'm not in need of tender ministrations.'

She was silenced.

She went to bed soon afterwards. Ethan didn't come. Unable to sleep, she tiptoed to the door of the living room about two in the morning to see him still sitting in the armchair, staring at the remains of the fire in the grate, his face like stone.

He was in the bathroom next morning when she woke. It was clear he had never come to bed at all. She went to the kitchen to start the coffee in its French jug, put bread in the stainless steel toaster.

When Ethan came to table he accepted the coffee eagerly but waved away the toast.

'But, darling, you've had nothing since . . .'

'Don't start fussing again.'

She heard the morning papers come through the letter-box. She went to fetch them. Instead of handing the *Financial Times* to Ethan, she set it aside.

'Whatever it was she did, she's made a barrier between us,' she said in a low, hurt voice. 'Isn't that just what she would want?'

He gave a startled exclamation, turned in his chair at the breakfast table and caught one of her hands. He pulled her down on his knee.

'You're absolutely right, dear heart,' he said, holding her close. 'I've been a brute, haven't I?'

'Yes, an absolute beast,' she agreed, but she was smiling now. The coldness was gone from him. Everything would be all right soon.

'I was upset,' he admitted. 'I'm sorry I took it out on you.'

'Are you going to tell me what happened?'

He shook his head. 'Let's just say Diana is never going to set me free to marry you,' he said. 'I suppose I was a fool to think she would.'

'But – what reason can she have for refusing the divorce?' She hesitated. 'She *does* love you, after all – is that it?'

'No, it's something utterly different. Don't let's waste time discussing it. What we have to do now is think about our future. I'm sorry, my love,' he said on a deep sigh, 'no divorce so no babies.'

She was silent. He drew back from her so that he could examine her face. 'I'm truly sorry, Ruth. I wanted your children.'

'Perhaps Diana will change her mind.'

'No.'

'Well then . . . well then . . .' She steadied her voice. 'We still have each other, Ethan. It doesn't matter.'

'It does matter,' he replied in a tone of sadness she had never heard from him before. 'I wanted another chance at being a father. I wanted to do it properly this time, and not make all the mistakes I made before.'

'Don't take the blame on yourself . . .'

'Oh, don't urge me to make excuses for myself. I realize after last night that I've been avoiding the truth for a long, long time. I married someone I didn't love, I tried to find consolation in burying myself in my work, in my hobby, in casual affairs. I should have done something sensible right from the start, if not for my own sake, for the sake of the children. I tell you, Ruth, if Antony's turned out a money-grubbing young stick and Martin's a thoughtless dilettante, it's my fault.'

'No it isn't.'

'We won't argue about it. There's something more important to talk about. I see now that perhaps we've been giving a wrong impression by the way we live.' He glanced about. 'This flat . . . It's all right, but it's the kind of place where a man might tuck away his ladylove. But that's not what you are, Ruth.'

'Then what am I?' she said, half laughing and half in earnest.

'As far as I'm concerned you're my wife. We can't go in front of an official and make it legal, but we can do what other newlyweds do – we can take a house, we can furnish it and live there openly, we can give parties and have friends in.'

'Ethan—'

'We're going to do it,' he told her.

They had a long discussion. When the porter announced from downstairs that the car was at the door to take him to the office, Ethan had Bignall come up. He instructed him to go to Fullerton, the family home, to pack up such clothes as were still there and to bring away the contents of the study desk. 'There are some books on the shelves I'll want by and by, but I haven't made out the list yet, you can go back for those another day.'

When the chauffeur had gone, Ruth said, 'Shall I ring the office to say you'll be late coming in?'

'Tell them I shan't be there at all. We're going out. Tell the porter to whistle up a taxi.'

She dared not ask where they were going. Although his cold rage of the night before had gone, he was still terse and somewhat unapproachable. But as she finished making ready to go out, he came into the bedroom to kiss her and ask her pardon.

'I'm sorry for barking at you. It's just that I've got a lot on my mind.'

'I understand, darling.'

He gave her the ghost of his wide, still boyish grin. 'You always understand. It's one of the reasons I love you.'

'So where are we going?'

'First we're going to an estate agent to tell him the kind of house we want. Then we're going to Tadsley and Gower to see if there's any way round Diana's refusal. I've just rung them to make an appointment. Are you ready?'

'Yes, Ethan.'

She was wearing the moss-green dress and matching shoes. He helped her into her coat, and they went out on this day of serious business.

The estate agent was delighted to hear their requirements – or at least Ethan's requirements, for Ruth sat in an almost frightened silence while he detailed them.

'It's got to be a house of character, in a good area of London, nothing new-built and brash, something dignified.'

'Quite so. How many rooms?'

'Well, there's got to be a drawing room and a good-sized dining room because we'll be doing some entertaining, and a study or library, and room for servants.'

'How many bedrooms, Mr Coverton?' A smiling glance at Ruth. 'Space for a growing family, perhaps?'

Ethan said brusquely, 'Two or three bedrooms will be quite enough, thank you.'

'Ah, I wonder – a terrace house – something late Georgian, early Victorian? Those have great character but they don't always appeal to clients because they tend to be tall and narrow. Shall I let you have details of a couple I happen to have on my books at the present time?'

'Where are they?'

'One is a bijou residence in one of the pretty little squares in Victoria; it dates from 1820.'

'We're not interested in living in Victoria.'

'The other is in Mayfair, Pouncey Square, perhaps you know it?'

'We'll take a look at that.'

'I'll have someone bring you the keys tomorrow.'

'What's wrong with now?'

'Now?'

'Do you want to lease this house out or don't you?'

'Of course, sir. Certainly. If you'll just wait a moment, I'll take you myself – my car is outside – just a moment while I fetch the keys.'

While he was gone Ruth whispered to Ethan, 'I don't want to live in a Mayfair house just to spite Diana.'

'It's got to be a decent house, Ruth. We've got a position to keep up. Let's at least look at it.'

She was determined to dislike it but when the agent opened the door to show her in, something in it spoke to her. The high narrow hall, the staircase with its elegant wrought-iron balustrade, the balcony outside the rooms on the first floor where, on a fine day, one could sit to gaze out on the square's gardens . . .

'Do you like it?' Ethan asked as the estate agent walked on up the stairs from the bedroom floor towards the servants' quarters.

'Oh, yes, it's beautiful. But what about furniture?'

'You walk into Harrods and order what you fancy.'

'But I wouldn't know what would look right in a house such as this, Ethan!'

'All right, we'll hire you a decorator.'

'But, Ethan, you were talking about servants' quarters—'

'Right, you can't run a house like this with just a daily maid.'

'But I don't know anything about hiring servants—'

'Don't worry about it. I'll get the Personnel Department at Covelco to sort some out for you.'

The estate agent, finding they hadn't followed, had returned.

'How much are you asking for the lease?' asked Ethan.

A sum was quoted that made Ruth draw in her breath in astonishment.

'I'll give you that less ten per cent for an immediate sale,' Ethan said.

'Less ten per cent? Well, I— I don't know whether our client would—'

'Telephone him and ask,' Ethan said, and taking Ruth by the elbow made for the door.

'Mr Coverton, I shall certainly do that but I don't think—'

'Just ask him. Cash in the bank tomorrow if he wants it. I'll be at my solicitor's office after lunch, you can reach me there, or at my own firm after about three. Here's my card, and I've written Tadsley and Gower's number on the back.'

The estate agent, staggered, hurried after them to open the car door. Ethan said, 'No, we'll walk, we're not going far.'

'Are you sure? It's no trouble to drop you anywhere—'

'Go back to your office and telephone the house owner,' Ethan said, and walked away with Ruth while the man still dithered.

Ruth was laughing as she hurried along at Ethan's side.

'What's the joke?' he inquired.

'It was a very good act,' she replied, 'but you don't really expect to get an answer to your offer today?'

'Yes, I do,' said Ethan.

At Tadsley and Gower's handsome Dover Street offices the receptionist rose at once to usher him in to Mr Tadsley. He proved to be a tall gaunt gentleman in the obligatory black jacket and pinstriped trousers. Also in the room was a much younger man, similarly attired, but with a freshness and vigour that had been long suppressed in Mr Tadsley.

'Let me introduce my young colleague, Mr Gillis. He's here to take note and offer opinion. I take it you have no objection to his presence?'

'I suppose not, but why is he necessary?'

'I gathered from your telephone request that this was further to your remarks about divorce, Mr Coverton. Divorce is not my forte. Mr Gillis has a more up-to-date overview on what we call family law. May he stay to advise?'

'Oh, very well.'

By this time they had shaken hands and been seated. Coffee was brought in. Mr Tadsley invited Ruth to pour, so under cover of this she was able to listen without colouring up while Ethan began.

'I spoke to my wife last night about a divorce. The answer was a very definite no.'

'As I recall, she would have been the innocent party?'

'Yes. But she adamantly refuses to bring a suit.'

'Aha. That is not entirely unusual, Mr Coverton. Perhaps if Mr Gillis approached her on your behalf and entered into negotiation . . .'

'No, you don't know Diana. It would be useless.'

The younger man cleared his throat.

'Yes?'

'Do I gather that she was indignant?'

'Oh, yes, you can gather that all right.'

'The request was a surprise to her?'

'It seems to have been, though God knows why – she knows Miss Barnett and I are living together. In fact, a short time ago she sent someone to try and buy her off.'

Ruth felt the young lawyer's gaze rest on her briefly, but was too busy with the coffee pot to need to raise her eyes. After a moment he got up to take a cup from her to pass to his senior partner.

174

'Cream?' inquired Ruth. 'Sugar?'

They sipped for a moment in civilized respect to the excellent brew – Mocha blended with Cuban, had Ruth but known it.

'In what way can we be of help to you, Mr Coverton?' asked Tadsley. 'The grounds for divorce are adultery, cruelty or desertion. It seems Mrs Coverton refuses to act on the first, I hardly think you would care to embark on the second, and desertion is a very long-term possibility. Moreover, it would still be up to your wife to take action over desertion if you persist in absenting yourself from the matrimonial home.'

'I wondered if there was any possibility of getting a foreign decree?'

'Foreign?'

'You mean in America, I expect,' said Gillis, taking up the discussion at a glance from Tadsley. 'In certain states – Nevada, for example – divorce is extremely simple and quick, a matter of days rather than months. Is that what you had in mind?'

'We-ell, yes.'

'There is a residence requirement. You would have to go to live in Nevada, Mr Coverton.'

'I could do that. Not immediately, as it happens, but next year.'

'There is a difficulty, though. In Nevada divorces, there is usually agreement between the parties. In other words, when the papers were served, Mrs Coverton would have to give her consent to your action.'

Ethan stifled a groan. 'No, she wouldn't give her consent.' He banged his cup down on the desk. 'I thought it could be done without consultation, that I could just go there and file suit and get a divorce.'

'Well, I believe there isn't the same strict jurisdiction there that there is here. But if it were by some means possible to push the case through without Mrs Coverton's knowledge, I rather doubt whether the divorce would be legal in this country. I should have to look that up. But if Mrs Coverton chose to contest the Nevada divorce, I'm almost sure she would win her case.'

'Damnation,' said Ethan.

Mr Tadsley moved pens and rulers about on his desk. 'I take it you want to be free to have a legal marriage with Miss Barnett.'

'Exactly.'

Tadsley shook his head. 'From what you say, it seems it won't be possible.'

'But it makes it all so hard on Ruth!' cried Ethan. 'I want her to have the right to call herself my wife.'

'There is a possibility,' Gillis said, with a glint in his dark eye that told of an Irish spirit ready for a fight. 'There are steps you can take that might ease the situation. Miss Barnett can call herself Mrs Coverton. There is no law that prevents her from doing so.'

'What?' Ruth said faintly.

'Certainly, Miss Barnett. You can call yourself Mrs Zoe Zooks and no one can prevent you.'

'Mr Gillis!' his senior rebuked him. 'This is not an occasion for levity.'

'Zoe Zooks?' exclaimed Ethan. 'How would you like that, Ruth?'

She smiled, thawing out a little and understanding that Mr Gillis's 'levity' had been for just that purpose. 'I don't think I should like to call myself by a false name, even if it were a bit less noticeable than that,' she said.

'Very well, another alternative is to change your name

legally. By deed poll. That is done quite often. You need only fill in a form claiming to intend using the name of Ruth Coverton from now on, and we can see to it that it is properly registered.'

'Really?' Ethan said.

'If Miss Barnett wishes to,' Gillis said.

'I don't know . . .'

'Losing your own identity is a big change,' Niall Gillis said with a sympathetic smile. 'Think it over.'

'I will. Thank you.'

They talked for about half-an-hour, but it became clear that the possibility of a legal divorce rested with Diana.

'Mrs Coverton may change her mind,' urged Tadsley. 'People do change, you know. Forty years in the legal profession has taught me that.'

'Not Diana,' Ethan said with despondency.

They were depressed by the interview. Even an excellent lunch did little to cheer them. Ethan parted from Ruth afterwards to go to the office. She took a taxi home to Crecy Court, where she walked from room to room with Mrs Monash making a list of all the essentials that might have to be bought if the house in Pouncey Square became theirs.

To her surprise, Ethan got the lease assigned to him by the end of the week. The decorator, Miles Springton, was allowed access to take measurements and get ideas. The wallpaper and paintwork were to remain as they were but there were to be new curtains and blinds. As to furniture, Springton would take Ruth to shops where he knew they would find the kind of chairs and tables needed to suit the house.

The property columns of the newspapers reported the sale of the lease. General magazines ran an item about

Springton's choice of antiques. Gossip columnists took it up: 'Car Racing Tycoon's New Home.'

Ethan took an advertisement in the personal columns of *The Times*. 'Coverton: Any private correspondence for Ethan Coverton should in future be addressed to 15 Pouncey Square, Mayfair. Business correspondence should go as usual to the Coverton Electrical Company, Holborn, London. Nothing for Ethan Coverton should in future be addressed to Fullerton, nr Hitchin, Herts.'

'Oh, Ethan!' protested Ruth when she saw the advertisement. 'Did you have to do that?'

'It's our wedding announcement,' he told her, and kissed her in celebration. He was fired with enthusiasm for the new life they were about to start. There was a recklessness about it, something of the kind that perhaps had taken him into motor racing.

A last batch of letters was given to Bignall at Fullerton to convey to his employer. He delivered it at Pouncey Square on the day Ruth was awaiting the arrival of the domestic staff. She took the big manila envelope from him in the hall, went up to the drawing room, sat down on Miles Springton's mushroom pink Regency sofa and opened it.

About a dozen letters in envelopes fell out on to her lap. Every one of them had been torn in four pieces.

It was Diana Coverton's way of saying 'Welcome to your new home.'

Chapter Eleven

Somewhat to Ruth's dismay, Ethan meant what he said about entertaining.

At first the guests were mostly from the motor-racing fraternity. These easy-going men brought their wives or girlfriends along and no one bothered about the relationship of their host and hostess.

When it came to Ethan's business friends, things became more sticky. The men were embarrassed at not knowing how to address Ruth: she wasn't Mrs Coverton and to call her Ruth was too familiar, yet to call her Miss Barnett drew attention to the irregularity of the situation. The wives were often worse, inclined to look down their noses at Ruth.

However, it dawned on the business colleagues that if you were snooty about Miss Barnett, you were dropped from Ethan Coverton's circle. This resulted in lectures to wives: 'None of that High Moral Tone nonsense! I'm in the middle of an important negotiation with Coverton, and if it falls through you won't get that sable coat you're so keen on.'

So diplomacy came into play. Ruth was not made to feel inferior or out of place by the British businessmen and their wives – those who continued to be invited.

As to Continental visitors, it was no problem. She was M. Coverton's mistress? *Très bien!* And by calling her madame, all difficulties were avoided.

It was a busy year. The Coverton III was entered for almost every European event in the motor-racing calendar. Ruth had plenty of work to keep her from worrying about her social position. Travel arrangements for herself and Ethan, the car and its team involved her in days of correspondence.

The car proved itself, but within its limits

'You see?' cried David Epps. 'She's a good little goer now we've worked the bugs out of the cylinders but you can tell the shape's wrong, boss, now can't you?'

Ethan tried to pooh-pooh this judgment. 'She's doing very well.'

'But not as well as the Renault cars with a lower wind resistance. We've got to slope that radiator back a bit, like theirs.'

'Dammmit, Dave, if we slope the radiator back, there won't be room for the camshafts.'

'Yes there will, if we shorten the supporting arm and—'

'If you shorten the supporting arm the camshaft will overheat against the combustion chamber.'

'Not if we alter the chamber—'

'What you're talking about is a complete redesign of the engine!'

'Yes,' said Dave.

'In other words, a Coverton IV.'

'Yes.'

'I'm not going to finance the building of a Coverton IV.'

'All right, get used to coming in second behind the Renaults.'

That evening, as they travelled home from Montlhery, Ethan said to Ruth, 'Do you think I should put money into redesigning the Coverton?'

'Yes, I think you should,' she replied without hesitation.

'My word, that was quick!' he laughed. 'Have you been giving it a lot of thought?'

'I've been watching *you*! You hate it when Peter Stokes has to fall behind to take advantage of someone else's windstream.'

'I should just say I do! The job of a racing driver is to get to the front and stay there!'

'But Peter can't always stay in front, particularly if the breeze is blowing against him. He gets buffeted – you can see it. So I think you should listen to Dave and let him show you some designs that would give the car less wind resistance.'

'Ha,' he said. 'That means you've already seen them.'

'We-ell, yes. I've seen rough sketches.'

'You and that boy spend too much time with your heads together,' growled Ethan.

'Then you take over and look at his sketches,' Ruth said, patting his hand in reproof. 'He only talks to me because you won't listen.'

'He talks to you because you're the prettiest girl on the track.'

Ruth smiled and shook her head. 'He's after some pretty blonde these days,' she said. 'He asked me last week what colour of scarf he should buy for a fair-haired girl.'

'Humph,' said Ethan.

She could never quite persuade him that the relationship between herself and Dave was more like sister and brother than girl and boyfriend. Sometimes his annoyance with his mechanic was so strong that she wondered if it would end in Dave's dismissal. Yet in his more reasonable moments Ethan agreed that he'd be sorry to lose such a good mechanic just because he smiled too often at Ruth.

As winter approached and the motor-racing season wound down, the pleasures of London life took over. A strange fact now began to emerge. Almost no matter where they went, a journalist would turn up.

During the summer months of racing, that hadn't seemed unusual. Sports writers were beginning to take a great interest in motor racing and Ethan was, after all, good journalistic copy. But why should journalists bother with them when they went to the theatre, or to a friend's birthday party, or the opening of a new art gallery? Why should the gossip columnists keep returning to them?

'They'll get tired of it,' said Ethan.

'I suppose so.'

'What baffles me is how they knew we were going to Sally and Brian's party last night.'

'I expect she let the newspapers have a copy of her guest list.'

'She said not. I asked her.'

'Well, that is odd, Ethan. Maybe it was just luck that that reporter was hanging about outside.'

'Maybe.'

Neither of them suspected the real cause. Which was that their servants, Mr and Mrs Worland, were selling tips to the newspapers.

Personnel at the Coverton Electrical Company had, in May, as requested by the boss, found him a suitable couple to act as butler and cook-housekeeper. The Worlands came from a reputable agency with excellent references. They were to join the household at the beginning of June.

However, the fact that Personnel were undertaking this task for Mr Coverton had become known on the office grapevine. Antony Coverton heard of it and reported it to his mother.

'Well,' said Diana. 'Isn't that just like him! As if you can hire domestic staff in that impersonal sort of way.'

'I suppose it's because Little Miss Muffet doesn't know how to go about it,' Antony suggested.

'Oh, very likely. A girl like her wouldn't know a good servant from a Mexican bandit.'

Antony was about to let the matter drop, but his mother seemed to be having further thoughts. 'Can you find out where they live?'

'Where who live?'

'These servants that are going to work for your father.'

'I expect so. But why should I?'

'Because . . . because, my dear boy, it would be useful to have someone who could keep us up to date with what's going on in that household, don't you think?

'I . . . er . . . I don't quite follow.'

'What I want you to do, Antony, is find out where these people are at the moment. I suppose they're either with an employer or else they're in lodgings waiting to take up this post. Drop them a line, arrange a meeting. See if they're open to suggestion of earning a little on the side.'

'Oh, Mother, I don't think they'd take that on,' Antony said, somewhat shocked. 'I hear the agency that's supplying them is one of the best.'

'My poor boy, servants are always on the make,' said Diana with an ironic smile. 'Pollard here, he sells bottles of wine left over after a party if he can get away with it. He regularly tells me lies about how much the guests have drunk. And Cook is in partnership with the butcher to overcharge us.'

'Really?'

'Of course! They're a kind of parasite, after all, living off other people, always got their feet under someone else's table. I shouldn't think there is a servant in the world who'll pass up a chance to make money on the side.'

Antony's suggestion to Eustace and Alice Worland might not have been well received in different circumstances. But the Worlands had accepted the post and committed themselves before they understood that Mr Coverton's lady was not his wife.

'It's belittling!' cried Alice Worland when the truth dawned on her. 'I'm not staying in a house where I have to say "Yes, madam" and "No, madam" to a woman like *that*!'

'Well, you've got to,' sighed Eustace, folding his belongings ready to pack them in their trunk. 'We've got to stay a month or lose a month's wages – take your pick.'

'All right, we take up the post but we give notice immediately!'

'Look, Alice, things are tight now,' he replied. He glanced about at their lodgings – comfortable enough, but nothing like the ease they could enjoy in a rich family. 'It's not so easy to get a first-rate billet, people are cutting down on staff. You know you expected Mrs Towers to keep us on when the old lady died, but you were wrong.'

'Well, we'll see how she gets on, running that great place with a general maid and two dailies,' sniffed his wife.

'But you see what I mean – that's an economy measure.

Everybody's economizing. We only got three offers worth looking at.'

'There's that post at Lady Magden . . .'

'Oh, if you want to go and live in the wilds of Shropshire! I thought you said you never wanted another winter in the English countryside?'

'You're not saying we should go to the Covertons and *stay?*'

Eustace examined a batiste jacket for stains. 'Think a minute,' he began. 'She's obviously as green as grass at this lady-of-the-house business, you can tell that by the fact that she hasn't interviewed us personally. You ought to be able to twist her round your little finger. And except for that Mrs Ginsley who's going to do the rough, we're on our own. Nobody to ask what we're doing. I think we'd be daft to throw it up without even giving it a decent try.'

'But, Eustace, she's not a *lady!*'

'Her money's as good as anyone else's,' murmured Worland.

So they decided to take the post and see how things would go. And while they were still in this uncertain state, Antony made his offer.

The prospect of extra income was irresistible. The Worlands hoped one day to retire from domestic service and run a pub. Any donations towards the buying of the pub were gratefully received.

So a regular written report was sent to Antony. A glance at Ruth's diary was enough to show her plans for the coming week and, in the case of trips abroad, these were signalled well in advance.

It dawned upon Eustace Worland, who had been in service since the age of sixteen and had learned how to gauge family relationships, that Mrs Coverton was the person really interested in his reports. Quite understandable. Her husband was openly living with Another Woman. By the time Ethan Coverton and his ladylove came back at the end of the motor-racing season to settle in for the winter, Worland had worked out that the real Mrs Coverton would be glad to hear of any discomforts they met.

From that it was an easy step to contacting a few newspapermen. A deal was struck. Ten shillings a time for any tips about what the millionaire and his woman were doing. It worked out at roughly two pounds a month, and what with the ten pounds the young Mr Coverton was paying, the bank account was beginning to look very healthy.

Antony Coverton at first had some problems of conscience with the surveillance. Public school notions of fair play troubled him. Yet it was pleasing to have this sense of power over his father.

Ethan had always been able to outdo him; even in handling money, which was Antony's forte, Ethan's inborn wisdom very often proved more reliable than Antony's formal economics.

Besides, Antony had another grudge against his father His blatant disregard for convention had cost them a knighthood. The idea of offering one to Ethan Coverton, for services in the technical field to the British Armed Forces during the Great War, had been floated last year for the June 1925 Honours List. But Diana, in a fury Antony couldn't assuage, had decided to prevent the award. A hint had been sent to the Palace in May that Mr Coverton was about to set up house in Mayfair with a woman not his wife.

Antony regretted his mother's action because it would have reflected glory on the Coverton Electrical Company to have a knighthood on its letterhead. But the blame lay mostly with his father, and so he deserved all he got in Antony's opinion. If that included having a spy in his own household, well, he'd brought it on himself.

Ruth never really took to the Worlands. She sensed that Mrs Worland despised her. Ruth's menu-planning seldom met with instant approval, Mrs Worland almost always had some alteration to suggest.

Ruth always fell in with her wishes. Neither she nor Ethan set great store by food and drink. So long as their meals were well cooked and well served, they were satisfied. When they had guests, Ruth was even more inclined to go along with the housekeeper's suggestions. She had no confidence in her own judgment.

The house was well run, the meals were on time. There was nothing to complain of. And yet she never felt at ease with her staff.

Once Ethan said to her, 'Isn't that butler of ours a bit of a queer fish?'

'How do you mean, dear?'

'Well, he always seems to be sort of hovering.'

'I thought that was what butlers were supposed to do, Ethan,' Ruth said, turning it into a joke, 'hover and spring to action when needed.'

'No, but really – is he all right?'

'Oh, yes, I suppose so.' There was no enthusiasm in her tone.

'You don't care for him either? Why don't we give him the push and get someone else?'

To Ruth, the idea of making someone unemployed was unbearable. She'd seen out-of-work men trudging round the farms at Freshton, hoping to be taken on at fruit-picking or harvesting.

'No, no,' she said hastily, 'he's all right.'

The next time Mrs Worland was patronizing about her choice of entrée and main dish, she rather regretted not taking up Ethan's suggestion.

But during the winter both of them had more important things to think about than unsuitable servants. They were taken up with the planning and construction of the Coverton racing car, Mark IV.

This involved many trips to the workshop near Croydon Aerodrome where Dave Epps and Peter Stokes consulted and argued. It involved examining blueprints drawn up by Ernest Patterwick, the Research and Development manager of Covelco, who did it in his spare time. In fact, everything was being done as a hobby: Dave had his living to make as a mechanic, Peter Stokes was a car salesman in Hanover Square, Patterwick had a department to run, Ethan had a whole business depending on him.

As yet, racing cars were still hobby projects in the main. Few manufacturers had woken up to the fact that important knowledge could be gained from them which could help in the construction of better family cars. Few British car firms invested in racing; it was left mostly to amateurs like Malcolm Campbell and Ethan Coverton.

So the money Ethan spent on building the Coverton IV couldn't be written off as official business research, which would have meant research into electrical engineering. Ruth sometimes tried to argue that there was a connection between the two. Research ought to go into the batteries used in cars and lorries in her opinion. And batteries were one of the things Covelco produced.

'One day, for instance,' she ventured over a sandwich lunch at the workshop, 'there ought to be a smaller battery for a radio set. Those great wet batteries make it impossible to produce a really portable set. And people are going to want portables.'

'What on earth for?' Peter Stokes inquired.

'Well, to take on a picnic,' she suggested, waving her sandwich in the air. 'If we were sitting on the bank of a river having a romantic lunch . . .'

'Ho, yes, in March, I can just imagine it,' said Dave, hugging himself against the cold in the workshop.

'It isn't always March. In June it's nice to go out into the country, or to the beach. Or, for instance, suppose you had to drive from London to Newcastle – wouldn't it be nice to have a radio to keep you company?'

'A radio in a car? You're cuckoo,' said Dave.

'Maybe that's a bit far-fetched,' Ethan said, as always protective of Ruth's ideas, 'but on the other hand maybe we should do a bit of research on smaller batteries. Have you any ideas on that, Patterwick?'

'Well, there's the dry-cell battery but you'd never get enough power from that to run a radio for long. Wet accumulators are cheaper in any case, and rechargeable. I don't know, Ruth. In theory your idea is right. I might see if any of our bright boys has any thoughts on it.'

'Not if it's going to cost any money!' she warned. 'We're spending enough as it is!'

She was the bookkeeper on the building of the Coverton IV. She had no way of knowing if they were spending money to the best advantage because no one had kept any proper books on the building of its predecessors.

By the beginning of April the car was finished. Peter Stokes had tested it rigorously at Brooklands. 'Well,' said Ethan, 'what are we going to enter her for?'

'What about the Duppigheim?'

'Why not?'

Ethan decided to ship the car to Strasbourg and then enter it for the Targa Florio in Sicily a couple of weeks later.

'Do you think you should put her through the Florio, boss?' Dave said in a tone of doubt and anxiety. 'I mean, it's pretty gruelling.'

'Look here, is this car race-worthy or not?'

'Well, of course it's race-worthy.'

'Then I'm going to race it.'

'But the Targa Florio is such a severe course . . .'

'What do you say, Peter? Do you have any problems with driving in the Florio?'

'None at all,' said Peter, as any racing driver would have said if asked the same question.

'Wait a minute,' protested Ruth. 'If Dave thinks it's too much—'

'Did we spend all winter building this car just to run it round easy concrete circuits? I thought this was supposed to be a really fast, strong car?'

'So it is, boss, I'm only saying—'

'There are other races we could enter it for,' Ruth said.

'Are you supporting Dave against me?' Ethan demanded, ready as always to get rattled if they seemed too friendly.

'No, of course not, love, I'm just saying be careful.'

'Oh, we'll never get anywhere in racing if we're *careful*.'

That was only too true, and Ruth was silenced. 'That's a nice problem in cargo-handling you've given me!' she sighed, to take Ethan's attention away from Dave at whom he was glowering.

'Keep you out of mischief!' he growled, then laughed.

It took her a week of hard work. She arranged to have

the Coverton IV taken by ferry and road transport to Strasbourg, then after the Grand Prix at Duppigheim it would travel by rail to Genoa. From Genoa it would go by sea to Messina.

The car arrived in Strasbourg in good time for the Duppigheim Grand Prix. Unfortunately, Ethan's hopes of seeing it come in first were dashed – both because it only came in fourth and because he and Ruth were unable to go.

Trouble was looming in Britain. Industrial unrest had been growing all winter. On 1 May 1926 the miners came out on strike, and two days later a General Strike followed.

It lasted only ten days, but the disruption and dislocation were enormous. Delivery dates had to be scrapped, cargoes couldn't be brought to or taken from ports, workers couldn't get to factories so factories went into temporary closure.

During those ten days, Ruth scarcely saw Ethan at all. He practically lived at the offices in Holborn. They spoke occasionally on the telephone but only briefly because other matters had to take priority.

On the morning of the day after the strike ended, he reappeared in Pouncey Square, looking thinner and tired, yet triumphant.

'Well, we survived that,' he announced. 'What I want now is a long hot bath, a change of clothes and a large breakfast before we set out.'

'Set out for where?' Ruth asked, at a loss.

'Sicily, of course.'

'But surely, Ethan, you're not thinking of going to the Florio?'

'I certainly am! I missed the French Grand Prix, I'm not

going to miss the Targa Florio!'

'But after the last ten days, darling, what you need is a good rest!'

'Don't be so silly, I'll sleep on the train! Oh, come on, poppet, don't look so worried – you know I recover quickly from any setback. I'm fine, only tired, and if you'll book a *wagon lit* for us I can soon catch up on my rest.'

'I really think you ought to—'

'Are you going to stand here arguing or are you going to get on the telephone to the railway company and book a sleeper? And tell Mrs Worland to cook plenty of bacon, I'm as hungry as a horse.'

It would take them two days to get to Messina in Sicily, near which was the starting point at Campofelice for the ninety-two-mile course of the Florio Gold Plate Race. There wasn't a moment to lose if they were to arrive in time to see the race. Shaking her head, Ruth went to the telephone.

The journey was uneventful and boring. Ethan slept through most of it, sometimes on the bed in their *chambrette*, sometimes over a newspaper he was pretending to read. Ruth was happy enough to watch the changing scenery outside the hurrying train – from the rich green fields of Northern France, past the vineyards, through the precipitous passes of the Alps, on to the flat plain of Lombardy and on into the yellow-beige land of Southern Italy. It was a relief to change to the ferryboat at Reggio and breathe the mixture of rope hemp, tar, seaweed and coal smoke scenting the fresh breeze from the sea.

Messina, on Sicily's northern coast, was to Ruth's surprise dotted with ruined buildings. When she inquired, she was told the city was still recovering from the damage caused by the earthquake of some twenty years before. This gave some idea of the pace of life in Sicily. The idea of a motor race for fast cars in such surroundings seemed bizarre.

But she already knew the reason. Count Vincenzo Florio, a keen motor-racing enthusiast, had wanted a testing terrain for the event bearing his name. He had chosen a circuit in the Madonie Mountains of the island, rugged, almost wild, the home of goatherds and men who lived by trapping and shooting game.

Messina was full of the scent of lemon trees – the growing of lemons seemed to be its only industry. In the clear air, the peak of Mount Poverello with its cap of snow dominated the landscape, and beyond that the smoking head of Mount Etna could be glimpsed from vantage points on the steep streets. Occasional whiffs of sulphur reminded strangers that the mountain was still capable of erupting. A rugged, imposing landscape.

The hotel into which Ruth had booked them, L'Estella, was reputedly the best in the city.

'If this is the best, heaven preserve us from the worst,' muttered Ethan as they watched an ancient, shabbily clad porter carry their suitcases up a worn stone stairway to their room.

Peter Stokes was waiting for them in the bar. David was in the hotel garage – a converted stable – tinkering with the Coverton IV.

'How was your journey?' Peter inquired politely.

'Slept through most of it. How was yours?'

'Oh, very smooth. Ruth certainly is an expert at sending out clear instructions.'

'And what about the car? How did she stand up to all the handling from shore to ship and so on? And why the hell didn't we do better at Duppigheim?'

'Well, the problem was overheating—'

'I told Dave that new bonnet would cause trouble by constricting the—'

'No, it wasn't that, it was the radiator. Dave thinks he's got it licked now.'

'Dave thinks,' groused Ethan. 'If the car is prone to overheating, how the devil is it going to stand up to the pressure on those uphill gradients in the Madonie?'

'Well, if you remember, boss, he did say he thought the Targa Florio was a bit much—'

'Are you saying Dave thinks we should withdraw?'

'No, no, boss—'

But Ethan had stamped off to find his mechanic, leaving his drink untouched on the table.

'It's all right,' Ruth said soothingly to Peter. 'He's just tired, that's all. While you've been away, you know we've had that big strike in Britain – he's been up to his ears in problems trying to cope with it.'

Peter nodded then buried his nose in his glass of local wine, called *zucco*. Ruth watched him.

'Something wrong?' she asked.

'Well, not really . . . Only Dave's got some scheme on his mind . . .'

'To do with the Mark IV?'

'No, I think it's something of his own. I'm not sure. He's been edgy, waiting for Ethan to turn up, seems to have something he wants to ask him.'

'I hope it's nothing serious. Ethan just isn't in the mood for unnecessary trouble.'

'No, no, I don't think it's *trouble*,' Peter said, wrinkling his brow and looking away. From which Ruth inferred that it probably was.

If it was 'trouble' it seemed to have nothing to do with the Coverton IV. From the bar they heard the rumble of its engine and emerged into the street to see it being gingerly driven out of the stableyard and on to the main street outside the hotel. Ethan was at the wheel, looking pleased, anxious and proud.

That evening, after a surprisingly good meal of local fish with a sauce from local lemons and surrounded by locally grown vegetables, Ruth persuaded Ethan to have an early night. As they prepared for bed she ventured, 'Did Dave have anything special to say this afternoon?'

'Huh!' grunted Ethan, brushing his teeth vigorously over a cracked china bowl.

Ruth waited.

'He wanted to bend my ear with some damn-fool scheme. I suppose he'd talked to you about it and you'd encouraged him.'

'No, not a word.'

'Then how did you know he had something to discuss?' he pounced.

'Ethan,' Ruth said, 'that's enough of this rubbish about Dave Epps. I only talk to him about the cars, just as I talk to Peter.' She gave a little laugh. 'Why do you have this thing about Dave? Why not Peter?'

Ethan made a grumpy sound and poured more water from the ewer into the cracked bowl. 'Because Peter isn't a lady's man,' he said, and immersed his face in the water.

'Oh, so you don't think I'm falling for every man I meet – just those that have a bit of a reputation.'

'I don't say you fall for every man you meet.'

'No, but you seem to think it!' she riposted. 'Once and for all, I don't give tuppence for Dave, and as to how I knew he wanted to talk to you, Peter told me because he was worried about it.'

Ethan came out of the bowl, groped about for a towel, and took the one she put into his hand. He used it vigorously. His face emerged from its folds, wearing a sheepish expression.

'I'm sorry, Ruthie. Am I an old grouch?'

'Yes, you are, and getting grouchier!'

'Not really?'

She laughed, and went into his arms. 'No, not really, and even if you were, I'd love you just as much.'

They had had a separation of almost two weeks due to the General Strike. That and the restrictions of travel. To Ruth it seemed as if he had not held her for aeons. As he put his arms about her she felt his desire flare up and knew again that sense of joy and wonder as she gave herself up to him. Why had heaven been so good to her? Why had it given her this marvellous man as her lover?

Early in the morning they set out for the starting point of the race. Others were wending their way along the coastal road to Campofelice, their precious racing cars mounted on lorries, trucks, wagons. Some who hadn't had Ruth's foresight in booking well in advance and paying good bribes had to make do with old carts drawn by oxen.

The road was very bad, rocky, full of potholes – yet this was the main road. What would the surface be like on the mountain circuit, Ruth wondered, as they jolted along in the cab of the battered but tough old lorry she had hired. Mountains loomed on one side, sometimes a sheer drop to the sea on the other, and where there was soil for cultivation, olive trees offered shade from the sun.

On the beach at Campofelice a motley crowd had gathered – racing drivers from most of the European countries, their friends and relations, mechanics, engineers and a large group of local peasants. The latter were clearly very amused at the proceedings. It was hard enough to travel up into the Madonie Mountains, but to do it simply to come down again – to do it for fun – only mad foreigners would undertake such a project. However, they had been coming each May for something like twenty years now, and there was money to be made by humouring them.

The May morning was becoming warm. Breakfast hampers were unpacked, spirit stoves were lit to brew tea or coffee. Makeshift viewing stands had been erected in the shade of the north-facing cliffs. Daisy-like flowers bloomed in cracks in the rock, samphire rose up to wave in the sea breeze, crabs scuttled about between the feet of the visitors. Local businessmen had taken advantage of the race to set up shop: there was an ice-cream vendor, and a bookmaker in a shack plastered with advertisements for Michelin tyres was offering miserable odds on Italian drivers.

'What are they offering on the Coverton?' Ruth inquired.

'Thirty to one,' said Dave.

'Damned cheek!' grumbled Ethan, though he smiled.

'What do they know?' Peter said with a shrug. 'This is the only motor race they ever see!'

Peter and some of the other drivers had driven the course in a convoy of trucks the previous day to get some idea of the hazards. 'There are villages up the road,' he said, 'the population all spills out to watch us go past – it's a nightmare to avoid them. And then there's the odd wild sheep that decides to wander across the track because it likes the look of a thistle on the other side.'

'What's the surface like?'

'Better than I feared – the locals have spent a bit of money on it here and there because they want to keep the

Florio coming back. But you know what hill-racing's like – you just have to take what comes.'

He got into the Coverton for trials. The race wasn't until the afternoon: at two o'clock the numbered cars would line up, one by one each would be summoned to the starting point, the starter would give the signal, the timekeeper would mark the time and each man would be off to test himself and his machine against the mountains.

All this would be accomplished so as to allow the Italian spectators at the starting line to get home for their siesta. The drivers would then head up into the mountains, up into the cool air and the snow zone, to drive hell for leather round roads that were scarcely more than farm tracks. At some of the better viewpoints, stands had been erected where for a fee enthusiasts could watch several of the bends at the same time, to see cars labour up the frightening gradients.

By two o'clock the approach from the beach to the mountain road would be roped off and strictly supervised by stewards. Meanwhile all the drivers were taking the opportunity of practising starts on the hard-packed sand, changing gear for the gradient on the road and steering hard for the immediate bend. They would roar off, disappear round the fold of the hillside, then return ten minutes later to make another try.

'What do you think?' Ethan inquired after Peter's fourth practice run.

'Well, it's not easy.'

'Hop out, boy, and let me have a go.'

'Ethan!'

'Now don't get in a fuss, Ruth, I'm only going to drive the blasted thing, not race it.'

'But you shouldn't even—'

198

'Come on, Peter, there are some fellows coming to rope it off.'

'Right you are.' Peter clambered out of the low-slung car and handed his helmet and goggles to Ethan.

'Now, Ethan, promise me you'll only go half-a-mile.'

'I promise, I promise.' But he wasn't listening to her. His fair-skinned face glowed with pleasure as the powerful new engine purred under his hands.

He reversed along the hard sand. David Epps stood by with his hand raised holding a handkerchief.

'*Now!*' he shouted, and brought his arm down fast.

Ethan was off. The Coverton zoomed past, sending up a hot hard spray of sand. Ruth heard the gears scream as he changed for the climb off the sand onto the steep rocky road. There was the bump that every car had made getting off the beach, then the car was leaping forward up the slope.

In a moment it was lost to view round the first bend. A faint cheer from above them announced that the spectators who had trudged up to the second bend had seen the car go past. Dave was looking at his stopwatch. Little would be learned from it, because the car could only go a few hundred yards up into the mountains, reverse at a convenient point, and race back down. But it was at least some measure of performance; time could be measured against mileage.

They waited. The car didn't reappear.

'*Don't* tell me it's broken down,' groaned Dave.

Ten minutes went by, a quarter of an hour.

'Something's wrong,' Ruth said. She started forward to the road.

From beyond the bend came a couple of men, running.

'Signora, signora!'

She needed nothing more. She knew what had happened. Ethan had crashed.

Chapter Twelve

She ran up the steep, rocky road. Spectators who had been scattered along the verge were running ahead of her. The sun beat down. Sweat moulded her silk blouse to her breasts, her shoulder blades. Dust rose up to coat her brow and cheeks.

The first bend, the second. Her breath was labouring. The third bend. A group of people stood on its shoulder, staring downhill, into the *garigue*. She stopped, gasping for air. Her eyes followed the pointing fingers, the staring eyes.

A few men were still making their way through the dust-leaved shrubs. They were following the wake of the Coverton. It had cut a swathe through hyssop, savory, rue and thyme. The scent of the crushed leaves reached Ruth as she stood, appalled.

The car had bounced against a clump of rocks and fetched up against a stunted cork oak. It was on its side, the undercarriage towards the road. Ruth couldn't see the driver.

She threw herself down the hill. Spiny broom and Jerusalem thorn snatched at her linen skirt, seared her legs. She smelt the benzine from the ruptured fuel tank. She heard herself cry, 'Ethan! Ethan!' But it was a mere gasp of despair, lost in the shouts of the men working at the car. One had a fire extinguisher, was dousing the machine and the surrounding *garigue* with its mixture of water and baking soda.

Behind her she heard the juddering engine of the first-aid vehicle. A motorbike and sidecar, it had a stretcher strapped along the side. It came jouncing down through the bushes, passing her. She called to the driver, 'Get him out!' He had no idea what she'd said, was too busy trying not to overturn. His passenger raised a hand in acknowledgement.

She reached the car a few minutes behind the motorbike. The sidecar occupant had leapt out, was haranguing the rescuers. Clearly he had medical knowledge; his gestures warned them they could harm the driver. A babble of tongues met him. Ruth threw herself among the men, forced herself to the front.

The sloping bonnet of the Coverton IV was stove in by collision with the tree trunk. Ethan was canting out of the cockpit, unconscious. His legs were trapped in the smashed aluminium of the bonnet.

'Oh, God,' groaned Ruth.

'*On a besoin d'un levier.*'

'A crowbar? A tree branch! But there's nothing strong enough.'

'*Perde molto sangue!*'

'Dammit, we can see he's losing blood, Giorgio—'

Blood was seeping through the thin leather of the racing helmet. The smashed goggles hung over Ethan's pale cheeks. Gashes on his chin flowed redly into the open neck of his shirt, to meet the red that came from chest wounds.

'*Signora, non guarda!*' cried Giorgo, trying to shield the

sight, out of an impulse of pity.

Too late to say 'Don't look!'

The horror of the scene jarred her brain. She felt her legs begin to buckle. Someone grabbed her by the shoulder. 'Steady!'

Yes, steady. No time to be foolish. They had to get Ethan out before he bled to death.

A well-known voice at her elbow.

'Let me,' cried Dave Epps. 'I can unfasten the screws—'

'We can't ferret about for screws.'

'I built the car, I know where they are!' Dave shouted, and threw himself on his knees by the wreck.

In his mechanic's overalls he had pockets for tools. He found a spanner, set to work. But the impact had bent the shanks of the screws. Cursing, Dave prised and pushed.

'*Avanti, avanti!*' cried the man from the first-aid team. '*Dobbiamo l'apportare in ospedale . . .*'

'What does he say?' begged Ruth.

'He says, signora, we must hurry, we must get him to hospital.'

'It's no use trying to hurry, I've got to get a grip on the screw-heads.'

'Try, Dave. Please, please try to be quick.'

She was kneeling by the side of the car, holding Ethan's dangling hand in both of hers. The first-aider was applying lint pads to the chest wounds. His partner was unstrapping and unfolding the stretcher.

Someone had run to the starting line and been driven back with a toolbox. He came dashing down the slope with a lever. In a tiny crack made by Dave's loosening of two screws, the bar was inserted. The hands of four men clamped round it.

'Heave!'

'*Soulevez!*'

A faint cracking sound from the wrenched aluminium.

'*Avanti!*' urged the medical student who was leader of the first-aid team. '*Il polso s'attenua!*'

'His pulse is fading! We've got to do it this time, chaps!'

The four men heaved on the iron bar. Ruth heard the little creaks of tension in the metal.

But, gasping, they had to let go.

'*Lass mich, Mensch,*' said a deep voice. A burly German mechanic stepped up, replaced one of the four. He spat on his hands, rubbed them. He gave Ruth a solemn nod as if to say, 'I will free him for you.'

'*Ein, zwei, drei – hebt auf!*'

With a scream of rending metal, the bonnet of the Coverton IV tore away from the chassis.

Ethan's legs were a mess of blood, torn and singed cloth and motor oil. Ruth looked round wildly for something with which to clean him up.

'*No, no, signora,*' chided the first-aider, pulling her away. He gave her an explanation over his shoulder as he lightly wound white muslin round the wounds. Ruth could only gather that it was unwise to touch broken bones.

Now she was forcibly led away. They had come to the business of moving Ethan to the stretcher. They knew it would be too painful a sight for her to see.

But she heard. She heard the groan of agony that he gave even in his unconsciousness.

When she was again allowed to be next to Ethan, he was lying on two boards laid along the motorbike and sidecar. The helpers were pushing it up the slope while the first-aiders kept the stretcher motionless. Ruth grasped the side with both hands and tried not to let it sway with their unsteady progress.

It took them twenty minutes to reach the road although Ruth had run down the slope in two. On the relatively good surface it was possible to start the motorbike engine. The driver carefully mounted the machine and in first gear it edged its way down the gradient with Ruth and six men holding it steady.

At the edge of the shore, they stopped. The transporters for the racing cars were lined up along the road towards Messina. The first in line, a flatbed truck with big wheels, edged up to the motorbike. A dozen willing hands lifted the stretcher aboard. It was laid on the bed of the truck. Ruth clambered up beside it. There some well-meaning soul tried to persuade her to get down again.

'Leave me alone!' she cried, lashing out at him in a fury that was almost like madness.

'*C'est son homme*,' explained one of the Frenchmen.

'Oh, I'm sorry, ma'am, I didn't understand it was your husband.'

She didn't correct the mistake. She hardly heard it. She was kneeling beside Ethan on the dirty planks in the back of the truck. Someone rigged a tarpaulin to give him some shade. She watched his pale face for the slightest sign of recovery, some flicker of an eyelash.

But there was nothing.

The journey to Messina hospital seemed to take a century. Some had gone ahead to warn the medical staff. At the door of the big stone building nurses in nuns' habits and a crew of white-coated men were waiting with a trolley. Once again, with agonizing care, Ethan was moved from truck to trolley. This time he made no sound.

Ruth scurried along at its side as it was wheeled to the casualty room. There she was barred from entering. When she tried to force her way in, a sister addressed her in halting English.

'Much must be done. You will only hinder. Go now, there is a – *un'anticamera* – where you can wait.'

'No, I must be with him.'

'Signora, it cannot be. You are not clean – not sterile – and besides you are fatigued – this may take long. Go, I recommend, wash and change the clothes, eat and drink, come back and sit in the *anticamera* where I will come to you. Yes?'

All opposition suddenly seemed foolish. Ruth nodded, a movement of her head that was almost like bowing it in defeat. She turned, walked out of the entrance to the casualty room, along the corridor and out into the heat of the early evening.

Someone took her arm and led her to a car. She was helped in, driven to the Estella. Later she never knew to whom she was indebted for this kindness, it went by in a blur.

At the hotel the plump manageress was waiting. After one glance she took Ruth's arm to help her upstairs. Murmuring kindly words in Italian, she unbuttoned the torn, dusty, bloodstained clothes, took the scarred shoes from her feet. An elderly maid came at her summons. Between them they bathed Ruth's scratches, applied salve, found clean clothes, helped her into them.

A tray was brought: fish soup, Italian bread. Ruth took up the spoon, but after the first mouthful pushed the plate away. But when soda water with lemon juice was brought, she drank thirstily.

It was about seven o'clock when she came downstairs. Peter was sitting in the hall waiting for her. He jumped to his feet at sight of her. 'Have you heard anything?' she asked in a voice she could hardly make audible..

'Not yet.'

'Where's Dave?'

'He's at the hospital.'

She nodded and went on to the door. Peter joined her, took her arm. She was glad of his support. On the short walk to the hospital her legs seemed ready to give way at any moment.

Peter apparently knew his way to the waiting room. Dave Epps rose as they came in. He shook his head before they could even ask. 'Nothing yet.'

Ruth gave a sudden little laugh.

'What's so funny?' Dave gasped in astonishment.

'I spent all last year learning French,' she said. 'It would have been more use to be learning Italian, wouldn't it?'

And she began to cry helplessly.

Neither of the men knew what to do. At last, awkwardly, Peter put an arm round her. They led her to a wooden chair with a seat and canopy of woven reed. There she collapsed, burying her face in its shade, and wept until she could weep no more.

For the next two hours they waited. From time to time members of the international contingent of racing enthusiasts came to ask if there was any news. Some of them were Italian and were able to approach the nursing sisters with questions. They were greeted with the same calm kindness that had been given to Ruth. Nothing could be told as yet. They must wait. The doctors were doing all they could and with God's help would succeed.

The same reply was given to the newspapermen who came in from time to time. It never occurred to Ruth to ask them whether the race had started, and if so who had won.

At about nine thirty, a doctor in a white coat came into the waiting room with the sister who had already spoken to Ruth. 'Signora Coverton?' she said.

'Yes?'

At a nod from the doctor, she announced: 'The procedures to deal with your husband's visible injuries are completed. I myself did not take part. I am here to explain because I speak English and will translate for Dr Andromi. Mrs Coverton, your husband is very ill. There were multiple fractures to the left leg, simple fracture to the right, one ankle is very badly damaged.' She paused, consulted Dr Andromi, then went on: 'Four broken ribs, the left clavicle also, and the humerus of the left arm but that is not so serious. There are internal injuries, their extent is still somewhat uncertain but we think the liver is in some distress.'

Ruth, who had risen at their approach, sank down again into her chair. A million questions shrieked for utterance but her throat had completely closed up.

'He was bleeding under his helmet,' Dave Epps said. 'He has a head injury?'

'There was bleeding from scalp wounds,' agreed the nun. She questioned the surgeon, who said a few dubious words. 'It seems likely there is some concussion. We believe there is no fracture to the skull but we have not made an X-ray because we felt it was more important for the patient to rest. At the moment he is still under the effect of the anaesthetic.'

Ruth found her voice. 'May I see him?'

'He is unconscious, signora.'

'But may I see him? Just see him?'

The nun repeated the question in Italian to the surgeon. '*Va bene*,' sighed the doctor.

The nursing sister led her along a stone-floored corridor into a room that was as austere as a monk's cell. White-washed stone walls, an iron bed with white coverings tented to be kind to the fractured limbs, a bedside table with a carafe of water, a pendent electric light and a crucifix on the wall. On a chair at the end of the bed sat another white-robed nun telling her beads. She looked up and smiled faintly as Ruth came in.

Ruth went up to the bed. Ethan looked almost like a stranger. His head was swathed in a turban of bandages. His cheeks were waxen, his blue-veined eyelids seemed dark against them. His left arm, bandaged and strapped to his chest, was visible. His right arm was on the side away from the door.

Ruth made as if to go there, to take his hand. The sister made a preventive movement, the nun by the bed stood up.

'No, signora. Let him rest.'

Slowly nodding, like a schoolchild who has learnt her lesson, Ruth left Ethan's room.

'How does he seem?' Peter Stokes asked.

She looked at him. 'Is this a good hospital?' she asked.

'What? I— I don't know— I suppose so.'

The sister joined them. 'I want to stay until he recovers consciousness,' Ruth said.

'No, signora, that isn't possible.'

'I must be here when he recovers consciousness.'

'No, signora, that might not be until tomorrow morning.'

'Then I'll stay the night.'

'Hospital rules forbid it,' she said, shocked.

'I *must* stay!'

But not even the kind-hearted Italians could alter the

rules. She had to be content with a firm promise that as soon as Ethan opened his eyes, Sister Febronia would telephone her at the Hotel Estella, no matter if it was the middle of the night.

In the event, it was bright morning when the chambermaid came knocking at her room door. 'Signora, signora, *telefono!*'

Struggling into wakefulness against the exhaustion that had engulfed her, she looked at her wristwatch. Eight fifty. She scrambled out of bed, ran barefoot to the door pulling on a wrap, and flew down the stairs. At the desk the receptionist was holding out the telephone.

'Yes? Yes?'

'Signora, your husband has just wake.'

'How is he? Did he say anything?'

'Oh, no, signora, he is too ill for saying anything. Only he wake and see Sister Tecla, and he fall asleep almost at once. So now he is in the hands of God to sleep and become better.'

'Oh, thank you! Thank you for telling me. I'll be there in an hour or so.'

'Very well, but a very short visit, and if Signor Coverton is sleeping, you must not wake.'

'Of course not!'

'Until later, then, signora.'

Delirious with joy, Ruth went back to her room. She took a long bath in the old-fashioned bathroom along the corridor, came down to find Dave and Peter at work on a vast Italian loaf of bread and a basket of fruit.

She joined them with the news that Ethan had been awake for a moment. 'What do they say about him?' Peter inquired, pausing with the coffee pot in his hand.

'They say he is in the hands of God.'

210

Peter nodded. Dave looked down. Neither of them was accustomed to being told that hospital patients were in the hands of anyone except the medical staff.

Ruth was allowed a glimpse of Ethan, but only that. It was two days later before she was permitted to sit by his bed and speak to him.

'You gave us a fright, darling.'

'Me too.' It was scarcely a whisper.

'You've got all sorts of broken bones. Does it hurt a lot?'

'Like hell.'

This sounded so much like the Ethan she knew that a lump rose in her throat.

'What happened in the race? Who won?'

'The Italian, Giandino.'

'Uh.' A long pause. 'The car's a complete loss?'

'Dave's had it hauled to the hotel garage so he can take a good look. But it doesn't seem likely he can rebuild it.'

Ethan muttered something.

'What was that, darling?'

'Money down the drain.'

'Never mind.'

'I do mind, though. Damn fool, lost control on the third part of my reversing turn.'

'S-sh, my love, don't tire yourself.'

'Uh,' sighed Ethan again, and dropped into sleep.

The recovery was long and slow. At the end of the first week Peter Stokes had to go back or lose his job at the showroom in Hanover Square. Three days later Dave remarked that as he wasn't doing much good here, he thought he'd drive with the remains of the Coverton IV back to London and get on with the reconstruction, if reconstruction seemed possible. Privately, Ruth didn't want the car reconstructed. It had nearly killed Ethan: she wanted nothing more to do with it and let Dave see how she felt.

'Just as well to let him go,' Ethan said. A faint shadow of his old smile glinted for a moment. 'Don't want him hanging round you while I'm *hors de combat*.'

'Now, Ethan!'

She looked forward to the day when he would be allowed to sit up. It seemed a long time coming. At length he was lifted into a wheeled chaise longue and taken out to the cool of the courtyard with its fountain and its crowded pots of geraniums.

He lay staring up at the sky for a while. His skin had a yellowish tinge due to a touch of jaundice from the shock to the liver during the crash, but his eyes had something of their habitual gleam. 'What's the date?'

'June 26.'

'Good lord, I've been here more than a month!'

'Yes, sweetheart.'

'My bones ache,' he complained. 'I suppose I won't mend as quickly as when I was a boy.'

'It'll come, darling, just be patient.'

'You know I'm not good at that.'

'Now's the time to learn, Ethan.'

Ruth had been told he could be allowed half-an-hour in the chaise longue. When it was time to have him wheeled indoors, he tried to put it off. 'Just a few more minutes, Ruth.'

'But Dr Andromi said . . .'

'I hate it in that room!' he burst out, his resentment almost childlike. 'There's nothing to look at except bare walls or that crucifix, and you have to agree, Ruth, there's nothing very cheerful about a crucifix!'

'I'll have you moved to a better room.'

'I think that *is* the best,' he sighed.

She could tell that time passed very slowly for him. He was too weak to hold up a book so he couldn't read but had to be read to. Ruth was only allowed in at visiting hours, so at other times Sister Febronia had to undertake the reading.

'Her accent's so thick I can hardly make out one word in ten,' Ethan complained. 'And there are bits in the books she refuses to read. She says it would be sinful. What's sinful about Arnold Bennett, for heaven's sake?'

With the coming of July, the temperature rose into the high seventies in the shade, the high eighties in the sun. The *sirocco* began to blow. The air became dry and hot, then would turn sultry and humid.

Ethan, perspiring on his hospital bed, asked Ruth to bring in an electric fan. When she did so, they discovered there was no power outlet in the room, so that it couldn't be plugged in unless they got a fitting to replace the electric light bulb. That done, it became clear Ethan could either have light or coolness at night, but not both.

'Get me out of here, Ruth,' he begged.

'But where would we go, darling? You're not well enough for a hotel.'

'Take me home!'

It hurt her to hear the note of pleading in his voice – he, who had once said of servants, 'You tell them to do something and they do it.' But she hardened herself to reason with him. 'You can't travel—'

'I damn well can! I can do anything but survive another week in this place!'

'Ethan, you can't even stand up.'

'I don't have to stand up, do I? I can be carried to an ambulance, and from the ambulance to the train.'

'But you know what it's like on a train, dearest! We'd have to take it easy, stop overnight somewhere – it could take three or four days, and it would be so *hot*.'

'We'll go by sea. This is a seaport, after all! Go to the shipping offices and make inquiries, Ruth.'

But her inquiries soon showed that the passenger ships which came to Messina were ferryboats, with very limited accommodation. Even changing to a coastal steamer at Reggio wouldn't be much help. What they needed was a stateroom in a passenger liner, and the nearest port for a liner was Naples.

When she put the idea to Dr Andromi in her halting Italian, he was horrified. '*No, assolutamente no!*' he exclaimed. 'Signor Coverton is not well enough for a long journey. I would be responsible for the consequences if I allowed it.'

'That's what *he* says,' Ethan responded when she told him. 'He can't keep me here. I'll discharge myself and he won't be responsible for my wellbeing.'

'But Ethan, he's right, you couldn't stand up to the stress of the journey.'

'I'm the judge of that. Look here, Ruth, are you going to arrange it for me or am I going to have to call in a travel agent from Via Santa Cecilia?'

She closed her eyes and ran her fingers through her heat-dampened hair. He was so *stubborn*!

Yet she couldn't help thinking that he was right. He was making no progress. The discomfort of his surroundings, the climate, the boredom, the lack of stimulation during the long hours when Ruth wasn't allowed to visit – none of these was good for him.

She argued against travel for the rest of her visit but only succeeded in making him angry with her. She started back to the hotel worn out and disheartened. In search of some cooler air she walked down to the Spianata and there leaned on the railing watching the boats setting out for the evening visit to the lobster pots.

Gulls wheeled and dived round the boats. How free and wild they looked, slicing through the air on wings like white scimitars. She wished she could fly with them, leaving behind her body with all its woes – no more prickly skin, no more perspiring brow, nothing but the freshness of the breeze and the cool sky.

By now anyone else concerned with the Targa Florio was long gone. She was the only single woman among the hotel guests. There was a married couple from Brindisi visiting a son at the local seminary and a sprinkling of businessmen.

She bowed acknowledgements and sat down to her solitary dinner with a book propped against the wine bottle. She was reading an Edna Ferber novel, *So Big*. It was all about what the Americans called a truck gardener, named Dirk. His problems with getting his crop to market seemed minuscule compared with her own. After all, he only had to get himself organized and find the right transport and his business would flourish.

Her gaze went past her book to the dining-room window. A gull swooped by.

She gave a cry that brought every eye in the room upon her. She jumped to her feet, knocking over her wine glass.

Of course. What a fool she had been!

Ethan wanted to go home. Very well.

She would fly him home.

215

Chapter Thirteen

On her frequent visits to Brooklands, Ruth had come to know some of the pilots who belonged to the Brooklands Flying Club. When she had worked with the project team on the Coverton IV, she'd made many visits to Croydon Aerodrome, and had become friendly with some of the airmen.

It was one of those owner-pilots whom she knew only by reputation that she was now going to summon.

She went to the hotel desk to ask the receptionist to get a connection to the telegraph office. Once connected, she dictated a reply-paid cable to David Epps: 'Hire Paul Envers to fly Blackburn Iris to Messina soonest stop. No haggle price stop. Advise estimated time arrival stop. Very urgent stop. Ruth.'

She had considerable difficulty getting this message across. When at last the phone call was completed Adriana, the receptionist, was studying her. 'There was some problem?' she asked in her slow, careful English.

'The telegraph clerk didn't seem to understand what I was saying.'

'Ah, signora, perhaps you need a translator?'

This was a decided hint. Ruth had dealt with Italians already and knew that besides the official fees, bribes had

217

to be paid. During the negotiations that she was about to enter, she knew she needed all the help she could get. It came as a surprise that even in the Office of Posts and Telegraphs, a little oiling of the wheels was necessary. But this seemed to be the case, so she said: 'Perhaps you could recommend someone, signorina?'

'*In fatto* – I have a cousin who speaks very good English.'

Ruth wasn't in the least surprised. Everybody in Messina had a cousin, or a nephew, or an uncle. 'Would you ask your cousin if he would like to help me, signorina?'

Adriana gave her a glance with raised eyebrows. Something more than a request for an introduction was expected.

'Of course,' Ruth went on, 'your cousin might have to give up some of his time – neglect his own business, perhaps. I would see that he did not suffer financially.'

'*Cosa?*' asked Adriana. Such English subtleties as 'suffer financially' were beyond her grasp of the language.

'I should be glad to pay him,' Ruth said bluntly.

'Ah. When do you wish to see him?'

'As soon as possible.'

'If the signora would be so good as to go into the bar, I will contact Renaldo and see if he can come.'

'Thank you.'

It was then about eight o'clock. After an hour of toying with a glass of *zucco*, she saw a young man come into the bar. He glanced about as if expecting someone but as Ruth was the only occupant, he gave up this ploy at once.

'Signora Coverton?' He bowed. 'I am Renaldo Pinturenzetto.' They shook hands formally. 'My cousin Signorina Gransini tells me you require a translator.'

'Yes, I expect to carry out some very important business in the next day or two, signore, and the language problem is beyond me.'

'Of course. It is a twofold problem, no? In the first place you perhaps do not speak good Italian, and if you did, signora, the local population speak Sicilian for the most part.'

'Exactly.' He waited, and she knew she must now mention money. 'I should like to hire your services, Signor Pinturenzetto, for the period of this business.'

'Two days, you said?'

'More or less. Can you spare the time?'

'Well,' he said, 'I am a philosophy student at the university, but of course the university is on holiday at the moment. Yes, I believe I could spare time from my studies, signora.'

'Perhaps you would let me know a figure I might offer you?'

He was very pleased. This was an extremely polite way of handling matters. If she had made an offer, he would have been obliged to haggle. But since he was naming his fee, she would hardly argue.

They came to a quick agreement. She then explained about her trouble over sending the cablegram. As if to illustrate the point, the reply was at that moment brought in by a boy of about eleven in a dusty uniform. He presented the envelope; Ruth opened it and tried to read the message. Either it was in Swedish, or half the letters had been left out of the words.

'Oh!' she exclaimed in annoyance. 'This is utterly incomprehensible!'

'May I, signora?' He took it from her, glanced at it, then excused himself to go out to the reception desk. She heard him on the telephone, speaking rapid Sicilian. After about ten minutes he returned with the message newly written out in his own handwriting.

'The signal was difficult to read, signora. Some problem with the machine.' Ruth stifled an angry laugh. Pinturenzetto gave the minutest of shrugs and went on: 'I took the liberty of asking the clerk to ask for a retransmission, and then he dictated it on the telephone. I hope that was what you would wish?'

'Of course. Thank you.'

The reply now read: 'Envers leaves 7 a.m. tomorrow stop. Estimated arrival 5 p.m. same day stop. What goes on query. David.'

Tomorrow evening! By tomorrow evening she would have begun on yet another travel plan – but this one would be the most unusual and the most important she'd ever undertaken.

'Signor Pinturenzetto, I have other important cablegrams to send. May I ask for your immediate help?'

'It will be my pleasure to assist you, signora.'

She signalled to the bartender. 'Please order some refreshment, signore. It will take me some time to write the messages.'

'Thank you, signora.'

In her room she wrote and rewrote instructions for those who would have to handle the London end of the journey. The house had to be made ready to receive an invalid, so she told the Worlands to empty the dining room and turn it into a bedroom for Ethan. He would be able to lie on the balcony that ran across the front of the house and watch the life in the square and the gardens while he recuperated.

She sent a lengthy message to Ethan's doctor in Harley

Street, Sir Bertram Yatesley, asking if he could be available to visit Ethan at home within the next two or three days. She asked him to send a private ambulance to collect Ethan and herself at a point to be determined later. She also requested him to have a nursing team in attendance at the house in Pouncey Square.

Next she wrote a message for Tadsley and Gower, telling them she would need their help within the next twenty-four hours to get permissions from the Port of London Authority.

The latter two messages were to be sent at once but to be delivered at nine in the morning, when Sir Bertram's secretary might have opened the consulting rooms and the lawyers' offices might be supposed to be functioning.

After some thought she sent a last message, this time a telegram, to a car-race contact in Naples, asking him to order supplies she felt would be needed and arrange for them to be sent at once by steamer to Messina docks.

By the time she had finished it was eleven at night. She went down to the bar, half expecting Pinturenzetto to have either fallen asleep or gone home. But he, like all sensible Italians, had had a good siesta in the afternoon and expected to go on in good working order until at least one in the morning. She handed him the messages, clearly written out on separate sheets of paper from Ethan's writing case.

'Can you understand all this?' she asked.

He read in silence. He was clearly very impressed. He'd thought her a young, innocent, English wife. Now she showed herself to be a considerable businesswoman. 'I understand perfectly, signora.' He hesitated. 'The telegraph office unfortunately closes at ten.'

It was quite untrue. She knew from her year of managing the Coverton racing team that cables and telegrams can be sent at any hour of the night or day. However, she understood the underlying message. 'Perhaps in view of the urgency you could find some way of seeing these are sent?'

'I could try, signora. But it would be at special rates.'

'I quite understand.' She opened her handbag and counted out hundred lire notes until her translator seemed to think it was enough. 'And any other fees, signore – you only have to let me know.'

He went off after promising to be with her immediately after breakfast. He was as good as his word. She knew her messages had gone before midnight, because the answer to the telegram to Naples was by her breakfast plate.

Until it was time to go for the morning visit at the hospital, she busied herself with further planning. She had Pinturenzetto hire a car and drive her to the docks. There they had an interview with the harbour master, who was much surprised at her request. So was her interpreter, who paused at least twice to make sure he was hearing correctly.

Then she had Pinturenzetto drive her to the hospital. 'Perhaps you would like drive to the telegraph office to see if any further replies have come for me, signore? Then if you would join me for lunch, we could see what more needs to be done immediately.'

'At your service, signora,' he replied, greatly pleased at being given the use of the car. He drove off in a roar of the engine and a plume of exhaust fumes.

Ethan was lying looking bored, with the electric fan going full blast. 'Is the breeze outside as hot as it is in here?' he enquired when she had kissed him good morning.

'Hotter. But never mind. I think you'll be going home in a couple of days,' she announced.

'Really? Thank the lord! By boat, I take it?'

'Well, almost,' she said. 'By flying boat.'

'Flying boat!' He lay for a moment in stunned silence. Then she saw him begin to laugh. 'By heaven! You don't do things by halves!'

'Now, Ethan . . .'

'Now, Ethan,' he mimicked. 'You're going to start telling me not to get excited. Well, dammit, I am excited. Why, the trip should only take twelve hours at most.'

'That's my estimate, allowing for a refuelling stop at Marseilles. We'll know better when Envers gets here – he'll have done the flight one way and he'll have a better idea of the fuel needs.'

'Hang on, Ruth! Where's Envers going to get aviation fuel for the flight back? There isn't an aerodrome in Messina.'

'No, but there's a port; and I've already arranged for drums of aviation spirit to be sent by boat from Naples.'

'Well done! You'd already thought of it.'

'I've had plenty of experience of foreseeing snags, darling. But I want you to leave it all to me. You mustn't start worrying about the details. I'll work it all out with Envers.'

'When's he due?'

'Somewhere around five this evening, give or take – if the sirocco decides to blow he may be delayed a bit.'

'Where's he going to land?'

'In the bay, of course. I went to see the harbour master first thing – it's all arranged. He's quite thrilled at the idea of having a flying boat land in his jurisdiction – it's never happened before.'

'I bet it hasn't! Ruth, it's great!'

'Now, Ethan, you promised not to get excited.'

'No, I didn't, but I'll try not to.'

All the same, they spent the visiting hour talking about the flight, with the result that he had a heightened temperature by the time she left. Sister Febronia tut-tutted at her as she went out.

'Will you come with me, please, Sister? I need to talk to Dr Andromi.'

'Now? It is better I stay with the signore and help to get his temperature down.'

'Very well, may I wait for you in the waiting room? I do need to talk to the doctor.'

In half an hour the sister joined her. Together they went to the office of Dottore Andromi.

'Dottore,' Ruth began, suddenly aware she was going to give him a tremendous shock, 'I want to tell you that Mr Coverton will be leaving here in a day or two.'

'No, no, signora, that is most unwise!' cried the sister, without even waiting to translate her words.

'Please tell Dr Andromi.'

Sister Febronia translated. Dr Andromi shook his head. 'I will not permit it. A long journey will do him much harm.'

'He's not going to have a long journey. It will only take a day to reach home.'

'What "home" do you take him to then? To Reggio? There is nothing in a Reggio hotel to improve his condition . . .'

'I'm taking him home, dottore. To London.'

'*Cosa?*' cried Andromi, annoyed. 'A foolish joke! Why

do you waste my time with this?' Sister Febronia translated this, making little placating gestures as she did so –
she thought his language too impolite.

'Dottore, I'm perfectly serious. Mr Coverton will be at
home in his own house well within twenty-four hours after
he leaves hospital. He is going to fly to London.'

When Sister Febronia had translated, both she and the
doctor looked at Ruth as if she had taken leave of her
senses. Then the doctor rushed into a tirade of Italian
while the nun shook her head in disapproval. At length
she turned to Ruth.

'Dr Andromi is very angry. He says he thought you
were a sensible woman. You know very well there is no
airfield at Messina . . .'

'No, but there is a bay of sea water, and a flying boat
can land there easily.'

'What?' gasped Sister Febronia. 'A – a flying boat?'

'Yes, an aeroplane that can land on the water. The
cabin is shaped like a boat.'

The nun turned to the doctor. '*Un canotto volente*,' she
ventured, in a tone that implied, 'Do you believe this?'

The doctor's face lit up. '*Un idroplano? Si, si, ho ne
letto!*' He made a great effort and said to Ruth, 'A flyeeng
boat, eet will come to Messina?'

She nodded, smiling.

'*Madonna mia!*' He seized her hand, shook it with
fervour. His plump brown face had lit up – even his bald
head seemed to glow with enthusiasm. '*Che miracolo!*'

For a further ten minutes he questioned Ruth about the
expected *idroplano* while his interpreter struggled to keep
up with him. After that, Dr Andromi's objection to
Ethan's leaving hospital diminished to almost nothing. So
long as he himself could accompany the patient to London

in the flying boat, he had no further protest to make. To travel in such a wonderful machine would make him famous, his career would be enhanced enormously. Although senior in Messina, he was a junior doctor with few prospects in the Italian medical hierarchy.

Nothing could have fitted in better with Ruth's hopes. She'd wondered how to find an attendant to take care of Ethan on the flight. Even Signor Pinturenzetto might have had difficulty finding one. If plump sedate young Andromi wished to risk it, she was only too happy to take him.

At about five that evening she was at the docks in a hired motorboat waiting for the arrival of the Blackburn Iris. This old three-engined flying boat belonged to Paul Envers who ran a cargo service for perishable goods. Built by Robert Blackburn during the Great War, it had been used for military purposes and bought by Envers after he had flown it during naval service on Malta. As reliable as a ploughhorse, it came swooping down out of the evening cloud rack into the Bay of Messina, settled like an eider duck on the choppy grey waters, taxied in half-a-mile or so on one engine, and cut power.

A cheer arose from the sightseers along the harbour wall.

Paul Envers and his co-pilot emerged from the open door as Ruth's boat drew alongside. 'Evening,' Envers said, touching his battered cap. 'On schedule, I believe?'

'Practically on the dot. How do you do, Mr Envers,' Ruth said. 'We've never met but I've heard of you.'

'Ditto,' said Envers. 'This is Andrew Fitzwilliams, known as Fitz.'

'Pleased to meet you, ma'am.'

'What now?' inquired Envers. 'Do I come ashore or do you want to come aboard?'

'May I come up? I want to look at the inside.'

'My pleasure.' He helped her up and she stepped into the flying boat.

It was a spartan interior, with only a thin partition between the pilots' seats and the cargo bay. The space was clean, had clearly been scrubbed and polished often to ensure that precious perishable goods wouldn't be contaminated by dirt or damp.

'What is it we're supposed to carry?' Envers inquired.

'A patient.'

'Ah. That could be a problem.'

'Why should it?'

'Well, there are very strict rules about infection. I take it the patient has something they won't allow on shipboard diphtheria, scarlet fever?'

'Nothing like that. The patient is Ethan Coverton who was injured at the Targa Florio some weeks ago . . .'

'Gee whiz, yes, I read about that,' Fitz broke in. 'Got his legs smashed up and things.'

'And he desperately wants to get home, and the doctors say he isn't fit for a long journey by train or ship. So I thought it would solve the problem if we flew him home.'

'Well, now, Miss Barnett, of course I want to help you. But I have to tell you I'm not keen to take a very sick patient unless there's medical attention. Neither Fitz nor I is qualified . . .'

'It's all right. Dr Andromi is coming.'

'He is? And who's he when he's at home?'

'He's the surgeon who treated Ethan's injuries. So I think we can say he's well qualified.'

'Well I never. You seem to have thought of everything,

ma'am,' Envers said with a twinkle. 'You seem to have thought of everything except the most important. Where are we going to get benzine for the return flight?'

'It will be here in the morning,' said Ruth. 'I'm having it sent from Naples.'

Because this was Italy and not a usual thing, therefore causing arguments at the loading point and misunderstandings on board, the aviation fuel did not arrive in the morning. But the harbour master bustled about importantly. The steamer, originally heading for Reggio, was diverted from its course to deliver the fuel drums. Ruth, of course, had to pay for the extra trip and the disruption to the delivery schedule. The fuel was brought to the Iris, and the flying boat was manually refuelled.

By then it was too late to start out that day, but Ruth had expected delays. She wanted to achieve the entire journey home in one day so that Ethan could leave his bed at the hospital yet go to a bed in his own home that same evening. There would have to be a pause at Marseilles, but he need not leave the cot in the flying boat.

Envers and Fitz had worked on the cabin of the Iris. They took out the bars and divisions which held cargo in place, and instead bolted to the deck an iron cot. They also fixed two seats, one for the doctor and one for Ruth.

Meanwhile Ruth was sending last-minute messages, paying off hotel and hospital bills, making a generous donation on Ethan's behalf to the religious charity which ran the hospital and settling accounts with Renaldo Pinturenzetto. Her interpreter was so delighted with her generosity that he kissed her hand several times and, clearly, wondered whether he should have asked for more in the first place.

The luggage she and Ethan had brought with them proved a momentary problem. She didn't want to take it on the flying boat because there was no place to stack it and it merely added to the weight. She gave it – suitcases and contents – to the staff of the Estella. The old porter, the dining-room waiter and the chambermaid stood amidst the expensive collection of Savile Row tailoring and Harvey Nichols dresses in a trance of happiness.

At five a.m. on the morning of 24 July, Ruth went to the hospital. Dr Andromi was awaiting her, with an overnight case and his medical bag. He was very, very nervous now that the moment had come. He had never flown in his life before.

But neither had Ruth.

She had kept that fact secret so as not to worry the doctor. She said in a voice of forced brightness: 'Now, dottore, we can't say much to each other. *Non potiamo dire molto l'un al altro – no?*'

He sighed agreement.

'So I only want to wish us *buon viaggio*.'

'Oh, *si, si, buon viaggio e buona fortuna!*'

She managed a smile. Sister Febronia came to say that the patient was ready. 'The doctor has given a light sedative, signora. It should last for about two hours. If more is needed, Dr Andromi will administer.'

'I understand.'

'The *idroplano* comes to rest at Marsiglia?'

'Yes. In about four hours.'

'For how long?'

'About three-quarters of an hour. I have arranged for fuelling facilities there.'

Sister Febronia passed on this information to the doctor, who nodded. 'Dr Andromi says some light food should be brought to Signor Coverton at that time. He has *aquavite* and other stimulants if they are needed. And when you reach London, what happens then?'

'I've had my lawyer contact the Port of London Authority for permission for the Iris to land in the Thames Estuary. From there we'll taxi up to the Pool of London.' Ruth had to repeat this once or twice so that the sister could translate for the doctor. The Pool of London was a term they couldn't understand but they were assured it was a harbour like Messina.

'And from there, what?'

'Ambulance to our house in Mayfair.'

'Good. Dr Andromi asks if you have made hotel arrangements for him?'

'Oh, dottore!' Ruth exclaimed. 'You'll stay with us, of course!'

Through his apprehension, Dr Andromi beamed with pleasure. This would be a thing to tell his children and his grandchildren when he had some – not only to fly in an *idroplano* with a rich mad Englishman, but to stay in his mansion – *che avventura!*

Ethan was carried out on a stretcher. He was drowsy yet fighting for consciousness. 'We're off, then?' he asked in a whisper when Ruth bent over him.

'Next stop Marseilles.'

'That's the stuff!' he caught her hand. 'You ever flown before?'

She shook her head. 'You?'

He gave her a sleepy grin. 'Never in a flying boat. Medals all round when we land, eh?' he murmured.

An ambulance took them the short journey to the pier. The Iris had taxied warily almost right up to the jetty and a temporary boardwalk had been built at the instructions of the harbour master, who had spent Ruth's money like water. The patient was carried aboard. Dr Andromi, clutching his medical bag to his chest, went next. Fitz came after carrying the doctor's valise.

Ruth went aboard in the clothes she stood up in. Her only luggage was a handbag containing money, cheque-book and passports.

When she stepped in, Ethan had already been settled on the cot bolted to the deck. Fitz was fastening webbing straps across him. 'Just a precaution,' he said as he saw Ruth's alarmed look. 'We have to make a climbing circle after takeoff, and he can't hang on to the sides of the cot because one arm is in plaster. So this is just to keep him from knocking himself about. All right?'

'Yes,' Ruth said, but she knelt on the deck beside the bed for the takeoff.

One engine began to turn. The flying boat shuddered in the water then began to move away from the pier. The crowd which had gathered to see this extraordinary sight waved and shouted *Brava, brava!* The big flying machine drifted through the waves, escorted by a little fleet of pleasure craft and fishing boats. After a few moments the two other engines joined the first, the boat surged through the water easily outstripping its followers.

Dr Andromi was gazing out of the window. He gave a startled exclamation in Italian. Ruth guessed they had lifted into the air.

The noise was great, the boat vibrated to the turn of the big airscrews. The sky tilted around them. Envers called back to them: 'Everybody all right?'

'Yes, thank you,' Ruth replied shakily. She took Ethan's hand. But Ethan was asleep. She gave a smoth-ered laugh. How he would complain when he realized he'd slept through the takeoff!

And then they were away, heading north-west, along the coast of Italy, towards the Côte d'Azur and Marseilles.

Afterwards, when people asked what it had been like, Ruth could only truthfully say it had been boring. Far below them the sea was rather like a blue silk bedspread dotted with toy boats, toys for a sick child. Above was a blue sky spattered with cottonwool cloud. Inside the aircraft there was nothing to look at except walls painted a metallic grey, and too much noise for conversation even if Dr Andromi could have spoken enough English.

Ethan woke at about seven thirty. As Ruth had foreseen, he felt ill done by at missing takeoff. He drank some milk and brandy, tried to talk to Ruth but grew tired at having to raise his voice. After a while he went back to sleep.

At ten fifteen they touched down in the Golfe du Lion. A tender came out at once with a harbour official who checked passports and issued a certificate of health. A little supply boat tied up alongside with metal food containers and coffee in vacuum flasks. Ethan was propped up on pillows so as to have breakfast. 'Ugh!' he said, screwing up his face. 'Vacuum-flask coffee! How about more of that brandy-and-milk?'

Dr Andromi shook his head reprovingly when Ruth haltingly translated this, but Ruth thought it encouraging. Ethan seemed to be suffering no ill effects from the journey.

As they set out on the final leg of the flight, the weather gave evidence that they were returning to England. The clouds thickened, a wind buffeted the aircraft. Dr

Andromi went pale. He made frequent visits to the rather primitive *cabine de toilette*. But he made no complaint and when Ruth inquired if he was all right replied valiantly that he was *eccellente*.

The flight plan took them over the mainland of France to Bordeaux and thence across the Brittany peninsula to the English Channel. The home port of the Iris was Southampton but on this occasion she bypassed it. Instead she flew on to the Thames Estuary where Envers let her down a few miles west of Southend.

Here a small fleet of officials came out to welcome them. First there was the Customs launch to check on the number of passengers and their luggage. Next came the Port of London officials to make sure the flying boat obeyed navigation instructions on her trip up to the Pool. There they had their passports examined.

As the door of the flying boat opened and Ruth stepped down into the tender, a cheer went up. She gazed about in astonishment. A dozen or so boats bobbed about in the murky waters of the Pool. Photographers were aiming lenses at her through the fine drizzle, reporters were calling questions, a film newsman was cranking the handle of his cine camera.

Ruth turned to try to retreat. The door was blocked by Dr Andromi backing out so as to allow the stretcher to be handed through.

There was nothing to do but step down into the tender. A hand came out to steady her. 'Welcome home,' said a voice. It was Niall Gillis.

'Good heavens! What are you doing here?'

'I thought you might need a hand. The newspapers got wind of your coming. I thought they might make a fuss.'

'But why are they *bothering*?'

'Because apparently nobody has ever done this before – used a flying boat as a flying ambulance to bring someone home into the Port of London.'

Seamen were handling the stretcher aboard. Ethan was trying to raise himself on an elbow to see what was going on.

'Look this way, Mr Coverton!' 'Mr Coverton, how are you feeling?' 'Miss Barnett, say a word for our readers!'

Dr Andromi gaped at the crowd. '*E famosa, lei?*' he asked Ruth, baffled.

'Let's get out of here,' called the skipper of the tender.

Fitz nodded and released the mooring rope. The tender edged away, the flying boat moved to open water where she made a circular turn and began to taxi back towards the estuary.

'Goodbye!' Fitz called.

'Goodbye, and thank you!' But the door of the Iris had closed before Ruth had finished her thanks.

The ambulance was waiting on the docks. Here again there was a crowd of reporters and photographers. Ruth fended them off as Ethan was carried from the launch. 'Go away!' she shouted. 'Can't you see he's not well enough for all this?'

With Niall Gillis's help she clambered aboard the ambulance. He closed the door on her with a quick encouraging wave. She sank down on the bench opposite the stretcher. Dr Andromi had gone in the front with the driver.

'Well,' said Ethan in a tired voice, 'home sweet home.'

'We'll be indoors soon, dearest. You can have a good rest.'

He nodded and managed a smile. 'I know we're home,' he said, 'that's a London drizzle out there.'

At the Mayfair house, the Worlands were waiting in a sort of excited frustration. Their income had been lowered considerably during Ethan's stay in Sicily – no titbits to sell to the newspapers, no reports to hand on to Antony Coverton. When the cable had come instructing them to move the furniture so as to give Ethan a different bedroom, they had brought in staff and had it done, but Eustace Worland considered the date of arrival was a mistake and had made no use of the information.

Only this morning, when the newspapers told him that Coverton and his friend Miss Barnett were due to arrive around teatime in a flying boat did he realize he had missed a chance two days ago of offering an exclusive.

But he and his wife took comfort in the fuss that was now going on around the house. Reporters everywhere, a policeman keeping the crowd in order, Sir Bertram Yatesley here in person awaiting the arrival of the travellers – oh, there was plenty of money still to be made out of this household.

Chapter Fourteen

Dr Andromi had brought with him the X-ray plates showing Ethan's fractures. He went next day in the Rolls to meet Sir Bertram Yatesley and have them examined on the viewer at the Prince Regent Hospital. Sir Bertram was on the whole pleased with them and with the state of his patient. However, he wanted Ethan to go into hospital for further X-rays.

'I'm not going into any damned hospital,' grunted Ethan.

Sir Bertram tried to persuade him. Ruth knew better. 'Is it urgent? If not, leave it for a day or two. Ethan's been away over two months. He needs to feel settled in his home before he'll want to leave it again.'

This wiser view prevailed. Ethan enjoyed himself for a week, ordering the nurses about, having them read the whole of the *Financial Times* to him, demanding that they put record after record on the gramophone, complaining about endless cups of beef tea and taking pleasure in the 'medicinal' champagne prescribed by Sir Bertram.

He progressed to sitting up and was taken out to the balcony. He watched the children playing in the garden of the square. He decided there ought to be a swing for them and was cross when he was told the bylaws forbade it. He discovered by observation that the housemaid next door had been having a romance with the postman. He began to make a try at *The Times* crossword.

'Ask him now if he'll go into the Prince Regent,' suggested Ruth.

Sir Bertram made his request. 'Only overnight,' he added. 'Just to get new X-rays, to see if the bones are knitting properly.'

'Hmm,' said Ethan. The idea of a trip out of the house wasn't unwelcome. 'I'm not going in an ambulance, though.'

'But why not, Mr Coverton? It's much the best . . .'

'You can't see out of the windows of an ambulance.'

Very well then, he could go in the Rolls. Dr Andromi and the day nurse would act as attendants.

Dr Andromi was having a wonderful time. He was being ferried about London at will in a luxurious limousine, he was hobnobbing with famous doctors at an expensive private hospital and the lady of the house treated him as if he were a distinguished guest.

It had come as a shock to the doctor to realize that the lady of the house wasn't the legal wife of Signor Coverton. To some extent he now understood the interest of the newsmen at their arrival and the mentions in the gossip columns that now began to appear. He couldn't read English well, but he recognized the names and some of the medical terms. 'Ethan Coverton the millionaire motor-racing enthusiast, his faithful companion Miss Barnett, Targa Florio, hospital examination—' These let him know that the British press considered Ethan and Ruth to be very newsworthy.

Not to be wondered at. Yet he was surprised that so much was common knowledge. He'd always understood that the British were very puritanical and this, the priests always explained, was because as Protestants they could not confess their venal sins and receive absolution. It followed that Signor Coverton and the signora – or signorina, as he now discovered her to be – were living in sin. In his own country, such things were better handled; a man's mistress was kept safely tucked away where no one could make a fuss about her. If not, the wife was apt to become very troublesome indeed.

In the case of Ethan Coverton, the wife seemed almost invisible. As far as Dr Andromi could learn, Mrs Coverton had not made any inquiry about the health of her husband, had not sent any good wishes for his recovery.

There was a son, the doctor knew, because messages came from him about the business, by telephone and sometimes brought by a secretary. Despite the protests of both Sir Bertram and Dr Andromi, Signor Coverton had begun to take an interest in business almost as soon as he was settled at home. But it was understandable that he should want to gather up the reins again: it seemed the business was very large and great sums of money were concerned.

The overnight stay in hospital was accomplished, the X-rays were taken and examined. Sir Bertram studied them, Dr Andromi 'consulted' – oh, the bliss, to be a consultant in a case involving a Harley Street specialist! Sir Bertram nodded his silvery head. 'Things are going well, signor,' he remarked. 'Very handsome work.' Then, remembering the poor man spoke almost no English, '*Mawlto benny.*'

'Thank you, Sir Bertram.' Andromi was wishing he could have it in writing to show the management committee of Messina hospital.

And in fact, when he left two days later, he had exactly that. Ruth, understanding his hopes and ambitions, asked Sir Bertram to write a few lines of commendation on his Harley Street writing paper. In addition, as a thank-you present from Ethan, she had bought and had engraved a silver cigarette box from Asprey's. The engraving said in Italian, 'To Dr Alessandro Andromi, from Ethan Coverton, a very grateful patient, May–July 1926.'

He had elected to go home by Channel ferry and then overland by train as far as Naples. Ruth ensured that he had first-class tickets together with a very handsome cheque. He kissed her hand many times as she saw him off at Victoria station. She, to his surprise and delight, kissed him gently on the cheek. 'Thank you for all you've done for us,' she murmured.

Ah, thought Dr Andromi as the train bore him away, perhaps the English are right after all. It would be a sin to hide such a jewel away in a back street.

Now Sir Bertram announced that the plaster must come off. The plaster on the arm, in his opinion, should have been removed before the end of Ethan's stay in the Italian hospital, but it was better not to mention that.

Ethan was delighted. He proposed going out for short walks round the square. But to his dismay, that proved impossible. The long period of immobility had weakened his legs so much that he needed a physical instructor to come and help improve the muscle tone.

Ruth could see that these periods were actually painful. 'Never mind, darling,' she soothed, 'Sir Bertram says it should only take about six weeks before you're mobile again.'

'It's so damned *undignified!*' groaned the patient. 'Like

being a baby again – I'm having to learn to walk as if I
were a six-months' child!'

'Patience, patience,' said Sir Bertram. 'You're very
lucky you've mended so well.' He was about to say, 'At
your age problems aren't unusual,' but checked himself.
He hadn't reached Harley Street by making tactless
remarks to his patients.

Now that things seemed returning to something like
normal, Ruth, to her own dismay, became ill. Nothing
serious, she kept insisting. But she found she couldn't eat,
couldn't sleep.

'Reaction, dear lady,' soothed Sir Bertram, 'sheer
reaction. You've been through a gruelling time, I imagine.'

'I suppose so. Can you give me a tonic or something?'

He prescribed iron tablets, Sanatogen and a mild sedative. He would have liked to say, 'Don't let things bother
you.' But it was difficult for a woman living in Ruth's
circumstances not to be 'bothered'. Her life seemed so
entirely entwined with Coverton's. She seemed to have no
one to turn to, no family of her own. What she really
needed, in his opinion, was six weeks of being cosseted by
a doting mother, but she didn't even seem to have kindly
servants to look after her.

'Is there someone you could ask to stay with you?' he
inquired. 'A woman friend?'

'I'm afraid not.' It came as a shock to her to realize that
she didn't have any friends. The girls from the Euphemia
Grey Hostel seemed to belong in another life, the colleagues from her short time in the office had receded from
her memory. Her friends were the people of the motor-
racing world, but she could hardly invite David Epps or
Peter Stokes to stay. Ethan would think she'd gone mad.

'Well, don't worry, you're only run down; it's nothing serious. But I think you should get out and about more. There's no need to spend so much time in the sickroom – the nurses are perfectly—'

'But Mr Coverton likes me to be there.'

'What Mr Coverton likes must take second place for a while.'

'No, no,' protested Ruth. And then, suddenly anxious, 'Don't tell him I'm under the weather!'

'Of course not, my dear.' He patted her shoulder. She was really a very nice child. 'But you must take care of yourself too, you know.'

'I'll be all right.'

She couldn't swallow the Sanatogen, but took the iron tablets and the sedative and tried to make herself eat more. But she still had this feeling of being at a loss, unanchored in a vast sea. Now that the enormous responsibility of looking out for Ethan had been taken from her, she seemed to have no *raison d'être*.

The work of organizing the motor-racing team remained. The Coverton III could still race, and she ensured that it arrived at the prescribed venues and that Peter Stokes was paid. But there were no prospects of travelling abroad with it for the winter season since the doctors had said Ethan must take it very easy until the spring at least. He was slowly regaining the ability to walk, but there were little recurrences of the jaundice which seemed to worry Sir Bertram.

As for the Coverton IV, Dave was still tinkering with rebuilding it after the crash, but without Ethan to give impetus to the work, it all seemed pointless.

When she came down to the breakfast room, she always found the morning post by her plate. One morning in

August she saw an envelope addressed in a hand she instantly recognized.

It was from her grandmother.

In the three years since she left home, she had had scarcely any response to the Christmas cards and birthday greetings she'd sent. Now, all at once and unexpectedly, a letter.

She felt a dart of anxiety. It could only be bad news. A death? She almost didn't want to open it. If Grandma was writing to say something had happened to Granddad, she felt in her present state that it would open a floodgate of tears which would drown her.

With trembling hands she slit open the envelope.

Dear Ruth,

Your grandfather and I have talked about you a lot in the last few weeks. We saw the newspaper pieces about how you had got Mr Coverton home from Italy after his bad smash-up and we thought it was very brave of you. Granddad has always said nothing would ever make him go up in an airplane and he has to admit it was brave, and so do I.

We can't pretend we approve of you living with a man you aren't married to and it's still wrong as the Bible says, but for all that the devotion you've showed deserves praise. So I thought I'd drop a line to say that in some ways we admire you.

Everything in Freshton goes on much the same. Elizabeth Goodcroft married that Tom Sisley and they're trying to make a go of a newspaper and tobacconist. If you remember Billy Grand that had a bit of a fancy for you, he got into trouble in a pub in Guildford and was up before the magistrate. Granddad is specializing a bit in fruit bushes for next year. I've nearly finished the patchwork bedspread so if you have any pieces of blue cotton I'd be glad of same if you ever have time to think of sending them. Kind regards, Grandma.

Kind regards. She read and reread the words. At last, after three years of silence, her grandparents had got in touch.

They hadn't forgiven her. She knew that if she were to go home on a visit, they would tell her that she had done exactly what they expected – gone straight to the bad. They would lecture her about her sinful life, warn her that hellfire awaited her if she didn't change her ways and generally show disapproval. How wonderful it would be to hear them berating her – she could hear Granddad's rusty voice: 'Is this our reward for bringing you up decent?' And grandma, a little tearful, adding, 'You've brought shame on us, Ruthie . . .' They were her family, people who disapproved and yet might listen to her when she tried to explain how she felt.

She left the breakfast table and went to the study. There she sat at the desk and began a letter home. She poured out all the terror she'd felt when she saw the men running down the hillside from the Targa Florio course. She related the hours, the days, the weeks of anxiety in Messina, the struggle with the language, the negotiations that were necessary even to buy an electric fan for Ethan. She described her loneliness now in the Mayfair house, no one to turn to, and the nights, the long nights without Ethan by her side.

About mid-morning the day nurse tapped on the door. 'Miss Barnett?'

Ruth looked up. Her hand was cramped from holding the pen. To her surprise she found her cheeks were wet with tears. She found her handkerchief, wiped her eyes and called, 'Come in!'

Nurse Timmins stopped in something like shock. 'Are you unwell, Miss Barnett?'

'No, no— It's just – it's nothing. What did you want?'

'It's ten thirty, Miss Barnett. Mr Coverton was wondering why you didn't come in as usual for morning coffee?'

She looked at her wristwatch. Ten thirty. She'd opened her grandmother's letter at eight thirty. From that moment to this, the world had passed her by completely.

It was the first time she had ever forgotten to join Ethan for the mid-morning break. It was an important point in the day because he moved with help from the nurses to the balcony and she would sit with him there.

'I'll be there in a moment, Nurse.'

She hurried up to her room. There she washed her face, applied some powder to disguise her red eyes and resettled her hair in its tortoiseshell clasp.

Nurse Timmins went out of the room as Ruth entered it. It was understood that this was a period when the day nurse could have some time to herself while Ruth kept Ethan company.

Ruth went through to the balcony. She busied herself pouring a cup of coffee. Ethan was watching her with a frown.

'What's the matter?'

'Nothing.'

'You've been crying.'

'No, I haven't.'

'Ruthie, don't be silly. Your eyes are all red. Come here.'

She set aside her coffee and came slowly to his chair. It was the kind made for use in the tropics, well cushioned, with wide arms on which to place a glass of rum, and a footrest. Around it stood plants in pots which Ethan had learned to take an interest in. On a table to hand lay the *Financial Times*, *The Times*, and an engineering magazine.

He patted the arm of his chair. She perched there. 'Now,' he said, 'tell me what's happened.'

'I— I had a letter from my grandmother.'

His frown of anxiety deepened to a ferocious glare. 'If that old hag has been upsetting—'

'No, no, Ethan! No, she wrote to say – it's a sort of like a reconciliation.'

'No!' He was surprised and pleased.

'Yes.'

'But I thought they washed their hands of you when you left home?'

'They've changed their minds. At least, not entirely. But Grandma says she thinks I'm not all bad, or words to that effect.'

'So why were you crying?' he asked, bewildered.

'It was just . . . I don't know . . . I've been feeling . . . I'd no one to talk to, no one to explain how awful things were when I thought I was going to lose you . . .'

He put his good arm around her and held her close. 'Poor little girl,' he said softly. 'I've been damned selfish, haven't I? It never occurred to me what a hard time you must have been having.'

'No, really, Ethan. It wasn't like that. I was glad to have a lot to do – it stopped me from worrying all the time. But now we're safe home, and you're getting well, and you don't seem to need me, and somehow it all seems so – so . . .'

'I know. I understand now. I was so taken up with being ill that I didn't think how lonely it must be for you.'

'But it doesn't matter! Soon you'll be better, and we'll be together again like before.'

'Yes, as soon as I can toddle a hundred yards without two sticks.'

'You're doing fine, Ethan, you mustn't try to rush it.'

'Ruthie, as soon as I can walk without feeling I'm going to fall over, we'll go down to – where is it? – and visit your folk.'

'Oh, no! We're not going anywhere until you're really fit again.'

'I'm getting stronger all the time. A week ago it would still have hurt my ribs to be hugging you like this.' He increased his grip to emphasize the words, and then laughed. ' "We must do this more often",' he said in a teasing quote.

'Oh, now you're laughing at me!' She sat up and shook her head at him. 'Drink your coffee.'

'You drink yours. You look as if you need it.'

'Yes, and I'm famished. I didn't eat any breakfast.' For the first time in weeks, she was hungry. She fell on the biscuits which came with the coffee tray.

Ethan watched her with loving amusement. She had changed greatly in the last few months, but she was still the most wonderful girl he had ever met.

By and by Worland came in to take away the coffee tray. Ruth removed herself from the arm of the chair: she always had the feeling that Worland disapproved of any show of affection.

'You write a reply to your grandparents,' Ethan

suggested, 'while I make a start on the crossword.'

'All right.' She went to the study and brought the letter for him to read. Her own letter she tore into shreds and put in her skirt pocket. Mawkish, self-pitying, idiotic – how had she ever thought she could write such things to Grandma.

Yet setting it down had helped her. In some way it had proved cathartic. She had recovered her balance, felt more in control of herself and her world.

'Well,' said Ethan when he'd read what her grandmother had to say, 'it's an olive branch, I take it, but it hasn't many olives on it.'

'You can't expect her to say she approves, Ethan.'

'No, I suppose not. Tell you what, why don't you invite her to stay?'

'What, here?'

'Why not? You'd like it, wouldn't you?'

'She wouldn't come, Ethan.'

'Yes, she would. Tell her you'll take her to Fortnum and Mason, give her tea at Gunter's.'

'She'd never go anywhere without Granddad. And Granddad can't leave the nursery garden.'

He pondered. 'All right, then, invite them for Christmas. Don't tell me there's anything doing in a nursery garden at Christmas! We'll take them to the pantomime.'

Laughing, Ruth sat down to write her letter. She said only that she had been very pleased to hear from Grandma, that Ethan was recovering from his injuries, and that he'd suggested her grandparents might like to come for a visit at Christmas. She knew they'd refuse, but they'd be pleased with the invitation.

One day, when Ethan was really recovered, they would drive down to Freshton together. She knew that once they had met him, her grandparents would like him.

On a day at the end of September, Ruth had made appointments to have her hair cut and look at some clothes for the winter. The team of day nurse and night nurse had been dispensed with by now, although the physical instructor who came in every morning reported to Sir Bertram on his patient's progress. Ruth felt easy at leaving Ethan, for some of his friends from the motor-racing world were coming to visit. She'd made him promise not to overdo things and had threatened Peter Stokes with dire reprisals if he let Ethan get overtired.

The hairdresser insisted on razor-cutting her light brown hair and giving her little curved side-pieces to lie on her cheeks. 'Very Clara Bow,' he enthused. 'Did you see her in *Kid Boots*? I'm telling all my ladies to follow her lead.'

The dresses and two-piece costumes at Leduc's had shorter skirts than ever. It seemed the wearer was expected to show the rolled tops of her silk stockings. Ruth ordered two dresses but asked for the skirts to be four inches longer. 'But it will spoil the line!' cried Leduc (born Harold Pinkton of Dover). All the same, he agreed when he discovered Ruth wouldn't buy them otherwise.

She had tea at the Ritz and then went shopping in Jackson's of Piccadilly. There was a special Gentleman's Relish that Ethan enjoyed. She returned home at about six and found, as she expected, that Ethan's guests were still there, filling the balcony room with cigarette smoke and arguing loudly about the new circuit at Le Mans.

'Out!' ordered Ruth, throwing out her arm in a gesture

of dismissal. 'Out, the lot of you! You ought to be ashamed of yourselves! Didn't I ask you, Peter, to keep this bunch in order?'

'You didn't really think they'd take any notice of me?' he said, shielding his head with a crooked elbow as if to protect himself from her onslaught.

'Come on now, fellows, it's time to go. Out with you.'

'Ruth, stop ordering my friends about—'

'As for you, Ethan Coverton, didn't you promise me you'd take it quietly?'

'I am quiet,' he said from his cane chaise longue. 'It's the others that are making all the row.'

Laughing and shaking her head, she ushered them out and down the stairs to the hall. There Worland was waiting with a pinched look to hand out their hats and canes. Mrs Worland showed similar disapproval when she came to clear the mess of tea things, whisky glasses and ashtrays from the balcony.

'I want this room thoroughly aired by the time dinner's over,' Ruth instructed.

The drawing room, which was at the back of the house, was now the dining room. Ethan was able to make his way there slowly for the main meal of the day. But this evening he showed little interest in his food.

'I think I'm a bit tired,' he remarked. 'I'll settle down for the night as soon as my room's tidied up.'

She knew that the visit of his friends had worn him out, but had too much sense to say so.

When she went into his room next day to say good morning, he was lying huddled up in the bedclothes although his morning tea was on the bedside table.

'Ethan, is something wrong?'

His flushed face looked at her over the top of the

blanket. 'I think I've got a bit of a chill,' he confessed.

She went at once to the ottoman at the end of the bed for an extra blanket. She spread it over him. 'Do you feel like drinking your tea?'

'It's too much bother.'

'I'll ring Sir Bertram—'

'No, don't, he'll only tell me it's my own fault for having half-a-dozen cronies to see me.' His voice was husky, as if he were starting a cold.

'Did you sleep all right?'

'Well, I've got a bit of a pain in my side. I think I bruised one of my busted ribs.'

'But how could you . . .'

'Oh, I was showing off how well I could walk without my sticks and toppled over. I suppose I hit myself on the table or something.'

'Oh, Ethan!' The reproach, suppressed until now, burst out against her will.

'I know, you're entitled to say "I told you so." ' He pulled the blanket closer round him then said, 'I think I'll just have a bit more shut-eye.'

She went downstairs to the breakfast room. To Worland, who was coming in with her tea and toast, she said, 'Please fill a couple of hot-water bottles and take them up to Mr Coverton's room.'

'What, now, madam?'

'Of course now.'

'But isn't Mr Coverton getting up?'

She ignored him, and went to the telephone in the hall. No matter what Ethan might say, she was calling Sir Bertram.

The surgeon's receptionist said he was at the hospital's orthopaedic clinic.

'Can you get in touch with him?'

'Well, in case of emergency, madam. Is this an emergency?'

Ruth couldn't say that it was. 'When will he be free?'

'At lunchtime, Miss Barnett.'

'Please ask him then if he'll come as soon as possible. I really feel he should take a look at Mr Coverton.'

'What seems to be the trouble?'

'I think he's starting a cold, and he may have damaged one of his ribs that had just mended.'

'I see. I'll tell Sir Bertram as soon as he comes in.'

When Ruth came back to Ethan's room, he was visibly shivering. She put the hot-water bottles next to him and tucked him in.

'Why is it so cold?' he asked. 'It's only September.'

'I think you've got a bit of a temperature,' she soothed. 'I'll get you some aspirin, shall I?'

'All right.'

He took two aspirin and swallowed half-a-cup of fresh tea. Then he fell into a restless sleep. Ruth sat with him, anxious and uncertain.

At about eleven o'clock, Milburn, the physical training instructor, arrived as usual. She heard him come up the stairs with the light running step he always used.

'The butler tells me Mr Coverton's a bit under the weather,' he said, advancing to the bed with his head cocked in inquiry.

'He overtired himself yesterday with a gang of his friends, and the result is he's got a bit of a chill, it seems. And he says he may have rebroken one of his ribs.'

'What?'

'He fell and banged himself yesterday.'

'Mr Coverton? Mr Coverton?'

Ethan opened his eyes. 'Yes, what?' he said in a crotchety tone.

'How're you feeling, Mr Coverton?'

'I'd be a damn sight better if you wouldn't wake me when I'm trying to sleep!'

'Miss Barnett says you hurt your ribs?'

'Yes,' said Ethan, giving a little cough and drawing a sharp breath, 'I've got a pain in my side.'

Milburn laid his broad hand on Ethan's brow. 'Temperature's up.' He went to his hold-all, brought out a leather case, produced a thermometer. 'Open.'

'I'm not having you fussing about like a nurse, Milburn . . .' But it was only a croak of defiance. He opened his mouth for the thermometer. Milburn took his wrist between his fingers until it was time to remove it.

'Ah,' he said when he'd read the point on the mercury. 'Well, I think we'll have to get a bit of advice on this, Mr Coverton.'

'Oh, go away,' muttered Ethan.

Milburn jerked his head at Ruth. They went out under the glass of the balcony as far away from the bed as possible.

'You ought to get Sir Bertram to look at him,' he said in a low voice.

'I rang him. He's at his orthopaedic clinic.'

'Ah. Well, if I can use your phone, I'll see what I can do.'

'Of course,' said Ruth, her heart leaping up into her mouth.

Milburn's phone call brought Sir Bertram to the house by noon. He sent Ruth out of the room while he examined the patient who was now very flushed and restless.

Milburn stood with her in the passage, his hands clasped behind his back, his gaze directed at the carpet.

'What's wrong with him?' she asked in a whisper.

'Not for me to say, miss.'

After what seemed a century, Sir Bertram emerged. He took Ruth by the elbow and led her into the study.

'I'm afraid Mr Coverton has pneumonia.'

'What? But that's impossible! He hasn't had flu or anything . . .'

'Miss Barnett, it's possible to pick up the pneumococcus, the germ that causes pneumonia, at any time. He's had people coming to see him for some weeks now – people from his office, friends and colleagues of all kinds. He has had some tendency to jaundice ever since the accident, and that makes him vulnerable. He only had to get overtired, get into a weakened state . . .'

'Oh, I should never have let Peter bring all those people yesterday—'

'You mustn't think like that. He may have been incubating the attack for a couple of days. But he's quite ill, Miss Barnett.'

'But he'll be all right?'

'Certainly, certainly, he's a tough character.' And has been recovering from a serious accident for weeks, he added to himself.

'What is the treatment?' she asked.

'Well, he'd be better off in hospital, but I don't want to move him while the fever's so high. The pain in his side is due not to the broken rib but to the lung catching internally against the pleura. I've given him a morphine injection to relieve the pain and that will allow him to sleep. If I may use your telephone?'

Once again she led the way to the phone. Sir Bertram

had quite a lengthy conversation with his receptionist then turned to Ruth. 'I'm bringing back the nursing team. Mr Coverton will need attendance night and day. Some equipment will arrive within the hour. Miss Barnett, this is an infectious disease so I should like you to gargle with a weak solution of permanganate of potassium which I will send. The domestic staff should be kept away from the patient.'

'Yes, Sir Bertram.'

It was like a nightmare. Just when everything seemed to be going so well . . . She clenched her fists against the desire to weep in pain and rage. Why should this happen to Ethan, who had fought such a good fight to get better from the crash?

The nurses came back, quietly taking over the running of the sickroom. The equipment Sir Bertram had promised proved to be a pneumonia jacket of flannel lined with cotton wool, and a sloping headboard to keep Ethan propped up in a sitting position: this was to aid circulation through the lungs.

Ruth was not allowed in the sickroom. 'But he'll want to see me!' she insisted.

'Miss Barnett, dear,' said Nurse Timmins, 'he's delirious, he wouldn't know you.'

'No!' cried Ruth in despair.

The nurse shook her head, gently detached her grasp of the doorknob, and closed the door of the sickroom.

Sir Bertram came back with a colleague at about six in the evening. Dr McDonaugh was a specialist in infectious fevers. The two men spent a long time behind the closed door and when they came out they looked grave.

'Dear lady,' said Sir Bertram, 'I want you to be brave.'

She stared at him in terror.

'Dr McDonaugh feels you ought to be warned . . .'

'No!' She put her hands over her ears. 'No! He's going to be all right!'

But at just after three next morning, while she sat outside in the passage, Ethan died.

Chapter Fifteen

When they allowed her into the room, she had a
moment of wild hope. He looked as if he were sleeping.
She half turned to Dr McDonaugh, an exclamation
rising in her throat. But he caught her hand and shook
his grey head.

'We did our best,' he said. 'He just wasn't strong
enough to fight any more.'

She went to the bed, leaned down to kiss his lips. She
was still sure they would be warm and responsive. When
she felt the chill of that contact, her heart seemed to give
one great throb of despair. After that, her body went
through the motions of staying alive but her soul was
absent – gone in search of the man to whom she had given
her love, her whole being.

She sat beside the bed. She was sure that if she listened,
she would hear his voice. He had always been so alive, so
vibrant – something of him must remain in the air around
her, he couldn't really have left her here alone.

They were kind to her, didn't ask her to take part in the
sombre formalities. Sir Bertram and his colleague murmured farewells, asked her to take care of herself,
reminded her that the death certificate was on the desk in
the study.

'Yes,' she said, trying to avoid hearing them. All her attention was on listening for the faint sound of Ethan's voice from the far country to which he had journeyed.

The night nurse moved quietly out of the room. By and by she touched Ruth on the shoulder. 'Miss Barnett, it's nearly dawn. You ought to go to bed.'

Ruth shook her head.

'I think you should go, dear. This is doing no good, you know.'

'I can't leave him.'

'But there are things to be done, you see. I really think you should go and lie down.'

The quiet authority of her manner called forth obedience. Like an automaton Ruth rose and was shepherded to her own room. She sat on her bed, Nurse Wimbush took off her shoes for her and made her lie down with a light blanket over her. She closed the curtains.

'Now you just go right to sleep,' she ordered, smiling down at her. She was a tall, middle-aged, heavy-bosomed woman, with a face like a benign turtle. Her eyes were small and alert, but kindly.

When the door had closed behind her, Ruth sat up. A pearly light was beginning to creep round the edge of the curtains. She went to the window, drew them aside a little. The window looked out on the back of the house, over Pouncey Mews and to the backs of the houses in East Pouncey Street. An autumn mist softened the outlines of the buildings. There was a blurred light in one of the windows. Someone else awake, someone else perhaps trying to come to terms with a catastrophe.

After a while there began the sounds of London coming awake for the day's work. A car was taken out of one of the garages in the mews. She heard the clip-clop of the milkman's horse, the rattle of the milk bottles. The paperboy put *The Times* and the *Financial Times* through the letterbox. A door opened and closed within the house – the Worlands starting the early-morning chores.

How strange that all this should go on, as if the world hadn't changed. Didn't people know that Ethan Coverton was dead? Nothing would ever be the same any more because of his passing. I ought to tell them, she thought, I ought to explain to them that they have to see the world differently today.

But how could she explain? How could she describe the emptiness, the utter void left by Ethan's going? Dark and cold as the sea under the Arctic ice – it would be unfair to tell them, it would frighten them too much. For her, it was different – she had to endure it because she was the one with whom Ethan had entwined his life. Wrenched apart, like two plants growing in the same patch of soil, one had died and one had been left to endure if it could. She need not inflict this on others, she would let them go on with everyday matters as if nothing had happened.

And she herself, she must try to go on. If she didn't, people would worry about her, express concern, try to be helpful. She didn't want that, she had to protect herself from that. Sympathy would crack the shell she was trying to build.

By and by she felt an urgent need to rouse herself from the chill that was encroaching upon her. She went into her bathroom, turned on the shower and stepped under it. The punishing torrent of hot water poured down upon her. She wanted it to wash away her grief and leave her dulled and insensitive, ready to face the future without the man she had adored. She leaned against the tiled wall, head bowed. I can't, she thought, I can't go on without him.

The water ran off her hair and into her eyes. She raised an arm to wipe it away, and realized she was still wearing her green silk dress of yesterday.

I'm losing my mind, she thought.

She dragged herself out of the shower, peeled off her soaking clothes. She put on a bath robe then sat on the edge of the bath.

What next? What should she do to begin the first day of her life without Ethan?

Nothing. Nothing was worth doing.

There came a tap on the door. 'Miss Barnett, dear, are you all right?'

She ought to reply. Someone was worrying about her.

But there seemed no energy to make her voice work. She shook her head. If she just said nothing, well-meaning Nurse Wimbush would go away.

'Miss Barnett? What are you doing? Can I come in, dear?' The bathroom door opened. In came the nurse, plain, kindly face screwed up in anxiety. 'Oh, I see, you've had a nice bath . . . ' Her gaze fell on the sodden clothes. 'Oh. Well, now, you probably want your morning tea. Mrs Worland's just bringing it. Come along now, dear, come and sit down – dear me, your hair's soaking, let me give it a rub for you. That's right, dear, this way, nice and comfy in your own little armchair.'

It was easier not to resist. Ruth went into her bedroom, allowed herself to be settled in the pale blue armchair and had her hair dried by Nurse Wimbush. Presently Mrs Worland came in bearing the tea tray. She set it on a table at Ruth's elbow. She left without a word, though her eye rested on her employer with something like scorn.

'There, now,' said the nurse, carefully pulling a comb through Ruth's short hair, 'that's better, isn't it? Nice and tidy. Now I'll just pour your tea and you must drink it up while I pick out something for you to wear. It's going to be quite a nice day once this mist's cleared. What about this, now, Miss Barnett? Navy-blue crepe de Chine, quite suitable, don't you think? Now where are your undies, dear? In the chest of drawers, I s'pose – oh, yes, here we are. And navy shoes, have you got navy shoes? Of course you have, silly me, here they are.'

Manfully chatting on to a woman who made no response, the nurse filled the cold silence with the warmth of her kindness. Ruth swallowed some of the tea. The first mouthful, hot and extremely sweet, almost choked her but she got it down and the next mouthful was easier. In the end she drank nearly a whole cup.

'Now, we'd better get dressed, hadn't we?' urged Nurse Wimbush.

'What for?'

'Well, Miss Barnett, I'm sure you're not the kind of girl who goes down to breakfast in her dressing gown, now are you?'

This seemed logical enough. Ruth put on the clothes that the nurse handed to her, combed her hair again, and regarded herself in the mirror.

Who was that person she saw reflected?

A nobody. No longer Ethan Coverton's woman, because Ethan Coverton had left her. How could he do that – surely he must have known how much it would hurt her? A hot surge of anger went through her, surprising her, leaving her gasping. Angry with Ethan? How could that be? Oh, God, how could that be?

'Come along now, this way,' said Nurse Wimbush, and

with her arm linked in Ruth's she made her way downstairs to the breakfast room.

Ruth was about to say, You don't expect me to eat? But Miss Wimbush was already sitting down and unfolding her own napkin. 'Now I'm sure you're not going to make me eat on my own, Miss Barnett, that would be very unkind.'

'Would it?'

'Of course it would. You know, we private nurses spend a lot of time having snacks in the pantry – it's lovely to have a bit of company.'

'Yes, of course.' It was her social duty to keep this chattering woman company. She picked up a dish on the table and handed it to her.

'Oh, look,' cried the nurse, taking the dish with great enthusiasm, 'wild-strawberry jam – how lovely, just like when I was in Switzerland last year. Toast and wild-strawberry jam, what could be nicer? Do have some, Miss Barnett.'

Ruth took a triangle of toast, buttered it, spread it with jam. Now what?

'Eat up, dear, while the toast is still crisp. I always say nothing is harder to eat than stale toast; it's like eating cardboard. There! When you've finished that, perhaps you'd like marmalade on the next piece. I alway say bitter-orange marmalade is so refreshing . . .'

By dint of urging and setting an example, the nurse got Ruth to eat two triangles of toast. At that, she felt she'd achieved enough for the moment. At least she'd prevented the poor girl from lying down to die of misery.

But her task wasn't finished yet. To get her to eat was something, to get her to engage in some activity was equally important. Nancy Wimbush had seen many a widow sit down in silence and with empty hands, giving up the struggle to live. And this girl, though unmarried, was a widow.

She asked her to go with her to the room she had shared with Timmins, the day nurse, when they had been living in. She had some belongings there. She said she would change into her ordinary clothes, and perhaps Ruth would help her by packing her uniform. 'I've got a taxi coming for me at nine, Miss Barnett, dear. Oh, look, there's my spare apron. Would you fold it for me? Thank you.'

Together they went down to the hall. A taxi arrived at the door.

'Don't go,' Ruth said.

'I must, dear. My mother's expecting me – she's a semi-invalid, you know. But before I go, is there anyone you'd like me to contact for you? Anyone who could come and stay with you for a day or two? Just give me the number, I'll call them up for you.'

'They're not on the phone,' said Ruth, thinking of her grandparents.

'Oh, well, now, what you ought to do is write out a telegram. And, of course, Miss Barnett, you'll want to put a notice in *The Times*?'

'*The Times*?'

'And The *Telegraph* too, I dare say.'

'I wouldn't know how to . . .'

'If you ring them up, they'll help you with how to word it.'

'Will they?'

'Oh, yes.' Nurse Wimbush thought hard. The girl seemed so alone, so vulnerable. 'Perhaps you should call your lawyer?'

'My lawyer?'

'Do you have one?'

'No. Oh – yes, perhaps I have.' Tadsley and Gower – the names swam into her consciousness.

'Well, you know – the death certificate – Sir Bertram said it was in the study. The death has to be registered, someone ought to deal with that.'

Ruth shivered, but nodded.

'So you see you have things to do, haven't you?'

'Yes, I suppose I have.'

'It's best to get on with things like that, I always think.'

'All right.'

Somewhat reassured that Miss Barnett was going to make at least some effort to restart her life, Nurse Wimbush shook hands warmly and took her leave.

Ruth went into the study. She looked at the telephone. She ought to ring David Epps. And Peter Stokes. And Ernest Patterwick.

A dreadful, awful thought occurred to her.

She ought to telephone Diana Coverton.

No, she could not. It was too much. Someone else must tell her.

But who? Who else was there?

If she delayed, Diana might learn of Ethan's death in the evening paper. Reporters might arrive on her doorstep. No, she couldn't allow that to happen. It would be too cruel to let that happen just because she shirked the task.

She had to look in Ethan's address book to find the telephone number. She asked the operator for it in a voice hardly above a whisper.

While it was ringing in the Hertfordshire house, she almost put back the receiver. But before her courage absolutely failed her, the instrument was picked up.

'Fullerton House,' said the voice of the butler.

'May I please speak to Mrs Coverton?'

'Mrs Coverton is at breakfast, madam. May I take a message?'

Tell her Ethan is dead. Ethan is dead!

'It's important that I speak to her. Will you tell her it's about her husband?'

The butler made a little huffing sound, which seemed to imply that he knew she was a gossip columnist after a nugget for tomorrow's column. 'I will inquire, miss,' he said, belittling her by his form of address.

There was a long pause. Then the phone was picked up at the other end and a high brisk voice said, 'Diana Coverton. Who is this, please?'

'This is Ruth Barnett.'

A gasp. A silence. Then Diana said, 'What do you want?'

'I have to tell you something, Mrs Coverton—'

'About my husband, I'm told. If this is some plea about getting a divorce—'

'Mrs Coverton, I don't know how to say this.' She took a quavering breath. 'Ethan died in the early hours of this morning.'

Another silence. About this one, there was something curious, as if Diana were listening to the echo of the words and studying them.

'Mrs Coverton, I'm sorry not to have let you know at once. I— I just couldn't bring myself to believe what the doctors were telling me. Only now – the nurse has gone – she said there were things I ought to do and I realized— I realized—'

'So he's dead, is he.'

'It was very sudden, very unexpected. He got lobar pneumonia. The doctors did all they could. I know this must be an awful shock. Mrs Coverton – Diana – please believe me when I say—'

'Don't you dare call me by my first name, you impertinent little bitch!'

'What?' cried Ruth.

'We're not on first-name terms and never will be! What do you take me for?'

'But we both loved Ethan—'

'Really? I don't think you have any idea what I felt about him. He was a hindrance to me all my married life, and worse still once he picked up with you! Now he's gone and can't stand in my way, I'm going to make you pay for all the shame and humiliation you heaped on me.'

'Mrs Coverton!'

'I couldn't get at you while he was still alive. He held the purse strings, oh, yes, always had his finger on the money bags. So we had to be discreet in what we did by way of reprisal. Pinpricks, that was all we were able to manage – even with inside information there wasn't much we could do. But now everything will go to Antony and we'll see who rules the roost, won't we?'

'Mrs Coverton, don't you understand, *Ethan died this morning.*'

'I understand perfectly. I told him when he came whining to me about a divorce, I told him I hoped he'd die soon so I could pay you out for what you've done. You'd better start packing, my girl, because before the day is out my lawyer will be at the door of your chi-chi Mayfair house with a strong-arm man to throw you out.'

'You can't mean what you're saying.'

'Every word, every word. I told Ethan I'd drive you back to the gutter where you belonged.'

'You said that?'

'He didn't tell you? Oh, too harsh for your dear little feelings, I expect. The fool, he really thought you were young and innocent, but I was never taken in and I told him you'd be back where you belonged the minute I had the power to deal with you.' Diana's voice was shrill with rage. 'No more fancy decorators to do up the drawing room, dearie, no more dresses from Leduc! You'll have to find yourself another fancy man to pay for all that.'

'You must be out of your mind,' Ruth said faintly.

'Perfectly sane, thank you, and equal to the role of the grieving widow when the time comes. But first things first – and the first thing is to get rid of you, you cheap little skirt! Put your things in a suitcase, get yourself out of there before I come and throw you out!'

The phone went down at the other end with a crash. Ruth stood holding the receiver against her ear in disbelief.

At last she hung it up and rose from her chair. She had better go and pack. If Diana Coverton were really to come here – the pain and distress of dealing with her – she couldn't bear it—

But she couldn't leave. Ethan was lying upstairs in the calm stillness of death. I can't leave him, she thought, it's not possible.

The names filtered again through the turmoil of grief and distress. She picked up the phone and asked to be connected with the offices of Tadsley and Gower. 'I don't know the number,' she said, 'it's in Mayfair.'

'Yes, caller, I have a number, it's ringing for you.'

After a moment the receptionist at the lawyer's office picked up. Ruth asked for Mr Tadsley. 'I'm sorry, Mr Tadsley has not arrived yet.'

'Who is available, please?' She had to have someone,

someone who would help. She needed rational advice to counter the mad rage of Diana Coverton.

'I could put you through to Mr Gillis?'

'Yes, I met Mr Gillis. Please tell him it's Ruth Barnett.'

Almost at once he was saying, in a tone he afterwards realized was much too bright: 'Miss Barnett? What can I do for you?'

'Mr Gillis, Ethan died— Ethan died this morning, and when I rang his wife to – to tell her – she said – she said . . .'

'What?' His tone changed completely. 'Miss Barnett, I can't make you out. What's happened?'

'Ethan is dead and Mrs Coverton says I must get out of the house at once. Mr Gillis, what shall I do? Ethan is still— I can't go— I can't leave him.'

'Miss Barnett? Miss Barnett, listen to me.' Niall Gillis tried to reach out over the wires to calm her. 'No one can turn you out of 15 Pouncey Square. The lease is in your name.'

'What? I don't understand.'

'Do you remember when you took the house? Mr Coverton brought you to the office and you signed some papers.'

'Did I? Yes, I remember. I witnessed something, did I?'

'No, you signed the lease. It's in your name. You can stay in Pouncey Square for the next twenty years if you want to.'

'But Mrs Coverton said—'

'Mrs Coverton imagines that the house is part of the Coverton estate,' he said, very lawyer-like to reassure her. 'That, I imagine, goes to the elder son, Antony. Tadsley and Gower never handled any of the family affairs, only business contracts and things of that kind, so I have no idea about the will. But Mrs Coverton is wrong if she thinks she has any control of your house.'

'But she said she'd throw me out.'

'She has the wish, no doubt,' Niall said with grim understanding, 'but she has not the power. The lease belongs to you and you have the right to remain there as long as you wish.'

'Oh!' It was a gasp of thankfulness. 'Oh, how like him to make a provision like that.'

'Miss Barnett, you sound as if you're under great strain.'

'No. I'm fine. No, that's not true. I'm feeling very strange – very shaky – I can't seem to get a grip on anything. And if Mrs Coverton came . . .'

'I'll telephone her solicitors at once. Let me see, it's Grenville Romstock, isn't it?'

'I don't know. Yes, I think so.'

'I'll deal with it. Mr Romstock will explain to Mrs Coverton that she has no power to carry out the kind of threat she's just made.'

'Thank you. It would be such a help.'

'Who's with you there, Miss Barnett?'

'Here?' Only my darling, my lover . . . And I shall never hear his voice again. 'No one, except the servants.'

Niall felt his throat close up at the emptiness of the words. 'I'll be there in half an hour,' he said.

He hung up, buzzed the receptionist to find the number for Grenville Romstock and put him through. He sat drumming his fingers on the desk until his phone tinkled.

'Mr Romstock?'

'Putting you through.' A moment later Romstock's heavy, sonorous voice spoke. 'Mr Gillis?'

'Yes, of Tadsley and Gower. Mr Romstock, am I

right in thinking you handle the family affairs of Ethan Coverton of the Coverton Electrical Company?'

'Yes, I do indeed. Is there something requiring attention?'

'Mr Romstock, Ethan Coverton died during last night, and his friend Miss Barnett telephoned to Mrs Coverton to give her the news a short time ago. Mrs Coverton uttered some threats about turning Miss Barnett out of the house she has shared with Ethan Coverton.'

'Ah,' sighed Romstock. 'Mrs Coverton is somewhat – headstrong, shall I say?'

'I of course don't wish to inquire into the family affairs,' Niall Gillis said, 'but I know for a fact that the house in Pouncey Square is not part of the estate because Tadsley and Gower drew up the lease and it is in the name of Miss Barnett.'

'I see. Ah, yes, you are right, if memory serves me, there is no such property in the list of items in Mr Coverton's file. In any case . . .' He fell silent.

Niall wondered what he had been about to say, but the important point was to keep Diana Coverton away from Ruth Barnett. 'May I ask for your cooperation in preventing Mrs Coverton from doing anything . . .'

'Embarrassing?' Romstock coughed and cleared his throat. 'Of course, of course. Dear, dear, so Ethan is dead . . .'

'I'm sorry, sir,' said Niall. 'I didn't think . . .'

'Quite all right. We had known each other ten or twelve years. An outstanding kind of man . . .' Niall could hear his heavy sigh. 'Well, you may rely on me. I will telephone Mrs Coverton at once and explain to her that she cannot make any change to the occupation of the Pouncey Square property.'

'Thank you.'

'Er . . . Mr Gillis . . . Are you acting for Miss Barnett?'

'I scarcely know, sir. She seemed in great distress when I spoke to her, I simply felt impelled to do something.'

'If you are in touch with her, will you give her my condolences? Ethan spoke of her with such warmth . . .' Niall could hear the other man falter, and understood there had been friendship between them. After a moment, Romstock resumed. 'No matter what the complexities of the marital position are, I gathered that Miss Barnett had made Ethan very, very happy. I would not want her to be more distressed than is absolutely necessary.'

'Thank you, Mr Romstock. I'll pass on your good wishes.'

He disconnected. As he passed through the outer office he said to the secretary he shared with another junior partner: 'Miss Wates, I'm off to 15 Pouncey Square and don't know how long I shall be. Will you tell Mr Tadsley as soon as he comes in that Ethan Coverton has died.'

'Ethan Coverton? The motor-racing man?' She looked up from her typewriter, affected by the news because in the newspaper columns he'd seemed so – so vital. But Mr Gillis's thin face, usually lively and ready to smile, was almost stern, certainly disinclined for gossip.

'Yes, Miss Wates, please let Mr Tadsley know. There may be some problems ensuing.'

He went out, knowing that the moment the door closed behind him the heads of the office staff would be together over the news.

As his taxi drew up, he espied a man loitering on the opposite pavement in the shelter of the privet hedge that surrounded Pouncey Square gardens. He knew at once he was a reporter. How did news pass so quickly to the Fleet Street grapevine? As Niall stepped out in his black jacket and pinstripes, the man approached him:

'You a lawyer, sir? You here from Mrs Coverton?'

Niall ignored him.

Worland opened the door. 'Miss Barnett is expecting me. Niall Gillis.'

'I'll inquire, sir.' He ushered him into the narrow hall. After a few moments he returned from upstairs. 'Miss Barnett is in the study.'

Niall expected to be shown the way. The butler, however, nodded at the stairs and went towards the back of the house. Frowning at the incivility, Niall took the stairs two at a time, made a guess at which door to tap on, and was lucky enough to choose the right one.

Ruth Barnett was sitting behind the desk with a pen in her hand, making a list. She was wearing a navy dress of heavy crepe de Chine which accentuated her pallor. Her grey-green eyes were shadowed by dark circles, her lips had almost no colour.

'How are you, Miss Barnett?' he asked, going in and sitting down uninvited in a leather chair near the desk.

'I'm making a list,' she said in a quiet, controlled voice. 'Things to do, people to inform. I've rung the Holborn office with the news, but they'd already heard. Mrs Coverton had rung Antony.' She half held out the paper towards him. 'Is there anyone else you can think of?'

He wasn't close enough to Ethan Coverton to know, but he took the list and scanned it. The top half was names, the lower half was actions. One of the lower items was Death Certificate.

'I can take care of some of these for you,' he suggested as he handed it back. 'If you feel you would like me to?'

'Oh, *would* you?' Her face changed almost as if she might smile if only the muscles remembered how to do it. 'I've never had to deal with – with – anything like this before now . . .' She faltered into silence for a moment, then added. 'The nurse said I had things to do. And I have. But I don't know how to do them.'

'Please let me help.'

The phone rang. She jumped and stared at it. She made no move to pick it up. 'Miss Barnett?' he prompted.

'It – it might be Diana Coverton,' she whispered.

He rose, picked up the phone. 'Pouncey Square,' he said. 'Who's calling please?'

'I want to speak to Ruth Barnett.' An angry woman's voice.

'I'm sorry, Miss Barnett is unable to come to the telephone. May I help you?'

'And who are *you*?'

'Miss Barnett's lawyer.'

'Ha! Quick off the mark to hire a lawyer! Some *innocent*! Well, you tell that little tart that she needn't think she's won. She may think she's safe in her little love nest but she's got another think coming. Is that clear?'

'Crystal clear, Mrs Coverton,' said Niall, and hung up.

Ruth gazed at him with huge eyes, dismay and horror mingled in them. 'What did she say?'

'Never mind,' said Niall. 'She doesn't mean it.'

'Thank you, Mr Gillis.' She frowned a little, as if trying to recall how she came to know him. In an office – but he'd been in the background then, rather shadowy. Her memory conjured up an arm reaching up to steady her as she stepped into the launch. A good voice, rich and deep, saying, 'I thought you might need a hand.'

'Oh, yes, at the docks when Ethan and I came home

from Sicily—' She broke off suddenly, sprang to her feet, and went to the window with her back to him.

Below, the doorbell rang. In a moment Worland came in. 'There's two reporters at the door to see her,' he said to Niall with a nod of the head towards Ruth.

'To see Miss Barnett,' Niall corrected him.

'To see Miss Barnett,' said Worland, with the faintest hint of a shrug. 'What should I tell them?'

'Tell them to go away. And bring some coffee.'

Worland inclined his head and turned to the door. Niall thought he heard him say under his breath, 'Hoity-toity!'

What kind of a servant was this? No wonder the poor girl looked so friendless and alone if even the staff were giving her no support.

Ruth turned back. 'What was that?' she said, as if coming to the realization that someone had come in and gone out.

'Your man says there are reporters at the door.'

'Oh, no!'

'It's all right, I told him to send them away. But you will have more coming. Mr Coverton was very much in the public eye.'

'I can't see them!'

'Would you like me to give them a statement? It would just say that Mr Coverton has died and at the moment you've nothing to add – something like that. It would hold them off for a while.' Not for long, he thought to himself. But every moment gained gave her time to recover enough to face them.

'All right.'

He studied her. 'Have you a headache?'

'No, but I feel this odd – sort of cottonwool effect – in my head.'

'Have you been out of doors recently?'

She thought about it. 'Not since the day before yesterday. I went to have my hair cut and things like that, so that Ethan could have time with his friends. They were all smoking and drinking when I got back.' She stopped for a moment. 'Five o'clock on Wednesday,' she said, as if it were something to write into her diary.

'Miss Barnett, let's go out for a breath of air.'

'Oh, no! No! I can't go out!'

'Come along. It will do you good.'

'But there are things to do—'

'We'll take the list with us, perhaps add a few names to it over a cup of coffee.' He thought about it. 'There's an ABC just round the corner – we could go there.' A humble enough place, but no reporter would think of looking for her there.

'Oh,' she said on a faint sigh, 'I haven't been in an ABC for two years.' Back in the days when she was an office girl, the ABC teashops had been important in her daily life. There was a certain nostalgia about them now.

'We'll go then, shall we?'

She glanced towards the door, as if the idea of going past a threshold were a great problem.

'You'll need a jacket or a coat,' he urged. 'While you get it, I'll write out a few words to hand to the reporters, shall I?'

'Yes, all right.' Obediently she went out and up to her room. From the wardrobe she took a short loose jacket and a felt hat. She picked up her handbag. She was going out. Away from Ethan.

But then Ethan wasn't really here any more.

When she rejoined Niall he took her arm and ushered her down to the hall. The butler didn't come to open the door. In fact, the coffee Niall had ordered seemed to have been forgotten.

As they went out, a man and a woman, each with a notebook, sprang forward. Niall handed them the note he had written. As they squabbled over it, he led Ruth away and round the corner.

It was only a little after ten. The ABC wasn't crowded. Niall chose a table towards the back and set Ruth with her back towards the door so that anyone glancing in wouldn't be able to see her features. He ordered two cups of coffee from the white-capped waitress. When it came it was the usual strange English brew, too much milk and not enough coffee.

Ruth brought the list out of her handbag. 'There are people I ought to get in touch with,' she began, frowning over it. 'I think Dr Andromi would like to be told. But he doesn't speak English, and I can't write a telegram in Italian.'

'Someone will translate for him if you send it in English.'

'Oh, yes, Sister Febronia.' She added the name to her list.

Little by little it lengthened. Niall suggested they should go to the post office to send some of the telegrams. When they'd finished their coffee they did so, walking amid the early shoppers in the busy thoroughfare to Heddon Street. The day was sunny, crisp and cool, a harbinger of autumn. It took them half an hour to write and despatch eight telegrams. When Niall suggested sending one to her relatives in Freshton, she shook her head. 'They'd be afraid to open it. Among the people I come from, telegrams only bring bad news. I'll write when I get back indoors.'

276

He was pleased with the improvement in her manner. Though there was no real animation in it, at least she was functioning again – not like the automaton that had greeted him when he first arrived.

When they got back to Pouncey Square, there was quite a group of reporters. They saw Ruth as she came along the pavement with her escort and crowded towards her. 'Miss Barnett, why did you go out? Couldn't bear to see it happen?' 'Miss Barnett, look this way!' 'What are your plans now, Miss Barnett?'

Niall ploughed a way through them to the front door. 'What did they mean, couldn't bear to see it happen?' she said to him as Worland opened the door to them.

'Never mind them. If you like I'll go out and talk to them in a little while. In the meantime, Miss Barnett . . .'

'What?'

'I'm afraid you ought to start thinking about the funeral.'

Worland, who had been taking their outdoors things and hovering somewhat as if he wanted to say something, now intervened. 'That won't be necessary, sir,' he said, the words addressed to Niall but the glance taking in both of them.

'What does that mean?' said Niall in perplexity.

'Mrs Coverton is, of course, seeing to all that.'

'What?' said Ruth.

'She's made all the arrangements. The undertaker's men left not ten minutes ago.'

'No!'

'Mrs Coverton rang first, of course,' said Worland smoothly. 'I was able to tell her it was quite a convenient time since you were out of the house, Miss Barnett

– it would have been an unpleasant moment for you, I imagine.'

'Unpleasant?' Ruth put up a hand to her head as if she felt it had received a wound. 'You mean . . .'

'The body will lie in the Chapel of Rest at the funeral home, miss. I have the address should you want it.'

Niall was staring at the man in horror. Ruth said, '*You let them take Ethan?*'

'Well, it was only right, miss. They were acting for the legal wife, after all.'

She looked at Niall. He nodded, appalled at what had happened. 'But I never imagined she'd do such a thing . . .'

There was a chest in the hall. She sank down on it and Niall said to Worland, 'Get some brandy.' She threw out her hand as if to say, Don't bother.

After a moment she slowly got to her feet. She faced the butler. He was tall and portly – it was one of his assets when job-hunting that he looked the part. He was regarding her with something of a smirk.

'Get out of my house,' she said, staring up into his face.

He looked a little startled, but held his ground. 'That's not for you to say. I regard myself and Mrs Worland as caretakers now for the rightful owner. I feel Mrs Coverton would want us to stay on.'

'Get out,' said Ruth. 'If you don't pack and leave within ten minutes, I'll call the police to throw you out.'

'I wouldn't take that tone if I was you, miss. They'd probably agree I've more right to be here than you have.'

'Wrong,' said Niall.

'I don't need you to tell me how things stand, sir, if you don't mind me saying so! Mrs Coverton was kind enough to say—'

Ruth gave a gasp. 'It was you!'

'What?'

'It was you she meant when she said she had inside information! "Pinpricks" – it was you who used to tell the reporters where Ethan and I were going! You've been spying on us!'

Worland lost some of his composure. 'I don't know what you mean—'

'You Judas!'

'Now look here, missy, hard names aren't going to help you! I'd advise you to pack up and go with some dignity while you have the chance.'

'Get out of my house! Get out before I call the police!'

'That's enough of that from *you*, you little nobody! I'm going straight to the telephone and tell Mrs Coverton—'

'Don't bother,' Niall intervened, stepping between Ruth and the man. 'The lease of this house is owned by Miss Barnett.'

Eustace Worland's eyebrows came together in a frown of alarm. 'That's not true.'

'The lease was drawn up in the offices where I am a junior partner.'

The other man drew back a little.

'I want you to leave,' said Ruth. 'You and that awful wife of yours who sneers at me all the time. Ten minutes – you'd better hurry.'

'Now, just a minute!' exclaimed Worland. 'You can't do that! You can't turn us out at a minute's notice!'

'Get out, get out! I can't bear to have you under the same roof.'

'Wages in lieu of notice,' he demanded loudly, standing his ground. 'I'll have you know we've got wages due—'

'Money? Is that what you want?' She pulled open her

handbag, found her notecase, threw it at him. It fell at his feet, the notes spilling out. 'Take it, take it and go!' she cried. 'Go, get out, get out!'

He knelt down to gather up the money. She stood over him, fists clenched, chest heaving with emotion.

Fury had taken over her entire being. That body which had been listless, that mind which had been dull – they were changed by the passion flowing through her.

In the cold desert of grief, a lightning bolt had struck. The icy rocks had been split apart. And from it now a life-giving stream was flowing.

Fuelled by anger, by scorn for the betrayers – unworthy feelings perhaps – but they made her pulse race, they brought the blood back into her cheeks.

She would not wither away because of her lover's death. She would not let go her hold on the world. She would live, and grow, and remember Ethan with love but without desolation.

Chapter Sixteen

Niall summoned a taxi to the mews door. He took up a guard position to see the Worlands off.

They came along the passage from the back stairs, lugging a trunk between them. Worland dropped his end. 'This isn't fair,' he whined. 'We couldn't possibly pack in the time. We've had to leave a whole lot . . .'

'Send someone to collect it. Ring first, don't try to come yourself.'

'We wouldn't demean ourselves,' sniffed Mrs Worland.

'And don't think of stopping to give the reporters a crumb or two. Your employment agency won't have many jobs on offer for staff who gossip to the press.'

The taxi driver came to take Mrs Worland's end of the trunk. As he was putting it aboard, Bignall came up the mews. His broad face lit up at what he saw.

'So she's given 'em the push,' he said. 'Shoulda done it months ago.'

'You mind your own business,' Mrs Worland said in an angry flash as she got in.

'Who are you?' asked Niall as the taxi took the Worlands away.

'Mr Coverton's chauffeur – was, anyway. Name of Bignall. Been hanging around head office since the boss was took ill. When I heard the news . . .'

'So it's reached there already?'

'You bet. The missus telephoned Mr Antony and he rushed round telling everybody. Can't wait to move into his dad's office. Next thing, he'd have wanted the Roller.' He nodded towards the arch where the mews began; the silvery roof of the Rolls was just visible. 'I wasn't having *that* so I got in and drove here.' He hesitated, a flush running in under his already ruddy complexion. 'You're that lawyer, ain't you? From Tadsley and Gower.'

'My name's Gillis.'

'How's she taking it, Mr Gillis?'

Niall shrugged.

'I just come – thought I might be some use – her and me – we really knew him . . .' His voice faltered. He cleared his throat and looked down.

Niall studied him. 'Are you doing anything at head office?'

'Nah, they use me and the Roller to ferry nobs about but that don't happen every day.'

'Miss Barnett needs someone. I can't stay all day, though I can put off some appointments. Would you consider acting as guard dog? She's not up to facing the press.'

'Bunch of hyenas!' Bignall blurted. 'I saw 'em round the front gate, dying to get at her. 'Course I'll stay, but she needs a woman around, someone with a bit o' heart, not like that snobby Worland.'

Niall sighed. 'There doesn't seem to be anybody within reach. Her grandmother is off in Surrey – no telephone.'

'There was that Mrs Monash,' Bignall mused.

'Who's Mrs Monash?'

'A decent body. "Did" for the boss and the lady while they was in the Kensington flat. I sometimes used to chat with her; she seemed a nice woman.'

'Is she on the phone?'

'Shouldn't think so, sir.' He hesitated. 'How about I go see if she'll come and you stay here till I get back, sir?'

'Right you are.'

Niall went back indoors to tell Ruth that the Worlands had gone. He found her in the balcony room, in a cane chair across from the chaise longue where Ethan had so often sat. Her face was sad but composed. She nodded with evident relief when he reported the departure of the servants.

'Mr Coverton's chauffeur was here,' Niall said. 'He's gone to see if a Mrs Monash . . .'

'Oh, yes. From Crecy Court.' She hesitated. 'I don't know if I'll be able to afford servants, Mr Gillis.'

'Don't bother about that now,' he soothed. He knew she owned the house and contents: she only needed to sell one of the antique Chinese pots containing the parlour palms to pay servants for a year.

In less than an hour Bignall was back with Mrs Monash, who at once took her apron out of her shopping bag and made her way to the kitchen. A tray of tea appeared within twenty minutes – not as elegant as Mrs Worland would have made it, but very welcome.

Niall took his leave. 'I really must go,' he apologized, 'because there are two clients who've been waiting in my office for over an hour.'

'I'm sorry! I should have thought!'

'It's all right, my secretary shunted things around. Bignall's going to stay. If you need anybody thrown out just call him.'

'Thank you for all you've done.' She was offering her hand.

'Nonsense, that's what I'm for.' As he walked down the front steps, the memory of that small square hand in his was very appealing.

Reporters crowded round him. 'When's she going to see us? What's she doing? Did anybody come in that Rolls-Royce? Was it a member of the family?'

'I've nothing to say,' Niall replied.

'You're her lawyer, right?'

'Yes, and I've nothing to say.'

'She going to court against the family, is that it?'

'I've nothing to say.' But they pursued him to the corner where he was lucky enough to get a taxi.

Mrs Monash came to clear away the tea things. 'I had a look in the larder,' she reported, 'to see about a meal. You could have cold chicken and salad or I could do an omelette . . .'

'I'm not hungry, thank you.'

'Now, Miss Barnett, dear, you've got to eat. Mr Coverton wouldn't have wanted you getting ill.'

'I know that, but I really don't feel hungry.'

'Righty-ho, then you tell me when you do, and I'll whip something up.'

'No, really.'

'I'm not leaving this house tonight until you've had dinner,' declared Mrs Monash, 'and what my Harry will say about that I daren't think, because he likes his supper over early enough to get down to the pub for a pint or two.'

Seeing there was no help for it, Ruth agreed that she would sit down to cold chicken and salad at seven o'clock.

When the time came she was still sure she couldn't eat, but Mrs Monash had provided a consommé with Melba toast as a starter, and to Ruth's surprise she found it tempting. After the soup she ate some of the chicken and also some of the fruit in a fine brandy sauce. She couldn't help agreeing she felt the better for it.

Mrs Monash left, promising to be back at eight the next morning. About half-an-hour later, Bignall tapped at the drawing-room door. 'I got to go, Miss Barnett. I shoulda reported back at head office to sign off and I better do that and get off home.'

'Of course,' she said, feeling a terrible sense of desolation at the idea of being left alone in the house.

'Them reporters have mostly packed up,' he said, 'so I don't think you'll have any trouble. You be all right?'

'I'll be fine.'

'Be here again in the morning bright an' early – Mrs Monash said she'd be here to let me in.'

'Thank you, Bignall. Thank you for coming.'

'Yeh,' he said. They stared at one another, and there was the glint of tears in the eyes of each. 'Don't you mind them, Miss Barnett,' he muttered, 'they just don't understand, that's their trouble.'

When he was gone she wandered round the house, switching on lamps to keep away the dark. As she closed the curtains she saw two stubborn reporters still hanging about in the square. They glanced up eagerly at her face in the window. She shrank back, holding the edges of the curtains together to blot them out.

The phone rang. She picked it up, expecting it to be yet another request for an interview.

'Hello, Miss Barnett? How are you?'

'Who . . .?'

'I'm sorry, did I startle you? It's Niall, Niall Gillis. I just thought I'd ring and check everything was all right.'

She felt a little rush of warmth. How kind of him to bother. 'I'm fine, thank you, yes, I'm fine.'

'Bignall and Mrs Monash are coming back tomorrow?'

'Yes, it's all arranged.'

'How are you feeling?'

Lonely. Uncertain. Rootless. 'I'm really quite all right,' she said. 'I'm going to have an early night.'

'That's a good idea. I thought I'd drop by some time tomorrow, if that wouldn't be a nuisance.'

'It's very kind of you. Thank you.'

'Are you sure you're all right?'

'Oh, yes, quite all right, thank you.'

But it was well into the small hours before she fell asleep.

She let Mrs Monash in at eight but by then she'd had something to eat and looked at the newspapers. *The Times* was too dignified to do more than report Ethan's death and offer a resumé of his career. *The Financial Times* went into some detail about the possible future of Coverton Electrical.

'Sources close to Mr Antony Coverton report that he has strong views about the development of the company. It is known that last year he put forward a proposal for a reorganization which implied taking Covelco into the international arena. Contacts in Northern Europe, notably Germany and Switzerland, recall conversations about expansion in those areas . . .'

And now of course he'll do it, thought Ruth. Even though Ethan thought the political situation in Germany was too risky and the Swiss wanted too big a share. And research and development will be sheared away so as to use the money to buy into foreign companies . . .

About eleven Niall arrived. Mrs Monash immediately brought coffee and biscuits as if she'd been primed. 'She's got an absolute obsession about making me eat,' Ruth said with a faint smile.

'She's quite right. Have a biscuit, they're awfully good.' They discussed the newspaper items. Niall let her know that the popular press had been more personal in its approach. 'But there are far fewer reporters outside today,' Niall declared. Privately he thought editors had redeployed their men to badger Diana who was more likely to blurt out something quotable.

After they'd finished coffee Niall cleared his throat. 'Did you – er – see the funeral announcement?'

'What?' She turned her grey-green eyes upon him in horror.

'In *The Times*?'

She shook her head. He showed her the page of announcements.

> Coverton, Ethan David, beloved husband of Diana,
> quietly after a long illness. Relatives and family
> friends only at the funeral which will be at 10.30
> a.m. on Monday 18th October in the private chapel
> at Flitchley Green Cemetery, nr Rivington,
> Lancashire.

It turned her to stone.

To break the stricken silence, Niall blundered on. 'When I saw it I rang her— I took the liberty— I said I represented you. Mrs Coverton said— I'm afraid she said—'

'She doesn't want me there.'

Diana had said, 'Tell that little tragedy queen to keep her crocodile tears for the press. If she turns up at the service I'll have her thrown out.'

'I'm afraid she said you wouldn't be welcome.'

'No, you couldn't classify me as either a relative or a family friend.'

'I'm sorry. But it's a long way to go in any case.'

'His parents came from Rivington – I think they're buried there. He said he'd take me one day to show me the factory his father began with – I think it was a glorified shed with a tin roof.' Her gaze had gone beyond him, to the past when Ethan used to talk to her about the days before she knew and loved him.

Niall smiled at the idea that it had all started in a shed with a tin roof. Tadsley and Gower handled all the business side of Covelco so that he had a fair notion of the extent of their property these days.

The telephone rang. Mrs Monash came in to say it was a lady asking for Miss Barnett.

'Diana?' Ruth said with a shudder. 'Tell her I'm not at home.'

'I don't think it's Mrs Coverton,' said Mrs Monash, uncertain about intruding on private ground and yet sure she was right. 'When I said a lady, it's more sort of a countrywoman. Not accustomed to the phone, by the sound of her.'

'Grandma?' cried Ruth.

She ran to the study. The receiver was lying on the desk quacking: 'Hello? Hello? Are you still there?'

'This is Ruth,' she said into the mouthpiece almost before she'd picked up the receiver.

'Is that you? Ruthie? Ruthie, girl, how are you?' Mrs Barnett was speaking at the top of her voice. 'I'm in the phone box outside the post office. I thought my tuppence would run out before you came.'

'Grandma, it's lovely to hear you.'

'Can't hear me? I'll speak up then. Your letter arrived first post this morning. I'm so sorry, Ruthie . . .'

The pips began to go for the end of the call.

'Grandma, give me your number and I'll ring you back.'

'Dash it, my money's run out.'

'Give me the number—'

'I'll put in a sixpence – that ought to be enough.'

By a miracle the connection survived. Ruth said, 'Before we go on, give me your number so I can ring you back if we're cut off.'

'What number?'

'The number of the phone in the phone box.'

'Oh.' Mrs Barnett read it off. 'What good does that do?'

'If your money runs out again I can ring you back.'

'You mean calls can come in as well as go out from a phone box?'

'Never mind, Grandma. It's lovely to hear you. Things have been so awful.'

'There, there. I knew how you'd be, which is why I said to your Granddad, I'll ring her, I said, because she'll be that low.'

'It was so unexpected, you see. After the good recovery he was making from the accident.'

'How did he go, then?'

'Oh, Grandma . . .'

There was a pause. 'Of course, you don't want to talk about it yet. You were always like that, grieved your heart out on your own when your kitten died.' Mrs Barnett sighed. 'Well, dear, just hold on a day or so and I'll be there.'

'You're coming to London?' Ruth cried, astounded.

'I certainly am. I said to your Granddad, I said, she needs somebody to be with her and I'm going, I said, but he said, we've got those fruit trees to dig out and deliver to Redhill, he said, and you know how he is when it's something important, Ruth, won't trust anybody but me to help him bag up the roots in sacking and all that, so it'll be a day or two, but I think I'll be on the train the day after tomorrow.' A slight hesitancy came into the loud, firm voice. 'Could you meet me at the station? Don't know as I'd be able to find my way to your house.'

'But a taxi driver would . . .'

'Take a taxi?' exclaimed Grandma in horror. 'What are you thinking of, Ruth Barnett? Do you think money grows on trees? No, no, you meet me and we'll go on the bus.'

It was no use arguing. 'Which train shall I meet?'

'It's the one that gets in at ten twenty-five – that's Saturday. Will you be there, Ruth?'

'Of course, Grandma.'

'All right then, I'm going to be on that train.' It was clear that the idea filled her with a sort of delighted dread. 'You look after yourself till I get there now, Ruthie, do you hear me?'

'Yes, Grandma and – thank you.'

'Yes,' agreed her grandmother, knowing she was being thanked for this tremendous leap into the unknown that she would be taking. 'Well, I'll ring off now. Goodbye.'

'Goodbye, Grandma.'

'Oh, just a minute! Are you there? Are you there?'

'Yes, I'm still here.'

'Granddad sends his love.' The instrument was hung up at the other end.

Granddad sends his love. After the years of disapproval, her grandfather had completely relented.

Niall was delighted with her news. Although he had no idea there had been a rift between them he had guessed there was a problem with the grandparents. But now they had rallied to the support of their grandchild – and no one needed it more.

When Mrs Barnett arrived at Waterloo on the Saturday, she was already in a fluster. Her feet in her best shoes were hurting, she had trouble at the barrier finding her ticket in the pocket of her mackintosh. She kissed Ruth in greeting and allowed herself to be shepherded out of the throng of Saturday visitors to the fearsome wonders of a cold, rain-soaked London.

When Bignall opened the door of the Rolls for her, she almost fainted.

'What's this?' she said, drawing back in alarm.

'It's Ethan's car, Grandma. I have the use of it for the time being.' Until Diana Coverton realizes what's happened and grabs it away, she added mentally.

'His car? What, for everyday?'

'Yes, he went to work in it every morning.'

'Lord,' whispered her grandmother, and allowed herself to be handed in.

Perhaps the splendour of the Rolls prepared her a little for the house in Mayfair. She followed Ruth in without hesitation and even allowed Bignall to take her suitcase from her to carry upstairs.

'Who's he?' she whispered behind his departing back.

'Ethan's chauffeur.'

'I see.'

Mrs Monash had coffee ready. The silver pot, the

ratafia biscuits in their china dish, the comfortable arm-chairs in their cheerful covers, the fine fire in the well-polished steel fire-basket in the marble fireplace – they were all duly noted.

Fortified by half a cup of coffee, Grandma said, 'This Ethan Coverton – he was really rich, then?'

'Very rich.'

'Goodness me. I knew he had money but I never imagined . . .' She let the words die then said, 'You and him – it was serious, was it?'

'We loved each other, Grandma.'

'But he was a married man, Ruth!'

'Yes. I don't expect to convince you so I won't try, but Ethan and I would have married if his wife would have agreed to a divorce.'

'A divorce! Ruth!'

'I'm sorry. I know it's against your beliefs.' She said no more, and her grandmother held out her hands to the fire for a moment.

When she resumed, it was on a totally practical point. 'When's the funeral?'

'On Monday.'

'I brought my black.'

'Oh, we won't be going, Grandma.'

'Not going?' She was shocked. 'Of course we're going.'

'No. Mrs Coverton's arranged it so it's impossible. The funeral's being held in Lancashire where his parents are buried, and the service is private.'

'But you have a right to go.'

Ruth was shaking her head. 'Not as far as Mrs Coverton is concerned.'

'She doesn't want you there?'

'No.'

'Well— I suppose it's understandable. But she must know how you felt about each other if he explained he wanted to marry you. It isn't very Christian, is it?'

'I don't think that comes into it.'

Mrs Barnett's view of life was simple. Death wiped out all ill-feeling, all bad remembrances. At such a time, in her view, there should be reconciliation – even if only temporary – so that the necessary rites could be performed with dignity.

'You've a right to be there,' she repeated with a nod of affirmation.

'I've been told she won't let me in if I go.'

'Let you in? How d'you mean?'

'It's a private chapel.'

'Oh, I see. A private chapel. Well, girl, when you've been to as many funerals as I have, you'll know that chapels may be private but a cemetery's a public place – open from sunrise to sunset every day by law. She can't stop you being there if you want to go.'

'What?'

'We'll go,' said Grandma. 'It's what you want, isn't it?'

'Oh, yes,' breathed Ruth. 'I need to . . . say goodbye.'

'Yes. That's what it's for,' the other woman agreed. 'Can't seem to get started on life again until the goodbyes have been said – it's always like that. Well, we'll go, that's settled.'

They went up to Bolton by train next day, stayed overnight at the best hotel (to the secret delight of Mrs Barnett) and by ten thirty next day were in the cemetery of Flitchley Green. They could hear the strains of the hymns from the chapel, a little Victorian building in red brick. By and by a small cortège emerged from the open doors. No one noticed the two women standing in the shelter of a juniper some yards off.

The words of the vicar of Fletchley came to them through the cold autumn air. 'Ashes to ashes, dust to dust . . .'

'There now, child,' murmured Mrs Barnett, 'be brave.'

'. . . Receive the kingdom prepared for you from the beginning of the world . . .'

'Not long now, dear.'

The vicar pronounced the blessing. The coffin was lowered into the earth. Antony Coverton stepped forward to throw a handful of soil on the coffin. His brother Martin did the same but Lorette turned away in dismay at the thought. The group began to disperse. The vicar shook hands. Within moments the mourners were getting into cars and being driven away.

The grave-diggers began to shovel soil into the grave. Ruth stood watching. The pain in her breast was so piercing that she needed all her strength to oppose it. Salt tears were drying on her cheeks.

Goodbye, Ethan, my darling, my love. Wait for me in your cold bed.

When the workmen were done, they put some of the wreaths upon the mound of soil. Others were placed around – and there were many, tributes from friends and colleagues forbidden by Diana's command from attending.

'There, lad, we've made ye tidy,' the elder of the men said kindly as they turned away.

Ruth waited until they had gone. Then she went to the graveside. She had in her hands a simple bunch of flowers, bought that morning in a shop in Bolton. Ethan had never cared much about flowers except as a gift to give to someone else.

She laid the chrysanthemums on the wreaths already on his grave. There was no message with them. Everything that needed to be said was known to Ethan before he died – that she loved him and always would. She stood by the heap of wreaths and flowers, straining to feel Ethan's presence one last time.

By and by her grandmother came to join her. 'Come along, child, it's time to go.'

'Yes. But it seems so – final.'

'But it is final, Ruth. What did you expect?'

'I don't know. Nothing. I just wanted to be close to him again, one last time. But they wouldn't let me.'

Mrs Barnett put her arm around her. 'Never you mind, dear,' she said in a voice of gentle certainty. 'They dragged his poor bones away to lay them in the earth, but his heart was always with you.'

Ruth turned to hide her face against the thin old shoulder. 'That's true,' she whispered, 'that's true.'

'And now you've said your goodbyes, he would want you to start a new life.'

'I don't know what to do without him.'

'It'll come, my love. Just wait.'

They were back in the London house by late that evening. Mrs Monash had gone, but had left a little pile of telephone messages in her own version of shorthand. Among them was one that made Ruth frown.

'Mr Romstock cld – wd lk you at his ofce tomor (Tuesday) 3 p.m. if conv. Ring to confirm.'

Mr Romstock was the solicitor to the Coverton family. Presumably he was going to demand the return of the Rolls-Royce. Well, she had expected that.

She rang next day to confirm the appointment. Because her grandmother longed above all else to see it, she took her to Selfridges next morning. She summoned Bignall and had them driven in the Rolls to the entrance. She didn't tell him that this would be the last time he would drive her. Bad news could always be left till later.

She and Mrs Barnett spent two hours wandering from department to department. 'Wait till I tell Elsie Manners I've actually been in the building,' crowed Mrs Barnett. 'She's always boasting about how she passed it once on a charabanc trip.'

They had lunch in a Lyons Cornerhouse, another 'must' for her grandmother. Afterwards Ruth put her in a taxi for the Mayfair house. She herself walked to Southampton Row, passing the headquarters of Covelco in Holborn on her way. She looked at the big, handsome building. By now Antony was settled in Ethan's office, preparing to carry out the changes his father had always opposed.

The receptionist at the lawyer's office was expecting her. 'This way, madam.' She tapped on a door and ushered Ruth into a handsome room with white panelling and a display of Chelsea ware in the alcoves.

'Good afternoon, Miss Barnett.' Granville Romstock rose to meet her. 'Though we have spoken on the telephone this is the first time we have actually met. Please sit down.'

'Thank you. If this is about the car,' said Ruth, having decided not to be cowed by the majesty of the law, 'there was no need to make a ceremony about it. I'm quite aware it isn't mine and I'm ready to return it.'

'The car?' said Romstock.

'Ethan's car. That's what it's about, isn't it?'

Mr Romstock was shaking his handsome grey head. 'Not at all, Miss Barnett. I know nothing about a car. In any case, you will not be returning it.'

'I beg your pardon?'

'The car is yours. Along with almost everything that Ethan Coverton owned.'

Ruth's lips parted in surprise, but no words came.

'It is my duty to make you aware of the contents of the will. I'll read it to you.'

'Just a moment. What did you just say?'

'I said that you have inherited Ethan Coverton's estate,' said Mr Romstock. 'With the exception of the house in which his wife lives with its contents and appurtenances, and some personal bequests to colleagues and employees, Ethan has left you everything.'

Chapter Seventeen

Mr Romstock took the papers from a document box to one side of his desk. 'It will be best if I read you the will in its entirety. It isn't very long—'

'Just a minute! Wait! This must be a mistake!'

The lawyer paused. He raised bushy eyebrows. 'What makes you say so?'

'Ethan couldn't possibly have left everything to me!'

'Why not?'

'Because everybody knows his son Antony is his heir.'

'Indeed?' said Romstock. 'Where could they get that information? The contents of a will are not published until after the death of the testator.' He leaned his portly figure back in his leather chair, waiting for her explanation.

'Well, what I mean is – everybody expects Antony Coverton to inherit.'

'Everybody's expectations will be confounded in that case.' He allowed himself a faint smile.

Ruth had recovered a little from the shock and confusion of the lawyer's first announcement. She gathered herself together to say, 'Let me sort this out. You're saying that Ethan hasn't left Covelco to Antony?'

'He has not. He has left him precisely nothing.'

'But he couldn't *do* that! Antony is the eldest son – he *has* to inherit.'

Mr Romstock could see she had some odd notions about the law. 'That would only be true in the case of an entail – and there is no entail of any kind on Ethan Coverton's estate. As the law stands at this time in this country, Ethan was free to leave his money to the roadmender if he wanted to. But instead he has left it to you.'

'But not all of it?'

'Except for some bequests to colleagues and employees . . .'

'But he couldn't leave his wife and children penniless?' Ruth cried in horror.

'Let me explain the background to you, Miss Barnett,' he said, showing no impatience. 'Diana Coverton and her children cannot in any sense be penniless. They already own shares in the Coverton Electrical Company. Ethan settled some on Diana at the time of their marriage. He gave five per cent to each of the children on their sixteenth birthday. Antony Coverton has since increased his holding to six per cent, whereas Martin sold some of his shares to back a theatrical venture and now owns only about three and a half per cent. Lorette Coverton's shares are held in trust for her until she is twenty-one.' He broke off to study her a moment from eyes that gleamed quite kindly under the bushy brows. 'You understand? Ethan's widow and children own about twenty per cent of Coverton Electrical. And so long as the company continues to do well, they receive a substantial income.'

'Yes,' said Ruth, nodding although still harried by doubt.

'I was about to tell you, when you broke in with your

protest about leaving them penniless—' he allowed himself another little smile, to indicate that it was a joke – 'that in his will Ethan leaves the family home Fullerton and its contents to his wife. She can either continue to live there or sell it. So you see that the widow and children are amply provided for.'

'Yes,' Ruth said again, uneasily accepting that part of the story. 'But the rest of the will – you said . . .'

'I said that you were Ethan Coverton's heir. There is a substantial capital sum invested with Zaretski Plomer, the merchant bank: the portfolio of investments is detailed in the folder which I will give you. There is the Coverton Electrical Company, in which you will have a holding of approximately eighty per cent. There is property of various kinds other than the factory and office buildings belonging to Covelco, and there are . . .' He broke off to glance at a sheet of paper . . . 'I see that there are three cars, one of which is in fact a Rolls Royce.' He looked faintly roguish as he said this.

Ruth was quite unable to take it in. Her head swam as if she had climbed to a mountain top where the air was too thin. She had at first gone hot with protest at the lawyer's words but now she found she was almost shivering with cold.

Her silence began to worry Romstock. 'Are you unwell, Miss Barnett?'

'I don't know. I feel funny.'

He rose quickly. He had had other clients who needed help in assimilating unexpected facts. From a cabinet in the white panelling he brought out a carafe and a crystal glass. 'Drink this,' he said.

She took the glass. The brandy filled her throat with warmth as it slipped down. Romstock surveyed her with anxiety. She looked wan in her dark coat and dress. She wasn't wearing black for Ethan, because Ethan had once told her he hated her in black, but her pallor was accentuated by the close-fitting, dark blue felt hat and the dark grey cloth.

By and by he was relieved to see a little colour come into her cheeks.

'This has been a shock to you,' he remarked.

She nodded.

'Ethan did say he'd no intention of telling you what he'd done. But I thought that in the course of two years, perhaps he'd give you some hint?'

'Not at all,' She set the brandy glass on his desk. Her hand was fairly steady. 'And, of course, I can't accept.'

It was the turn of the solicitor to be shocked. 'What on earth do you mean, Miss Barnett?'

'I couldn't possibly take the legacy. Think what would happen! Antony expected to get it all – he would hate me! And as for Diana . . .' Her voice faded into horrified silence.

'I don't think you understand, Miss Barnett. This isn't something being offered for approval. Ethan has left his fortune to you. There is no alternative.'

'But he couldn't really have meant it.'

'My dear, I was Ethan's friend as well as his solicitor,' Romstock said, sighing as he looked back on the years of their acquaintance. 'He was never in the habit of saying what he didn't mean.'

'Then you must have misunderstood him!'

He said nothing to that, and after a moment she said, 'I'm sorry. Of course, you wouldn't make a silly mistake like that.'

'Certainly not.' He was forgiving. Poor child, she

looked as if a dragon had suddenly stepped in her path. 'Let me say that when he came to make this will Ethan had already written out a rough draft. I still have the handwritten note here in the document box. There were some very frank remarks about his wife and children in it which I persuaded him to leave out of the final version. You see, we both thought he would live many years more . . .' Mr Romstock paused, drew a deep breath to steady himself then resumed, 'Many years more, and things might just possibly have been patched up between him and his family. He would not then have wanted these rather critical sentences to remain. However, the substance of the bequests is exactly as he noted them down here.'

He took a sheet of paper from the document case, holding it towards her so that she could see it was the blue-edged writing paper Ethan used for private correspondence. She looked at it. She could see Ethan's untidy scrawl covering both sides of the sheet.

'Yes,' she said, 'I see you couldn't have made any mistakes. But he must have meant to change it all back one day.' She went slowly red before she could nerve herself to say, 'You mentioned that he did all this a couple of years ago. Was it – was it about the time that – that we went to live in Mayfair?'

'Yes, it was.'

'Well, he was very angry with Diana around then. I don't know the ins and outs of it, he would never talk about it. But he wrote that will because he was angry with them, that's all. He could never have meant to let it stand.'

'I think you are mistaken.'

'No, think of Antony! Ethan wouldn't have taken

Covelco away from Antony.'

'Yes, that was one of his express purposes, Miss Barnett.'

'What?'

Mr Romstock looked uncomfortable. 'I never envisaged having to talk about such matters,' he muttered, almost to himself. 'I shouldn't like it to come to the ears of Mr Antony Coverton. But Ethan had a very poor opinion of his son. He confessed to me he'd made a hash of bringing him up but that it was too late to mend matters. It is true that on the occasions when I have dined with the family, I found Antony somewhat obsessed by his own personal theories. But I have never come to know him well.'

Ruth could hear Ethan's voice in her mind: 'Antony swallowed an economics textbook at university and he's been spitting it up bit by bit ever since.' And what she heard of his plans always had a tinge of the grandiose.

'I gather,' resumed the solicitor, 'that Antony is very much under his mother's influence. He shares her view that Covelco isn't impressive enough. Apparently he had made no secret of his intention to use the firm as a bargaining counter to get into international commerce, an idea that Ethan strongly disapproved of.'

'Yes, that's true,' Ruth agreed. 'I expect he's been making a start on that by now, to tell the truth.' She stopped. 'Does he know?' she asked in dismay. The idea frightened her.

'Certainly. He and his mother were here this morning, at their insistence – they made the appointment as soon as Ethan's death was known,' he said with disapproval. 'But decency demands that the will should be kept until after the funeral. Antony had taken it for granted, as you had, that he was the heir. He reacted very badly. I'm afraid he had already been in contact with people abroad, making promises he will now have to retract.'

'It's dreadful,' said Ruth. 'I don't have any great regard for Antony but he must have been absolutely shattered.'

'Quite so,' the lawyer agreed. 'And his mother even more so.'

The scene, in fact, had been quite horrendous. They had arrived in almost holiday mood. They accepted morning coffee. Diana made conversation about plans to go and see the latest theatrical hit, *The Constant Nymph*.

Then he read them the will. Diana jumped to her feet, spilling coffee down the front of her Patou dress. Antony demanded to have the document in his hands to examine and having read it crumpled it up and threw it at Mr Romstock. Both shouted that it was a lie, a fraud, illegal, wicked, unnatural, immoral, not to be borne and likely to be overturned by a better lawyer the moment they could hire one.

'You must, of course, consult another lawyer if you wish to do so,' Romstock told them with hauteur. 'But the will is entirely legal.'

'I'll never let it stand!' Diana cried. 'I'll never let that little strumpet get her claws on my money!'

'Mrs Coverton, is it not *your* money . . .'

'No, but it's *my* company!' Antony broke in. 'And I've got plans for it.'

'I believe it was because of those plans that your father decided to leave it elsewhere.'

'Good God,' Antony shouted, 'even from the grave he's spoiling everything!'

'Mr Coverton, I must ask you to control yourself.'

'Control myself! Why, you stupid old dodderer, you aided and abetted him in making a fool of me!'

Mr Romstock pressed the intercom on his desk. His

secretary, who could hear the uproar even through the mahogany door, replied at once. 'Yes, Mr Romstock?'

'Please send young Mr Villiers to show out my visitors.' Young Mr Villiers was a rugby-playing articled clerk, already on his way across the office at a gesture from the secretary. He appeared in the doorway almost before Romstock had flicked the switch back. 'Mr Villiers, Mr Coverton is leaving.'

'No, I'm not, not until this farce of a will is put in the waste basket and we find out the truth . . .'

'Mr Coverton, your imputation is slanderous, and you have uttered it before a witness, a member of my staff. I advise you to moderate your tone. Mr Villiers, would you be so good?'

Antony realized he was about to be thrown out bodily and became less uncivilized. 'I'm going,' he said. 'But I want a copy of that will!'

'You are not mentioned in it. Your mother, however, is a legatee and I give you now a copy of it, Mrs Coverton.'

She snatched it from his hand and for a moment he thought she too was going to crumple it up. However, she merely stood for a moment with her fist clenched round it.

Antony went out, with Villiers in close attendance. His mother made as if to follow him, then paused. 'Well,' she said with a thin smile, 'I told him I'd be glad if he died soon. Strange to say, I was mistaken.'

Much shaken, Romstock had comforted himself with a good lunch and a glass of excellent claret. Meanwhile the office caretaker had tried to clean the coffee from his carpet. The damp spot still remained, close to Ruth's feet. And the echoes, too, of the hatred and resentment. But he had no intention of telling Ruth what had happened that morning. Instead, he tried to tell her what he thought had been in Ethan Coverton's mind.

'Ethan had realized that his elder son was not the right person to run Covelco. He made his new will not on the spur of the moment, but after several days of consideration. I will agree, my dear, that the stormy interview with his wife helped to bring him to a decision, but in my view, Ethan wasn't out for revenge or retaliation. He decided to give his estate to the person who really cared.'

The measured statement brought tears to Ruth's eyes. She blinked them back.

'But what am I to do?' she said.

'I don't think you have to do anything today, or even tomorrow.' There was kindness in the dry voice. 'But within, say, a week, there are problems that have to be faced, decisions that have to be made. For instance, if Antony has done anything that you think unwise, there is no one in a position to rescind his orders – except yourself.'

'But I can't do that!'

'You need time to come to terms with it. Is there someone with whom you could discuss it? A friend? An adviser?'

'No one. Except – there's a lawyer at Tadsley and Gower who has been very helpful.'

'By all means get in touch with him. Here is your portfolio of documents. Please read the will through at leisure. You understand that it has to go for probate? But I foresee no problems there, although it may quite likely take some months. Shakespeare spoke of the law's delays, did he not?' He smiled. 'Everything is here – a list of properties, a copy of the investment schedule, some insurance policies, other items of lesser moment but which are part of the estate.'

'Thank you.'

'Did you come by the famous Rolls-Royce? No? Then shall I have a taxi called?'

'Please.'

He gave the instruction to his secretary. He walked with her to the stone staircase outside his office door, and then, despite her protests down to the big hall. The doorman opened the heavy door for her.

'Please call on me for any information or help,' he said. 'Of course, I could not act for you – I am still the solicitor for the Coverton family although—' he gave a grim smile— 'I think not for much longer. But as a friend of Ethan's . . .'

'You've been very kind. Thank you.'

'Good afternoon, Miss Barnett.'

'Good afternoon.'

When she got home, Bignall was hovering in the hall. 'Your grandma said something about you having to go and see the boss's solicitor. Getting his property sorted, are they? We're losing the Roller, I suppose?'

'No, Bignall,' she said, rather faintly, 'it seems we're keeping it.'

'Never! Left it to you, did he? Well, that's great!'

'Bignall, how would you like to work for me?'

His square ruddy face took on a perplexed expression. 'I am, ain't I?'

'No, I mean permanently.'

'Permanently? Chauffeur the Roller?'

'Yes.'

'Oh! Oh, Miss Barnett! Oh! You mean it?'

'I do. It seems money isn't going to be a problem after all.'

In the drawing room Grandma was reading and knitting. She put down the steel needles, stabbing them through the ball of wool, and closed her magazine.

'Well, Ruthie, what was it?'

'It's unbelievable, Grandma.'

'Well, what?'

'Ethan's left everything to me.'

Grandma gazed about. 'The house, you mean? But I thought it was yours already?'

'I mean everything. *Everything*. The house, the office, the factories, the money in the bank – everything. Everything, everything!' And she threw herself into the sofa, buried her face in the cushions and burst into tears.

It took Mrs Barnett and Mrs Monash a quarter of an hour to calm her down. At length they had her tucked in among the cushions with a blanket over her legs and drinking strong sweet tea. Mrs Monash exchanged a worried glance with Mrs Barnett as she withdrew.

'Now, dearie, tell me.'

'See for yourself.' Ruth gestured at the portfolio given her by the solicitor. Her grandmother opened it gingerly, took out the top document and read it. It was the will. Within minutes she understood the reason for her granddaughter's outburst.

'We-ell,' she said. 'What are you going to do?'

'I've no idea! That's the point. I don't have any idea what to do!'

'What did this lawyer chap say you should do?'

'Get advice.' Ruth set aside the empty cup. 'And, of course, he's right,' she said with a return of firmness to her voice. 'I must ring Tadsley and Gower.'

'Who're they, when they're at home?'

'They're the firm who sorted things out when Ethan's

wife tried to have me thrown out of this house.' She went out and along to the study. It was just after four in the afternoon: quite possibly the solicitor's office would be closing for the day.

But, no, the phone was answered quickly and she was put through to Niall Gillis.

'Miss Barnett? Has anything happened?'

'Not here at the house. But— Mr Gillis, I went to Ethan's lawyer this afternoon and he read me the will.'

'Yes?'

'I'm the chief beneficiary.'

She heard him draw in a startled breath. Then he said, very calm: 'You say *chief* beneficiary. Meaning what?'

'He's left me everything except for the family house and a few personal bequests to friends.'

'By everything you mean – the company? Coverton Electrical?'

'Yes.'

His firm handled the Covelco business. He knew just how much it meant.

'I congratulate you,' he said.

'Oh, don't!' she begged. 'I don't feel as if it's something to be pleased about. Mr Gillis, I'm scared stiff. What am I supposed to do?'

'Well, I— I imagine you and Mr Coverton must have discussed—'

'No, not at all. I had no idea what was in the will. Mr Gillis, will you come and help me sort myself out? I simply don't know what to do.'

'Of course. I can't come immediately, I'm expecting someone in a few minutes. May I come when the day's business is over? Say, six o'clock?'

'Would you? I'd appreciate it very much.'

'Until six, then.'

Mrs Monash presented herself a little later to say that the evening meal was prepared and would be ready to serve at eight. She hovered.

'Is there something else, Mrs Monash?'

'I . . . er . . . Bignall said . . . That's to say . . .'

'Yes?'

'He said you'd asked him to stay on permanent.'

'That's right.'

'I was wondering if . . . that's to say . . .'

'Yes?'

'I was wondering if I might ask . . . It would be handier for me . . . But then of course you may want someone "live-in" . . .'

'Are you asking if I want you to stay on too?'

'Well, as a matter of fact, Miss Barnett, yes, that's what I was after. Seeing as Bignall's had the word.'

'I didn't know that you'd want to be permanently employed here.'

'Oh, Miss Barnett, dear, no question! Far easier for me than "doing" for all those bits and bobs at Crecy Court! And they come and go so much, I hardly know who I'm working for half the time. But the trouble is, you see, my Harry isn't in the domestic service line, being a plumber, and so I couldn't "live-in", and I expect you'd prefer that.'

'Not at all, Mrs Monash. I'd very much like it if you'd consider yourself a fixture. It seems silly to me to have a couple installed here as servants just to look after one woman.'

'All the same, miss, I couldn't handle all the work on my own – this is a big house in its funny way.'

'We'll hire whoever we need to do the rough work, Mrs Monash. You give it some thought and let me know how much daily help you feel you'll need. We'll talk about wages then.'

'Well, that's first-rate. That's really nice. Wait till I tell my Harry. Well, thank you, Miss Barnett. That's a real pleasure to me.'

'Oh, Mrs Monash—'

'Yes?' said the maid, her hand on the doorknob.

'Will you bring in the sherry? And some of those biscuits you served to Mr Gillis last week? He seemed to like them.'

'Right you are, miss.'

Ruth's grandmother had listened to all this in wry silence. 'Well, fancy *you!*' she remarked when the door had closed. 'Hiring servants! Who'd have thought it?'

Ruth flushed a little but shrugged. 'It's something you learn to do, Grandma.'

'Mmm. I never have,' Grandma said, and there was something almost like envy in her tone.

Niall came with the moisture of the autumn drizzle on the shoulders of his black jacket and on his crisp black hair. His blue eyes were full of friendly interest. 'I'm a little late. I couldn't get rid of my client,' he explained. 'Silly man with a grudge against his next-door neighbour. Good evening, Mrs Barnett, how are you enjoying London?'

'It's a big enough place,' Grandma acknowledged.

Niall sank with a sigh into the chair he was offered. He had had a busy day, and in truth had an engagement for the evening. But the friendly room with its fire was soothing, and he wanted to do what he could for Miss Barnett. 'Now, how can I help you?'

Ruth hesitated. 'Would you please read the will?' She handed it to him, and while he began on it she poured the

sherry. He accepted it absently, his mind on what he read.
When he had finished, he raised his gaze to her. 'As a
legal document, I'd say it's watertight.'

'But Mr Gillis, from what Mr Romstock said, it seems
I'm expected to do something with the Coverton Electrical Company.'

'Such as what?'

'Prevent Ethan's son Antony from wrecking it as far as I
can gather.'

'Ah. There's no mention of that in the will. You're
simply left the controlling interest in the company. If you
wanted to, you could sell it.'

'*Sell* it?' The mere idea was shocking to her.

'If that was your preference.'

'I couldn't do that, Mr Gillis!'

'Why not?'

'Because – because Ethan wouldn't have wanted that.
He wouldn't want Covelco sold off to just anyone.'

Niall was nodding. 'I didn't know Mr Coverton very
well. His business was dealt with by the senior partners,
naturally. But I did have some contact with him – you
remember I was present to advise when you came in
together?'

'I remember.' When they had gone to ask if Ethan
could somehow get a divorce.

'And there have been other occasions when I was called
in to consult. So I suppose I had some acquaintance with
him. My impression is that he had a particular view of the
way his company should be run. It may be that in leaving
it to you he hoped or expected that you would carry on in
that way.'

'But I can't run a million-pound company! I don't know
how to do it.'

'Now, just a minute, Ruth,' her grandmother intervened. 'Haven't you been telling me how you took notes and made phone calls for him while he was convalescing? And sat with his business friends in the balcony room while he discussed things? You can't say you don't know how to do it.'

'But that's entirely different, Grandma! Listening and taking instructions . . .'

'But you've never been slow off the mark, child. You'd have picked up a lot.'

'Not enough to be able to handle Covelco.'

Niall set down his sherry glass on a nearby table. 'Let's look at the alternatives,' he suggested. 'You could refuse to accept the bequest.'

'Mr Romstock said I had no choice.'

'That's not entirely true. You could refuse, but that would mean the estate would go into chancery, and it might be years before the courts decided how to settle it. Meantime,' Niall said, gesturing in the air to show how long the slide would be, 'the business would be running downhill and might possibly be in a worse mess than if Antony had inherited.'

'No, it would be wrong to allow that.'

'Well, then, you can sell. Not to just anyone – I daresay there are business colleagues of Mr Coverton's for whom he had respect?'

'As businessmen, yes, but there's the research side. Ethan felt that the electrical industry was at the very threshold of great new things. He encouraged research, it was his main interest. I don't know of any company in this country who gives the same encouragement to the R and D department.'

'That does present a problem,' Niall agreed.

'There's Cedric Glass, of course,' mused Ruth. 'But he's practically a one-man affair. He could never raise the money to buy Covelco.'

'What it amounts to is that those who have the money to buy Covelco don't have the interest in research and development, and those who have the interest don't have the resources to buy.'

Ruth's grandmother gave him a bright glance over her knitting. This young man had his head screwed on the right way. Speaking for herself, she'd never had any truck with lawyers, but what she'd heard of them had not been encouraging. Still, this young fellow seemed decent enough.

The young fellow was studying his client from thoughtful Celtic-blue eyes. 'Well, the last alternative is that you keep it and run it yourself.'

'But I've told you, I don't know how.'

'You could hire people,' he said.

'What?'

'You don't have to do it yourself. At least, not to the same extent as Ethan – I mean Mr Coverton. He had his fingers on all the pulses, but no one could expect you to understand the scientific side . . .'

'No, certainly not!'

'There's a Research and Development Department?'

'Of course.'

'With someone at the moment in charge of it?'

'Yes, Mr Patterwick – Leonard Patterwick – he's first-rate. Ethan thought a lot of him.'

'He's one of those to whom Ethan has left a personal bequest, I seem to recall.'

'Yes, they had a lot in common.' She paused. 'I see,' she murmured.

'It's more than I do, child,' muttered her grandmother. 'What's all this about Leonard Patterwick?'

'Don't you see, Grandma? He's been running R and D for years. If anyone had Ethan's confidence, he did. And then there's the company secretary, William Gooding. He's as reliable as the Rock of Gibraltar. And Miss Krett, of course. Miss Krett is Ethan's private secretary – was, I mean. She never approved of me but she knew all there was to know about Ethan's business routine.'

'She figures in the will too,' prompted Niall.

'Yes, because she and Bignall and Mr Patterwick were the kind of people Ethan knew he could rely upon.'

'How many of these business friends are mentioned in the will?' asked Mrs Barnett.

Ruth took the document back from Niall to run through it for the names while Mrs Barnett completed a row of heather-mixture sock she was knitting for her husband.

'There were eight bequests in all, seven if you exclude Bignall because he's not strictly Covelco staff.'

'People you know?'

'I've met most of them, worked with some of them – Patterwick, Gooding, Henderson who runs the factory in Stiggley . . .'

'Your man relied on them. Do you think you could?'

'Of course. But don't you see, Grandma, that's not the point. How would they feel about *me*?'

'You'll never know if you don't ask them.'

Niall Gillis flashed her a brief, brilliant smile. No fool, this old lady.

'But I wouldn't know how to ask them. What would I do – write to them? Telephone?'

'Surely you can do what you like,' her grandmother said. 'You're the boss, aren't you?'

'Oh, no. Not in the sense that Ethan was.' Ruth was shaking her head, seeing in her mind's eye the boardroom with Ethan in the chair. 'He built up the company, he had a right to ask for their trust and to give them orders. But me – why should they listen to me?'

'Because Ethan chose you, dear.'

There was a little pause.

'Is that true?' murmured Ruth. 'Is that what he wanted?'

'Listen to me,' said Mrs Barnett, laying aside her knitting. 'You said to me, when I told you you had to start a new life, that without Ethan you didn't know how to. Seems to me he's showing you how.'

'But it's such a big thing to do. What do you think, Mr Gillis?'

'If you had people you trusted, you might feel able to handle the business . . .'

'No, it's too big an undertaking.'

'Ruth,' her grandmother said, 'what more do you want? It's like a voice speaking to you from beyond the grave.'

She stared at her grandmother, her hands clasped almost as if in prayer.

'He's telling you to take hold of what he's left you and make it work, child.'

She turned her troubled gaze on Niall.

'Yes, Ruth,' said Niall Gillis, 'I think he really is.'

Chapter Eighteen

The boardroom of the Coverton Electrical Company was buzzing. Eleven men sat at the table. In front of each was a blotter on which lay a writing pad and two freshly sharpened pencils. Scattered along the centre of the table were ashtrays, some of which were already half full of crushed-out cigarettes. Many of those present were nervous enough to be chain-smoking. Their jobs were on the line.

They sat the length of the rectangular oak table. They were sombrely clad, some in black jacket and pinstripe trousers, some in dark grey worsted suits. Ties were in general grey or navy or plum – no note of gaiety was allowed. They were mostly well past their thirties. A few, like Leonard Patterwick, were approaching their sixties.

This was not a board meeting. The 'board' of Covelco – a private company – had consisted of only two members, Ethan Coverton and his son. But it had been Ethan's habit to call managerial meetings every month to discuss progress and make plans. These men were managers or department heads with the exception of Antony Coverton who was the deputy managing director.

They had been summoned by Miss Krett on Friday. She had telephoned them all with instructions that the new owner of Covelco, Miss Ruth Barnett, wished to have a discussion about the future of the company beginning at eleven o'clock Monday morning.

Miss Krett herself sat at a table a little to one side, shorthand notebook at the ready. She was clad in her best black silk rep frock with new lace cuffs and collar. She couldn't quite tell why she'd felt impelled to put on her best dress just because Miss Barnett was coming to the office.

One or two of the men had already been informed that they had received a bequest from Ethan Coverton. They were wondering if that ought to be regarded as a farewell present. It was the general consensus that the new owner had brought them here to tell them she was about to sell up.

'After all, what else can she do?' Antony wondered aloud. 'She doesn't know anything about running a business.' And she only took up with my father for the money anyway, he added internally, although he had the sense not to say it aloud.

He couldn't help thinking that Ruth Barnett had had very good luck. When Ethan began to take an interest in her she would have been flattered and pleased. A millionaire – a fine catch. She'd have expected to have a year or two of lush living as his mistress. When it became clear that he was besotted enough to want to marry her, that was even better. But the marriage had never been possible, and perhaps she had been looking ahead to several more years of being tied to an old man who, though fond, must often seem boring and tiresome.

Then fate steps in, thought Antony, Ethan Coverton dies, and there she is, not only well provided for, but with a big industrial company in her possession. All she has to do is sell out, and she could live in luxury for the rest of her life on the proceeds – and in complete freedom.

Antony, like all those present, was sombrely dressed and looking serious. He'd talked things over with his mother and decided his role was the grieving son, the concerned executive. He kept his sharp hazel eyes somewhat downcast, his light voice was husky with controlled emotion.

But the emotion he was feeling had nothing to do with grief. Since Friday morning when Miss Krett told him about the meeting, he'd been on the telephone to friends and contacts in the business world. He knew he could summon up the backing to buy the company as soon as the Barnett girl put it up for sale. What he was feeling was triumph. *Now*, at last, he was going to come into his own.

Glances were directed towards the pendulum clock on the boardroom wall. Eleven o'clock. She was late. Of course, women were usually late.

The door opened and Miss Barnett walked in.

Some only knew her through newspaper photographs. They saw a slender girl of middle height, with short light brown hair held to one side in a tortoiseshell clasp. Her grey-green eyes gazed straight ahead. She was wearing a very dark green crepe dress with a single string of pearls. In her hands she held a portfolio.

She took the chair at the head of the table. 'Good morning, gentlemen,' she said.

'Good morning,' they responded in a ragged chorus.

Except for Antony, who said nothing.

Ruth was so nervous she thought they must see her shaking. She laid the portfolio down so as to press her hands on the blotter to steady them. She cleared her throat.

'I imagine that since the death of Mr Coverton you've been wondering what would happen to the company. None of you could have expected that it would be bequeathed to someone like me. I didn't expect it myself.'

When she paused here, she looked momentarily towards Antony. He was looking at his notepad and affected not to see.

'Since I was made aware of the contents of Mr Coverton's will, I've been getting advice and giving the matter a lot of thought. I've called you together – and thank you for coming—' Here some of them shifted a little, as if to say, We had no choice but to come. She made a little apologetic shrug and continued: 'I called this meeting to ask your opinion of what I've decided. I say decided – if any of you should have something better to propose I'm prepared to consider it.'

The manager of the Sales Department, who liked to be regarded as an ideas man, decided to speak. 'I've had one or two thoughts,' he said.

'Very well. You can put them forward when you've heard what I have to say, Mr Chalfont.' She waited to see if anyone else wished to stake a claim. 'Right, then I'll tell you what I've been thinking. Those of us who knew Ethan well – I mean, Mr Coverton . . .' She broke off, colouring up. Only one or two of these men had ever addressed Ethan by his first name. By using it, she had accentuated the irregularity of her position. It was a bad opening. But she had to go on, there was no help for it. 'Those of us who knew him know that he loved this company. It wasn't just because it made a lot of money, although he enjoyed the money he made. What he loved was the adventure of pushing forward into new fields of technology.'

'Hear! hear!' murmured Leonard Patterwick, stifling a sigh.

Ruth flashed a glance towards him. This angular, grey-haired man was one of the few she knew well. He had come to dinner several times while Ethan was fit, had come sick-visiting regularly while he was convalescing. Ruth had heard him discuss the results of the Research and Development Department with an enthusiasm and delight that made him look like a boy.

Others were nodding. She felt a little encouraged. 'I've thought about it for days now, and I've come to the conclusion that what Mr Coverton would have wanted was for the company to continue along the same lines—'

'What?'

That was Antony, startled into exclaiming aloud.

'You don't agree, Mr Antony?' she asked.

'I think we have to look at the situation as it is now, not as the late owner would have looked at it.'

'Is there anything in the present situation that prevents the company going on as before? We still have the same staff, the same departmental heads. All that has changed is the ownership.'

'Just a minute! A lot has changed! The ownership, as you call it, has gone into hands which have no experience—'

'I absolutely agree with you. That's why I brought you here. If I try to run this company the way Ethan would have wanted, I'm going to need help.'

'You're going to run it?' cried Antony.

Hubbub broke out. Ted Chalfont could be heard saying that he thought the prestige of the company would be better served if it went public. The personnel manager wondered aloud if Miss Barnett intended to come into the office.

Ruth heard the question. 'That's an important point, Mr Daniels,' she agreed. 'I've thought about it. I believe that I shall be in the building every day at first, although once we've established the new team I may take more of a back seat.'

There was a very awkward silence. Everyone in the room knew that Antony Coverton had moved into his father's office within two days of his death. If Miss Barnett was going to come every day, Mr Antony was going to have to move back to his old office.

No one dared to turn a glance upon him. Antony glared down at the table. His mother had said so airily, 'You've got experience and education, she's got nothing – you'll run rings round her.' Not at all. She was not only cutting the ground from under his feet, she was going to turn him out of his office.

'Gentlemen, you didn't let me finish what I was trying to tell you. I believe that Mr Coverton wanted me to keep Covelco going along the same track, and I'm going to try to do that. I don't know yet quite what it will involve, but I can only do it if you help me. I admit I know nothing about the scientific side, and although in the past I've typed up financial reports, I don't know much about finance.'

'So you're admitting you're a complete amateur,' Antony blurted.

'Yes, I am. But someone said to me the other evening that I didn't have to do everything *myself*. I could hire others to do things for me. And when I came to think about it, I realized that Ethan didn't in fact do everything himself. He relied on Mr Gooding, for instance, to keep the books and prepare them for audit. He relied on Mr Patterwick to run R and D. It seems to me that if the heads of departments are willing to give me the same support that they gave to Ethan – or perhaps a bit more because I don't have the same basic knowledge that he had – we ought to be able to keep Covelco going in the same way.'

She turned her head towards Alfred Gooding, the company secretary, who was sitting two places down on her right. He took off his glasses, polished them, then returned them to his nose. 'I . . . er . . . I must admit this is a complete surprise to me. The idea is startling. A woman in charge?'

'There *are* businesses that are run by women.'

'But not on the scale of Covelco. Dressmaking establishments, nursing homes.'

'There are women running university colleges.'

'Those are outside the commercial arena, Miss Barnett. Life is much more fierce outside the dreaming spires of Oxford.'

'You think my idea is a bad one?'

'Er— I didn't say that, Miss Barnett. I merely say that I'm surprised by it.'

'I should think anybody with any sense would be astounded by it,' Antony remarked. 'The idea's absurd. Nobody would take us seriously.'

'Why not?'

'A woman running an industrial company?' Antony's tone implied. And a woman of this particular kind?

It was as bad as Ruth had expected. The men in their business suits sat on either side of the table looking sceptical, disapproving, some of them even annoyed. Ted Chalfont in particular seemed to take her proposal as a personal affront. Antony, as she expected, was opposed to anything that she put forward on principle. She could guess why. If he himself wasn't to be in charge, then he wanted Covelco sold – to some group of backers who would *put* him in charge.

'Let's leave aside the point about whether it's right for a woman to be in charge of a company,' she said. 'Does anyone have any objection to the idea of trying to keep the company running in the way Mr Coverton did – that's to say, with new ideas getting a lot of emphasis and investment?'

'I'm against that, for one,' declared Antony. 'It's no secret, I always have been. To me Covelco's done enough in developing wireless and domestic electrical appliances. The time has come to drop research, and instead go in for mass production on a big scale. And the only way to do that is to go international.'

'But your father never agreed with that.'

'Well, he let himself get out of touch with the financial situation. He spent a lot of time thinking about things outside the company.'

For instance, about the affair he was having with a girl half his age, was the implication.

'Things outside the company,' said Ruth. 'You mean his enthusiasm for racing cars? I've decided to close down the Covelco racing team. So nothing will distract my attention from running the company.'

There was a murmur of amusement at the riposte. Leonard Patterwick smiled widely. Good for you, he was thinking.

'I would like to think aloud for a minute,' he announced, taking up the initiative. 'I knew Ethan Coverton as well as any man sitting at this table, and my opinion is that he'd have approved of Miss Barnett's plan. I know he would have wanted to keep research going. Last time I was with him, we had a long discussion about electric storage batteries – we've been trying to make them smaller and less cumbersome. He said he thought there was a killing to be made by any firm producing a battery that would keep a wireless set going without the need for hydrochloric acid. I agree with him.' Pointedly, Mr Patterwick addressed Antony. 'He saw how much money there was to be made by a dry battery if we could really get one going. No lack of vision about money matters, as far as I could see.'

The company secretary was nodding. 'Of course it is true that a very large sum goes into R and D. But over a ten-year period, you can see that almost each investment has returned a sizable profit . . .'

'A ten-year period,' Antony snorted. 'If we used that money in the financial markets, we could treble it in ten years.'

'That supposition is based on Professor Zakov's premise, and no one has yet been able to test—'

'Anyone with a mind above mere book-keeping knows that Zakov's theory of the balance of the international trade—'

'There are other theories, Mr Antony, which are completely in opposition—'

'Look at South America! Zakov has been proved right—'

'Gentlemen, gentlemen.' Ruth tapped on the table to get their attention. 'I've never heard of Professor Zakov or his theory, and that's not what we're here to talk about. My question to you was, do you in general agree with me, that Ethan Coverton wanted to retain an emphasis on research? We know that Mr Antony is against that. Is anyone else against, and if so, why?'

'Well,' began Chalfont the sales manager, 'my chief problem is having enough goods to fill orders. I tend to agree with Mr Antony – we ought to turn our attention more towards mass production of what we've already got.'

'If you would stop promising production dates to customers that are impossible to fill,' retorted the production manager, Dick Watters, 'your orders would be filled. I keep sending you production deadlines, and you keep ignoring them!'

'Are you in favour of going over to mass production, Mr Watters?'

'I'm in favour of expansion of the production line. But it can be done within the company, without involving ourselves in mergers.'

'Can I have a show of hands? Those in favour of taking the company away from research and into mass production?'

Anthony put his hand up at once. Ted Chalfont, after a moment's thought, did likewise. The manager of the Northern Area, who supervised the buying or enlargement of factories, signalled agreement by a brusque flagging of his finger: he wasn't pleased at having a woman demanding to know his opinions. But mass production meant more power in his hands, so he had to be in favour of that.

'Three against eight. Do I take it that the eight agree with me, that we should try to keep Covelco as it always has been, in the forefront of invention and development?'

Murmurs of assent, noddings of the head. Ruth began to feel less shaky. On the whole these were men who had been picked by Ethan. For that reason they were likely to share his views.

'Very well. I'm glad, because that's my wish and intention. If you'd all been heavily against it, I'd have had to go away and think again.' She allowed herself a smile, and to her surprise one or two of those around the table smiled back.

'Well, now we come to the matter of being taken seriously if you have a woman running the company.' There was a murmur, and she knew it was a very big hurdle for her. They really didn't want a woman in charge. It would have been bad enough if she'd been a mature career woman with a record of business experience behind her. But a chit of a girl? And one with a bad reputation?

Oh, Ethan, she sighed inwardly, what a problem you've laid on me . . .

'I'm not experienced enough to "run" the company,' she said. 'I know that and you know that. But I believe I can put together a team who could do it.'

'You can't run a business by committee,' Antony objected. 'It's been tried and it never works.'

'But a board of directors is a committee.'

'Huh! Most directors only turn up for the fee they get. In any case, Covelco only had two directors – myself and my father. And *he* took all the decisions.' The resentment was barely concealed.

'Of course, we've got to find a new system. I'm not equipped to make decisions about research, and you don't even agree that we should go on with it. We can't make it work with a board of only two directors. What I'm suggesting is a management committee—'

'But who's going to select the members of such a committee?'

'I am.'

Antony glared at her. 'And what makes you think you've the right to?'

'The fact that I own eighty per cent of the shares.'

Everyone present was jolted by the starkness of the response. For the first time, they began to suspect that there might be steel beneath that gentle exterior.

They listened to the echo of the words. They ought to be careful about how they treated her. She was no mere country girl with a village-school education. She was the inheritor of all that Ethan Coverton had built during his business career. She had the power to change their lives if she wanted to. And it was clear she intended to use her power.

Watters, the production manager, began a long proposal for selecting a committee. The personnel manager, Daniels, objected that managers were hired to manage and not sit on committees. The argument went back and forth across the table.

At length Ruth looked at her watch. 'Gentlemen, I suggest that we break now for lunch. I've ordered sandwiches and drinks to be brought in but there's no obligation to stay here if you'd rather go out. I've made arrangements to eat with a friend at the Automobile Club so if you decide to stay here you can discuss what I've said without restraint.' She gave a faint smile. She could well imagine the kind of thing they would say about her.

'At what time are we resuming?' Miss Krett inquired, pencil poised.

'I think two thirty, Miss Krett. And gentlemen—'

They paused, attentive.

'I think it's clear I intend to take an active part in running the company. Think it over during the lunch break. If you feel you couldn't be happy with that arrangement, you can rest assured your departure from the firm will be marked by good severance pay and good references. But when it comes to assembling the team to run Covelco, I want to be sure I have people who can work with me.'

She smiled, nodded and walked out.

'My God,' muttered Dick Watters, 'didn't we underestimate *her*!'

Ruth's lunch date was with David Epps. He and Peter Stokes had telephoned and sent messages of condolence, but she hadn't seen either of them since Ethan died. She'd been glad of it, because they belonged to a part of Ethan's life that she couldn't bear to think about.

It was at Dave's invitation that they were meeting. She'd tried to avoid it, but he had pleaded for a chance to talk to her. She had a fair idea of what he was going to say.

'You look peaky,' he remarked when they had settled at their table in the stately dining room. The patrons at the other tables were mostly men, yet there were a few women present, probably guests like herself. She never felt at ease in such places.

'I'm all right,' she said.

'They're talking about putting up a plaque to him.'

'What? Where?'

'Brooklands. Not getting to go to the funeral, you see – a lot of chaps thought that was pretty rotten of his missus. So they want to do something to compensate.'

She shrugged. 'Ethan would think that was pretty silly.'

'I suppose so.'

Their soup came. They made small talk. David couldn't settle. Someone had clearly told him that you ought not to talk business until the sweet course, but she could tell he was going over in his mind what he really wanted to say.

'Why did you want us to meet, Dave?' she asked, to put him out of his misery.

'To find out what plans you've got for the winter season, of course. I've pretty much rebuilt the Mark IV . . .'

She was shaking her head.

'What?' he begged. 'What's the matter?'

'Covelco isn't going to support motor racing any more, Dave.'

'I suppose Antony's got control, has he?' he said bitterly. 'He was always against Ethan's racing cars.'

'Antony isn't in control. It's my decision.'

'But Ruth!'

'Racing cars killed Ethan.'

'That's not true! He died of pneumonia.'

'He'd have got over that if he hadn't been so badly weakened by the crash. He just hadn't the strength to fight it off.'

'Ruth, you can't shut down the team.'

'I can and I am. I never want to be near a racing car again as long as I live.'

'But you're throwing away all we've achieved!'

'No, I'm just taking Covelco's name off. You can have the car, Dave. You can have both of them, the Mark III and the Mark IV.'

'What?'

'I don't want them. I don't want to have to think about them. So take them and do that you like with them.'

'But, Ruth, I can't afford to run a racing team!'

'Somebody else might take you up. You know a lot of people on the racing scene, Dave.'

'Not many have got the sort of money Ethan had,' he mumbled. 'It's no good giving the cars to me – I can never race them.'

'Get Peter Stokes to go in with you.'

'Peter's got no money, you know that. He wouldn't be selling cars in Grosvenor Square if he had any money.'

'Then sell them. There are buyers for racing cars.'

'Not unless they're race winners. The Mark III didn't do all that marvellously, and the Mark IV was smashed before she'd done anything.'

'So you don't want them, then?'

'I didn't say that,' he said quickly. 'Mebbe I can't race them, but I could always strip 'em down. You see, Ruth, that's another thing I wanted to ask you about. I've got this idea, see, about going into business for myself – engine design – high-performance stuff. I'm good at it, but I need premises, testing beds, that kind of thing. I was wondering whether . . . you know, seeing you're in the money now . . .?'

'No, Dave.'

'Don't just turn me down like that! Good heavens, Ruth, we've been friends a good while now! Don't just say no without thinking about it!' He turned his dark good looks upon her, hoping to melt her determination. It usually worked with other women.

Ruth had always been proof against his charms, and seemed almost indifferent now. 'I don't need to think about it. I don't want to be connected with high-performance cars. I told you, racing cars killed Ethan.'

'Oh, that's nonsense and you know it.'

'I'm not going to give you money.'

'I don't want it as a gift,' he said hotly. 'I'm not asking for a hand-out. Just lend me a bit . . .'

'No. I'm not going to help you to design engines with which men will risk their lives. That's final.'

'But men have to risk their lives, or there'll never be any progress! That flying boat you brought him home from Sicily in – don't you think men risked their lives before we got flying machines that worked?'

'I understand all that. I know there's physical danger in testing new things. But there's no need to keep going faster and faster round a track – it's useless, silly – it killed Ethan and I'm not going to help kill anyone else!'

Their voices had risen. Other people in the dining room were staring at so much emotion among the white-covered tables.

'Keep it down, you'll get me thrown out,' Dave said, embarrassed. 'I never expected you to take up a silly attitude like this.'

She almost laughed. 'You'll never win any prizes for tact,' she retorted. 'You're trying to get a loan out of me and you tell me I'm silly?'

'I didn't mean it like that. But you know very well Ethan would never agree with what you've just said.'

'Ethan was entitled to spend his money in whatever way he liked,' said Ruth, 'and to risk his life if he wanted to. In just the same way, I'm entitled to think what I like about it, and what I think now is that Ethan would be alive today if he hadn't fallen in love with speed.'

'Well, I still think you're wrong in that. Ethan died in his bed.'

'Stop it,' she said, suddenly unable to go on with the conversation. 'Don't say "He died in his bed" as if it was a good thing. He's gone, I've lost him! He's gone for ever!'

Dave Epps was silenced. In the face of so much grief, he had nothing to say.

His problem was that for the first time in his life he wanted to use his talents to make money. Until now he'd been happy – no, delighted – to live from day to day, devoting all his energies to making cars run faster. Diversion had always been available -- there were a lot of pretty girls around the motor-racing tracks.

But now, alas, David Epps had fallen in love.

Hitherto Dave had thought love was pretty silly. Ethan's devotion to Ruth had struck him as absurd, and the jealousy Dave himself had evoked by flirting with Ruth was pretty incomprehensible. Now, as he looked back, he regretted his carelessness. His behaviour towards Ruth had alienated him from Ethan.

He'd approached him for a loan while they were in Sicily and got a very dusty answer, but then next day Ethan had sent him a note saying he was sorry. At that point he'd been pretty sure of getting the money from him to start a business of his own. And then Ethan had crashed, and after that it was no use thinking about new ventures – it just didn't seem appropriate.

Of course, no one had expected Ethan to die. Anyone who knew him expected him to live for ever. So Dave had bided his time about repeating his request for financial backing.

And now it was too late, and Ruth was off on some emotional idiocy over racing cars, and he'd lost his chance completely.

So now he would have to resign himself to losing his girl. She was the sort you couldn't expect to pig it out in the kind of digs Dave could afford, or to live the sort of hand-to-mouth existence that had seemed fine to him.

The fact was, David Epps had fallen hopelessly in love with Lorette Coverton.

He didn't want to be in love with her. It hampered his activities and spoiled his hobbies. In times gone by he could finish a long day's work on some temperamental motor, wash and change, have a few pints and pick up a girl for the evening.

Now he hung around after work hoping she'd be able to meet him. But Lorette's family had this 'full social programme', from which she couldn't absent herself without causing trouble with her mother.

'Good heavens, just tell her you're going up to London to meet a friend,' Dave urged.

'When she expects me at home to make up numbers at the dinner table?' Lorette replied. 'You don't know Mother!'

Dave's mother was a timid widow-woman living in Kent. He couldn't imagine being dominated by her. He and Lorette would quarrel about her cowardice, and they wouldn't see each other for a week or so, and then Dave's heart would have this strange ache in it, and he'd know he had to see her and he'd ring and leave a message with her girlfriend Rose Dellafield, and it would start all over again.

He was never sure if she cared for him beyond the 'adventure' of going out with someone from a different social class. They'd met at a car rally where her twit of a boyfriend had taken her. The boyfriend, idiot that he was, seemed keener on showing off his Buick Opera Coupé than giving Lorette a good time. Dave had put himself out to entertain her, just because she was the prettiest girl there. And, of course, because there was a bit of a thrill in flirting with Ethan Coverton's daughter.

How it had got so serious, he couldn't quite tell. It was quite against his nature to get serious. Yet here he was, trapped. And from the way Lorette always seemed happy when they made up after a quarrel, he sometimes felt it was the same for her.

They never talked about marriage. That would have been useless. Dave had made money in the past, but had never saved any of it. Besides, even a well-paid job as mechanic to a rich patron in the car-racing game wouldn't be enough. Mrs Coverton was never going to let her precious daughter be wasted on a car mechanic.

No, he had to have a business of his own. Even that wouldn't impress Mrs Coverton, he well knew. But it was a start, enough for Lorette to be able to say, 'No, I won't get engaged to Eustace Sutcliffe, or Viscount Luce— I'm going to marry a man who's building up a business of his own.' If she could just keep refusing the men her mother lined up until she was twenty-one, then she could please herself who she married.

That's to say, if she had the courage to defy her mother so completely.

And, of course, there was no certainty that she'd wait. And the uncertainty was like a pain that could never be eased.

Dave told none of this to Ruth. It wasn't that he felt she wouldn't understand – she, more than anyone else, would know what he was going through. It was just that he couldn't talk about it. He'd never taken love seriously, he'd certainly never talked about his intimate feelings. He didn't know how to do it and, more than that, he didn't want to. They were too precious to share with anyone, even Ruth.

Ruth's refusal to patronize the Covelco racing team was a tremendous blow. But Dave knew enough about women to realize argument would get him nowhere. No matter how silly her notions about racing seemed to him, he could tell she believed in them. And when a girl got a silly idea in her head, logic was useless.

For her part, Ruth was eager to end the meal. Her emotional energies had to be saved for the argument in the Covelco boardroom. By and by she might get around to offering Dave some help, but only if he chose a career other than racing cars. About that she was adamant: she would never finance the sport that had killed her man.

The waiting Rolls-Royce whisked her back to Holborn. She was a little ahead of some of the others. The meeting at last assembled about five minutes late. Ruth tapped with her pencil on the table.

'Well, gentlemen, I hope you had a pleasant lunch. And I hope you gave some thought to what I asked. Can you work under the direction of a woman?'

There was an uneasy mutter. Some of the men glanced at one another.

'Perhaps we'd better do it this way. Anyone who would rather not continue in the employment of Covelco in the new circumstances had better say so now and leave – with no hard feelings.'

She waited. After a long moment Ted Chalfont said, 'I think I'd better make the move. Nothing personal, you understand. I just never have taken orders from a woman and I don't think I could now.'

'Very well, Mr Chalfont.'

Hitherden, the Northern Area manager, stood up. 'I'm going too. At my time of life and seniority, it just doesn't seem right to have to accept the new regime.'

'I quite understand.'

Ruth looked at Antony. She was expecting him to go. He felt her glance upon him and raised his eyes to meet it.

His mouth set with stubborn determination. She understood, and didn't put the question into words. Antony was staying – perhaps in the hope she'd make such a mess of things that she'd have to turn to him for salvation.

The two others nodded round the table and made for the door. With his hand on the knob, Hitherden paused.

'Have you any idea what you're taking on, Miss Barnett?' he demanded, and without waiting for a reply went out. Chalfont, shrugging apologetically, followed.

The rest turned their faces towards Ruth. She had brought them here, she had asked for their support. Now she must say what she wanted.

Well, she'd lost only two out of eleven. That wasn't bad. She felt encouraged, rewarded. 'Gentlemen, thank you for your loyalty to Ethan's firm,' she said. 'Here's what I propose for the future . . .'

Chapter Nineteen

Forming the management committee offered few difficulties. All the men Ruth approached were delighted to be asked. Leonard Patterwick, after some hesitation, accepted the post of managing director; he needed reassurance that he could first choose his successor as head of Research and Development. Alfred Gooding remained as company secretary but with increased responsibility and a salary to match. Dick Watters, bursting with ideas for increasing production, practically demanded to be included.

Three others, recommended by either Patterwick or Watters, joined the committee. Ruth, shying away from the title of Chairman, appointed herself Administrative Officer.

The only problem was Antony.

'We ought to keep him on the board,' Patterwick mused, at a meeting of what Ruth thought of as the 'inner cabinet'. 'After all he's got the boss's name and that helps the feeling of continuity.'

'And he does own some of the shares,' Gooding added. 'And I suppose would represent his family's holdings too.'

'But I can't have him as deputy managing director,' Patterwick said, embarrassed. 'I know it sounds as if I'm throwing my weight around, but I don't think I could work with him.'

'No, he's got quite different ideas,' Ruth agreed. 'We must find a role for him, but not as deputy managing director.'

'He's not going to like it.'

'No.'

'He's got to have some sort of a job that sounds important . . .'

'But which won't allow him to make any moves to change the company . . .'

There was a long pause while they considered the point.

'How about Director of Development?' Patterwick suggested.

'But that's your province, Leonard.'

'No, not scientific development, financial development.'

'I don't want him going into negotiation with those cronies of his—' Gooding began with indignation.

'It's all right, Alfred, he'd have to get your agreement to anything he did before it got to contract stage.'

Ruth was nodding. 'After all, he does know a lot of people in the City. He might be able to do us some good if we were urgently looking for funds.'

'We don't need to look for funds.'

'I know, I know, Alfred,' Patterwick soothed, 'the boss left us with a lot of money in the bank. But you never know – one day we might want to expand and it's always good to have the right contacts.'

Gooding wasn't entirely convinced, but in the end accepted the idea because they could think of nothing better. Antony's training had been in economics: they had to offer him something to do with finance or planning.

It was then Ruth's difficult task to give the news to Antony.

When Miss Krett showed him in, he looked full of determination and suppressed anger.

Why, thought Ruth, he thinks I'm going to tell him he's fired! The thought gave her a launching point for the interview.

'Please sit down, Antony,' she invited, and when he had done so went on, 'you and I aren't exactly friends, are we?'

He was taken aback. 'No,' he agreed.

'And naturally now that I've taken over, I have to think whether or not I could work with you.'

'I suppose so. There's no denying you have control of the company and I accept that. But let me tell you, you know nothing, *nothing* about running a business and if you push me out you'll be making a big mistake. People know me, I have friends throughout the financial community—'

'Exactly. That's why the management committee have decided to use your talents in that direction,' she said, pouncing on the words.

'What?'

'We talked it over and decided that, of course, we wanted you to be a member of the team.'

She had thrown him completely off balance. He'd been so sure she was going to tell him he had to go that all his prepared speeches were about that. He felt his brain whirling.

Play for time. What had she just said? Something about teamwork. He gave a snort of derision. 'I think the idea of a team to run the firm is nonsense.'

'Well, I hope you'll at least give it a try, Antony. We

decided to invite you to take on the role of Director of Financial Development.'

The title rolled off her tongue. He could scarcely believe his ears. Director? He'd still be on the board – or team – or whatever they chose to call this stupid arrangement. He'd still have a chance to influence things.

All the same, he'd had an even better title. 'That's a bit different from—'

'No doubt you'd have preferred to stay on as deputy managing director, but Mr Patterwick feels your ideas are too strongly opposed to his – and mine. So . . .'

'So who's going to be deputy managing director?' Antony demanded, ready for the fight he'd been expecting, ready to throw up objections to any name she might mention.

'We're dispensing with that post.'

'I don't think you've the right—'

'Oh, yes we have, Antony. The letters of administration give me the right to run the company until probate is completed, and once probate's registered I'm the major shareholder – the vastly major shareholder. So it comes to this.' She forced herself to put some steel into her manner. 'The management committee is offering you the post of Director of Financial Development. The salary is somewhat less than you were receiving as deputy MD but you would remain in the office you now occupy. If you wish to travel abroad to study international stock markets, or hire university teams to make studies for us, Mr Gooding might very well be agreeable to that.'

'I'd have to get Gooding's *permission?*'

'Yes, Mr Gooding is in final charge of financial matters.'

That was the biggest hurdle. She could see he was

almost ready to baulk at that. He despised Alfred Gooding. Alfred Gooding had come up the hard way, through the cashier's office and night school. He knew nothing of the 'larger picture', the waves and graphs of university economics.

'Mr Gooding always had your father's confidence,' she pointed out, seeing him struggle with the notion. 'If we want the outside world to see Covelco going on as before – and that's what I want – Mr Gooding is an essential part of the team. The rest of the management committee are happy with him.'

Implied was the sentence, and if you're not, it's up to you to back out. She'd kept her tone resolutely cool. This was the make-or-break point: Antony had to come to terms with Gooding's superiority or his services would be dispensed with.

Antony didn't want to be dispensed with. His post at Covelco had brought him prestige and influence at an early stage in his career. He didn't want to go back to the beginning with a different firm, and certainly no one else would take him on at the level his father had given him.

He wondered what his mother would prefer him to do. She'd commanded him to put up a big fight if 'that woman' gave him the sack, but there'd been no advice on what to do if he was offered a different job.

It was better to accept. After all, he could always stage a big scene and walk out in the future if it became advisable. The essential thing, so his mother said, was to keep some sort of surveillance on Ruth Barnett.

'Very well,' he said with as much grace as he could muster. 'I do, of course, want to remain associated with the firm which my father built up.'

'Good, I'm glad,' Ruth said politely. 'Miss Krett will

give you a file of information on the management committee and its decisions so far. There will be a meeting on the first Tuesday of every month to review policy – the next one is in two weeks. I hope you'll attend.'

It was a dismissal. He bowed stiffly and went out, fuming at the way she ordered him about. It didn't occur to him that she'd given him no orders, only invitations.

Ruth watched the door close behind him. Well, that was over. But really, she couldn't help wondering if she'd have been better advised to get rid of him. He was not on her side, and it would be absurd to expect it. Worse still, he was under the influence of a woman who hated her. In other words, he was an enemy spy in the camp.

There was no one to whom she could confide these personal fears. The management committee were strongly on her side where the running of the firm was concerned, but she couldn't discuss Diana Coverton with them. Not even to her grandmother could she speak of Diana's behaviour.

Mrs Barnett had gone back to Freshton, promising to return for a Christmas visit and bring Granddad. This she did, rather to Ruth's surprise. Her grandfather had always been stern in his attitude over what he called loose morals.

Yet even his iron uprightness had bent a little. Ethan's accident and Ruth's steadfast care for him had touched him, and Ethan's death had shocked him. Then his wife had come back with these tales of splendour in London and, truth to tell, he was a little curious to see it for himself.

The Mayfair house impressed him. He couldn't help being pleased when Ruth had them all driven out to Kew to look at the winter wonderland of its plants. He enjoyed the simple pleasures of the Christmas pantomime. But what made the biggest impact on him was the office in Holborn.

Somehow it seemed absurd to say that the Coverton Electrical Company was the 'wages of sin'. The business-like atmosphere, the respectable attire of the workforce, the sheer size of the place and its efficiency – these were far from the scarlet rewards of vice as he'd always pictured them. No scarlet satin, no lolling about on divans. Nothing but the clatter of typewriters, the hurrying about of messengers.

So as the new year began, Roger Barnett went home to Freshton with a new opinion of his wayward granddaughter. He even kissed her goodbye on the platform at Waterloo. It was a comfort to Ruth to be reconciled at last.

And, as 1928 advanced, she needed all the comfort she could find.

The problems began with a telephone call from Tadsley and Gower. Mr Tadsley would like to see Miss Barnett as soon as possible. Ruth rang back to inquire and was put straight through to Keswick Tadsley himself. This was significant, because as a rule Niall Gillis dealt with her affairs. There had been no conscious choice in this; it somehow just seemed to have happened.

'I've had a communication from Mrs Coverton's law-yer,' said Tadsley. 'I think we ought to discuss the matter.'

'What sort of communication?'

'Let us talk about that when we meet,' he replied, in a tone that told her he wasn't in the habit of discussing important matters on the telephone.

She got through her afternoon's work so as to leave early and go to her lawyer's office in Dover Street on her way home. Niall was waiting for her in the reception area.

'Is it something bad?' she asked nervously when she saw his troubled expression.

'Well, it's not good.'

They went into Keswick Tadsley's inner sanctum. He rose to greet her. 'Dear lady, I hear you've been doing great things at Covelco!'

'Well, not quite. But we've picked up what we lost through the General Strike.'

'Excellent, excellent – a remarkable achievement.' When they were seated he went on, 'Unfortunately we may now be in for some stormy weather.'

'In what way?'

'Mrs Coverton now has a new lawyer – I understand she parted from Mr Romstock on the grounds that he had not looked after her interests properly. The new firm is Lethwaite Montgomery, an excellent partnership – John Lethwaite is the son of an acquaintance of mine, Rodney Lethwaite.'

Ruth cast a glance at Niall, as if to ask him for help. He responded by saying, 'Mr Tadsley is explaining that Mrs Coverton's solicitor is to be taken seriously, Miss Barnett.'

'I see. And you've heard from him?'

'He has entered a caveat to probate,' said Mr Tadsley. She waited.

'You realize, of course, that Ethan's will had to go for probate. This is seldom a swift procedure and involves making a statement of all the estate of the deceased. That meant including the house and contents of Fullerton, which was left to Mrs Coverton.'

'Yes, of course.'

348

'I explain this so that you understand Mrs Coverton's lawyer had to be kept *au fait* with what was going on. Everything was proceeding normally. Then this morning I received a letter informing me that John Lethwaite has entered a caveat, which means that he has some objection to probate.'

'But what objection?' Ruth asked, bewildered. 'What does that mean?'

'We have no way of knowing at present. The caveator, that's to say, the person entering the objection, has no obligation to spell out his reasons until he wishes to do so. It's a politeness, of course, on the part of Lethwaite to let us know the caveat has been obtained.'

Once more Ruth sent a glance of appeal towards Niall Gillis. What did all this legal jargon mean?

'The point is,' Niall said, 'that the caveat is valid for six months. Probate can't be completed until the caveat is withdrawn.'

'I suppose not. But in the meantime the letters of administration are still in force? The company can still operate?'

'Oh, yes, the courts would never allow the viability of a commercial enterprise to be jeopardized.'

'But Mr Tadsley, if everything can go on as before, why is the caveat so important?' Ruth asked.

'Because it augurs something more. Mr Lethwaite has some objection which must be amplified to us before too long.'

'An objection to what?'

'To the will itself, we presume.'

She sat in silence.

'The point is, Miss Barnett, that as everything concerning the title deeds to Fullerton and so forth was perfectly straightforward, Mr Gillis and I are led to the conclusion that there is some objection to the substance of the will. We have re–examined it, of course, since we received Mr Lethwaite's letter, and so far as we can see there is nothing dubious in its intentions or instructions. We are somewhat at a loss as to what to say to you.'

After a moment Ruth asked, 'Have you spoken to Mr Lethwaite? To ask his reasons?'

'Not yet. It was our duty to speak to you first.'

'What do you think it means?'

Mr Tadsley looked embarrassed, Niall said, 'We think it's Mrs Coverton making mischief.'

I should have known, thought Ruth, her heart sinking. She was never going to let me just take over Ethan's firm without trying to hinder me somehow.

'What should we do?'

'Well,' said Mr Tadsley, shrugging, 'we must, of course, ask Mr Lethwaite what he intends. When we discover that, we shall be better able to see our next step.'

Legal procedures are seldom swift. It was well into February when Mr Lethwaite responded to the request for information. Ruth went once more to the lawyer's office.

'My dear Miss Barnett,' said Mr Tadsley, quite unable to hide his distress, 'I fear this is going to grieve you very much. I have this morning a letter from Lethwaite Montgomery with the information that they have taken counsel's opinion in the matter of Ethan Coverton's will and are entering suit against you on the grounds of undue influence.'

She glanced from him to his junior partner. Niall was looking very serious. 'What does that mean?' she inquired.

'It means Mrs Coverton is accusing you of cajoling, coaxing or pestering Mr Coverton into making a will in your favour.'

It was so absurd that she almost laughed. 'That's nonsense,' she cried. 'Anyone who knew him would say at once that nothing could coax or cajole Ethan into doing anything he didn't want to do.'

'But,' Niall said, 'a judge in court would not have known Ethan.'

'In court? You're saying there's to be a court case?'

'I'm afraid so. And quite a good case can be made against you. At the time that Ethan made the will, he had just had a tremendous quarrel with his wife. He might then have been in a frame of mind to be cajoled.'

She stared, then gave a shrug of rejection. 'Is that what Diana is saying?'

'We have no idea what Diana is saying. We're simply going by the dates. Ethan went to Romstock and made a new will at about the time that he came to us to ask about the possibility of obtaining a divorce in some way, perhaps going abroad. At about the same time he bought the lease of the house in Mayfair and you moved in together. You'll recall we had several conferences here in this office.'

'Yes, I remember only too well!' How hateful it had been, to sit here trying to scheme up a way to get Ethan free of his marriage.

'My partner is laying out for you,' Mr Tadsley said, 'the kind of case that *could* be made. Ethan was in the grip of what they will call an infatuation . . .'

'No, that's not true.'

'Miss Barnett, I'm merely telling you what might be produced,' soothed the lawyer. 'Ethan wanted a divorce, his wife refused, he was angry and upset – I recall some of the expressions he used when talking about the situation – I have no doubt he was very angry.'

'Yes, he was,' Ruth acknowledged, 'and that may have been the reason he changed his will. It doesn't mean I had anything to do with it.'

'Nicely answered,' Tadsley said with a smile of approval. 'You have a head on your shoulders, Miss Barnett. However, the appellant will imply that while Ethan was in this state of emotional chaos – angry, frustrated, easily influenced – you made him write a new will.'

'It's not true,' she cried. 'It's absolutely not true! I knew nothing about the will!'

'That is exactly what the appellant's lawyer will expect you to say.'

'But I *didn't* know! Ask Mr Romstock. When he told me about it on the Tuesday after the funeral, I couldn't believe it!'

'Anyone can act as if they're surprised at good fortune, Miss Barnett.'

'Mr Tadsley!' She was too shocked at his words to do more than gasp in dismay.

'I'm only putting to you what the prosecution is likely to use. This is, of course, all supposition, but it's based on experience,' sighed the lawyer. 'Mrs Coverton will assail your character – and your character is not of the kind to influence a High Court judge in your favour. You were the mistress of a man much older than yourself. You lived with him in flagrant violation of convention. You tried to break up his marriage. When that failed, you persuaded him to make a will in your favour. That's how it can sound in court.'

To Ruth's horror and shame tears began to brim over and run down her cheeks. She put up her hands to hide her face. She heard a sound, and a hand touched her shoulder gently.

'Now, now, Ruth, that's not what *we* think. We know that it didn't happen like that. Don't cry, Ruth.'

The voice was Niall's. The kindness had the opposite effect from what he intended and she found herself sobbing helplessly. She opened her handbag, sought about blindly for a handkerchief. His hand stilled hers, found the scrap of cambric, and gave it to her. She mopped at her eyes.

When she was at last able to look up, Mr Tadsley was looking at her with a shamed expression. 'I'm sorry, my dear, perhaps I was somewhat too forceful in my enactment of the prosecution,' he muttered. 'I just wanted you to understand how very serious this is.'

'I – I understand,' she said between the dying sobs. 'I'm sorry, I shouldn't have made such a fool of myself.'

Niall was standing over her. If she could have looked up at him she would have seen that he was glaring at his senior partner.

'Don't let it worry you, Ruth,' he urged. 'We'll hire a first-rate barrister and he'll sort them out for you.'

'Aha!' cried Tadsley, taking refuge in the normal routines of the law. 'Let us order some tea and decide whom to hire, my dear boy!'

In her bewildered state Ruth almost giggled. When her entire world was being threatened, Mr Tadsley recommended tea and discussion.

But Niall patted her shoulder in reassurance. She made a big effort and pulled herself together.

She must prepare for a fight. There was no way she was
going to let Diana Coverton say that Ethan had been a
weak fool who could be talked into doing something
wrong.

For Ethan's sake – and for her own – she had to fight.
And win.

Chapter Twenty

By the time Ruth got back to her office in High Holborn, bewilderment over the train of events had given way to anger.

She said to Miss Krett as she swept past, 'Tell Mr Antony I want to see him.' Not 'Please ask Mr Antony if he can spare a minute,' nor 'I'd like to have a word with Mr Antony if he's available': it was a direct order.

Miss Krett, who had had dealings with Mr Antony in his moods before this, relayed the message to his secretary with some trepidation and was surprised to be told that he would be there directly.

He came into Ruth's office looking defensive and yet combative. He sat down, leaned back as if very much at ease, and said: 'I won't pretend I don't know what this is about. But if you think you can use it as an excuse to push me off the board of directors, think again.'

Ruth studied him. His fair good looks were marred by the sulky expression. He was avoiding her eye.

'I've no wish to get rid of you,' she said. 'Your name makes you a valuable asset to the company.'

'I'm glad you have sense enough to see that.'

'But it would be quite impossible for us to work in anything like harmony while this court case is pending.'

355

'We're not in harmony and never will be. I'm completely against your small-scale ideas.'

'My ideas aren't small-scale. Keeping Covelco in the lead of research in British wireless communication is not small-scale.'

'We need to go international if we're to compete with the United States.'

'We're not competing with the States. We've got our own line of products that no one can touch and we've got more to do with those before we rush into overseas investment. Your father—'

'My father only had half his attention on the business.'

'You're wrong there, Antony. He understood the importance of having outside interests. I think that's what's wrong with you – your whole attention is so concentrated on making yourself a big name in the international business world, there's nothing else in your life.'

She could see she had startled him. The sharpness of her manner was entirely new. And there was enough truth in what she said to make him pause.

'In any case,' she went on curtly, 'I didn't send for you to have a wrangle about your view of how to run Covelco. I sent for you to say that I don't want you around in the building until this case has been decided.'

'What do you mean? If you're trying to fire me . . .'

'I'm not talking about firing you. I just don't want to have to see you. Take a leave of absence.'

'Oh, yes? And when the court decides in my favour, I find you've let the whole thing run down with your crackpot notions.'

'Don't be absurd! I'd never do anything to harm your father's firm! In any case the management committee have the final say.'

'And a fat lot *they* know – a bunch of middle-aged has-beens—'

'Well, maybe they see you as a young never-was!' she riposted. 'All you've ever done is hang around waiting to step into your father's shoes, and let me tell you you're never going to be big enough to fill them.'

He gasped, as well he might. This girl he'd always thought of as some little country sparrow of his father's suddenly seemed more like a hawk.

'I want you out of the building by six tonight,' she went on, her grey-green eyes flashing with a momentary glint of hard emerald. 'The press will be here in hordes, I've no doubt, so you're to prepare a statement.'

'I'm what?'

'Think up some excuse for not being available. You're going to take a six-months' leave of absence.'

'I am not!'

'If you dare to enter this building tomorrow, you'll find your office locked.'

'Well, I'll unlock it.'

'You'll have a hard time because I'll have the locks changed.'

'You can't stop me from coming in—'

'No, but I can make sure you have no place to hang your hat!' She hardly cared what she said to him, she was so full of contempt for him. 'If you feel like working from a table in the canteen, that's your affair. But Miss Gunster will be transferred to other duties and no secretarial help will be afforded from the typing pool.'

'You can't do that!'

'I can and I will.' She stood up behind her desk, leaned on it with both hands, and stared at him. 'If you think you can bring an action against me suggesting I somehow tricked the man I loved into giving me his fortune and *not* earn my complete disgust, you're living in cloud-cuckooland.'

'You twisted him round your little finger.'

'Antony, the thing I hate most about you is that you can suggest things like this about your father *in public!* You and that domineering mother of yours are bringing this case without a thought of how it makes him look. *You* know and *I* know he wasn't a weak man – even when he was ill he had twice the strength of the likes of you!'

'He was a stupid old fool who didn't want to see that the world is changing around us! No foresight, no overview of the business battle – no, he was too busy cavorting round the world with his sugar-baby!'

'Calling me silly names isn't going to help you,' she said. 'I've heard them all and I know they don't refer to me. Now . . .' She paused and drew a breath, and to his own surprise Antony found himself waiting with trepidation for her words. 'I don't want to set eyes on you again until we meet in court. Don't dare to show your face.'

He'd expected a row when he came into her office but he'd been sure he would have the upper hand, chiefly because days ago he'd thought out what he was going to say. But, taken by surprise though she was, she'd somehow managed to take the initiative away from him. She wasn't scared, she wasn't confused – she was just contemptuous.

'I'll have a writ taken out ensuring I have access to my office,' he said, plunging at what he thought might work. 'Until the case is settled, you've no real right—'

'Yes, I have. Before I left Mr Tadsley he checked with the Office of Probate. Until probate is settled – and it can now only be settled in the Law Courts – the grant to me of power of attorney will remain in place.'

'That's what *you* say.'

'That's what the Office of Probate says. So go back to your room, pack up your personal belongings and get out!'

'If you think you can order me about like a filing clerk—'

'You have until six o'clock this evening. At six o'clock the Maintenance Department will lock up your office. If you're still inside it, you'll be locked in. So you'd better make sure you're on the outside of the door.'

'Who do you think you *are*?'

'I'm the woman you and your mother are accusing of trickery. Did you think I wouldn't be angry? You fool,' she said almost dismissively, 'you're so much under her thumb you didn't even look ahead to what it would be like once the suit was brought. Well, this is what it's like – you're *persona non grata* in this building until the matter's decided in court. So clear out.'

He too was on his feet now. He was in a rage – with her, with himself, with his mother. Why hadn't they thought about the months that had to pass before the case reached the courts? It hadn't occurred to him that Ruth Barnett would take any personal action against him: he'd thought he had the ascendancy over her when it came to the in-fighting of business. He'd intended to intimidate her, lord it over her, and by so doing, weaken her determination to take part in running the firm.

Ruth had rung the buzzer on her desk. Miss Krett came in. 'Mr Antony is going to dictate a statement,' Ruth said.

The atmosphere in the room was electric. Uncertain, a little scared, Miss Krett looked from one to the other.

'Sit down, Antony. Miss Krett, get your notebook.'

'Yes, Miss Barnett.' She scurried out.

'I'm not dictating anything.'

'If you don't supply some sort of reason to the press for your prolonged absence, I'll have to do it for you.'

'Don't you dare put out any statement in my name.'

'Very well, do it yourself. And have some sense, Antony. Don't say anything to damage Covelco. Don't forget, you're hoping to get it back from me in a few months, so you don't want commercial confidence to be shaken.'

'I'm not dictating any statement!'

Miss Krett came in, notebook at the ready. 'Miss Krett,' said Ruth, 'the heading is, Statement by Mr Antony Coverton and the date. "In view of the forthcoming lawsuit . . ."'

'Stop!' shouted Antony. 'I won't allow you to put out anything that I haven't written myself.'

'All right, get on with it.' She glanced at her watch. 'It's four o'clock. If you don't dictate something within the next two hours, you'll have no one to dictate it to.'

'Then the press will understand that you're forcing me out—'

'Quite right, that's how it will look. Is that how you want to appear to the City and the Stock Exchange? As someone who was forcibly ejected from the building? As someone who came whining to the office in the morning only to find his desk in the corridor?' She shrugged. 'Please yourself. But it doesn't seem to me to suit the young tycoon image.'

For answer, he stormed out of the room, almost knocking Miss Krett over as he went.

'Well,' faltered the secretary, picking up her notebook and pencil, 'this is a mood I've never seen before . . .'

'Go to his office,' Ruth commanded, 'and don't leave until you get a statement from him. Bring it straight to me.'

'Miss Barnett, what's going on?'

'The Siege of Mafeking,' Ruth said grimly. 'And there's probably worse to come.'

Antony's statement, when it was brought to her, was better than she'd hoped. He announced that he was taking a six months' sabbatical in order to write a book on economics 'which he had long planned'. With more good sense than she'd given him credit for, he left the building at four thirty by a side door. The reporters gathered in the hall missed him entirely.

But that scarcely mattered because those at Fullerton House, the Coverton family home, got good copy from Diana. She went on record as having always thought that her husband had been tricked into making the disputed will, that Ruth Barnett had only been one of a long string of women in her husband's life, that no doubt he'd made other silly bequests in his time but had generally come to his senses and cancelled them.

COURT BATTLE LOOMS, ran the headlines. WIFE AND SON SUE MISTRESS.

The hearing was put into the Michaelmas sitting of the Probate, Divorce and Admiralty Division before the Right Honourable the President, Lord Waitford, on 4 October, a Tuesday. For the plaintiffs, Mr Goodrich Reeder. For the defendant, Mr Merton Stillington.

Ruth had two meetings with Merton Stillington, her KC, both rather short. She had a feeling he disapproved of her personally. All the same, that didn't affect his determination to win the case. At their first interview he questioned her closely about her relationship with Ethan: she answered with perfect truth.

'It's just nonsense to say I persuaded him against his will. He was impossible to persuade about anything he'd already decided.'

'When he told you he'd changed his will in your favour, what did you say?'

'He never told me.'

'You didn't know you were his heir?'

'No.'

He narrowed his eyes to study her. He was a short man, with a pointed face rather like a fox. There was a long silence. Ruth sat waiting. Perhaps he thought she was lying. Perhaps now he'd decide not to take the brief.

He said: 'Very well. I'll discuss with Tadsley how to get depositions from witnesses.'

At the second meeting, he said, 'Mr Coverton's secretary is now working for you.'

'Miss Krett? Yes.'

'The plaintiffs are calling her as a witness. Can she damage you?'

'I don't see how.'

'Perhaps you'd like to transfer her out of your office.'

'Oh, no, I rely on Miss Krett.'

'Then you must assure me that you won't try to influence her about the evidence she intends to give.'

Ruth stared at him, colouring up. 'What kind of person do you think I am?' she said faintly.

To her surprise, he smiled. 'That will be all for now,' he said. 'We'll meet again on the fourth.'

The Law Courts, a Gothic façade at the eastern end of the Strand, must have looked rather charming when first built in the 1870s. The light-grey fretwork of stone would then have had airiness and a certain majesty. Half-a-century of London smoke and fog had darkened it so that even on a sunny day in early October, with the plane trees only just beginning to turn golden-brown, it had a forbidding look.

There were reporters on the shallow steps in front of the great oak entrance doors. By this time Ruth was accustomed to them. She had discovered there were two ways of handling them. She could stop and smile and say a brief word that told them nothing, or she could hurry through in silence. Experience had taught her that the second way was the better, because any word she uttered was likely to be distorted.

If she said she wasn't worried over the coming court proceedings, the headline would run: SMILING MISTRESS SHRUGS OFF CASE. If she said she had confidence in her counsel, the journalists translated it into: MILLIONAIRE'S WOMAN TURNS TO NEW MAN.

The central hall of the Law Courts formed a vestibule to the courts themselves. It had a mosaic pavement over which hung a marble gallery at each end. The vast ceiling was arched like a cathedral, but there was nothing cathedral-like about the echoes of conversation, footsteps, the calls of the court usher and the opening and closing of heavy doors. It was a very businesslike atmosphere.

Mr Tadsley came forward to meet her as she stood glancing about.

'Good morning, Miss Barnett,' he said. 'Mr Stillington is in court, we'll join him there when the usher beckons.'

The big plain clock in its box-case on the wall of Court Number Seven showed twenty-nine minutes past ten when the door opened and the official leaned out to murmur, 'Coverton versus Barnett?'

Mr Tadsley took Ruth with him into the court. She was relieved to find she wasn't asked to mount a special platform or appear in the box, but instead was shown to a seat in the row just behind Mr Stillington. The tall man along from him, also in wig and black robe, was presumably Goodrich Reeder, counsel for the plaintiffs. There were a couple of young men in wig and gown also sitting in the front bench, presumably minions of the lordly King's Counsels. In the row in which Ruth was sitting with Mr Tadsley there were men in black jackets and pinstripes: Ruth guessed them to be the lawyers of Diana and Antony Coverton.

The clerk of the court called it to order. 'Anyone having business before the Right Honourable the President of the Division of Probate, Divorce and Admiralty this Fourth day of October 1927, let him give attention. God Save the King.'

The judge appeared from a door behind the main bench set above the rest of the oak-panelled room. His robe was scarlet trimmed with ermine. He bowed, all the barristers and lawyers bowed in response, he sat down and surveyed the gathering. The time was exactly ten thirty.

There was no jury. This had surprised Ruth when she first heard of it, but Mr Stillington had explained that in the civil courts, juries were only used in actions for libel or slander. Ruth was glad. The fewer people who heard the awful things being said about Ethan, the better. But, of course, there were the reporters crowded around a small table in the well of the court and already scribbling eagerly.

'Gentlemen?' the judge said.

Mr Reeder rose, tall and imposing. 'If it please Your Lordship. I appear on behalf of the appellants, Mr Antony Coverton and his mother Diana Marianne Coverton, widow of Ethan Coverton of Fullerton House in Hertfordshire. My friend Mr Stillington appears for the defendant, Ruth Barnett of 15 Pouncey Square W.1.'

The judge nodded, adjusted his wire-rimmed glasses, and picked up his pen.

'My lord, the case against the defendant is that she used undue influence upon the late Mr Ethan Coverton to cause him to change his will in her favour.' He picked up a document on the desk in front of him. 'Your Lordship has a copy of the relevant document, dated 14 April 1925.'

'Quite so, Mr Reeder.' Lord Waitford picked the will out of a small pile before him on the bench.

'Until the death of Mr Ethan Coverton last year, it was accepted as a known fact that Mr Antony Coverton was the heir to the Coverton estate, that estate consisting not only of the family home and its contents and grounds, and Mr Coverton's private funds, but the electrical components firm known as the Coverton Electrical Company, or Covelco to use its trade acronym, together with its factories, warehouses and offices in various parts of the country. This estate has a value of well over one million pounds.

'My lord, the late Mr Coverton entered into a liaison with Miss Barnett of which his wife and son, and indeed the general public, were well aware. My client Mrs Coverton will give evidence to show that Miss Barnett had persuaded Mr Coverton to ask his wife for a divorce, and I will offer proof that in revenge for Mrs Coverton's refusing the divorce, Miss Barnett decided to obtain a hold on

Mr Coverton's fortune, no doubt as a bargaining counter to force Mrs Coverton to agree to the divorce.'

Ruth made a movement of repugnance. Mr Stillington glanced round at her and gave a minute shake of the head. He had told her that the case against her would be based on attack on her reputation. 'The relationship between yourself and Mr Coverton can be made to look very black,' he had remarked, with the air of a man quite used to dealing with such problems. 'So sit very quiet and look very demure.'

He had even advised her what to wear. 'Something dark with a little white trim,' he mused. 'And a smart but plain hat — no decoration on it, no bunches of flowers. The judge who'll preside doesn't approve of women who spend a lot on clothes.'

'Very well.'

'And gloves, of course, and plain shoes – no gold clips or diamanté buckles.'

So here she was in a two-piece costume of dark green rep, with a white blouse to show at the neck. Her hair was neatly tucked under a dark green felt cloche. Her shoes were of dark green suede to match her gloves and bag.

Mr Reeder laid out the bones of his case, bowed, and sat down. Mr Stillington rose.

'I appear for the defence, my lord. My client utterly refutes the idea that she ever discussed his will with the late Mr Ethan Coverton and moreover that anyone could persuade him to do anything that he did not wish to do. The defendant's case does not rest on many facts that can be brought before Your Lordship, but rather on the refutation of any supposed facts offered by the plaintiffs.'

He bowed and sat down. The bailiff called: 'Mr Antony Coverton.'

Antony came in and, sworn in by the bailiff, stood in the witness box, a large railed-in enclosure up a short flight of steps and just to the left of the judge's bench.

Mr Reeder rose.

'You are Antony Coverton of Fullerton House near the village of Fullerton in Hertfordshire?'

'I am.'

'Are you in some way concerned in the Coverton Electrical Company?'

'I am. Until the death of my father I was deputy managing director.'

'You father appointed you to that post?'

'Yes.'

'What was his reason?'

'He wished to give me a good grounding in the running of the company so that I could take over from him when he retired or in the event of his death.'

'Did he tell you this was his reason? In so many words?'

'Oh, yes. Often.' Antony hesitated.

'Go on,' urged his counsel.

'We didn't see completely eye to eye on the running of the firm. I, of course, had the opinion that his ideas were a bit old-fashioned.'

Ruth understood that Antony had told his counsel of the disagreements. Mr Reeder had thought it best to get them out into the open as soon as possible and account for them.

'The young are inclined to think so of their elders, I imagine,' Reeder said easily. 'How did this show itself?'

'When he talked of my taking over the company in due course, he would say, for instance, "By that time I shall have knocked some sense into you" or, "You've plenty of time to get the better of these notions before you step in"

– he was half joking, of course, but serious in the prediction that I would be taking over.'

'Did he at any time – after he became acquainted with Miss Barnett, for instance – say that he had changed his mind about leaving you the company?'

'No, never.'

'It was your understanding that you were his chief heir?'

'Yes.'

'Thank you, Mr Coverton.'

Antony relaxed, but only momentarily, because Mr Stillington rose to take Mr Reeder's place. Mr Stillington was in no hurry to begin his examination. He glanced through some papers in his hand, cleared his throat, arranged his robe more comfortably on his shoulders and then said, 'A will is in general a confidential document, is it not?'

'Yes.'

'You had never actually seen a copy of the will that you supposed would leave you the entire estate?'

'No. But I knew there was a will. Mr Greville Romstock, the family solicitor, had it in his keeping.'

'Mr Romstock approached you after the death of your father, in order to let you know the contents of the will?'

'Er – no – as a matter of fact,' said Antony, 'we approached him. My mother and I, I mean.'

'And he then apprised you of the will's contents?'

'Yes.'

'You were surprised?'

'Astounded.'

'You had no reason to think your father might have changed his intentions?'

'No.'

'You were on good terms with your father?'

'Yes.'

'You said before, that you and he didn't agree about how to run the firm?'

'But that was only in the ordinary way of business. It's impossible for two people to be in the same business without having occasional disagreements over planning or production.'

'Occasional disagreements?'

'Yes.'

'After Mr Coverton Senior became attached to Miss Barnett, you never had disagreements about that?'

'Well . . .'

'Yes?'

'I tried to talk some sense into him. My mother was very upset. I tried to make him see he was making a spectacle of himself.'

'How did he take your suggestions?'

'He shrugged them off. He'd done the same over other women in the past.'

' "He shrugged them off." You never had a serious row over the relationship with Miss Barnett?' asked Miss Barnett's counsel.

'No.'

'I call to your mind a day in February of 1925. Your father sent for you to his office and there followed a very violent argument.'

'No.'

'You deny that Mr Coverton sent for you and that you had an argument?'

'Well – we may have had a disagreement.'

'About Miss Barnett?'

'Yes.'

'During which Mr Coverton told you that you were

never again to go to Crecy Court, where she lived, or if you did, he would have the doorman throw you out?'

'No, he didn't say that.'

'He further said that if you were disrespectful to Miss Barnett, he would dismiss you.'

'That's not true.'

'You had been to Crecy Court to see Miss Barnett and had created a scene.'

'I— I went to see her to ask her to break off the affair.'

'The daily maid came into the room because she was alarmed for Miss Barnett, isn't that true?'

'No. Well, yes, she came in, but I was leaving and she came to show me out.'

'The doorman at the block of flats was given instructions not to let you in if you came again.'

'I don't think that's so.'

'We can easily call the doorman, James Johnson, if necessary. You were not to go near Miss Barnett, and at the argument in your father's office he told you this, isn't that true?'

'Well, he said he didn't want me to see her.'

'And if you persisted in interfering, he would dismiss you.'

'He didn't say that! We were only together a few minutes.'

'A short interview, but a very heated one.'

'That's not true. He never even raised his voice.'

'No, but when you went into the room you left the door unlatched, and what you were saying could be heard in the outer office.'

For a moment Antony looked appalled, but recovered. 'The discussion was not heated. It's true my father asked me to stay away from Miss Barnett. He explained his feelings about her and I left. That's all.'

'I see. And you were on amicable terms thereafter.'

'Yes. We worked together at the office.'

'At the family home?'

Antony looked up at the arched windows of the court as if seeking inspiration. 'No,' he said at last, 'but then he was seldom there.' Quickly, he went on. 'He had always stayed away a lot – sometimes on business, sometimes to attend racing-car events. When he was at home, we were on amicable terms.'

'Your father continued to come to the family home from time to time?'

Antony knew it was no use saying Ethan had been near the house in Fullerton in the eighteen months before his death because the servants, if summoned as witnesses, would have to say he had not.

'No, he stopped coming.'

'Never came?'

'No-o, but we still saw each other at the office.'

'And you were good friends?'

'We got on all right.'

'A close working relationship?'

'I wouldn't— I wouldn't say "close". But the distance between us had nothing to do with the business side. I was his deputy, the assistant managing director. Nothing changed in that respect.'

'He continued to talk about the time when you would take over?'

'Yes.'

'Indeed?' said Mr Stillington sceptically, and moved on to something else. 'Your father was seriously injured in a racing-car crash in Sicily?'

'Yes.'

'When he was brought home by flying boat, you were at the Thames dock to greet him?'

'Well . . . no.'

'He was taken to his house in Pouncey Square and over some months was convalescing there?'

'Yes.'

'Did you go to visit him?'

'No.'

'When Mr Coverton began to feel better, he took up the reins of business from his home. Members of the firm were asked to visit him to discuss the firm. You were aware of this?'

'Yes.'

'Were you invited?'

'No.'

'Your father sent instructions about forward planning and on some matters to do with the purchase of a new factory?'

'Yes.'

'How did you receive these instructions?'

'Mr Patterwick, the research manager, brought them.'

'Did you agree with the instructions?'

'Well, more or less.'

'Did you do anything about those with which you disagreed? Did you go to see your father?'

'I telephoned and we sorted thing out.'

'A man who was going to inherit the business ought surely to have closer contacts with the owner and managing director?'

'Not necessarily.'

'It didn't occur to you that your father had changed his mind about your future role in Covelco.'

'Certainly not.'

'Thank you, Mr Coverton.'

There was a slight delay while Mr Reeder looked through some papers. Then the next witness was called.

'Mrs Diana Coverton!'

If Diana had been given advice about how to please the judge by her choice of clothes, she'd chosen to ignore it. She was wearing a light brown coat trimmed with red fox against which her glossy dark hair showed up beautifully. Her hat was small, so that her fine aristocratic features could be well seen.

She took her son's place in the witness box. Mr Reeder smiled at her as he rose to begin his examination. She returned his smile while agreeing she was Diana Marianne Coverton of Fullerton House in the county of Hertfordshire, the widow of Ethan Coverton of 15 Pouncey Square in Mayfair. Having to agree Ethan's address as Pouncey Square clearly annoyed her.

'Did your husband discuss his will with you?' asked Reeder.

'Yes, he said he was leaving the firm of Covelco to Antony, and that his private fortune was to be divided between myself and my other two children, Martin and Lorette.'

'When was this?'

'It was about the time that Antony left university and joined the firm. Ethan said that he was grooming Antony to take over one day, and that as Martin showed no interest, he wouldn't expect him to go into the firm but he must have enough to live on. And, of course, my daughter Lorette – well, he wanted to provide for her although he always said she'd marry well.'

'Did he tell you later that he had changed his will?'

'No.'

'Were you surprised that he did?'

'More than surprised. I couldn't believe it. I couldn't believe that Mr Romstock – that's our solicitor – would let him do such a thing.'

'You are aware of the date on which the new will was drawn up?'

'Yes, it was a few days after Ethan and I had had a dreadful row about *that woman*.' She glared across the court at Ruth. 'He came to Fullerton to ask me for a divorce. I, of course, refused.'

'You have strong views on the sanctity of marriage?'

'Of course. "Whom God hath joined let no man put asunder." '

At this point the judge could be seen to be nodding to himself in agreement.

'Your husband was aware of your views?' Reeder asked.

'Mr Reeder,' said the judge gently, 'Mrs Coverton's views on matrimony are scarcely to the point.' Though he agreed with her sentiments, he didn't intend to let that mislead them.

'If Your Lordship will allow, I will bring out the point. Mrs Coverton, you thought your husband knew your views, I imagine? So what were your feelings when he put the request?'

'I knew he would never have done it if that woman hadn't put him up to it. She wasn't the first, of course, but he'd never been so infatuated as to want to *marry* one of them. This time he was so much under her evil influence he came to talk about divorce though he was well aware I thought the mere idea disgraceful.'

'How did he take your refusal?'

She hesitated and allowed herself a little shudder of

distaste. 'I can only say he was a changed man. He stormed at me, and when I refused to give in – because you see I knew he didn't really know what he was doing—'

'M'lud,' said Mr Stillington, rising, 'I don't believe Mrs Coverton has been shown to be an expert on psychology or mental conditions?'

'Quite so, Mr Stillington. Mr Reeder, your witness's view of her husband's mental state is not germane.'

'Very well, m'lud. Mrs Coverton, your husband was nevertheless very angry at your refusal?'

'Yes,' agreed Diana, looking a little confused at the exchange between the judge and the defending counsel. 'He was very angry and declared he would never enter the family home again.'

'When you were made aware of the contents of the new will, and of its date, you associated these events?'

'Oh, yes, I think when he got home to that woman and she heard she'd lost that round, she got at him to—'

'M'lud, this is mere supposition.'

'I agree. Mrs Coverton, you must restrict yourself to answering counsel's questions.'

'Let me go back, Mrs Coverton. You associated the date of the new will with the date of the row over the divorce?'

'I did.'

'Until that time your husband had been on good terms with his family?'

'Oh, yes.'

'He ran his business efficiently?'

'Yes.'

'There was nothing in his manner or demeanour to make you think he was losing his grip in the days before the row over the divorce?'

'Nothing at all. But there's an element of revenge in disinheriting his family – and Ethan was not a vengeful man.' As she said this she gave the judge a hesitant smile, as if to say, 'Will you allow me to say that?'

'He never got his own back on people?' asked Reeder.

'Never. Only pressure from someone else could have made him behave in that way.'

'Thank you, Mrs Coverton.' Reeder sat down.

Diana watched the defence counsel get slowly to his feet.

'Mrs Coverton. Quite some years ago, your husband settled on you some of the shares in his company, the Coverton Electrical Company?'

'Yes.'

'Your sons Antony and Martin and your daughter Lorette, also received shares?'

'Yes.'

'They bring in a substantial income?'

'Yes,' snapped Diana.

'So, when Ethan Coverton changed his will, he didn't leave you penniless.'

'No, but Antony—'

'Antony's expectations were disappointed. But he has the income from the shares and a salary from the company?'

'Yes, but he would have had it all if that woman hadn't pushed him out.'

'Have you ever met Miss Barnett, Mrs Coverton?'

'Certainly not!'

'Then you have no way of knowing whether she could influence your husband to change his will.'

'She changed him! He made a spectacle of himself with her! She was different from the others he'd played about

376

with – she got her claws into him so that he didn't know what he was doing!'

'He continued to run the company successfully—'

'The company ran itself! He was off with her at motor-car racing here and there all over the world – you can't say he was running the company. Antony was doing that.'

'He had always given a lot of his time to motorcar racing. Your son testified that he was seldom at the family home long before he met Miss Barnett.'

'The difference was that she went with him everywhere. The others before her, he just saw them now and again in London but that woman went everywhere with him. Of *course* she influenced him. He was besotted with her.'

'Did your husband have a high opinion of your son Antony as a businessman?'

'Of course he did. Antony took a good degree in economics at Cambridge. Ethan thought highly of that, he himself only went to one of the Northern universities.'

'Your husband wanted to see Antony put his economic theories into practice in the firm?'

'Yes.'

Ruth couldn't help a start of surprise at this blatant lie. She leaned towards Mr Tadsley to murmur, 'That's completely untrue. Ethan thought Antony was talking nonsense.'

'Your son testified that they didn't see eye to eye on such matters,' remarked Ruth's counsel.

'Oh, Ethan would have come round. But that woman made sure it didn't happen.'

'How could she do that, Mrs Coverton?'

'Well, when he was supposed to be so ill in that house in Mayfair, people went to see him. But *she* made sure that Antony was never invited.'

'But, Mrs Coverton, the will disinheriting Antony was made long before that – before the accident, before your husband ever went to Sicily.'

'Yes, but— But she prevented them from making up.'

'She did? There had been a major quarrel and she prevented them from making up?'

'Yes, of course.'

'What was the quarrel about between your husband and son?'

'Why, her, of course!'

'But your son has told us there was no quarrel.'

'Well, he . . . I mean, Ethan could be . . . You have to understand how difficult . . .'

'No further questions,' said Mr Stillington, and subsided smiling into his seat.

The judge consulted the clock on the wall. 'Mr Reeder, how many more witnesses do you intend to call?'

'Two more, m'lud – Miss Lorette Coverton and Miss Krett.'

'Then I think we may adjourn now for lunch. Before we go, Mr Reeder . . . This case depends on the state of mind of the testator at the time that he changed his will. Is there any medical evidence on that?'

'M'lud, Mr Coverton was not under the care of any doctor at that date.'

'The domestics? Are they being asked to give evidence?'

'Unfortunately, m'lud, at the time when the new will was executed – at and around the date 14 April – Mr Coverton was in process of moving into the house at Pouncey Square. The servants were quite new to the household and could have no useful opinion of Mr Coverton's state of mind at that time.'

'A servant was mentioned as intervening at the former

address . . .' His Lordship sought among his notes. 'Crecy Court. Is that servant to be called?'

'Her name, I believe was Mrs Monash – yes, Mrs Monash,' said Reeder, verifying it. 'She was a daily maid who left the premises every evening before Mr Coverton came home from the office. She therefore never got to know him.'

'I see.' The judge debated with himself. 'His lawyer, then? Let me see.' He shuffled through his papers. 'Mr Romstock?'

'We are not calling Mr Romstock, m'lud,' said Reeder in a dismissive manner. 'The Coverton family is very dissatisfied with the conduct of Mr Romstock in allowing this iniquitous will to be made. They did not wish him to testify. In fact, they are taking the matter to the Law Society.'

'Mr Stillington?' said the judge, cocking his head at Ruth's counsel. 'Are you calling Mr Romstock?'

'M'lud, we approached Mr Romstock but he was very unwilling to appear in view of the ill will being expressed against him by the Coverton family. He felt his evidence would seem biased.'

'A very discreet stand to take. All the same, I think I would like to hear Mr Romstock. I shall ask him to come in the role of *amicus juris*, and to appear as one of your witnesses. But that will not be until tomorrow, I imagine. Well, we will resume at two o'clock this afternoon.' He rose, everyone rose with him, he bowed and walked out.

'What does that mean?' Ruth asked Mr Tadsley as he escorted her out to the hall.

'What, *amicus juris*? Friend of the court. It's rather like an expert witness.'

The reporters clamoured for quotes as they went out to

the Strand. There the faithful Bignall was waiting with the Rolls to speed them off to the Savoy for lunch.

Ruth could eat very little. Mr Tadsley and the barrister chatted easily, as if nothing of great moment were involved. By and by Niall Gillis joined them, eager for news.

'Sorry I had to miss the morning session,' he said, 'something came up at the office. How's it going?'

'Very well, I think,' said Merton Stillington. 'They're going to have a hard time proving there was any undue influence.'

'I don't just want it *not proved* that I talked him into it!' Ruth burst out. 'I want to be proved innocent!'

Everyone was silent. Then Tadsley said sadly, 'Ah, my dear, that's not a very common event in an English court of law.'

Chapter Twenty-One

The hearing resumed with Lorette Coverton on the witness stand. She told Mr Reeder her name and address in a voice so timid and nervous as to be almost inaudible. Ruth felt an impulse of pity for her. It must be frightening to be the target for the questions of the barristers, and she remembered that she too would have to take her place on the stand, perhaps today, perhaps tomorrow.

'Speak up, Miss Coverton,' said the judge kindly. 'The proportions of this court aren't helpful to easy listening.'

'Yes, sir,' whispered Lorette.

'Now, Miss Coverton . . . You have met Miss Barnett?'

'Yes.'

'Will you tell us when this was?'

'At Easter two and a half years ago, at a *concours d'élégance* for motorcars. My father was there with his Rolls-Royce, and Miss Barnett was with him.'

'Did you speak to them?'

'I spoke to *her*,' muttered Lorette. 'I went up to tell her how awful she was making things.'

'And what did she say?'

'She had the cheek to tell me that nobody had loved my father until she came along!' Resentment made Lorette put more force into her voice. She looked up and around the court for the first time, her blonde complexion almost angelic in the dark room. 'And later, when I got to know Dave Epps, he told me—'

'One moment. Who is Dave Epps?'

'David Epps – he was the chief mechanic on my father's racing cars. He was always with him, both before and after Ruth Barnett came along, and, of course, he saw them together a lot, and he told me—'

Mr Stillington was getting to his feet. 'M'lud? This evidence?'

'Quite so. Mr Reeder, where are we going with this?'

'M'lud, this *concours d'élégance* was at Easter. Mr Coverton changed his will ten days later. My intention is to show Miss Barnett's influence over him at that time.'

Lord Chief Justice Waitford took off his spectacles, to swing them by one side-piece and look thoughtful. 'Miss Coverton, was your father with Miss Barnett when you spoke to her?'

'No, sir, he'd gone to look at someone else's car.'

'He rejoined Miss Barnett while you were speaking to her?'

'No, sir, it was Dave who came up while we were speaking.'

'Dave – er – David Epps,' supplied Mr Reeder, for the sake of the court record.

'Yes, and later I got to know him and he told me quite a lot about what was going on. He said they were practically in each other's pockets.'

Ruth was astounded to hear that Lorette even knew Dave, let alone set any store by what he told her. Of course, Dave was always one for the ladies . . . But this relationship, if it had begun at the Easter meeting, had lasted much longer than usual.

And what, she wondered, did the family think of it? David Epps, a mere mechanic, a man who got grease on his hands, who wore overalls . . .?

Mr Stillington was back on his feet. 'M'lud?'

The judge put his spectacles on again. 'Mr Reeder, let us see where you are going with this, but please ask the witness to restrain herself only to what she knows of her own personal knowledge. What she heard from someone else is of no use.'

'As Your Lordship pleases. Miss Coverton, can you give us more of the conversation between *yourself* and Miss Barnett?'

'Well, she said if my mother was bitter she'd no right to be.'

'How did it come into the conversation, the remark about your mother?'

'I said Mummy was bitter about *her* – Ruth Barnett – and she took out her bitterness on others and it made me very unhappy, and *she* said that Mummy should have more concern for me than to take out her bitterness on me. And later Dave told me—'

'Mr Reeder,' said the judge, frowning, 'the witness must not report hearsay from Mr Epps.'

'M'lud, I felt it important you should hear from the only member of the family to have met Miss Barnett other than Mr Antony Coverton.'

'Can she give, from her own observation, anything concerning the state of mind of her father at or about the time he altered his will?' The judge transferred his gaze to Lorette. 'Miss Coverton, can you offer direct evidence of the defendant's power, if any, over your father?'

'Well, she went absolutely everywhere with him.'

'Did you meet her on such occasions?'

'No, sir, only the once at the *concours d'élégance*,' replied Lorette, puzzled because she thought she'd already made that plain.

'On that occasion did the conversation turn to her intentions with regard to Mr Coverton's money? Or about the family business?'

'Oh, no sir, she'd hardly talk about that out in the open.'

'What did she say, in general?'

'She said Martin shouldn't have written that silly song that was sung in the nightclub.'

'A song!' repeated Lord Waitford, astonished.

'Yes, my brother Martin wrote a silly song about my father. I *did* think that was a bit much, actually.'

The judge looked as if he was trying not to laugh. 'Mr Reeder,' he said, relinquishing the witness to the barrister.

'Miss Barnett expressed animosity towards your brother Martin?' asked Reeder. 'Towards your mother?'

'Yes. No . . .' Lorette floundered. 'Well, anyway, Dave told me she thought we were a dreadful bunch . . .'

The judge had had enough. 'I fear I must rule that what this witness wishes to tell us is mostly second-hand information and quite inadmissible even if it were to the point. To be clear – she met the defendant once?'

'Yes, m'lud.'

'Her father? Miss Coverton, did you speak to your father at any time after his liaison with Miss Barnett began?'

'Well, now and again, when he was at home.'

'Mr Reeder?' urged the judge, having set up a train of questions he would admit.

'After he met Miss Barnett, did he seem different?' Reeder asked.

Lorette's unlined forehead creased in thought. 'I don't think so . . . He and I never had much in common. I wasn't interested in the business or in racing cars, you see. So we never had much to say to each other and I don't know that he was any different . . . I'm sorry,' she added, knowing she had disappointed him.

'Thank you, Miss Coverton,' sighed Mr Reeder, and sat down.

The judge glanced at Mr Stillington, who shook his head. His Lordship said kindly, 'You are excused, Miss Coverton.' Lorette, gasping with relief, blundered down from the stand.

Niall Gillis had accompanied Ruth and Mr Tadsley to the court for the afternoon session. He said in an undertone to his senior partner, 'If that's the best Reeder can produce, he must be in a bad way.'

Meanwhile the usher was calling for Maisie Krett. Miss Krett came in, clutching her handbag. She mounted the stand, was sworn, and agreed she was Maisie Elizabeth Krett of 23 Mudeford Gardens, Epping.

'Miss Krett, you are employed by the Coverton Electrical Company?' inquired Mr Reeder, leaning back and taking hold of the folds of his gown as if for a long session.

'Yes, I joined the company when my then employer Mr Bullock of Oxylee Components was directed into their research department at the outbreak of the war.'

'You later became Ethan Coverton's secretary?'

'Yes.'

'How long did you hold the post?'

'From 1919 until Mr Coverton's death.'

'You knew him well?'

'As an employer, yes.'

'At a certain date in 1924, did you break your wrist?'

'Yes, and this made me unable to take shorthand dictation. A junior was sent from the typing pool to help me in that respect.'

'And the junior was—?'

'Miss Barnett.'

'When you recovered the use of your right hand, what did you do?'

'I recommended to Mr Coverton that he could dispense with the services of Miss Barnett.'

'What was his reply?'

'He said he wished to keep her attached to his office.'

'What was your view of that?'

'I thought it improper.' The reporters at the press bench scribbled furiously, 'Improper!' but crossed it out when Miss Krett added, 'A girl so junior should not have had preference over others of greater seniority.'

'What followed with reference to Miss Barnett?'

'Quite suddenly she resigned.'

'Did that surprise you?'

'Very much. To give up such a good job was strange and ungrateful.'

'Later did you have a view of this action?'

'I realized that Miss Barnett had resigned because she and Mr Coverton were carrying on an affair. Her resignation then became understandable – it would have been difficult to keep their relationship a secret if she had remained in the office.'

'Was the relationship much talked about in the office?'

'Regrettably, yes. I learned that Miss Barnett had *volunteered* to come and take dictation from Mr Coverton in the first place. This was seen by many as her way of getting to the executive wing.'

'She had manoeuvred herself into the position?'

Miss Krett stood silent for a moment then replied, 'That was being said.'

'So as to begin a relationship with Mr Coverton?'

'I can't say what her motive was.'

Mr Reeder consulted his notes. 'When Mr Coverton's liaison with Miss Barnett became known through the press, what was your opinion?'

'M'lud,' intervened Mr Stillington, 'the opinion of the witness—?'

'I will allow it, Mr Stillington. The witness was in a good position to observe. You may answer, Miss Krett.'

'I was shocked,' Maisie Krett said roundly. 'Mr Coverton had had other lady friends—'

'Indeed?'

'Yes,' Miss Krett confirmed, looking at a point near the ceiling.

'How did you know of them?'

'I was often called on to send flowers or chocolates in Mr Coverton's name. But it was all very discreet, there had never been any publicity about these ladies although in the office their existence was known or suspected. I was shocked and surprised to see that he took Miss Barnett with him openly to motor racing and social events, both at home and abroad. That seemed to imply she meant more to him than the others.'

Ruth felt a stab of pain at the words. Their truth was a sorrow and yet a joy. Yes, she had meant more to him than any of the others. He had given her an inestimable gift – his trust, his confidence, his love. Later, as a last token, he had given her money – money and property that she didn't want, scarcely knew how to cope with. She would have given it all back just to have Ethan at her side again, sharing his laughter over some absurdity in the world around them, hearing his shouts of encouragement to his car's driver.

But he was gone, and she was here, in this gloomy courtroom, wrangling over his fortune.

'She was not *like* the other ladies in Mr Coverton's life?' Mr Reeder was asking Miss Krett.

'No. From the little I knew of those, they appeared to be satisfied with far less of Mr Coverton's attention. But then they didn't share his interest in motor racing, as Miss Barnett did.'

Mr Reeder didn't look very pleased at this reply. 'Motor racing? Miss Barnett was really interested in *racing cars*?' This was said with amazement, and expected the answer 'No.' But counsel should never ask questions to which they don't already know the answer, for Miss Krett surprised him.

'Oh, Miss Barnett was devoted to motor racing. I believe she originally met Mr Coverton on a racing track.'

'Hmm. You said you were shocked that Miss Barnett went about publicly with Mr Coverton. You felt it harmful to Mr Coverton's reputation, I take it. Did the office staff speak of him with disrespect?'

'Not to *me*,' Maisie Krett said sharply.

'No one ever expressed an opinion on the newspaper reports?'

'Miss Giles, Mr Antony's secretary, remarked to me that Miss Barnett was feathering her nest, and good luck to her. I reproved her.'

This was more to the questioner's taste. ' "Feathering her nest," ' he quoted, savouring the thought before moving on to his next angle. 'Before she left the office, how did Miss Barnett get on with Mr Antony Coverton?'

Miss Krett said unwillingly, 'Not very well.'

'Can you give us an instance of this?'

'She was often ordered to take dictation from him and would come back saying he was "difficult".'

'So she had something of a grudge against him?'

The witness allowed herself a small smile. 'Not especially. Mr Antony wasn't regarded as easy to take dictation from.'

Ruth heard Diana snort 'Disgraceful!' at this disclosure. Antony himself was shaking his head as if to say, You simply can't expect loyalty these days.

The barrister moved briskly away from that unsympathetic view of his client. 'Mr Antony was generally considered to be Mr Coverton's heir?'

'Oh, yes.'

'Was this just hearsay, or did you know this from Mr Coverton himself?'

'Well, he would say things like, "One day that boy will grow up enough to be able to handle this firm." Or "Before I shuffle off this mortal coil I've got to teach him how to run this desk."'

'In other words, his general attitude was that Antony Coverton would inherit Covelco?'

'Yes.'

'Thank you, Miss Krett.'

'Thank you for nothing!' muttered Diana Coverton.

Mr Stillington gave the secretary a little bow of respect when he stood up. He had understood that she had been called to give evidence she would rather have kept to herself. 'Miss Krett, when Mr Antony's secretary said Miss Barnett was feathering her nest – implying that her liaison with Mr Coverton was a matter of commerce – did you agree?'

'I did then. But later I changed my mind.'

'Why was that?'

'The devotion that Miss Barnett showed when Mr Coverton was injured made me feel I was wrong.'

'On a day in February of 1925 – this is going back to a time just after Miss Barnett had left her job and was known to be the companion of Mr Coverton – did Mr Coverton send for his son into his private office?'

'Yes.'

'When Mr Antony went in, did he accidentally leave the door unlatched?'

'Yes.'

'Did you hear the ensuing quarrel?'

'M'lud,' protested Mr Reeder, rising.

'Quite. Don't lead the witness, Mr Stillington.'

'I apologize, m'lud. I will rephrase. Did you hear the ensuing encounter?'

'Yes.'

'Would you please give us what you consider the main point that you heard?'

'Mr Coverton told his son to stay away from Miss Barnett or would dismiss him from the firm.'

'Did he sound as if he were in earnest?'

'Very much so.'

'Did he raise his voice? Shout at his son?'

'No. He spoke in very level tones.'

'But you heard him?'

'Oh, yes. I had been taking dictation from Mr Coverton for years – I was accustomed to all his tones of voice.'

'Had there been disagreement between father and son before that?'

Miss Krett hesitated. 'There had been some incidents— Mr Antony could be obstructive to his father's wishes.'

'In what way? Can you give us an example?'

'I don't know whether I have the right to discuss Covelco business in public.'

'Miss Krett,' said His Lordship, 'we are here on Covelco business. We are trying to decide the rightful ownership of Covelco. Anything you can tell us to make matters clear would be helpful and should be said.'

'I see. Well, for instance, there was a property in Lancashire that Mr Coverton wanted to buy. It would have enabled us to enlarge one of our factories there. He left the negotiations in Mr Antony's hands because he, that is, Mr Coverton, was going to a motor-racing event in France. Mr Antony let the property go to a rival buyer. Mr Coverton was vexed.'

'Indeed?' said Stillington. 'Vexed because the property was lost to him?'

'That was one reason. The other was that he felt his son had allowed the purchase to fail by intention.'

'He said so to you?'

'He said, if I remember rightly, "That young fool just wants to make life difficult for me these days." '

'Miss Krett, just to keep the record straight – you are still employed by Covelco?'

'Yes.'

'In what capacity?'

'I am now Miss Barnett's secretary.'

'Have you and Miss Barnett had any conversation about the evidence you would be asked to give today?'

'Certainly not!' declared Maisie Krett with great indignation.

Ruth smiled. No one who knew the upright, fastidious Miss Krett would have needed to ask that question. It often crossed Ruth's mind to wonder why the secretary stayed on in the firm. Fundamentally, she knew, Maisie Krett disapproved of her and the past liaison with Ethan. Yet she stayed on, and served Ruth faithfully. Perhaps she was being faithful to Covelco. Whatever her reason, she was an excellent secretary.

'When the contents of Mr Coverton's will became known, was there a great deal of talk in the office?'

'I'm sorry to say there was.'

'What were the expectations of the staff?'

'They thought Miss Barnett would sell up and live comfortably on the proceeds.'

'That would have been the reaction of what is commonly called "a gold-digger", would it not? Thank you, Miss Krett.'

Mr Reeder rose again. 'Miss Krett, you've said there was some friction between father and son. Surely that is quite common in business – little disagreements are bound to occur?'

'That's quite true. Mr Coverton and Mr Antony had often been on opposite sides of an argument even before Miss Barnett came on the scene.'

'So if Mr Antony decided to disobey his father's orders regarding the property in Lancashire, it may well have been that he had a different view about the business possibilities in it.'

'That may have been part of it. But while Mr Coverton was absent I reminded Mr Antony that there was a deadline for making a bid. His reply made me think he was being careless on purpose to annoy Mr Coverton.'

'That was only *your* interpretation of what he said,' Mr Reeder said in haste, intending to close a line he was sorry he had opened.

'Let us not rely on interpretation,' said Lord Waitford.

'What was Mr Antony's reply?'

'He said, as near as I can recall, my lord, "If the boss can't be bothered to give up his little trip with his bit of fluff, why should I bother to do his job for him?" '

Counsel for the plaintiff made an effort to retrieve the situation. 'In other words, Miss Barnett's influence over Mr Coverton was taking him away from important matters of business.'

'Oh,' said Miss Krett with complete sincerity, 'Mr Coverton was always one for going off to motorcar events, long before he met Miss Barnett.'

Mr Reeder had had enough. 'Thank you, Miss Krett,' he said. To the judge he bowed. 'That concludes the case for the prosecution.'

Rather than have the defence open at once, Lord Waitford decided to adjourn so as to hear direct evidence of the testator's state of mind from Mr Romstock. 'We will resume at ten o'clock tomorrow, gentlemen,' he told the barristers, 'in hopes of getting something to the point.'

Mr Tadsley was beaming as he went out with Ruth to the car. 'You seem pleased,' Ruth said in some surprise, for to her it was utter misery to hear the problems of the Coverton family and the Coverton business aired in public.

'Of course, he's pleased,' said Niall. 'You heard what His Lordship said – he hopes tomorrow to get "something to the point". In other words, he's very irritated with the plaintiff's case. Up till now he thinks they've been wasting the court's time.'

'Do you really think so?'

'Good heavens, my dear lady,' Tadsley exclaimed, 'it's all a string of nonsense! They need to bring solid proof that Ethan Coverton was persuaded against his better

judgment or while in a vulnerable state to change his will.
There isn't a scintilla of evidence.'

'The marvel to me is why the case was brought at all,'
Niall said.

'I can only suppose Mrs Coverton and her son insisted
on bringing it against protests from their advisers.' Tadsley glanced at Ruth. 'You've had some dealings with the
lady. Is she headstrong enough to insist even when she's
warned against it?'

'Oh, yes,' sighed Ruth. She was thinking that Diana
Coverton hated her enough to do anything if she thought
it would harm her. And though her lawyers seemed
optimistic, Ruth could find little comfort in that. Tomorrow she would have to take the stand after Mr Romstock
and talk in court about Ethan, and she felt she would
rather die, rather take the first boat across the Channel
and hide somewhere until it was all over.

Yet she couldn't do that. She had to speak about her
love for Ethan and Ethan's love for her, otherwise Antony
would be given ownership of the company, and that was
clearly against Ethan's wishes.

For Ethan's sake, she would go to court tomorrow and
wait her turn to be put on show.

The car dropped the solicitors off at their office. Niall
leaned in to say, 'Get a good night's rest, Ruth. And don't
be afraid, things are going well so far.'

So far. But what would the judge think of her, he who
had almost nodded agreement when Diana Coverton
repeated the words, 'Whom God hath joined let no man
put asunder'? He had, she was almost sure, the usual
prejudice against 'the other woman'. His first instinct
would be to support the general view of society, that a
man should leave his property to his wife and children, not

to some rapacious creature with whom he'd been living *in flagrante*.

Ruth had no illusions. She knew how strongly most people felt against her, firstly because she appeared to have broken up a marriage and secondly because she had *profited* by it. True, a High Court judge was supposed to be impartial, not swayed by prejudice or gossip. Yet even a High Court judge was unlikely to have an unbiased view of 'the millionaire's woman'.

Mrs Monash had afternoon tea waiting, and a folded copy of the early edition of the *Evening News* on the tea tray. 'Want to read it?' she asked as she set the tray before Ruth.

Ruth shuddered. 'No, just tell me what it says.'

'Well, they concentrate on Mrs Coverton. SOCIETY LEADER IN COURT, TYCOON'S WIDOW SPEAKS OUT. Then there's quite a lot about what everybody was wearing. Young Miss Coverton,' Mrs Monash said with irony, 'seems to have been very appealing in dark blue that matched her eyes.'

The phone rang. Ruth was sure it would be the press but Mrs Monash announced it was Mr Epps. Ruth went to the instrument.

'How'd it go, Ruthie?' he asked. 'The papers are having a field day!'

'Mr Tadsley and Mr Gillis seem hopeful. Listen, Dave, what's been going on between you and Lorette Coverton?'

There was a shocked silence at the other end. At length he said, 'How d'you find out?'

'She was trying to tell the court what you thought about Ethan and me. The judge ruled it inadmissible.'

'Thank the Lord for that!'

'You mean you were saying bad things about us?' Ruth said, hurt.

'No, no, listen, you've got to understand. Lorette's been taking her opinions from her mother all her life so far. She was determined to think you were – well – you know . . .'

'And what did you say?'

'I tried to explain it wasn't like that. I mean, I told her about how close the two of you were, how he liked to have you around all the time . . .'

'And the barrister was trying to get her to say I'd gained power over him.'

'Nah!' said Dave, scornfully. 'I never told her that!'

'Well, luckily, it was all hearsay so it got struck out of the evidence. But look here, Dave, what do you think you're up to with Lorette?'

'I'm not "up to" anything.'

'Because if you're playing fast and loose . . .'

'I'm not, I'm not, I swear it!' He hesitated, then plunged on. 'Thing is, Ruth, I'm stuck on her.'

'What?'

'I'm serious about her.'

'About Lorette Coverton?'

'Yes, I want to marry her. But her mother would come after me with a hatchet as things are, and I can't say I'd blame her. I mean, I haven't anything to offer her, I'm just a garage hand, aren't I?'

'So that's what you wanted the money for? To have a business and gain some respectability with the Covertons,' Ruth said, suddenly seeing it all.

'Well, yes.'

'Why didn't you tell me that? About Lorette and everything?'

'Well, tell the truth – I— It hurts me to talk about it, Ruth. It's all so hopeless— I mean, even if I can start my own business, it's still a long way below what "Mummy" expects for her darling daughter.'

'How does Lorette feel?'

'Scared,' said Dave succinctly.

'But does she want to marry you?'

'Sometimes yes, sometimes no. Her mother is the big noise in that family, as I dare say you know. Whatever Mummy says is right. It's taken Lorette a long time to agree that the boss probably didn't take up with you just to spite Mummy.'

Despite herself Ruth laughed. 'Poor Lorette. I think you've got your work cut out for you there, Davie.'

'Oh, the blinkers'll come off one day. I just hope it's before Mummy gets her married off to some aristocratic twit. Listen, Ruth, I didn't mean to get into all this. I only rang to say, chin up, you'll come out on top. I'm sure.'

'Thank you, Dave.'

Dave's troubles were enough to keep her mind off her own at least while she had tea and looked through the afternoon post. Her grandmother had written to wish her well, and there were notes of support from some of the motor-racing fraternity. Later Patterwick rang to say that everything was going well in Holborn.

I've got lots of friends, she thought. Yet she felt lonely, forlorn. There was no one person to whom she could turn, no one to talk over the day's events with.

She thought of ringing Tadsley and Gower. There would still be someone at the office. Perhaps Niall Gillis would come to the phone.

But that was unfair. There were other clients besides

herself. She ought not to expect to monopolize his attention.

She had no idea, of course, that Niall was sitting looking at his telephone telling himself she needed rest and quiet and that he ought not to disturb her.

She slept badly, her dreams haunted by images of the courtroom: Diana's haughty glance and her voice calling her '*that woman*', the judge smiling kindly at Lorette, Mr Stillington's foxlike features with the dim light of the arched windows upon them.

In the morning, heavy-eyed and pale, she got into the car for the journey to the court. Niall Gillis was already waiting for her at the door of Court Number Seven.

'A bad night?' he asked with sympathy as he saw her.

'Do I look as bad as that?' she parried, summoning a smile.

He cursed himself for a blundering idiot, but she was already going in to take her seat.

Mr Romstock was called at once. When he had been sworn and taken the stand, Mr Stillington rose to establish his identity and his credentials.

'I understand you wish to make a short statement to the court, Mr Romstock.'

'Thank you. My lord, I should like it to go on record that although I am appearing at your request and on the list of witnesses for the defence, I had already *declined* an invitation from Mr Stillington to give evidence.'

'Quite so, Mr Romstock.'

'Your Lordship heard yesterday that the plaintiffs refused to consider taking testimony from me, accusing me of bias against them.'

'Indeed, and I also understand they have entered a complaint with the Law Society.'

'Yes, my lord, on the grounds of negligence. In those circumstances I felt it wrong to take any part in the court case, but of course at Your Lordship's invitation I felt I had no option but to come.'

'I'm very glad to hear it,' said Lord Waitford in tones that implied he might well have sent a constable for him if he had refused. 'Mr Stillington? If you're ready.'

'Thank you, m'lud. Mr Romstock, you have been the solicitor of the Coverton family for some years?'

'Something like twenty-five years.'

'You have also been a family friend? Invited to their house and so forth.'

'Yes.'

Diana Coverton was heard to mutter that she wished she'd never had him in her house. Her lawyer made soothing noises.

'You drew up a will for Mr Ethan Coverton?'

'I drew up two wills for Mr Coverton.'

'I mean the will which, by general belief, left Mr Coverton's fortune to his wife and family.'

'Yes, I drew up that will, although I prefer not to specify its contents.'

'You subsequently, in April of 1925, drew up another will?'

'Yes.'

'Leaving almost everything except the house at Fullerton to Miss Ruth Barnett?'

'Yes.'

'Can you tell us something about the meeting at which Mr Coverton asked you to draw up this will?'

Mr Romstock sighed and straightened his shoulders. 'I was extremely surprised at his request. I remonstrated with him. He told me to stop arguing and produced a handwritten version of what he now wanted. It was almost exactly in the terms he'd already mentioned.'

'Did you agree to draw up the new will?'

'I first of all asked him to explain why he was making this tremendous alteration. I felt it my duty both as a friend and as a lawyer – I could not understand why he felt Miss Barnett a fit person to inherit both his private fortune and the firm which Antony had always regarded as his by rights.'

'Did he give you his reasons?'

'Yes.'

'What were they?'

'He had been two days previously to see Mrs Coverton, to ask for a divorce so that he might marry Miss Barnett. He said that his wife had responded in such a manner as to make him decide to alter his will.'

'What was his state of mind?'

'He was very calm, very firm.'

'Nothing unbalanced about him?'

'Not at all.'

'Did you fall in with his wishes after having heard his reason?'

'I tried to dissuade him. I said that while he might at that moment be angry with his wife, he would get over it. He said he was angry but he would not get over it. His wife had used expressions to him that he could never forgive. I then said . . .'

'Go on.'

'That if he was angry with Mrs Coverton, that was still no reason for disinheriting his son. I tried to show that Antony had done nothing to deserve the change in the will.'

Diana Coverton at that point made sounds of contemptuous disbelief. It earned her a glance of rebuke from the judge.

'What did Mr Coverton say about his son in regard to the new will?'

'He said that Antony was under his mother's thumb, that recently he had behaved in a very unbusinesslike manner merely to make life unpleasant at the office, probably at his mother's instigation.'

'Utter nonsense,' huffed Diana. Her lawyer and her counsel both bent towards her to urge silence.

'Please go on, Mr Romstock.'

'Mr Coverton said his wife had always thought that making electrical components was plebeian, and that Antony had no interest in research, only in the financial side of the business. He said Antony would like to use Covelco as a bargaining counter in financial deals which would be to the detriment of the research side of the company.'

It was Antony's turn to show annoyance. Mr Reeder turned to shake his head warningly at him.

'Mr Coverton was telling you that he felt his wife and son to be unsuitable heirs?'

'That was his view. I then said that, if what he said was true, that seemed no reason to make *Miss Barnett* his heir.'

'And what was his answer?'

'He said Miss Barnett was the only person close to him who saw the aims of the Coverton Electrical Company in the same way as he did.'

'Did you continue to argue against it?'

'I did, but he was adamant. In the end I said I would draw up the will and let him know when it was ready. My view was that meanwhile he would reconsider.'

'And did he?'

'No. Two days later, before he signed and had the will

attested, we went over the ground once again. I was very insistent that he think deeply before making these new legacies and perhaps made him see I needed to be convinced. He said he was changing his will because his wife had said she hoped he would die soon.'

'That's a lie!' cried Diana. 'I never said any such thing!'

'Silence!' called the court usher.

'But it's not true! Ethan made it up!'

'Silence in court!'

The judge thumped his desk with the gavel. 'Mrs Coverton, please remain silent.'

'But it's a travesty—'

'If you will not behave, Mrs Coverton, I shall have you removed from the court.'

Diana sank back in her place. Ruth could feel the fire of her glance as she glared at Romstock. But she had no time to pity him. Her mind was still reeling at what the lawyer had reported.

Diana had told her husband she wanted him dead?

It's my fault, thought Ruth. If Ethan had never met me, Diana would never have come to hate him.

'Mr Romstock,' continued Mr Stillington, 'did you believe what Mr Coverton told you?'

'I did,' Romstock replied. 'Mr Coverton was a hard-headed businessman. He was not given to fantasy.'

'Mrs Coverton's remark was part of the quarrel over the divorce, I take it?' Stillington urged.

'Yes. She refused to set him free to marry Miss Barnett. She said that Miss Barnett was under the protection of Ethan Coverton but if he died, there would be no one to look after her. Therefore Mrs Coverton said she hoped he would die soon so that she could harry Miss Barnett. This was the sense of the scene as he related it to me.'

Mr Stillington let a little pause ensue. 'Did you then give up the attempt to prevent Mr Coverton from signing his new will?'

'Yes, because in view of what he told me, it seemed a waste of time. I certainly couldn't argue in favour of a wife who had hoped for an early death for her husband. However, I still felt Mrs Coverton had spoken in the white heat of the moment and had not really meant it. I felt that in due time Mr Coverton would understand that it was an outburst of anger and indignation on her part, not intended seriously. I said so to him. He replied, "You don't know Diana." As later events showed, he was right.'

'What events do you mean, Mr Romstock?'

'I refer to events on the day of Mr Coverton's death a year ago.' Mr Romstock stopped for a moment to find a handkerchief and pat his brow. He was clearly very unhappy at being where he was.

'When you are ready, Mr Romstock,' said Mr Stillington, sensing the suspense in all the listeners.

'I received a telephone call from a junior partner in the firm of Tadsley and Gower. I knew the firm by name – it was the one Ethan Coverton used in general for contractual matters at Covelco. The caller, a Mr Gillis, said Miss Barnett had been in touch with him in great distress.'

'For what reason?'

'Miss Barnett had rung Mrs Coverton to tell her of the death early that morning of Ethan Coverton. Mrs Coverton had responded by saying that she wanted Miss Barnett out of the house in Pouncey Square immediately or she would have her turned out.'

All eyes turned to Diana, expecting another outburst.

But this time Diana sat transfixed, eyes half-closed, one hand up to her mouth. It was just possible she was looking into the past and realizing her mistakes.

'How were you involved in the matter, Mr Romstock?'

'Mr Gillis asked me to contact Mrs Coverton and make her aware that she had no power to turn Miss Barnett out of the house. His firm had dealt with the matter of the lease, and he informed me that it was (and still is, I imagine) in the name of Ruth Barnett.'

'What steps did you take?'

'I telephoned Mrs Coverton at once to tell her that Miss Barnett owned the lease.'

'Yes?'

'I . . . er . . .'

'To remind you of your train of thought, you introduced this topic because it concerned your view of Mr Coverton's wife.'

'Thank you. Yes. I'm afraid I found that day very distressing. It distresses me still to recall it. Mr Gillis had had to tell me of the death of my friend and I was in some grief over the matter. I began my telephone conversation with Diana Coverton by offering my condolences. Her reply was . . .'

'Yes?'

'Her reply was, "Never mind that. I was just going to ring you. Send someone to get that girl out of that house." '

A little silence ensued.

'Did you explain the situation to her?'

'I did. It was not an easy task. She expressed herself with what I can only describe as vindictiveness towards Miss Barnett. I could not help remembering as we spoke that her husband's body was not yet cold. When I put the telephone down, I felt that Ethan had been right – where his wife was concerned he had changed his will for good reason. And, having accepted that, I felt that he had probably been right on the matter of his son's unsuitability to inherit the firm.'

Antony Coverton gave a faint groan of despair.

'You are saying that when he made the will Ethan Coverton knew what he was doing, and was not influenced in his action by Miss Barnett?' asked Mr Stillington.

'He was influenced in his actions by his *wife*, and knew what he was doing.'

'Thank you, Mr Romstock.'

The reporters were writing hard. One of them got up and scuttled out, clutching copy to read over the telephone for the noon edition. Mr Reeder got up and stood staring at the brief on his desk before at length beginning his re-examination.

'Mr Romstock—'

The lawyer met his gaze squarely.

'You were concerned when Mr Coverton told you his wife had said some unkind things to him.'

'Very.'

'When Mr Coverton told these things to Miss Barnett, no doubt she too would have been concerned, and urged him to take some reprisal.'

'M'lud,' said Stillington, 'that is purely hypothetical.'

'Quite right, Mr Stillington. Mr Reeder, please—'

'Your Lordship, if I may?' Mr Romstock intervened.

'Mr Romstock?'

'May I answer the question?'

'Ahem. Answer it and I will see whether to allow the question and the answer.'

'Miss Barnett could not have given Mr Coverton any urgings about reprisals. Mr Coverton never told Miss Barnett about the changes to his will.'

'How can you possibly know that?' Reeder asked with great scepticism.

'He told me so. When we were having the discussion just before the signing, I asked him what Miss Barnett thought about it. He replied that he hadn't told her and never would, because it would mean telling her what Diana had said. He said he would never hurt her by repeating that kind of thing to her.'

Mr Reeder looked towards the judge's bench, as if wishing His Lordship would now rule the whole thing inadmissible. The judge merely sat in attentive silence.

'Let us leave the ill will between Mrs Coverton and Miss Barnett—'

'Objection, Your Lordship,' exclaimed Stillington, half rising.

'On what grounds?'

'The phrase "ill will between Mrs Coverton and Miss Barnett" implies it was mutual. While I have heard many expressions of ill from Mrs Coverton towards Miss Barnett, I have heard none from Miss Barnett.'

His Lordship favoured Stillington with a slow nod of appreciation. 'A very neat point,' he acknowledged. 'Rephrase, Mr Reeder.'

Reeder chose to drop the matter. 'Let us turn to Mr Antony Coverton,' he said. 'Given that Ethan Coverton was angry with his wife, it seems perhaps reasonable that he should leave his private fortune elsewhere. But the family firm, which everyone expected Antony to inherit: it seems hard that his son should suffer so great a loss?'

'That was for Ethan to decide.'

'But does it not seem likely he had some help in making that decision? We have heard evidence that Miss Barnett disliked Mr Antony—'

'M'lud, we have heard no such evidence!' cried Mr Stillington, leaping up.

'Mr Reeder?' inquired the judge.

'We have heard that Mr Antony went to see Miss Barnett and in some way offended her. It is reasonable to think that she disliked him, m'lud.'

'Well, I will allow it. Go on.'

'Miss Barnett would have shaped Mr Coverton's thinking about his son?'

'I'm not sure I understand what you mean,' said Mr Romstock.

'Mr Coverton followed his own wishes with regard to provision for his wife. The change with regard to Antony is due to Miss Barnett's influence.'

'I don't think so, because when I read the will to her, she was astonished.'

Mr Reeder shrugged. 'Play-acting.'

'I have been a lawyer for thirty years and have read the contents of wills to hundreds of people. I am a fair judge of their reactions.'

'Who does he think he is?' hissed Diana to her lawyer. 'The man's a fool!'

'I put it to you, Mr Romstock,' Reeder persisted, 'that when you take part in a moment of crisis, you can be misled. For instance you have given us a very unlikely account of what Mr Coverton said when he came to give instructions for the new will.'

'Is that an imputation against my integrity?'

'I'm merely suggesting that your memory has played you false.'

'I think not,' Romstock said with immense dignity. 'I still have the handwritten note he brought, and because I was so concerned I took copious notes of our conversation. I still have them.'

'You brought them with you?' inquired the judge.

'Yes, my lord, they are in my briefcase. I can produce them immediately if you wish.'

'Thank you, I should like to see them.'

'No further questions,' said Reeder, baffled.

'Mr Romstock,' said the judge, 'in order to help me understand the scene – what did Miss Barnett actually say when you read her Mr Coverton's will?'

'She said, my lord, "It's a mistake, everybody knows Antony is the heir." '

'Thank you, Mr Romstock. You are excused.'

Ruth had heard it all with feelings that fluctuated between horror and dismay. She longed to run out of the courtroom, to splash cold water on her face, to breathe fresh air. But in a moment she would be called to the stand. She braced herself.

The judge was speaking in low tones to the clerk of the court, who was standing up at his desk to listen. He turned, and Ruth expected the usher to be told to direct her to the witness stand.

Instead the clerk came from his desk to speak to the front row of barristers. The bewigged heads were together for several moments. Then there were noddings, and the barristers sat back in their places.

The clerk spoke to the usher. The usher stood up and called, 'Clear the court! Please clear the court!'

'What's happening?' Ruth asked Niall.

'I'll ask.' He went behind the barristers, leaned over to confer. In a moment he was back at her side. 'The judge wants to speak to counsel in Chambers.'

'And what does *that* mean?' she asked, not the least enlightened.

'Everyone has to leave the court except counsel and His Lordship.' He was urging her out as he spoke. 'The judge wants to discuss some point of law with them in private. We'll be told when they've finished. Come on, let's get out on the steps for some air.'

But it was a vain hope, because the reporters ambushed them outside the door of Court Number Seven.

'What did you think about Mrs Coverton wishing her husband dead?' 'Is that true, she tried to throw you out of your own home?' 'Look this way, Miss Barnett, look at the camera, Ruth!'

The hall bailiffs came to quell the throng. 'Silence! There are cases going on in other courts! Be quiet!'

The crowd around Ruth suddenly melted away. It had become obvious that Diana Coverton was having an almighty falling-out with one of the clerks from her lawyers. Ruth slipped away into the shadow of an arched hallway leading to a flight of steps. Here she stood with her forehead against the cool stone until, after what seemed a very short time, she heard her name being called.

Niall took her arm. 'We've been called back into court.'

'What do you think is coming now?'

'God knows, after a morning like this,' he said in bewilderment.

It took some time for the court to reassemble and settle down, despite repeated cries of 'Order!' and 'Silence in Court!' The public gallery in particular was seething with impatience.

The judge came in, took his place and surveyed the barristers at their bench.

'Gentlemen,' he said, 'after hearing the evidence of the last witness, and in view of the lack of anything like hard facts in the case for the plaintiffs, I have come to a decision.

'This case is an example of the most frivolous behaviour I can ever remember in a court of law. It is clear to me the suit was brought out of a desire for revenge. While this desire is all too human, and perhaps understandable on the part of a wronged wife, the justice system is not the place for a vendetta.

'I have found not a shred of evidence that Miss Barnett influenced Mr Coverton in the making of the will now at Probate. On the contrary, I am convinced that she knew nothing of its existence until Mr Romstock read it to her after the death of Ethan Coverton. I have read Mr Romstock's notes taken at the time and they bear out all he said.

'Whether Mrs Coverton and her son believed Miss Barnett to have influenced Mr Coverton over the making of the will, I very much doubt. From the evidence of Miss Krett and Mr Romstock, Ethan Coverton does not sound like a man who could be influenced against his better judgment, and I am sure both wife and son knew this.

'Antony Coverton hoped perhaps to get back his inheritance, but his mother was not motivated by anything so logical in bringing this action. I have inquired, and find that she was advised against bringing it to court because of the lack of grounds. That she insisted, to my mind, demonstrates she merely wanted to damage Miss Barnett if she could.

'I have stopped the trial at this point because the

evidence of Mr Coverton's solicitor, who drew up the new will, was to my thinking conclusive. It showed decisively that Mr Coverton's mind was not at all clouded by infatuation for Miss Barnett or any weakness of that kind. Rather it was inspired by a wish to take away any reward to a family from which he felt alienated. Some may say that it is wrong to leave an estate away from one's own kith and kin, but the law of England allows a man to dispose of his property in any way he chooses, and Mr Romstock was constrained to follow Ethan Coverton's instructions.

'Had the plaintiffs dealt sensibly with their former solicitor and listened to what he could have told them about the making of the new will, they would have seen there was no case. But good sense has been sadly lacking in their behaviour.

'I have decided to stop the trial at this point because the time of the court and its officers should not be wasted in this absurd manner. My belief is that Mr Coverton knew what he was doing when he instructed his solicitor and felt he had good reason for it.

'I therefore dismiss the action against Ruth Barnett as being groundless. I give judgment *against* the plaintiffs Antony Coverton and Diana Coverton in the matter of the accusation of undue influence against the defendant and, in the belief that the action was brought from reasons of malice, I direct that costs be given against the plaintiffs.

'The business of the court is closed. Thank you, gentlemen.'

Chapter Twenty-Two

The judge rose, bowed, and left the bench.

The courtroom erupted.

The public gallery rang with cheers and shouts of 'Serves you right!' The reporters rose en masse to rush at the principals of the trial. The ushers called for order, shoved people towards the doors.

Niall cried: 'Perfect!' Mr Tadsley jumped to his feet to shake hands with Stillington.

Antony Coverton was sitting with bowed head groaning: 'Oh, God, oh, God.' His mother was weeping hysterically into a lace handkerchief.

Only Ruth Barnett sat unmoving.

The first feeling that surged through her was one of utter relief. It was over! Over! And she was completely exonerated.

The next impulse – and later she had to admit it to herself and feel ashamed – was triumph. She couldn't help feeling exultant at seeing the humiliation of Diana Coverton.

And then came joy, a surge of pure, unadulterated joy. Ethan's love for her had been shown to be real and vibrant, not due to some failure of reason or foolish infatuation. She had not had to take the stand to talk about dear, intimate things. Mr Romstock had saved her from that by his account of the making of the will.

The man himself pushed his way through the reporters to offer his hand. 'I'm glad it has ended well for you,' he said. 'Ethan spoke of you with so much affection.'

'Thank you, Mr Romstock, thank you.'

'Miss Barnett! Miss Barnett! What are you going to do now?'

'Are you going to sue, Miss Barnett?'

'Did you know what Romstock was going to say, Ruth? Ruth, can we have an interview?'

The reporters were yelping at her. The usher was trying to get them out of the room. 'Gentlemen! Ladies! This is not allowed!'

With Niall's help they were eventually out on the steps. He said in her ear, 'I think if you could answer a few questions and give them a smile or two, they might back off a bit.'

She saw the sense in it. She had avoided them during the trial itself, uncertain whether she would be strong enough not to break down in front of them. Now she paused while the reporters and cameramen grouped about her.

'Are you going to bring suit against Mrs Coverton?' asked the man from *The Times*.

'Whatever for?'

'Well . . . Slander? Harassment?'

'I have no intention of bringing any kind of action. As far as I'm concerned, the matter's closed.'

'What about the son, Ruth? Are you giving him the push from the firm?'

'Of course not.'

'Ruth, Ruth, give us a smile, Ruth! This way, look this way!'

'What are your plans now, Miss Barnett?' This was *The Sketch*.

'To get back to normal as soon as possible. To run Mr Coverton's company the way he'd have wanted it run.'

'How d'you feel, Ruth? Tell us what you felt when you realized you'd won?'

'If you'll just be quiet a minute I'll tell you how I felt and how I look at things.' They huddled round her, pencils at the ready, cameras pointed. 'I'm happy, of course, very happy, but I've hated it all because it seemed so – so *unworthy*. Now I want to put it behind me and get on with things. I'm sure the other members of Covelco feel the same as I do, that we owe it to Mr Coverton to get back to real life. We've been living in limbo these last few months while the trial was pending.'

'But what about Mrs Coverton? Don't you want to make her pay?'

'She's paying now,' Ruth said in a voice so low they had to bend close to hear her.

'Ladies and gentlemen,' Niall intervened, seeing the glint of tears on Ruth's lashes, 'I think that's enough, don't you? Thank you for your co-operation.' He began to force a way out to the pavement.

'Ruth, Ruth! Are you going to celebrate now?'

'My paper would pay well for an exclusive, Miss Barnett!'

Shrugging them off, they got to the car. Bignall was standing there with the door open, an enormous smile on his face. 'Fell into her own pit, didn't she?' he murmured as he helped Ruth in. 'Lovely to see you come out of it so well, miss.'

At the house there was a different crowd of reporters. Once more, at Niall's suggestion, Ruth paused to make a short statement, much like the one she'd made outside the Law Courts: that she was happy and relieved it was all over, that she intended to put it behind her. She was asked if she would be celebrating and to this, this time, she said she thought she would. 'A few friends this evening, perhaps,' she said. The idea pleased her.

As Niall was leaving she said to him, 'Will you come this evening? Nothing elaborate. Ask Mr Tadsley if he'd like to come.'

'I'll be there,' he assured her, grinning with pleasure.

Inside, Mrs Monash was so transported with delight when she heard the news that she almost threw her arms round Ruth. 'Oh, miss, miss, it's great, it's just what I have prayed for! Oh, marvellous, wonderful! I bet you're happy, dear!'

'I am, Mrs Monash, and that being so, I'm going to give a little party this evening. Can you order in some food? Nothing fancy – just cold meat and salads and stuff. Bignall, would you go into the cellar and bring up some wine?'

Mrs Monash darted to the kitchen to write out a list of requirements. Ruth went to the study to ring Covelco's headquarters. But Patterwick had already heard the news. The financial columnists had been on to inquire about Covelco's plans.

'I congratulate you, Miss Barnett, I really do. It's the very best result we could have hoped for – not just proved not guilty, but proved that there never was a case against you in the first place.'

'Thank you, I feel the same.' She invited him and the rest of the management committee to the celebration, and Miss Krett and a few others from the executive wing.

Then she rang David Epps who whooped with delight at

her news and accepted the invitation to the party at once.

'I'll bring a few of the boys, shall I?' he asked, meaning drivers and mechanics from the racing world.

'Please do. The more the merrier.'

Mrs Monash volunteered to stay so as to look after the catering. 'But what about your husband?' Ruth inquired.

'Could I ask him too, miss? He's always so interested in everything I tell him, and he'd be handy for bringing up the wine and opening bottles and things.' So Harry Monash in his best suit went about beaming and offering trays of food when the guests started arriving.

Niall was one of the first. He brought her a bunch of hothouse carnations wrapped in green tissue paper with white ribbons and a card saying, 'Here's to the future!'

Quite what it meant, she wasn't sure. Now that everything was settled, she wouldn't be seeing him much. He must mean the future of the company, she supposed.

If Niall had hoped to spend much time with her that evening he was disappointed. By eight o'clock the race driver of the Covelco car, Peter Stokes, had arrived with a covey of companions from the racetrack and assorted girlfriends. They made a strange mix with the sober-suited men from Covelco's head office and the black-clad secretaries. I must bring in a regulation allowing girls to wear coloured dresses, thought Ruth to herself in a moment's quiet. I must do something about brightening up the canteen too.

Her mind seemed unable to settle. When neighbours dropped in to congratulate her on the result of the hearing, when someone started putting on gramophone records for dancing, it all seemed to be happening on another planet.

If only Ethan could have been here . . . That was the

thought that returned oftenest to her mind.

David Epps turned up rather late, about nine thirty when the party was in full swing. He had a girl with him, a girl who hesitated behind him in the crowded hall and seemed almost unwilling to appear.

Ruth was just about to say, 'Who's your shy girlfriend?' when a movement of people revealed her.

To Ruth's amazement, it proved to be Lorette Coverton.

And what was even more amazing – and startling – was the fact that behind her were Antony Coverton and a young man whom Ruth had never actually met but knew to be his brother Martin.

At sight of Antony she stiffened. 'No one invited you here,' she began.

'Hang on, Ruthie,' Dave interrupted. 'Lorette and I had a date this evening and when you invited me I told her about it because I had to arrange to meet her later than we'd planned. But then she asked me . . .'

'I begged him to bring me, Miss Barnett,' Lorette took it up. 'I felt so awful when I heard what was said in court. I had no idea— I mean I was led to believe— I mean, you just don't know what Mummy is like . . .'

Martin Coverton stepped forward. Clearly, would-be playwright that he was, he'd rehearsed what he wanted to say. 'Miss Barnett, I was never in favour of this court case from the outset. Believe me, as far as I was concerned it was an idiocy . . .'

'Martin, that's no comfort to Miss Barnett,' his sister broke in. She tried to put on a smile. 'Martin always tries to take a lofty tone, you see. But us mere mortals have to live among other people and *I've* had to live with Mummy – and you've no idea how difficult that's been.'

'I can imagine, but that's no reason to go into court and distort things that you'd heard from Dave.'

'You're right, you're right, but I didn't know they were distorted. Dave used to tell me how you badgered Daddy not to take risks, and made him wear his driving goggles, and things like that, and when I told Mummy she sort of made it seem— I can't explain— I've always thought she knew best, you see. But now I begin to think – perhaps she's been terribly wrong all along.'

Some of those in the hall were too engrossed in their own amusement to hear this. The gramophone in the upstairs drawing room was grinding out 'My Blue Heaven' for the sixth time and to some extent masked the conversation. But some of Ruth's guests were listening with curiosity.

'Come into the breakfast room,' Ruth said, and led Dave and the contingent from the Coverton family there. Mrs Monash was laying out yet further supplies of food on trays. She looked surprised when she recognized Antony and ready to call her husband to throw him out again, but at a nod from Ruth she went out.

'Now,' Ruth began with a calmness she didn't quite feel, 'I'm prepared to believe that you, Lorette, were young and misled. And that your brother Martin was too bound up in his own affairs to care one way or the other. But you—' she let her gaze rest coldly on Antony – 'you knew better.'

Antony couldn't meet her eye. 'You don't know what it's like,' he said. 'Mother's such a – such a *force*! Whatever she takes up, she does with all her strength, and she sweeps you along with it.'

'Come on, you're not a baby! You're a grown man and touting yourself as a financial leader! You're telling me you couldn't stand up to your mother?'

'You don't know how it is when she gets the bit between her teeth,' Martin put in glumly. 'She's absolutely *prehistoric* in her belief that she must down all before her. That's why I got out as soon as I could. And Antony should have done the same, only she'd got her claws sunk further into him than anyone else. First-born, you know . . .'

'It's true,' urged Lorette, tears in her eyes. 'Dave'll tell you— I had to lie and twist things so as just to get out to meet him.'

'Never met her, of course,' Dave said with a shrug. 'But she certainly sounds like a bit of a monster – she's got what these psychological fellers are calling an "ego" or something. A warrior queen, that's what she shoulda been.'

'When Lorette told me she was coming here tonight with Dave to apologize, I asked to come along,' Antony said.

'And what did your mother say to that?'

'Oh, God,' muttered Martin, 'if she knew . . .! No, no, she retired to her room when she got home from court and she's been there ever since, with her maid taking in little bits of dry toast and sips of brandy. Believe me—' for the first time some real emotion entered Martin's drawl— 'whatever was said in court today has really shattered her. She's talking about going abroad to live, the maid says.'

'Well, I shan't go!' Lorette declared. 'I'm not going to potter about Menton for the rest of my life!'

'I hope not, sweetie,' whispered Dave.

'I don't care where Mrs Coverton goes or what she does so long as she stays away from me,' Ruth said. 'As for the apology – if that's what it is – I accept it. And now perhaps you'd all go and let me get on with the celebrations.'

'Aw, come on, Ruthie, don't be huffy,' Dave said with one of his most fetching smiles. 'Lorette's with me, you know. You don't want *me* to go, do you?'

'You'd no right to bring this gang . . .'

'You said you wanted bygones to be bygones. It says so in the *Evening News*. What's this you're doing, then – living up to your word?'

'Dave, I don't need lectures from you.'

'Of course, we didn't intend to stay,' Martin interrupted. 'I just came along to try to put myself in the clear. I'm sorry for the legal vendetta and I assure you, Miss Barnett, I kept right out of it.'

'No, no,' said Ruth, suddenly ashamed. 'You must have a drink. I'm sorry, my mind's in a muddle since the end of the case. It would be wrong of me to blame you . . .'

And after all, she thought, these are Ethan's children. His blood runs in their veins, some part of his strength and spirit must live within them somewhere. If we could be friends, it would be what he'd want.

'Please,' she said, 'take off your coats and hats and help yourselves to food. Mrs Monash!'

Mrs Monash had vivid memories of the encounter with Antony at Crecy Court. She'd remained within earshot and now bounced in, ready for action. When asked to take outdoor coats and fetch wine, she looked dubious but obeyed. Ruth went out with her: she'd had enough of the Coverton family for the moment.

'Was that Antony I heard in the hall?' Patterwick asked as she rejoined.

'Yes. Come to apologize,' she told him with raised eyebrows.

'Thank heavens for that. Makes it easier about having him back in the office now his "leave of absence" is up.'

'Yes, but . . . His apology blamed everything on his mother's dominance. That proves what Ethan believed – that Antony wasn't fit to lead Covelco.'

'Did you need to have it proved?' Patterwick asked gently. 'I thought you knew that.'

Niall walked up at that moment to invite her to dance. Now the gramophone was playing 'Let a Smile Be Your Umbrella' so they foxtrotted as well as they could in the tiny space afforded by the crowd in the drawing room.

'Happy?' he enquired.

'Oh, yes.'

'That doesn't sound very convincing.'

'The Covertons are here.'

'What!' he stopped so suddenly they were a momentary tangle of feet. 'Here? Of all the nerve . . .'

'No, no, they came to apologize.'

'They? Who's they?'

'Lorette and Antony and the brother who took no part, Martin.'

'And what did you say?'

'I asked them to stay for a drink.'

'I hope it chokes them,' Niall said. Then after a moment, 'Ruth, you've got to stop thinking that because they're a part of Ethan you owe them something.'

She started, stared up at him. 'How did you know that?'

'Oh, I know a lot about you,' he replied.

Dancers were bumping into them. They retired to a couple of chairs in a corner by the writing desk. Harry Monash, passing, offered Côtes du Rhône. They each took a glass but more for something to do than because they wanted it.

'What did the Covertons say to you?' he inquired at last.

422

'Oh, they're sorry for the way Diana went on, they didn't want it to happen . . .'

'Oh, didn't they? They wanted it to happen enough to come to court and tell lies.'

'No, Lorette didn't tell any lies.'

'Antony did. Didn't he? About the time Ethan warned him off. Miss Krett's evidence showed him up as a liar.'

'Well, yes, but that was because his mother put hiim up to it.'

'Don't make excuses for him. Of course, they all want to put it off onto Diana – they want to make her look the villain so they can seem less culpable themselves.'

'You don't know them, Niall. I really feel pretty sure that Lorette had no idea what she was doing. And Martin stayed right out of it.'

'All right, that's one and half that didn't really mean you any harm. But Antony was so determined to get back the firm that he'd have lied up hill and down dale to get it, and don't let him persuade you otherwise just because he bears Ethan's name.'

'Why are you so anxious about it?' she asked in some surprise.

'Because, as far as I can gather, Antony's going to be back in the office now that the case is over. I think you're crazy to let him.'

'But he's part of the family that founded the firm.'

'The Kaiser founded the German Army but the Germans got rid of him fast enough after the war! You owe Antony *nothing*, Ruth.'

Miss Krett appeared coming through the dancers in search of them. 'If you don't mind I'd like to be off home now, Miss Barnett. By the time I get home to Epping it'll be after eleven.'

'Oh, Miss Krett, let Bignall run you home.'

'Not at all, not at all, the Underground will get me there in good time.'

'No, I insist.' Ruth had risen and was now urging Miss Krett away. Niall watched her go with regret. He could only hope his warnings about Antony would have some effect.

Others were following Maisie Krett's lead. The party thinned out, Niall said his rueful goodbyes, but the contingent from the motor-racing circuit remained, dancing, laughing, drinking and generally having a good time. Martin Coverton had found himself a pretty girl and was telling her lies about his success in the theatre. His brother was matching drink for drink with one of Ruth's neighbours. Lorette was dancing in Dave's arms, oblivious to everything else.

A little after midnight even the most assiduous partygoers had begun to think it time to go. Tomorrow was, after all, a working day for most of them. Ruth waved them off, tucked a fiver into Harry Monash's pocket as he and his wife left, and was looking for Bignall to report back from Epping so she could lock up. She went up to the drawing room, gathering up empty wine glasses and crumpled napkins en route.

To her surprise someone rose from a sofa as she came in. It was Antony Coverton.

'I thought you'd gone?' she said, startled.

'No, I waited on purpose. I wanted to speak to you alone. I didn't get a chance to make m'self clear when we all arrived in a bunch.'

'There's no need,' she said, rather quickly. She didn't want to hear any more apologies.

'Oh, yes, there is. We've never really had a chance to

424

speak to each other without all the fam'ly troubles hanging over us . . .'

'Really, Antony, it's very late. I'd rather leave this till another time.'

'No, I want to say it! I want you to know that I've always thought you a lovely girl, even when I was s'posed to disapprove of you entirely . . .'

'Antony, please! This is—'

'I always thought you were wasted on him,' he said, and the solemn spacing of the words told her he had had too much to drink. 'I mean, a pretty young girl like you and an old man like him – it was *stupid!*'

'That's enough! I want you to leave.'

'No, no! No, no, no. Not till I've had my say. We got off on quite the wrong foot, didn't we? Mother sent me to buy you off, which was quite the wrong thing to do because you weren't int'rested in money. Not the mercen'ry type. No, no, I put myself in the wrong, I see that now, and I just had to speak to you and make you unnastand. I knew from the first I'd made a mistake, and then of course Mother got carried away and I couldn't stop her, and you think I'm silly and weak but I'm not, y'know, and if we could start all over again, Ruth, get to know each other, y'know, because I really admire you, I think you're a lovely girl, a really lovely girl . . .'

'You're drunk,' she said in disgust. 'Come on now, Antony, your coat and hat are downstairs.' She moved towards him to guide him to the door, and it was a big mistake.

He threw his arms around her. 'You're lovely,' he repeated and planted a slobbering kiss on her lips.

Ruth was horror-stricken. Repugnance and anger raced

through her. She struggled in his drunken embrace. 'Let go! Let me go!'

'No, no, I wanna show you – I wanna make you unnastand – Ruth, Ruth . . .' His mouth was seeking hers but she writhed in his arms so that his wet touch landed on her neck. He was dragging her as close as he could against his body. She could feel him entangling her with his legs, forcing her off balance.

She managed to get her arms up. She shoved against his chest with her fists. He staggered momentarily. 'Naughty!' he chided. 'Don't be rough! Just be nice, Ruthie, just be nice—'

'You loathsome ape, let go of me!' She pushed against him with all her might.

'Silly girl— What's all the fuss about? You did it with *him!*'

'Don't dare—!'

'And plenty of others, I'll bet! You don't fool me, little Miss Innocent! All wide-eyed and demure in court – who did you think you were fooling? And now it's *my* turn.'

'Stop it! Stop it!' But the breath was knocked out of her as he overbalanced her on to the couch. His heavy weight landed on top of her.

Next moment he was wrenching her skirt up, fumbling at the delicate flesh at the top of her stockings. She thought, with despair and revulsion, It's going to happen! She fought for one last moment of freedom, pulled her head free of his shoulders and screamed at the top of her voice.

'Help! Help!'

'Shut up!' he growled. For a moment he halted his efforts at intimacy to unleash a hand. He clapped it over her mouth. She bit at it. He swore loudly and snatched it away.

Just for a second she thought he was going to hit her. She managed a muffled scream. The pounding of feet could be heard on the stairs.

Voices: 'Ruth?' 'Miss Barnett?'

Someone surged into the room. An arm came round her attacker's neck. He was hauled off, grunting and thrashing.

Ruth squirmed away from him, into the corner of the couch. Someone leaned over her.

'My God, Ruth – are you all right?'

She was trying to pull down her crumpled skirt. She'd lost a shoe. Her hair had come loose from its clasp. Luckily it covered her face for a few seconds. It gave her time to hide and recover herself.

When she was able to look up, she found Niall holding her hand. A large male figure was dragging Antony out of the room.

'How – how did you get here?' she quavered.

'I couldn't get a taxi— I was strolling along— Ruth, for God's sake— I'll get you a drink!'

'No – don't go— Niall—' She began to weep.

He sat down beside her, put an arm about her. She buried her face in his jacket. Sobs shook her.

'Don't. It's all right. He's gone. It's all over. Ruth, Ruth, don't cry.'

But she couldn't help herself. She wept helplessly, not only for what had happened but for all the days of stress and strain before and during the trial. She wept for Ethan's son, who had so much hidden envy of his father that he wanted to possess his woman. She wept for herself, facing a future without the man she had so dearly loved.

By and by the storm abated. Bignall appeared bearing a tray. On it was a teapot with cups and saucers. He set it down, poured tea, added milk and then sugar in large quantities.

'Drink it,' he said.

'No, I don't want—'

'Drink it. Best thing in the world for shock. Learnt that in the trenches.'

The tea was like sweet tar. But he was right, it was the best thing in the world for shock. She began to feel better.

She glanced about, shuddering. 'Where is he?'

'Picking himself up out of the gutter, I reckon.' Bignall added under his breath, 'Bastard!'

'Right,' agreed Niall with angry fervour. 'Thank God we got here when we did.'

'How did you come to be here?' Ruth asked again, trying to make sense of it.

'Mr Gillis here was walking along looking for a taxi as I drove back from setting Miss Krett down in Epping. I says to him, I says, if you'll just come back with me for a minute while I report in to Miss Barnett, I'll give you a lift home afore I put the car up for the night. And the minute I opened the side door we heard the ruckus from upstairs.'

'What the hell did he think he was doing?' Niall grated.

'He was drunk.'

'That's no excuse.' Niall was pacing up and down. 'I'll kill him if I ever lay hands on him.'

'I'da give him a oncer,' said Bignall, 'only you can't hit a drunk, it ain't fair.'

'Fair? I'll give him fair!'

'No, please,' begged Ruth. 'Please, I don't want any trouble over this.'

'What – because he's Ethan's son? All the more *reason!*'

428

'Niall, please – I'm terribly tired; all I want is to put this aside and get to bed.'

'Of course.' He was instantly contrite. 'Shall we fetch Mrs Monash, to spend the night?'

'No, no, she'll be in bed by now.'

'But I can't just leave you here alone.'

'I'll be here, sir,' said Bignall. He grinned sheepishly. 'Not the same as a woman's touch, but at least it's someone in the house for safety.'

'Yes, I'll be all right with Bignall here. Thank you, Niall. You've been very kind.' But her voice was fading, and he could see she was dead on her feet.

He took her hand, pressed it, looked for a moment as if he might do more, then said goodnight and left. She heard his footsteps running down the stairs and the closing of the front door.

'I'll just lock up behind him,' said Bignall. He hesitated. 'He's all right, is Mr Gillis.'

'Yes, he is.' But she was beyond thinking of Niall or anyone else. She dragged herself to her room, dropped on her bed, pulled the quilt about her, and fell into sleep as if into an abyss.

She was very late at the office next day. Miss Krett made no remark upon it but proffered the morning's post and several notes about telephone calls of congratulation.

'Has Mr Antony come in?'

'No, Miss Barnett. He rang to say he was taking the day off. He says his mother isn't well.' And I can well believe it after yesterday, Miss Krett's expression added.

'Ring him and tell him to come in.'

'I beg your pardon? He said he needed to stay with—'

'Tell him I want to see him.' He's used his mother as an excuse once too often, Ruth thought to herself.

She had dealt with the post, discussed some new arrangements with Patterwick and made some preliminary moves to set those arrangements in motion when Miss Krett announced that Mr Antony had arrived.

'Tell him to wait.'

Miss Krett looked a little disturbed at the tone of voice: this, after all, was the son of Ethan Coverton who was being spoken of, a former member of the board of executives. But something in Miss Barnett's attitude warned her not to demur; she withdrew and passed on the message. Something serious was clearly in the wind.

Out of the corner of her eye she watched Antony Coverton sit and fidget all though the twenty minutes that Ruth kept him waiting.

When he was summoned into her office, he looked shamefaced, self-protective – and quite ill. He clearly had a bad hangover.

And that was his justification. He began at once. 'I'm terribly sorry about last night, Ruth,' he said. 'You know, of course, I'd had too much to drink.'

'That was obvious.'

'I was upset. Everything had gone wrong for me. I don't really remember what happened.'

'*I* remember,' Ruth said.

'Well, look, I hope you'll accept my apologies. Whatever I may have said or done, it was the wine speaking.'

'*In vino veritas*.'

'Don't be so hard,' he begged. 'I've had a hell of a time for the last few years, and particularly this last year since Father died.'

'Don't speak to me about your father,' she warned. 'You're not fit to speak his name.'

'Oh, look here, don't make a saint out of him . . .'

430

'Antony, I didn't get you in here to talk about how much you resent your father or even about last night. I got you here to tell you what I've decided about your future.'

'Oh, I see!' Anger flared in him. 'I made a fool of myself and gave you your chance. Well, if you think you can fire me from the company because I tried to get you into bed, forget it. I'll fight you every inch of the way for my job.'

'I'm not firing you. I want you to remain part of the company. You bear the name of its founder and that's worth something. But I can't have you here in this office.'

'Just a minute! What d'you mean, you can't—'

'I never want to set eyes on you again if I can help it.'

'Oh, you're going to fall back on feminine sensitivity, is that it?'

'Be quiet and listen to what I tell you,' she commanded, and her tone made him fall silent.

'There's a lot of opportunity for extra sales of our products in America,' she said. 'I mean both the United States and South America. I want you to go to New York and set up a Transatlantic Sales Office.'

'Sales Office?' he blurted. 'You can't put me on the sales staff!' The mere idea shocked him. It was a terrible demotion.

'I can and I have. As from the beginning of November your post will be in New York. I've already sent some cables to find out about suitable premises in the business section of Manhattan – the real estate agents will be expecting you when you get there.'

'When I get there!'

'You can travel on the *Mauretania*, sailing at the end of the month. Your passage is booked.'

'My passage!' He felt like an idiot parrot, only capable of repeating her words.

'You will have the same salary as you've been drawing here, plus, of course, quite reasonable expenses. You can hire office staff as required and sales staff as you make inroads into the market.'

'I don't want to be on the sales staff! I'm a financial executive—'

'You're what I say you are. If you refuse this post, that's grounds for dismissal.'

'You can't do this!'

'Antony, you've coasted along on your so-called abilities as an economic adviser. Now you're going to have to try a real job of work. Mr Gooding and I will discuss what your targets should be. We won't expect too much in the first year, but we've heard there's plenty of demand in Argentina and Brazil . . .'

'Gooding's an old woman! He knows nothing about the real world—'

'Mr Gooding is a very efficient company secretary.'

'Anyhow I don't want to live in America! London is where I belong—'

'If you wish to stay in London, then you can't work for Covelco.'

'If you think I'm going to let you push me around—'

'You have until the end of the month to make your mind up,' Ruth said. 'If you decide against it, you must consider your connection with Covelco as terminated. I have the backing of the management committee on this.'

He was stunned. Ever since the humiliation yesterday in the Law Courts his mind had refused to work properly. When Lorette, with her schoolgirlish sense of honour, announced to him that she was going to Ruth's house to apologize, he'd latched on to the opportunity. Apologize and get into her good books; he knew she was soft-hearted about keeping his father's name going in the company.

Then somehow a mix of emotion – things he couldn't identify – desire, resentment, frustration – they'd swept him away like an avalanche.

He truly didn't remember all that had happened the previous night. He knew he'd tried to kiss her, and that seemed strange because she wasn't his type at all – none of the county background, none of the Knightsbridge polish he looked for in a girl. He had a feeling he'd gone a bit far: he had the tactile memory of soft flesh, of soft contours under his body, and he had a mark on the palm of his left hand that stung and rankled.

Whatever he'd been up to, it must have been pretty bad because he'd found himself sprawled on the pavement outside her house. His coat and hat were lying beside him. He had a pain in his elbow where he'd hit it on the kerb and his neck felt sore as if someone had half throttled him.

A bobby on the beat had found him weaving about at the corner. He'd been put in a taxi and driven home to his London flat. The taxi driver had to find his key for him and unlock the door. He'd fallen asleep on the carpet of his living room.

He woke about six thirty to the shrilling of his telephone. He had a terrible crick in his neck and a taste like brown boot polish in his mouth.

It was his mother on the phone. 'Where have you *been* all night, Antony? I stayed up till two expecting you home. How could you be so thoughtless, after what I've been through?'

'I've been through something too, Mother . . .'

'Young people are all alike! Lorette's always off on her own these days and Martin's *never* home! Well, you'll miss me when I've gone to live abroad, that's all I can say.'

'Mother, don't get in a state, please. It's practically the crack of dawn and I'm not in the mood—'

'Not in the mood? Not in the mood? How do you think I feel, held up to public ridicule yesterday and left alone all evening after it? I want you to come home *now*, Antony. You know I'm no good at dealing with travel arrangements and I want to be off and away by tomorrow at latest.'

So he'd gone home to Fullerton with an aching head, made worse by his mother's tirade about injustice and ingratitude. He'd been almost glad to be delivered from it all by the summons to head office.

And now this! To be sent away like a naughty child, to be banished abroad like the black sheep of the family. To be downgraded to the sales staff when he had been a board member, a chief executive.

His head was throbbing worse than ever. He lurched to his feet. 'I won't go,' he said. 'You can't make me.'

'I think I can. I can let it be known that I'm trying to get rid of you because you tried to force yourself on me—'

'That's a lie!'

'I have witnesses, Antony. They had to drag you off me.' She studied him with grey-green eyes that he found as cold as the North Sea in winter. 'What will your mother say when she hears that? Her darling son trying to make love to the woman she hates most in all the world?'

The full horror of it hit him like the blast of a flame-thrower. He whirled and stamped out of the office. The door slammed behind him.

A moment later Miss Krett dared to open it and peep in. 'Is anything wrong, Miss Barnett?'

Ruth shook her head. 'I think I've just done some tidying up after the courts, Miss Krett,' she said with a sigh that held a mixture of relief and distress.

Chapter Twenty-Three

Niall spent all of that day refraining from ringing Ruth. He wanted to find out if she was all right and what she'd done about Antony, but she was, after all, supposed to be only a client. If she decided to bring an action against Antony, it was up to her to come to him about it.

By evening, however, he'd had enough of being an upright lawyer. He wanted to know how she was getting on. He dropped by her house after the office.

Mrs Monash, to his surprise, was still there. When he remarked on it as she took his coat, she looked vexed. 'If I'd stayed last night,' she muttered, 'he never would have got his hands on her.'

'Bignall told you?'

'Not the first time that one's stepped out of line,' she said. 'We practically had to have him thrown out of Crecy Court.'

'How is Miss Barnett?'

She shrugged. 'Edgy. She was steady enough when she got home but then she saw the flowers.'

'What flowers?'

'*He* had the nerve to send her flowers! I'm glad to say she told me to put 'em straight in the dustbin. The nerve of it! Well, I'll just hop up and say you're here, sir.'

When he was shown in, Ruth was sitting by the light of a single table lamp. Dusk had fallen. The flicker of the fire gave the room an uneasy atmosphere – or perhaps he sensed something in Ruth's mood.

'Niall, how nice to see you.'

'I thought I'd just drop in to see if everything was all right.'

'I suppose it is.'

'What does that mean?'

'Antony sent me flowers, and a note of apology. Very touching and humble, but it just— I threw it on the fire.'

'Best thing for it,' Niall agreed. 'Did he expect a reply?'

'The messenger waited. I told Mrs Monash to say I had nothing to add to our previous conversation.' Her voice had an edge to it. 'Even if I thought he really felt regret . . . But it's only because he doesn't want to be sent out of London.'

'Is that what you decided?'

'I told him this morning. He's going to New York for the firm – that's as far away as I could manage.'

He couldn't help thinking Antony had got off lightly. If he'd been asked for an opinion, he'd have said, 'Sack him.' He said, 'New York sounds rather grand. He doesn't want to go?'

'He thinks it's beneath his dignity to have anything to do with sales. I'm sending him to open a Transatlantic Sales Department and if he refuses he knows he'll be dismissed.'

'Great!' said he before he could stop himself. 'I hope he refuses the post. Then you can chuck him out.'

'Oh, he'd do almost anything rather than leave London. He wants to be near at hand so that he can grab any opportunity to get back control of the company.' She seemed to shake herself. 'But that's enough about the troubles of Covelco. I haven't offered you a drink. Please help yourself. The drinks tray is on the side table.'

'I'll have something if you will?'

'No, thanks, I don't feel like it. But please, you go ahead.'

Something in her voice told of depression and loneliness. He said on an impulse, 'Are you doing anything this evening?'

'What? Well, I have some papers to look over . . .'

'I meant, about dinner – are you dining at home?'

'Well, yes.'

'Alone?'

'Yes.'

'Come out for a meal,' he urged. 'Nothing special – we could go to the Dorchester Grill.'

She sighed. 'But that would mean I'd have to change, and really . . .'

'Well, then, how about a little place I know in Soho – very informal, French provincial cooking, nobody cares about dinner jackets or that sort of thing – would you like that?'

'But Mrs Monash has got things ready . . .'

'Mrs Monash won't mind putting it all in the larder for tomorrow,' he assured her. 'Come on, just put your coat on and come out.'

So she did, and instead of an evening by herself moping about whether she was doing the right thing over Antony, she spent it listening to a hair-raising account of Niall's childhood in County Tyrone. Poaching trout and salmon, causing pheasants to fall into gunny sacks at night, stealing apples and pears out of orchards – how he ever came to be a respectable lawyer was a puzzle to which he could offer no solution.

'I just like the law,' he acknowledged. 'I just enjoy legal conundrums.'

He was happy to hear her laugh at some of his tales, and to see a lighter shade in her eyes when he returned her to her door later that evening.

And she too, as she went upstairs to her room, was better pleased with life. For a whole evening, she'd been able to lay aside the problems of running Ethan's firm.

Next day was Saturday, a half-day. She spent the afternoon writing notes to well-wishers, and a long letter to her grandmother. Niall telephoned about eight o'clock to ask if everything was all right and she said everything was fine, and then after she'd put the phone down, rather wished she'd said something less self-sufficient, so that perhaps he might have suggested calling in person.

Next day was Sunday. She woke unreasonably early. Mrs Monash didn't come in on Sundays so she went down to the kitchen to make tea and toast. Bignall was there in his shirtsleeves reading the *News of the World* at the kitchen table.

'I'll do that for you, miss,' he offered.

'No, no – I had enough of your kind of tea the other night!'

'Go on with you, that was Gunpowder Grog, eight spoons of tea in half a pint of boiling water, special for shock! I can make proper tea when I've a mind to.'

'Well, you make the tea while I make the toast.'

She had just taken it from under the gas grill when a bell tinkled. Both she and Bignall looked at the box on the kitchen wall. The hall door. Who could be here at this hour of a Sunday morning?

'I'll go,' said Bignall, picking up his jacket and hurrying out.

In two minutes he was back. 'Miss Barnett!'

She knew by his tone that something was wrong. 'What's the matter?'

'It's that solicitor – him that spoke up at the trial.'

'Mr Romstock?' she asked, startled.

'Him and that pair you got shot of – the Worlands.'

'*Here*?'

'I was just going to tell them to sling their hook – saw them first as I opened the door, you understand – then the gentleman steps forward, and he says, "May I speak to Miss Barnett?" And I was that taken aback, I've let them in. Them Worlands, I mean, as well as the solicitor.'

Ruth looked at the kitchen clock. The time was ten minutes to eight. On a Sunday morning.

'I'll go back up and throw 'em out, shall I?' said Bignall, flushed at his mistake. 'Rotten pair – what the devil are they up to now?'

'But they're with Mr Romstock . . .'

'That's a puzzler, I'll admit. I'm sorry, Miss Barnett, I shoulda told them to wait on the doorstep.'

'No, no. I'll go up.'

He looked unwilling, but could see no help for it. 'I'll be just by the back-hall door,' he told her, following her as she went out.

Her three morning visitors awaited her in the hall. Mr Romstock took off his hat, came forward, and after a moment's hesitation took the hand Ruth held out.

'Good morning, Miss Barnett. Forgive me for this early call, but the matter only came to my attention late last evening and I felt there must be no delay in following it up.'

'What matter?'

'I . . . er . . .' He glanced about him in embarrassment. 'I've been given reason to believe that Ethan Coverton wrote another will, cancelling the provisions he made in the will that has just been accepted in the courts.'

Ruth drew back. 'That's not true.'

'Miss Barnett, the Coverton family brought this to my attention yesterday. Mr Antony rang to tell me he had proof that there was a will rescinding the bequest under which you inherit the firm.'

'*Antony* said this,' she said, with contemptuous disbelief. It was just a ploy – to pay her back for daring to send him abroad. 'And where is it, then, this will?'

'That is as yet undetermined. But it does exist. We have a statement from the persons who witnessed it for Ethan.'

'And who . . .?' But she had no need to finish the question. The Worlands presented themselves. formal and dignified in their Sunday best.

She looked from the lawyer to the two servants who had always despised her. She could sense hidden triumph in their impassive faces. 'These two?'

'I have their signed deposition.'

'You're not going to believe anything *they* say?' she said in disbelief. 'I dismissed them for their disloyalty just after Ethan died. They're simply paying off a grudge.'

'If you'll excuse me, miss,' Mrs Worland intervened. 'There's no call to be making accusations of that sort. No complaint was ever made against us, if you remember, and we've got references from the best families, so if you don't mind we want to be treated with a bit of common decency.'

Mr Romstock sighed at the tone of voice but had to pursue his point. 'Miss Barnett, whatever you may feel, these two good people have nothing to gain by coming forward with the information.'

'No, and we wouldn't be here now,' Worland took it up, 'if it wasn't that the judgment in the case went wrong and Mrs Coverton and her son were done out of what's rightfully theirs. Mrs Worland and I have had sleepless nights ever since. I couldn't reconcile it with my conscience to let it go without telling what my wife and I know. So . . .'

'This is a pack of nonsense. I don't believe you would lose a minute's sleep over the rights and wrong of anything—'

'Miss Barnett, please, may we go somewhere more comfortable and talk about this?'

Reluctantly, she led the way up to the drawing room. She offered chairs. Everyone sat down.

'Well,' she said, in a tone that let them know she would disregard what they said. 'What is this story about a new will?'

'It was during Mr Coverton's convalescence,' Eustace Worland began. 'You went out one afternoon and the master rang for me so I came upstairs to the garden room where he was lying on his chaise longue like he usually was. He told me to fetch Mrs Worland up, so of course I did—'

'Although it was most inconvenient,' his wife put in, 'because I was in the middle of making puff pastry—'

'Alice, my love, that's not to the point,' he reproved her gently. 'Well, to go on, he showed us this sheet of paper and told us it was to revoke the will he'd written when he'd had a big row with Mrs Coverton. He said to us, he said, that he realized he'd been unjust and wanted to put it right.'

'Mr Coverton told you all this?' Ruth said with utter incredulity. She couldn't imagine Ethan ever mentioning his marital disagreements to the Worlands.

'Yes, he did, miss, and he had this sheet of notepaper with his wishes written out. He put it on the little table beside his chair and asked us to watch him sign it, and when he'd done that asked us to sign our names.'

'Which we did,' said Alice Worland, 'Eustace first and me after.'

Ruth smiled. 'And where is this will, then?'

Mr Romstock looked distressed. 'You have not found it while going through Mr Coverton's papers?'

Eustace Worland gave a snort, as if to say, 'Stupid question'.

'No, I have not. And in the course of taking over the running of the firm, I assure you I've been through every document in the house.'

'Miss Barnett, would you allow us to search for it?'

'Absolutely not!'

The lawyer flushed. 'I'm afraid I must insist. It is a matter of law—'

'And how does it come about that you're involved in this, Mr Romstock?' she broke in, angry with him. 'Why are you acting as lackey for the Coverton family? I understood they dismissed you from their affairs a year ago!'

He frowned and gave a little gesture of appeasement. 'That is quite true. But I am still the solicitor of record with regard to the disposal of the Coverton property. Mrs Coverton felt she could not have confidence in the solicitors who prepared her case for the courts so has brought this matter to me. She felt it was my duty to find the new will. And I feel that she is right in that – Ethan would wish me to settle his affairs in the manner he had chosen.'

'You're wrong, Mr Romstock,' Ruth said helplessly. 'There is no new will.'

'You're quite entitled to refuse to allow us to search. But in that case I shall have to go to the police, because concealing a valid will is a criminal offence.'

'Concealing a will? What are you saying?' she flashed. 'There *is* no will! Why can't you listen?'

'A search must be made, and if you refuse to allow it now, I'm afraid I must then ask the police to apply for a search warrant.'

Ruth was hot with anger, with dislike of the Worlands, with astonishment that they dared to come back to her house, with dismay that Romstock should listen to them. But even in this welter of emotions, she recognized the voice of authority. Mr Romstock would get a search warrant. Police cars would roll up to the door. The press would get to hear of it.

The last thing she wanted was to let the Worlands paw through her belongings. But there seemed, at that moment, no help for it. She made a gesture of unwilling invitation.

'Go ahead, if you must.'

To tell the truth, Mr Romstock was at a loss. In all his years as a solicitor, he'd never had to search for a missing will. He had no idea how to go about it. His momentary hesitation gave the upper hand to Eustace Worland.

'If I may suggest, sir?' he murmured. 'Mr Coverton was an invalid, you know—'

'Of course I know that,' snapped Romstock.

'Well, sir, what I mean is, he couldn't hardly get from his bed to the chair he spent his day in – I mean he had to be helped. I myself helped him to his chair many a time.

didn't I, Alice? And sometimes you lent a hand.'

'That I did, I'd carry his newspaper or his book.'

'So what I'm saying to you, sir, is that as he couldn't get about the house at the time he made the will, it isn't likely to be anywhere except in what we call the garden room, where he spent his nights and days until the day he died.'

Ruth's throat seized up at the memory. She stood in frozen silence as Worland led the way to the room at the front of the house, the room, once the dining room, but converted to a sickroom for Ethan.

Nothing had been changed since. She'd never yet had the heart to do it. Mrs Monash kept it clean and tidy, but if Ruth ever went into it, it was only to stand on the balcony and look down at the garden in the square, seeing the view that Ethan used to see and thinking that the seasons came and went, the rain fell and the grass grew, the trees turned green and shed their leaves even though he was not here to watch them.

Down in the hall, Bignall was desperately looking for the piece of paper on which Niall Gillis had scribbled his home telephone number the night Ruth was attacked. What the devil had he done with it? He had to find it, for the poor kid needed somebody here to stand up for her.

Bignall had been eavesdropping shamelessly. Never trusted them Worlands, a rotten pair they were and always had been. He hadn't been able to hear everything but he'd caught the words 'police' and 'warrant' and that was enough. He'd scuttled down the stairs to the hall phone.

But where was Mr Gillis's number? They'd been in the hall when he wrote it down, and Bignall had tucked it – here it was, under the bowl of the table lamp.

In a low voice he gave it to the operator. A short pause,

four or five rings, and a surprised voice said, 'Who's ringing me at this unearthly hour on a Sunday?'

'Mr Gillis, sir, this is Bignall . . .'

'Bignall!'

'Can you come at once, sir? Please, I think it's urgent.'

'Is that swine bothering her again?' Niall's voice rose several tones.

'Not him, sir, it's that lawyer – him at the trial, Romstock – he's here, searching the house.'

'*Searching the house?*'

'Please come, sir. I didn't know who else to call.'

'I'm on my way.'

Bignall went back upstairs, without concealment this time. The door of the garden room was open. He marched in. Miss Barnett was standing at the far side, near the windows that opened onto the balcony. She was watching with shocked amazement while the three others moved about the room.

Bignall had no idea what they were after. They were opening drawers, shaking books by their spines, lifting cushions.

They were searching for something, but what?

He crossed the room to Ruth's side. 'You never had your tea and toast, miss. Shall I make fresh?'

'No, thanks, Bignall.' The words were scarcely a whisper.

'What's going on?' he asked out of the side of his mouth.

She shook her head. It was beyond her to explain.

'I telephoned Mr Gillis,' he said softly.

She looked directly at him. She didn't smile, but something about her expression seemed less stricken.

The chauffeur shifted from foot to foot. He didn't know

what to do next. Mr Romstock's eye rested on him for a moment, a puzzled look crossed his face, and then he went back to his search as if Bignall were a piece of furniture.

Embarrassed, Bignall left the room. Ruth made a move as if to prevent him, but really, what good could he do? Only it would have been nice to have someone – a friend, a supporter – in this hideous scene.

Everything had been examined. The few ornaments had been picked up and inspected. Worland had looked behind the picture frames. His wife had got down on her hands and knees to feel under the edges of the rugs.

'It's not here,' Worland said at last. 'Sorry, sir.'

'It was in this room he called you to witness?'

'Well, no.' The butler raised a hand to attract his wife's attention. She rose from her knees, dusting the edge of her coat. She stood watching him as he considered. 'It was out on the balcony, wasn't it, Alice?'

'Of course it was!' she agreed on a note of surprise. 'A warm day in September, don't you remember, Eustace? Mr Coverton was fanning himself with *The Times* when you brought me in.'

'So he was! That's right, Mr Romstock, he was out on the chaise longue on the balcony.'

As it happened, Ruth was standing by the French doors that gave on to the balcony. Through the glass, the palms and oleanders were silhouetted against the light from Pouncey Square.

It was now full morning. Clouds were strung out against a sky of pale autumn blue. Church bells were chiming for the early service.

Ruth opened the door of the balcony. She stood aside in invitation to let them pass.

The three went in. She remained in the opening of the French windows. The balcony ran the width of the front of the house but was only about four feet in depth. Some of the floor space was taken up by the large pottery tubs which held the plants. The chair which Ethan had used was at a slight angle in the left-hand corner against the house, with on one side a little table and on the other a decorated pottery jar holding a big flowerpot with a Kentia palm.

Mr Romstock and the Worlands stood in a huddle on the balcony. Clearly they were undecided where to start. Mrs Worland made the first move, picking up the cushions of the chaise longue and feeling in the cracks of the woven cane.

Despite herself, Ruth felt a faint amusement. If Mrs Worland really believed that anything could still be there after a year of Mrs Monash's cleaning operations, it showed she didn't know Mrs Monash.

They moved about, getting in each other's way. They lifted the flowerpots off the windowledge to look under them. They looked under the rush mats. They picked up everything on the little table by Ethan's chair – cigarette box, lighter, ashtray.

Nothing.

'You won't find anything,' Ruth said. 'There's nothing to find.'

'But these people say there is,' Romstock replied in a weary voice.

'And the next question is,' said Alice Worland, staring at Ruth, 'did you find it first?'

Ruth gasped. Mr Romstock said in distress, 'Now, now, Mrs Worland . . .'

'Let's think sensibly,' the butler said, almost as if he

were in charge. 'He was sitting here, wasn't he, Alice?'

'That's right.'

'With this piece of paper held steady on a book on this table.'

'Right.'

'He said, "I'd like you to witness my signature," wasn't that it, Alice?'

' "I'd like you to witness while I sign this," that's what he said, Eustace.'

'So he did. So we came up to him, and he signed with the pen he was holding.'

'That's it. "Ethan Coverton", just as always. And while he was doing that, you got out your fountain pen, Eustace . . .'

'Did I?'

'Yes, don't you remember, because I gave you a nudge to pay attention to the signature.'

'Did you? I don't recall that but – I think I did get out my pen – ' He put his hand inside his jacket pocket and brought out a black fountain pen.

'So you signed, and then I signed when you handed me the pen, and I was just going to hand it back to you when Mr Coverton said, "You'd better add the date," so I did that.'

'And he was sitting here? And used this table?' Mr Romstock said.

'That's it, sir.' Worland glanced about as if in search of ideas. Then he said: 'I wonder . . .?'

He stooped by the chair. Mrs Worland said, 'What, Eustace?' and stooped beside him.

They both straightened. They looked at Romstock. 'There, sir,' said Worland, moving aside.

Romstock took his place, stooped over the chair. Ruth

saw his hand go to the big plant container. Something gleamed pale in his hand. He straightened.

He held out his hand to her. To her utter amazement she saw between his fingers a sheet of Ethan's private writing paper, folded in four and somewhat stained with damp or soil.

She heard herself begin to say something – a protest, a sound of disbelief – she hardly knew what.

'It was tucked down between the pot and the container,' he said in a wondering tone. 'Still there, after all this time.' He unfolded it. He read it, glanced at her with frowning inquiry, and held it out.

She put out her hand to take it. He drew back. 'I think I had better retain it,' he said. 'Please read it.'

She stood at his elbow and read:

I've thought things over seriously. I see now how wrong I was to react so angrily and I'd like to set matters right before it's too late.

I want the former arrangements to be reinstated because I can't bear to think I've been unjust. My lawyers will put it all into formal language.

It was signed Ethan Coverton and witnessed by Eustace and Alice Worland. The date was 12 September of the previous year.

Chapter Twenty-Four

The shock of unexpectedly seeing Ethan's writing wiped out everything else. Her breath seemed to leave her. She felt herself swaying.

Her shoulder met the frame of the French window. She half closed her eyes, breathed deeply. Don't be silly, she told herself. Stand up. Face this.

Romstock was speaking. With a great effort she sorted out his words.

'. . . Can say from my own knowledge that this is Ethan Coverton's handwriting.'

'Of course it's his writing,' Worland replied. 'We saw him do it.'

'No, no, Eustace,' said his wife, 'we only saw him sign, now didn't we?'

'Oh, of course.'

Romstock said, 'Miss Barnett? Do you agree this is Ethan Coverton's handwriting?'

She summoned her strength, stood straight. 'Yes, certainly. It's Ethan's writing.'

'In that case, I feel I must point out to you that although this is holograph, it can be considered a legal will. Holograph wills are acceptable so long as they are properly signed and witnessed.'

'I understand.' She nodded in acceptance. Of course it was Ethan's handwriting. Of course his wishes must be accepted. All the same she burst out in distress, 'You don't understand! I had no idea that sheet of paper was there! More than once I've considered altering this room – I might have thrown everything out!'

'I bet you wish you had,' Mrs Worland said in an undertone.

'Now, now, Mrs Worland,' Romstock reproved. 'I understand that you and Miss Barnett didn't part as friends, but there's no need for that kind of remark.'

'Huh,' sneered Mrs Worland, 'you can't tell me she's glad the will's been found. If it hadn't been neatly hidden, she'd more than likely have done away with it.'

'What?' gasped Ruth.

'Mrs Worland, that's slander,' Romstock said in a pained voice.

'Well, I— Well— I didn't mean anything by it. All the same, it stands to reason. Why else did he hide it? To keep it out of her sight.'

Ruth was too confused and upset to take offence at the implication. She was trying to come to terms with the discovery of the paper. 'I don't understand,' she whispered. 'Why was it tucked away like that? If it was a will, why didn't he send for you, Mr Romstock?'

'I can't explain it, Miss Barnett.'

'He had only to ask me to telephone you . . .'

'Oh, yes?' said Mrs Worland. 'I heard you dozens of times telling him such and such a visitor would be bad for him. You had the final say who came to the house! He was under your thumb and you know it.'

'But that was because the doctor told me to keep things as quiet as possible.'

'We can't ascertain his reasons,' said Mr Romstock, shaking his head. 'All we have is this statement of his wishes. My dear, I wonder if you would fetch an envelope to put this in?'

'Of course.'

Ruth went along to the study. She took a long envelope out of the stationery holder. Coming back into the passage, she was aware of sounds below in the hall. As she went to the door of the garden room, there was Niall Gillis rushing up the stairs with Bignall at his heels.

'Niall!'

'What's going on?' he said, taking her free hand. 'What's in the envelope?'

'Nothing. It's for the will.'

'What will?'

'We've just found a new will – this is to put it in.'

'Not till I've seen it!' he declared, and preceded her into the garden room.

'Romstock, this is outrageous!' he said at once. 'You had no right to make a search.'

'We had Miss Barnett's permission, Mr Gillis.'

'But Miss Barnett should have had a legal representative here.'

'Mr Gillis, Miss Barnett was not being accused of anything. She had no need of legal protection.' But Romstock was flustered. Beneath his silvery hair, his face was pink.

'Do I understand you've found a document?'

'A holograph will.'

'May I see it?'

The older man handed the sheet of writing paper to him. There was a moment's strained silence while Niall read it through.

'This isn't a will!' he exclaimed, flicking it with his finger. 'There's nothing in this to say it concerns the Coverton estate.'

'Excuse me, Mr Gillis, it is to be regarded as a will. It is signed, witnessed and dated, and the witnesses were informed it was a will retracting the bequests of its predecessor.'

Niall gave the Worlands a contemptuous glance. '*They* claim it's a will? I wouldn't believe what they said if they swore it on a stack of Bibles.'

'Oh!' cried Alice Worland.

'That's slander!' cried her husband.

'It's a statement of fact. I wouldn't believe a word you said on any inducement. Look here, Romstock, you weren't around when this pair were given their marching orders. I was present, and I can tell you they had behaved disgracefully—'

'That's not true,' Worland interrupted. 'All we did was give due respect to the widow when she sent for her husband's body.'

'You let Ethan Coverton's body be taken out of the house while Miss Barnett was away, when anybody with a spark of decency would have waited for Miss Barnett's permission. Added to that, you'd been spying on her.'

'We had not!'

'You didn't deny it when she accused you of it.'

'It was beneath our dignity,' Worland said, putting his nose in the air. 'We're not used to dealing with persons of Miss Barnett's type. We were glad to go, weren't we, Alice?'

'My dear Mr Gillis,' Romstock put in, having gathered himself together, 'this is neither here nor there. The document we have found is a legal will.'

'No, it's not.'

'It is a handwritten statement of intention, stated by the testator to be a will, signed by him and properly witnessed by two people to whom he made his intentions known. That is a legal will.'

'We'll see about that,' Niall said. 'I refuse to accept it. I certainly want a handwriting expert to examine the document.'

'Don't, Niall, don't!' Ruth cried. 'It's Ethan's writing, it's his will, there's no doubt about it. Don't make a battle out of it, I couldn't bear it!'

'But Ruth . . .!'

'I want Ethan's wishes to be carried out. I don't understand how he came to write them down in this way or why he hid it from me—'

'That's clear enough,' Mrs Worland said. 'We wouldn't be looking at it now if you'd found it first!'

Ruth put her hands up to her face as if to protect herself from a slap. Niall advanced on Mrs Worland. 'Out!' he ordered. 'Get out! You too, Worland – get yourselves out of this house!'

'Mr Romstock!' Worland appealed. 'Am I to be spoken to like this? I'm only here because I felt it was my duty.'

Mr Romstock shook his head. 'I think we have all overstayed our welcome,' he said with gravity. 'If I may have the envelope, Miss Barnett?'

She gave it to him. He put the sheet of paper into it. He led the way to the door of the garden room. There he paused. To Niall, he said, 'I must inform Antony Coverton and Mrs Coverton of the existence of this document. I will advise them that, in view of your objections, nothing should be done at once. I will ask an expert to examine the writing but I am certain it is

Ethan's – I've seen it often and have in my files, as I told the court, a very similar sheet of paper on which he noted down the bequests in the will which was contested.'

'Yes,' Ruth said.

'Look here, Ruth, don't just give in like this.'

'It's best, Niall. I can't bear it if we haggle over it.'

'I thank you for your forbearance, Miss Barnett,' Romstock said, and with the faintest of nods towards the Worlands as they filed out ahead of him, added, 'They mean well.'

'No, they don't,' said Niall.

'Mr Gillis, you know very well that lawyers have to accept facts. Truth sometimes comes to us in very painful packages.'

Bignall followed the party downstairs to make sure they left the house. Niall stood looking at Ruth.

'You've made a mistake, Ruth,' he said.

'No.'

'Ethan Coverton could never have intended to go back to the original will. It means he's left you nothing.'

'He left me the lease of this house,' she reminded him. 'It always seemed to me a very generous thing in itself.'

'Ruth!' Niall almost shouted. He felt like shaking her. 'You can't just let it all go like that! Antony Coverton is going to get Covelco back.'

'That's what Ethan intended, after all.'

'No, he didn't!'

'Yes, otherwise he wouldn't have written that will.' Tears brimmed over. She sat down on one of the cane chairs.

'Ruth . . . Don't cry . . . We'll contest it . . . We'll put it right.'

458

She was shaking her head. 'It's not that. I don't care so much about Covelco . . . At least . . . I do care about that but . . . What really hurts is that he hid it from me.'

'No, no, dear . . .'

'He did, he got those two to witness a will while I was out of the house, and then he hid it. He hid it, Niall. As if he was afraid I'd see it.'

Niall was stooping over her, patting her shoulder, murmuring comfort. 'I'm sure it wasn't really like that, Ruth. If he *did* change his mind, it was while he was ill and confused. Perhaps the medication he'd been given—'

'His mind was always quite clear,' she objected. 'He always knew what he was doing. You knew him, Niall, he was a man who would never have taken action unless he was sure he was right.'

Niall could think of nothing to say. He couldn't imagine Ethan Coverton doing anything while confused or fuddled.

'I have to accept it,' Ruth said. 'I *do* accept it. He changed his mind and decided to make Antony his heir again. And that's only right,' she added, nodding to convince herself. 'He's the eldest son. He *should* inherit.'

They both knew that she didn't believe this. Events had shown that Antony was not the right heir for the Coverton estate.

Bignall reappeared. 'Them Worlands,' he said, 'grinning like cats that had got the canary at last. If I ever run across 'em again, I'll knock 'em for six. Miss Barnett, I'm sorry I let 'em in.'

'No, it's all right, don't blame yourself.'

'But I can see they've done you a damage, miss.'

'By God they have,' Niall agreed grimly. He sighed.

'Ruth, think it over. You have rights, you know. Don't sign them away without a lot of thought.'

'Yes, thank you. I know your advice is good, Niall. And in any case, Mr Romstock said he wasn't going to do anything straightaway.'

'His conscience is bothering him,' said Niall. 'He can say what he likes about truth coming in painful packages but the fact is, the Covertons hauled him over the coals about negligence in the contested will and he's afraid of putting a foot wrong this time. He was a lot too lax with the Worlands, their attitude was more than unfriendly to you and he ought to have controlled them.'

'What does their attitude matter?' Ruth sighed. 'Facts are facts. They had witnessed a new will and no one can deny it.'

Bignall picked up the words. 'Is that what they were looking for? A new will?'

'I'm afraid so.'

'And they found it?'

'Yes, Mr Coverton had tucked it down between the pot of that big palm and the Chinese jar it stands in.'

'Why the devil should he do that?' Bignall cried in amazement.

'I don't know, Bignall, I don't know,' stammered Ruth and began to cry again.

'Shut up, you fool,' Niall grated to the chauffeur.

'I'm sorry, sir. Miss Barnett, don't take on! I never meant to – oh, Lord, I better make myself scarce!' He plunged towards the door but then stopped. Turning, he addressed Niall. 'I tell you this. I drove Mr Coverton's cars for him for nigh on ten years, and chatted with him on many a long drive. And I never knew him do anything hugger-mugger or creepy-crawly. And if them Worlands say he hid his will in a plant pot, you can take it from me it's not true.'

With that he stamped out.

Niall waited until Ruth recovered her composure. 'What do you want me to do?' he asked.

'I don't know. Nothing.'

'We can't just do nothing, Ruth.'

She put away her wet handkerchief. 'It's up to Mr Romstock, isn't it? He has to write to us officially and say a new will's been found?'

'Yes, and then, of course, if you don't contest it, it will have to go to Probate. It's quite likely, you know, that the Court of Probate won't accept it. It's not a usual sort of document.'

She was shaking her head. 'I hope they do accept it. I couldn't bear a long wrangle, especially now that I know Ethan had changed his mind. I'd feel like an impostor, giving orders at Covelco.'

'I can't stand it that you're just caving in like this!' he exclaimed with an anger he found hard to control. 'You can't let that bounder Coverton take it all away from you!'

'You don't understand,' she said. 'If it's what Ethan wanted, it's what I want too.'

There was no arguing with her. She had accepted defeat – had decided there wasn't even a battle in which she could be defeated. She was stepping aside without objection or resistance.

In the end he saw he was only wearying her. He himself had an engagement for that Sunday afternoon. He thought it best to leave her, to let time and distance bring a new view of the matter. It was very hard to be a knight errant to a princess who didn't want to be rescued.

Ruth spent the morning and afternoon alone. She

pottered about doing things that she'd intended to do – putting things out to go to the cleaner, sewing on loose buttons, writing personal replies to notes of congratulations on her victory in the courts. Her victory in the courts . . . How ironic that seemed now.

Around six she had a headache. She took some aspirin and then thought that probably the headache was due to a sort of exhaustion. She hadn't eaten all day.

She changed from her blouse and skirt into an after-six dress and went out. It was a fine evening of late October, the shadows cool as the sun went down behind the houses of Mayfair.

She ate dinner in the Savoy Grill. It occurred to her that she wouldn't often do this in future. When the new will had gone through, she would be back where she'd been before: no money, no job, her only assets a few unimportant pieces of jewellery and the house she couldn't afford to keep.

She tried to think about tomorrow. Obviously, she couldn't go in to Covelco head office and behave as if she still owned the firm. Antony would probably be there, ready to triumph over her. Well, she wouldn't give him the satisfaction. She would write her letter of resignation tonight.

But when she got home she was all at once so weary that she went to bed. She slept heavily and long. Mrs Monash woke her by bringing in a tray of tea and toast.

'Good morning, miss. Thought you'd like a bit of breakfast in bed.'

'Good morning, Mrs Monash.'

She settled the tray across Ruth's legs. 'Bignall told me, miss.'

'Yes.'

'I never met them Worlands—'

'I don't want to talk about it, Mrs Monash.'

'No, miss. I just wanted to say, from what Bignall tells me, they're a bad lot.'

She made no response. Mrs Monash fidgeted with the tea things then burst out, 'Don't you give in to them, Miss Barnett, dear!' and hurried out, her cheeks aflame with embarrassment.

When she had dressed, Ruth went into the study to write a letter to Miss Krett. She found she had decided to delay sending in her resignation, but in the meantime, since she wasn't going to the office, there were engagements for today that must be cancelled and plans that had to be altered. Rather than telephone her secretary with explanations, she sat down at the desk, listed the points that needed attention, signed it, and reached for an envelope in which to put it. Bignall could take it to High Holborn.

As her hand was closing on the envelope, she paused. She looked at the stationery container. It was an upright box of fine walnut with dividers. The back slot held writing paper, the next slot held envelopes, the nearest slot held postcards and memo pads.

There was none of the writing paper on which Ethan had written the new will.

Ethan had had private writing paper. It was edged with pale blue the exact shade of the Covelco racing cars, and his name and private address were encased in a little box of the same colour. The envelopes matched the paper: they fitted it exactly when it was folded in four and had an edging of a light blue line. The blue line was on the 'follow-on' sheets too.

In the stationery holder there was only heavy cream

writing paper with the Pouncey Square address in black engraving. The envelopes that fitted it were long and narrow, intended to take the paper when it was folded from the top into three.

Ruth pulled the contained towards her. There was no blue-edged paper in it. She knew this for a fact but she needed to verify it.

There had been none for a year. The blue-edged paper fitted into a leather writing case that Ethan used to take with him everywhere. Before they set out for the Targa Florio in Sicily, he had taken the last of the blue-edged paper out of the desk supply and put it in the writing case. He had taken it with him to Sicily.

And she had left it there when she flew him home in the flying boat.

When she had arranged the trip home by flying boat the pilot had warned her that they had to lighten the load. She had left everything behind except the clothes they stood up in.

There was no blue-edged writing paper in the house in Pouncey Square. She had meant to reorder it from the supplier in Bond Street, but with more important matters on her mind during Ethan's illness, she'd never got round to it.

True, Ethan had scribbled notes. Notes to his production manager, notes to friends, to racing colleagues. He'd used the memo pads. She had put a supply of those on his bedside table and on the table by the chaise longue. He never wrote anything very long, he'd found it tiring to scribble more than a few lines, so the memo pads had been quite adequate.

After his death, while clearing up his papers, she'd collected up all the pads from their various resting places in the sick room and returned them to the desk in the study.

She sat and thought about it.

In the first place . . . In the first place, the Worlands were implying that Ethan had written the will in her absence because he didn't want her to see it. Supposedly, she could persuade him to change it back. She was supposed to have him 'under her thumb'.

Well, *she* knew that was not true. Ethan had always been in command. He had practically browbeaten her into bringing him home from Sicily. He had won that point, and he had won the next: if she could have persuaded him, he'd have come home to a hospital, not the Pouncey Square house.

In the second place, if he wanted to make a will, Ethan would have called in Mr Romstock. It was nonsense, sheer nonsense, to suggest she could prevent him from seeing whoever he really wanted to see.

And thirdly, even supposing he hadn't wanted to ask her to summon his family lawyer, he could have asked one of the nurses. He could have asked one of his frequent visitors, such as Leonard Patterwick. He could even have asked one of the Worlands to make the call.

As she cleared her mind and ordered her thoughts, she realized it was idiotic in the first place to say that Ethan had written a muddled, handwritten will. But if he had done so, he would have handed it to Romstock to be made official. He would never have tucked it out of sight in a Chinese plant jar.

She picked up the telephone and asked the operator for the office of Tadsley and Gower. She told the receptionist she was Miss Barnett, calling Mr Gillis. Yes, she said, it was urgent.

When she was put through, she said: 'Niall, the Worlands are lying.'

Chapter Twenty-Five

When Niall arrived, his first words were, 'The will's a forgery, right?'

Ruth was shaking her head. 'That's Ethan's writing, Niall.'

'But, Ruth . . .'

'Please accept that fact. The words on that sheet of paper are in Ethan's writing.'

'Then what are you saying?' he demanded, perplexed.

'I'm saying that though he wrote it, he didn't write it when the Worlands say he did.' She explained about the blue-edged notepaper. 'The last few sheets were in Ethan's writing case in Sicily. We left all that when we flew home. I never got around to ordering a fresh supply. So you see, there's none in the house and hadn't been for over six months when the Worlands claim he wrote those words.'

Niall thought about it. 'Can you prove that? That Ethan had no access to his private writing paper?'

She sighed. 'No, but I know it's true. *I left it all in Sicily.*'

'He couldn't have brought some home in his pocket or something?'

'You saw him when we arrived, Niall. He was in pyjamas and dressing gown.'

'Where did that sheet of paper come from, then?'

'Perhaps the Worlands stole it while they were working for us?'

'Well, that's possible. Bignall says they were into every fiddle you could think of. But then— how could they get Ethan to write what he did?'

'They never could,' she said with conviction. 'That's one of the absolutely vital things, Niall. You've got to believe me. Ethan would never have brought the Worlands into his private affairs, nor been influenced by them in any way.' She looked at him. 'You do believe me, don't you?'

'Of course. But it isn't *evidence*, Ruth. You and I both know that the Worlands are a rotten pair but . . .' His voice died away.

'What?' urged Ruth.

'Why are they doing this?'

'To get their own back on me for throwing them out.'

'But why now? If they've had this document in their possession since before Ethan died, why have they only surfaced with it now?'

'Well, they said they waited until the outcome of the trial and then when they saw it had gone against Antony and his mother . . .'

'Huh! Out of nobility of mind, is that it?'

She almost laughed. 'No, it's not that. I don't know why they're doing it. They're not getting anything out of it.'

'Oh, no?' Niall was frowning. 'A good question to ask is, *cui bono*?'

'What does that mean?'

'Roughly translated it means, "Who benefits?" '

'Well, who?' Then she looked at him and they said together, 'Antony.'

After a moment of shocked silence Ruth said, 'Do you really think he'd plot with people like the Worlands?'

'Do you really think he wouldn't?'

'We-ell . . .' She was shaking her head, but had to add: 'I think he'd do almost anything to avoid being demoted to the Sales Department. I made a mistake there – it really hurt his vanity.'

'And if that sheet of paper is accepted as a legal will, he'll get back the whole company and his mother will get Ethan's personal fortune. It's a lot, Ruth, it's not only a case of winner takes all but he pays off his score against you.'

'But he wouldn't . . .'

'I think you think he would – if he could get away with it.'

'Well, it looks as if he will. Because I can't prove that there was none of that writing paper in the house nor that Ethan wouldn't have turned to the Worlands for help.' Her feelings on the point were absolutely confident, but what use was that in legal terms?

'How did they get hold of that paper?' she burst out.

'Yes. More interesting, how did those words come to be on it?'

'I don't know. I can't imagine.' After a moment she added, 'I'll tell you something else that's odd. It's not a first sheet, it's a follow-on sheet.'

'I'm not with you.'

'The first sheet had his name and private address printed on it. Then if he wanted to write something that would take up more than one sheet, he'd use a follow-on sheet which *didn't* have the heading. And that sheet of paper Mr Romstock found in the Chinese pot had no heading.'

'No, you're right,' he agreed, picturing it again in his mind as Romstock had handed it to him. 'It was a plain sheet of paper with a faint blue line round the edge.'

'As if – it was – *part of a letter!*'

'By heaven,' Niall exclaimed, 'that's it!'

They went over it excitedly, with a sudden feeling that they could turn the tables on the Worlands. But after a few minutes the excitement died.

'How are we going to prove it?'

'Yes, where's the rest of the letter?'

'Could Ethan have written it to Antony?' Niall suggested.

'Never in a million years! If it's a letter, it's a letter of apology. And Ethan would never have apologized to Antony, never.' This was beyond doubt in her mind.

'But maybe he felt he'd been unjust to him over his inheritance.'

'But then if he wrote to Antony and said he felt he'd been unjust and wanted to go back to the original will, why didn't Antony come forward with that letter at the outset?'

'Oh, Lord, yes, why not? What we seem to have is part of a letter that Ethan wrote to someone, saying he was sorry and wanted to go back to the way things used to be. You knew him better than anyone. Who could that be, Ruth?'

But even she, who had his trust and love, couldn't say she knew every single thought that passed through his head. 'I don't know,' she confessed. 'He had a lot of friends . . . He might have had a little squabble with somebody . . . Yet it must have been something fairly important.'

'And the problem remains, how would Antony or the Worlands get hold of a letter from Ethan to someone else?'

It seemed insoluble. They discussed it for almost an hour. Ruth showed him the place where the note was found between the flowerpot and the rim of the Chinese jar, showed him the desk in the study with its store of only cream-coloured paper.

Mrs Monash, unasked, brought coffee. Niall drank a cup but had one eye on his watch. 'I must dash. I've got a client coming in about ten minutes.'

'Are we going to do anything about all this?' Ruth asked as she rose to show him out.

'You bet we are! Mr Tadsley's busy this morning, but after lunch I'll get hold of him and explain it.'

'Is there really anything to explain?' she asked uncertainly.

'There certainly is. I'll tell you one thing that's staring us in the face – poor old Romstock found that document because it was put there for him to find—'

'But by whom, Niall?' she broke in, confused.

'By the Worlands, of course! They were here, weren't they? To show Romstock where they'd been when they supposedly witnessed this "will"?'

'Yes, of course. They came with that piece of paper in their pocket!'

'And used poor old Romstock as witness when it was "found". I don't fancy suggesting that to him, but Keswick Tadsley has enough prestige to do it.'

Ruth felt sad. She liked Mr Romstock.

Keswick Tadsley himself telephoned Ruth in the early afternoon. 'Miss Barnett, I am very much perturbed by what Mr Gillis has recounted to me,' he said in his stately way. 'If he is right, there is a conspiracy to pervert the course of justice.'

'Do *you* think he's right, Mr Tadsley?'

'Hm . . . I have a high regard for Mr Gillis. On the other hand, there is so much public interest in the affairs of the Coverton family that I hesitate to go to the police – to make it public in any way. One must not do anything rash . . .'

'I agree with you.'

'I have instructed Mr Gillis to make some discreet inquiries. In the meantime, Miss Barnett, I think you should carry on as if nothing had happened.'

'But that's impossible, Mr Tadsley! Antony Coverton is probably taking over already at Covelco.'

'If that is so, he is acting very unwisely.' Mr Tadsley ahemmed to himself for a moment then said, 'There is enough doubt in the matter of the newly found document for us to prevent any changes being made in the *status quo* for the present. I shall apprise Mr Romstock of my opinion and in the meantime, if I were you, Miss Barnett, I would carry on as usual.'

This advice she nerved herself to follow. She had not sent Bignall to head office with the note for Miss Krett, so, though it was well after lunch, she called for the car and was driven to work.

In a way it was pleasing to see how well everything was going on without her. Unasked, Miss Krett had rearranged her appointments: she'd supposed Miss Barnett had a headache or something of that kind.

'Is Mr Antony in the building?'

'I believe he came in about ten, Miss Barnett, but left again. He told his secretary he had a business meeting and wouldn't be back today.'

A token visit – just to let her know he was disregarding her command that he stay away until it was time for him to leave for New York. He's nervous, she told herself. If he thought himself secure he'd have been in today altering everything he could. He's nervous . . . So what is he nervous about? Is there some way he feels he can be caught out?

And so matters remained for the next three days. Antony would come in about mid-morning and leave again without encountering Ruth. They didn't meet or communicate. Leonard Patterwick was curious enough to inquire, 'Is he packing up ready to go to the States?' but not curious enough to pursue the matter.

Late on Thursday afternoon, Mr Tadsley rang Ruth at the office. 'If it is convenient to you, Miss Barnett, I should like to have you present at a conference tomorrow, Friday.'

'A conference? Where?'

'At my office, at two thirty. I have invited Mr Romstock and the members of the Coverton family.'

'Oh.'

'That displeases you?'

'The whole family? Including Diana Coverton?'

'I understand you are unwilling to meet her, Miss Barnett, but I think it's necessary.' Mr Tadsley hesitated, then added, 'Mr Gillis has pursued some inquiries. I gather he has spoken to Lorette Coverton and her brother Martin. There is enough in their replies to make him feel that some sort of plot was recently hatched, but whether by Antony or by Mrs Coverton, he cannot be sure.'

'You mean he was able to question them on my behalf? I'd have thought they were regarding me as the enemy again, if their mother has told them Ethan had to hide his new will from me.'

'I have no knowledge of what Mrs Coverton may or may not have told her younger children,' the lawyer said in faint reproof. He had a distaste for the family relationships of the Covertons. 'From Mr Gillis, I gather that Lorette and Martin Coverton were by no means unfriendly. Martin Coverton said that his mother and his brother "had their heads together and seemed full of glee". The date appears to have been just before Mr Romstock was asked to search for the new will.'

'And the Worlands? Did Martin or Lorette know anything about the Worlands?'

'Martin Coverton heard the name mentioned recently. He admitted to Mr Gillis that it troubled him, because in the days when your liaison with Mr Coverton was – ahem – somewhat in the public eye, Antony Coverton seemed to get information from the Worlands. Martin Coverton seemed to think this was "caddish" of his brother. So that is why I have invited the whole family to the conference – it might be helpful to us to have them all present, if the younger members are not precisely in agreement with their mother and Antony.'

'Very well.' But she hated the thought nevertheless.

On Friday she cleared her desk by lunchtime. She tried to eat a meal but she was in such a state of nervous dread that she could hardly swallow a mouthful. At two fifteen she was driven from the restaurant to Tadsley and Gower.

Niall was waiting for her in the hall of the building. He gave a little frown when he saw her. She was wearing a dark dress he had seen before with a jade necklace and earrings that heightened her pallor. 'Are you all right?' he asked.

'Do we have to do this, Niall?'

'You're not afraid of the Covertons?'

'I don't want to meet Diana Coverton. She dislikes me so much.'

'It'll be all right.'

'Have they arrived yet?'

'Oh, yes, all together in a taxi with Romstock. Their willingness to come to this meeting is really interesting. When Mr Tadsley suggested it, he thought they'd propose a day next week, but no, Romstock said he would consult Antony and came back suggesting Friday.'

'Do you think it means something?'

'I think it means they're worried. Which is another reason for you not to be afraid of them.'

He escorted her upstairs but instead of going into Mr Tadsley's office they passed it. He opened the door to a room which must have been the dining room when the house was a mansion. The main items of furniture were a long oval table, at one end of which sat Mr Romstock with the Coverton family on either side, Martin and Lorette on his right, Antony and Diana Coverton on his left. A secretary was seated two seats down from Diana so that she was halfway between either party.

The men rose as Ruth was shown in. Mr Tadsley was at the other end of the table and it was to his left that Niall ushered her.

Ruth sat. Down the length of the table, Diana Coverton was watching her. It was almost more than Ruth could do to raise her eyes and meet that piercing, avid glance.

A glance of hate.

Chapter Twenty-Six

If Ruth had suffered from the effects of the court case, they had taken their toll on Diana Coverton too.

She was still a beautiful woman, yet there was a haggard look to her now. Crowsfeet that the beauty salon couldn't hide had gathered at the side of her eyes. There were lines that seemed to draw down the sides of her mouth. Her dark eyes, always her best point, had a quality almost wolflike in its ferocity.

Today she was wearing no bright colours, no ostentatious style. Her intention seemed to be to impress the lawyers with her gravity and dependability. Her soft, fawn wool dress and matching hat were unrelieved by any touch of contrast. Only the rings on her third finger – the fine hoop of diamonds, the broad platinum band – had any brightness.

Her son was in a city suit: black jacket, pinstriped trousers. His tie was pearl grey.

They made a sombre pair. Yet there was about them an air, an atmosphere of muted triumph, sparkling expectation.

They think we've come here to admit defeat, thought Ruth. She drew in a deep breath. She would give in, hand over everything, if anyone could truly prove to her that it was what Ethan had wanted.

If not . . . If not, she would fight to the death to prevent his will being made the object of a fraud.

When they were all settled, Tadsley picked up the top paper from the pile in front of him. 'Ahem, we're here to discuss the matter of the document found at Miss Barnett's residence in Pouncey Square on Sunday last, 28 October.'

He looked over his glasses at his colleague, Romstock. 'I have not yet seen the document,' he went on gently. 'May I examine it, please?'

'Certainly.' Romstock handed a folder to the secretary, who passed it on to Niall, who handed it to his senior partner. Ruth felt an impulse of irritation. What a charade! Why couldn't they be open and brisk with each other?

The triple folder opened out flat. 'You will see,' explained Mr Romstock, 'that in the centre there is a document written on blue-edged writing paper, with three signatures at the foot – those of Ethan Coverton and of Mr and Mrs Worland. This is the document found on Sunday last at Pouncey Square.'

'Yes,' said Mr Tadsley, placing a finger on it.

'On the left-hand side you will see clipped to the folder another piece of paper of the same kind,' continued Mr Romstock, 'with the heading of the Pouncey Square address in a little box. The writing on the paper is that of Ethan Coverton and gives details of the alterations he discussed with me when he changed his original will. It was brought to my office by Mr Coverton himself and has been in his file since then.'

'I see,' Mr Tadsley said.

'On the right-hand side of the folder you will see a

typewritten letter signed by Alexander Gardener and some papers clipped to that. Gardener is a handwriting expert who often gives evidence in court concerning the validity or otherwise of signatures. You will see that he gives his expert opinion that both pieces of the blue-edged paper carry the handwriting of Ethan Coverton.'

'Thank you, Mr Romstock,' Tadsley said with exquisite courtesy, 'the writing is not in question. Miss Barnett accepts, and we therefore accept, that this is the handwriting of Ethan Coverton.'

There was a stir among the Coverton family, as if this wasn't quite what they had expected. Antony shifted uneasily. His mother frowned inquiry at him but he made no sign of attention. Martin Coverton and his sister seemed at a loss entirely.

'What we do not accept,' Mr Tadsley went on, 'is that the document we have here is a valid will.'

'Nonsense!' said Diana at once. 'My husband's intention is quite clear.'

'Mrs Coverton, forgive me. His intention is not clear to me. The wording states that he wishes to go back to the way things were and that his lawyers can put it into legal terms, but there is no indication as to what "things" he is talking about.'

'But the Worlands, who witnessed the document, have stated that they were told it was a will,' Romstock said.

'Forgive me once again, Mr Romstock. But what a testator believes to be a will is sometimes ruled invalid by the courts. My view is that, whatever Mr Coverton said to the Worlands, this is not a valid will.' He paused, then added, 'I imagine you have consulted with others on this point?'

It's like a dance, thought Ruth. One advances then

retreats, the other advances and retreats, and it's all dignity and politeness. She longed to cry, Get on with it! She wanted it to be over, to get away from the ill will she could feel like a blade of cold steel thrusting at her from Diana.

'I have shown the will to colleagues and learned colleagues.' Ruth took this to mean fellow lawyers and, perhaps, former judges of the Court of Probate. 'Opinion is not entirely unanimous but—'

'I should imagine it's far from unanimous,' Niall put in. It was the first time either of the lawyers had been interrupted, and Ruth could sense that the gloves were about to come off. 'For instance, did you tell your colleagues that the only witnesses were two people who have a considerable grudge against Miss Barnett?'

'Nothing is to be gained by disputing about the feelings of the witnesses.'

'Excuse me, sir, that is one of the key questions. We have only the Worlands' version of what happened. They say, for instance, that Mr Coverton called them to the garden room at a time when Miss Barnett was out of the house – the imputation being that he didn't want Miss Barnett to know he was making a new will.'

'Of course, he didn't want her to know,' Diana exclaimed. 'And that's why he hid it afterwards!'

'Mr Romstock,' Niall said, 'you testified in court that when you told Miss Barnett the contents of Mr Coverton's will, she was surprised.'

'Yes.'

'Very surprised?'

'Astounded.'

'You therefore took it that Mr Coverton had remained true to the intention he stated to you, not to tell Miss

480

Barnett about the will's contents?

'Yes.'

'Very well. Miss Barnett was in complete ignorance of the bequests Mr Coverton had made. Why then should he take pains to conceal the fact that he was altering them? If she didn't know of them in the first place?'

There was a little silence. Then Romstock let out a slow breath. He half shook his head. 'I'm getting old,' he said with sadness. 'That point had not occurred to me.'

'May I take it a stage further? Since Miss Barnett didn't know of the will by which she was made heiress to the Coverton fortune, and since there was therefore no need to keep a new will secret, we may ask ourselves why Mr Coverton is supposed to have hidden it in a plant pot instead of having the Worlands post it to his solicitor.'

Romstock made no reply. But Diana was ready with hers.

'This all depends on whether you believe that woman hadn't found out she was going to get it all. You can take it from me, she'd wheedle it out of Ethan. He was besotted by her—'

'Mrs Coverton,' Romstock said, giving her a little shake of the head. 'Please don't speak in such personal terms.'

'What do you expect? You and Mr Tadsley prose on as if it was all about noughts and crosses. I'm trying to get back what rightfully belongs to us! My son has been shamefully treated—'

'May we return to the discussion?' Tadsley said in a manner that quelled even Diana. 'My colleague has just pointed out that the story told by the Worlands is not entirely without its inconsistencies. I believe he wishes to go further.'

'I certainly do. I want to state here and now that I

believe the piece of paper found in the garden room under very odd circumstances is not a separate document intended as a will, but that it's part of a letter, taken out of context.'

Ruth heard Lorette make a startled sound. The girl gave a questioning glance towards Antony who ignored it stonily.

Ruth could see the folder containing the so-called will. Something about it, compared with the note that had been so long in Romstock's possession, struck her as odd. 'May I see the document?' she asked, making to draw the folder towards her.

'Don't let her touch it!' cried Diana. 'She'll tear it up!'

'Mother,' said her son Martin in embarrassment, 'do be reasonable.'

'The document will be quite safe, I feel sure,' Romstock remarked with old-world courtesy. 'Please, Miss Barnett, examine it.'

She unclipped it from the folder. It was soiled along the lines where it had been folded. 'It seems rather grubby,' she remarked.

'Naturally,' Romstock said. 'It has been down the side of a plant-pot holder for more than a year.'

But the stain was more than could result from dampness and soil. She held the piece of paper to her nose. 'It smells like car oil,' she said.

Niall turned his head quickly to look at Antony just a moment after she said the words. He saw a flash of panic cross his face.

Got you, he thought. Though how, he still didn't quite know.

'Car oil?' said Mr Tadsley in amazement, and took the paper from Ruth. He sniffed it. 'I'm not familiar with . . .

482

But certainly, yes. Mr Romstock?' He passed the folder along to Romstock who in his turn inspected the paper then sniffed it. He then held it up to the light.

'I would say there *is* grease or oil of some kind . . .'

'So what?' cried Diana in the tone one used to nincompoops. 'Everybody knows Ethan was mad about cars.'

'Excuse me, Mrs Coverton,' Niall said, thinking fast. 'We have to go back to the Worlands again. Their story is that they witnessed this so-called will and that it was then hidden by Mr Coverton in the plant container by his chaise longue.'

He waited. Diana, confused, hesitated. In the end it was Antony who said, 'Yes.'

'It remained there, hidden and unknown, until last Sunday?'

'Yes,' said Antony.

'Your father was too ill to go out. Never left the house after he came home from Sicily . . .'

'He did once,' Ruth interrupted, 'to have X-rays taken.'

'When was that?'

'The day after he came home from Sicily.'

'Long before this "will" was supposed to be written.'

'Oh, yes.'

'After that, did he go out?'

'No, he got fresh air by lying on the balcony with the windows wide open.'

'I believe,' Mr Romstock observed soberly, 'that the Worlands told me Mr Coverton could only get from his bed to the chaise longue with help. The implication was that he was more or less immobilized.'

'Can we agree that Ethan Coverton never left the house at Pouncey Square after that one excursion to the hospital for X-rays?'

Lorette and Martin Coverton, who both looked as if they longed to be elsewhere, nodded. Diana, still at a loss, said nothing. Antony said, 'Yes,' in a sullen voice.

'Miss Barnett, is there any motor oil in your house at Pouncey Square?'

'Of course not.'

Niall looked round the table. 'It does seem unlikely, doesn't it?' he said. 'There isn't any motor oil in most homes. Now, we agree that Ethan Coverton was unable to leave the house. How then did a streak of motor oil get on to the will he is supposed to have written in September of last year?'

There was a little exclamation of understanding from the secretary who was taking notes. Lorette Coverton put both her hands to her mouth and shook her head as if to deny something only she could hear. Martin Coverton, totally at sea, said, 'I don't understand . . .'

'It's perfectly simple,' said his mother, shrugging and shifting about in annoyance. 'It's not car oil, it's salad oil or embrocation or something like that.'

'It will be perfectly easy to have the oil analysed,' Mr Tadsley said, after a glance of consultation at Niall. 'There must be a great difference between motor oil and culinary oil.'

'But – but—' said Martin, still baffled.

'My contention,' said Niall to him in explanation, 'is that this document had nothing to do with changing your father's will. I think it's part of a letter written to someone who folded it up and put it in a grubby pocket.'

Lorette Coverton jumped to her feet, almost overturning her chair, and rushed out of the room.

'What are you saying?' Martin gasped. 'That the Worlands have been trying to pull a swindle?'

'*Someone* has been.'

'I think it would be a good idea to question the Worlands,' Mr Tadsley announced. 'They may wish to make a further deposition.'

'I've no doubt they'll wish to make a further deposition,' Niall agreed, to hammer home his senior partner's point. 'They could face a very serious charge if they knowingly presented this document as a will. And, of course, the police might want to think about whether or not the Coverton family were aware—'

'How dare you!' cried Diana. 'What are you saying? That we took part in a—'

'In a swindle, Mother,' Martin said. He stared at her. His face was pale. 'Did you really believe that scrap of paper was a will?'

'It *is* a will!' She had risen to her feet. 'Isn't it, Antony?' she appealed, throwing out a hand to him.

Antony made no reply to her. Instead, he turned to his solicitor. 'Do we have to listen to all this supposition? Anyone can make claims about its not being a will, that it's a part of something else . . .'

'My advice to you, Mr Coverton,' said Romstock with a heavy shake of the head, 'is to break off the discussion at this point.'

'But they're saying that we've been playing a trick!' Martin exclaimed. 'You've got to clear this up, Antony. Come on, sort it out – where did those people, what's their name, Worlands – where did they get that piece of paper?'

'I strongly advise you to say nothing more at this moment, Mr Coverton,' Romstock insisted to Antony. 'You asked me to act on your behalf and I am giving you good advice.'

But Martin kept up the protest. 'What you seem to be saying, Romstock, is that my brother . . .' He hesitated, glanced from the lawyer to Antony, and fell silent.

Tadsley held his peace. Niall murmured to Ruth, 'They're hoist with their own petard.' Ruth sat with her gaze averted from the Coverton family. She didn't want to witness the confusion and dismay that was growing upon them.

'I suggest,' said Mr Tadsley rather grandly, 'that we break off for a recess. My client and my colleagues and I will leave you, Mr Romstock, to confer with your party. Shall we say fifteen minutes? Then you can tell me whether you wish to resume or withdraw until a future date.'

'I think that would be useful, Mr Tadsley,' Romstock said. He sent a warning glance towards the members of the Coverton family. 'Fifteen minutes, then.'

'I will have some tea sent in,' Tadsley said, and nodded at the secretary who hurried out to carry out the order.

They were following her out when she turned back. 'Mr Tadsley,' she said in a low voice, 'the young lady seems very upset.'

They found Lorette sitting on a wooden chair in the passage with her handkerchief over her face in floods of tears.

'Lorette!' cried Ruth, hurrying up to her. 'Lorette, what on earth's the matter?'

'It's too awful. How could they – I'm so ashamed,' wept Lorette, her voice choked with sobs.

'My dear, don't go on like this,' said Ruth. She turned to the two men who were standing helpless behind her. 'Is there somewhere I could take her?'

'My secretary's room. Miss Payling, would you . . .?'

'Yes, sir.' She showed the way to a cubicle of a room with a typewriter and filing cabinets and very little else. 'I'll just go and see about the tea,' said Miss Payling, and made herself scarce.

Ruth thought it best not to force words out of the sobbing girl. She put an arm round her, soothed and patted her, and after about five minutes Lorette began to calm down.

'Feeling better?'

'I s-suppose s-so. But it was such a shock.'

'What was?'

'The letter.'

'Yes?'

'When they said – c-car oil – I knew at once it was the letter . . .'

'What letter?'

'The letter Dave sent to Antony.'

Chapter Twenty-Seven

Miss Payling came with two cups on a tray. Ruth thought it best to say nothing more to Lorette until she'd drunk some tea and recovered her composure.

Then she murmured, 'You said the letter was to Dave. You mean Dave Epps? Your father's mechanic?'

'Well, I— I don't really know for sure – but I think it's the letter Dave gave to Antony.'

'But why should Dave give Antony a letter in Ethan's – your father's handwriting?'

'Not to do anything dishonest!' Lorette flashed. A sob rose again but she checked it. 'Dave . . . You know Dave and I . . .'

'Yes,' agreed Ruth as the younger girl blushed and faltered. 'Dave spoke to me about his plans a while ago.'

'He did? I didn't know that.' The blue eyes were thoughtful. 'Poor darling, he's so desperate to get something together by way of a living. I keep telling him it doesn't matter, *I've* got money. But he feels – he feels— Oh, men are so ridiculous!'

Ruth couldn't think it was entirely ridiculous in Dave not to want to live off his wife's investments. But this wasn't the moment to try to make Lorette Coverton face the economic facts of life. 'How does the letter

489

come into it?' she prompted.

'Well, as far as I can gather, while Dave and my father were in Sicily for that car race, they had a bit of a falling-out. I don't know what it was about,' Lorette said with a sigh.

Ruth thought she could imagine. She recalled how Ethan had had one of his little spats of jealousy over the way Dave spoke to her.

'They had a falling-out?'

'Yes, and so Daddy told Dave he wasn't going to invest any money in the racing-engine firm that Dave wanted to set up. But then he thought better of it and scribbled a note and sent it to Dave at his hotel. Then there was that awful accident . . .' Her words trailed off. When at length she resumed, her voice was laden with self-reproach. 'Goodness knows what you must have thought of us, not coming to see him when he was so ill – not even telephoning. It's difficult to explain. You see, Mummy can make things look so awful. And we weren't really close to him, Martin and I . . .'

'Don't upset yourself by going over things like that,' Ruth soothed. 'It was all a big misunderstanding.'

'Oh, yes, when we saw how Mummy behaved in court over the will – I can tell you, it was a terrific shock to Martin and me! I mean, it hadn't ever occurred to us to doubt what Mummy said. Well, at least, I think Martin had his doubts . . .'

'So Dave had this note from your father and he kept it?' said Ruth, trying to get back to the point, for she knew the lawyers would want to resume the conference.

'Well, yes, but not intentionally, you know, it was just in his overalls when he got back from Sicily, I think. Anyway, when Dave couldn't get anyone at all to come up with the money for the engineering firm, he said he thought he'd try Antony as a last resort, because the letter was a sort of a promise to invest. You know?'

'But he knew Antony and your father didn't get on.'

'But he'd *tried* everything else!' Lorette cried in despair. 'I told him it was no use, but he said the letter promised to make the investment. He said it was like a contract. He said Daddy wanted it all put back the way it was before.'

'Ah!' cried Ruth.

'Yes,' said Lorette, nodding her blonde head and sighing. 'Your lawyer mentioned that, didn't he? "Going back to the way things were before" —I'm not quick on the uptake, you know. I didn't realize . . . It was only when they said about the motor oil. Of course, that came from the pocket of Dave's overalls. It's the note Daddy wrote for Dave in Sicily. It must be.'

'Yes,' Ruth said. 'And then, of course, he was so ill, and in any case Dave went home with the remains of the car, to see if he could put it together again. And then I suppose it went out of Ethan's head because – well – he *was* ill, Lorette, and it took him all his time to pull himself up.'

'Poor Daddy,' Lorette sighed. 'Oh, I *wish* I hadn't been so beastly to him. Well, after Daddy died and *you* said you wouldn't invest, Dave was at his wits' end. He tried everyone he knew in the motor-racing game but no one would take it on. So as a last resort he wrote to Antony and enclosed the letter as evidence that my father had intended to back him.'

'And Antony took the second page and got the Worlands to add their names at the end. Then they slipped it in the jar beside the chair where Ethan used to sit, ready for Mr Romstock to find it.'

Lorette began to cry again. 'How could he?' she sobbed. 'Oh, how could he? And Mummy too – do you think Mummy knew it wasn't a real will?'

'I'm sure she didn't know,' said Ruth. She believed it – Diana's behaviour had been that of a woman who felt sure she was in the right.

The whole idea had been Antony's. Disappointment over his inheritance, resentment at Ruth's taking his place and perhaps also at her rejection of his advances, humiliation over being demoted and sent away – one thing on top of another had driven him to the point where he was willing to use fraud to get the better of her.

And he had been shrewd enough to see that she would participate in her own defeat. She *knew* the handwriting in the 'will' to be Ethan's. She would have accepted it as a legal will on that ground. Had Antony been just a little cleverer, a little more subtle, she would have stepped aside because she could have been made to believe it was the wish of her dead lover.

Not now. Nothing in the world would ever make her let Ethan's company fall into hands like those. A fraudster, a cheat and a liar – he was unfit to step into Ethan's shoes.

When Lorette had mopped her eyes, they went together out into the passage. Niall and his senior were already there, glancing at their watches. 'Time is more than up,' Niall urged.

'Lorette has something she wants to tell you,' said Ruth.

'Yes?' The two men looked at Lorette in expectation.

'That piece of writing paper . . .'

'Yes?'

'I think it's part of a note my father wrote to David Epps in Sicily just before the car crash.'

'What!'

'Can you prove that?' Niall said quickly.

'No, I never saw it. But Dave told me he was sending it to Antony, and it sounds like the same note. Daddy was patching up a quarrel he'd had and promising to stay as a backer in Dave's new business.'

'We-ell—' sighed Niall.

There was a long hesitation.

'I think it's over,' Mr Tadsley said. 'If there's any idea of keeping on with this absurd claim I think we need only suggest contacting Mr Epps.'

'Quite.' Niall looked grimly delighted. As he ushered Ruth back into the conference room, he murmured in her ear, 'You can sue Antony for every penny he possesses if you want to!'

Once more they settled themselves round the oval table. Mr Romstock looked extremely weary.

'I think it right to make a statement on the situation,' he began. 'My clients and I have had a talk. I have not asked them any further questions on the provenance of the document in the folder. But I have made it clear to them that I do not believe it to be a will made under the circumstances described by the Worlands, and that I cannot represent them in any such claim.'

'We concur in your view,' Mr Tadsley announced. 'Further, we believe that by inviting Mr David Epps to join us we could clear up the matter of how that document came into the possession of Mr Antony Coverton.'

Antony drew in a sharp breath. Martin Coverton said in bewilderment, 'David Epps? Lorette's boyfriend? How does he come into it?'

'Who is David Epps?' Diana Coverton demanded. 'Lorette, isn't he that dreadful young man I forbade you to see?'

'Oh, Mummy,' groaned Lorette.

Mr Tadsley waited. Antony began to speak then changed his mind.

'Shall we telephone to Mr Epps?' Tadsley inquired.

'That won't be necessary,' Antony said.

'Antony, what's the meaning of all this?' his mother demanded. 'You're not just giving in?'

'Mother, there's nothing more to be done.'

'But we can make the Worlands explain—'

'It's nothing to do with the Worlands.'

'How can you say that? They told us about the new will.'

'Mrs Coverton, I must, as your lawyer, insist that you accept the facts,' interrupted Mr Romstock. 'That piece of paper is not a will. The Worlands can claim what they like, but they almost certainly did not witness it in the presence of your husband. It came to light somehow *outside* the house in Pouncey Square after his death and they then wrote their signatures on it for reasons I prefer not to go into.'

'You mean they . . . they tried to swindle us?'

'Someone tried to swindle someone,' Niall took it up.

'But that's outrageous!' cried Diana. 'How dare they make fools of us like that! Coming to us with a tale that sounded so noble and high-minded . . .'

'I believe if we were to speak to the Worlands with a certain amount of severity, we might find that they did not in fact approach you, Mrs Coverton,' Mr Tadsley remarked. 'It's more likely that they were sent for.'

'Nonsense!'

'It isn't nonsense,' Ruth said. 'I don't think you'll bother to deny that you were paying them all the time they worked for me, to spy on us and report back to you. You know the Worlands very well.'

Diana didn't bother to deny it. 'That's all gone by,' she said, shrugging it off. 'But why should we send for them now? How could we know they had a new will?'

'Mrs Coverton,' said her lawyer, 'I advise you not to ask any more questions on this matter nor to argue the case any further. I have given you my view. The piece of writing paper is not a will and was not witnessed as such by the Worlands. That is my opinion. My urgent advice is that you withdraw any claims based on it.'

'But – but—'

'My God,' gasped Martin. 'I've just twigged! What you're saying is that someone put the Worlands up to it! And since Mother seems to be in a fog, it could only have been—' He broke off abruptly, aware at last of where he was heading. 'My God,' he said again, staring at his brother.

'I am not saying anything of the kind,' Romstock insisted, colouring. 'My sole aim is to bring this meeting to an end by getting the Coverton family to withdraw any claims based on the so-called will.'

'That is good advice, Mr Antony,' Tadsley put in. 'Please listen to it.'

'Hold on. It's not quite as easy as that,' said Niall, thumping the table with his fist. 'All kinds of aspersions have been thrown at Miss Barnett over this paper—'

'No, Niall, please.'

'Don't let them get away with it, Ruth! They deserve all they get!'

'My young colleague is quite right,' Mr Tadsley

remarked with what looked like a smothered smile. 'If you wish to give me any instructions on the point, Miss Barnett—'

'Not only that, but there's a legal fraud here that ought to be investigated—'

'Stop it, stop it,' begged Ruth, as distressed as any member of the Coverton family. 'Do you think Ethan would have wanted this? It's all got to stop, *now!*'

Mr Tadsley allowed a moment to go by so that emotion could die away. 'It's a very generous view,' he observed. 'I'm sure you agree, Mr Romstock.'

'I do indeed, and I urge my clients to agree also.'

'Agree? Agree to what?' Diana cried, looking from one to the other, understanding only that somehow she had lost and furious at the thought. 'Are you implying that *we* have done something wrong? What's the point you're making, Romstock?'

'If I must spell it out for you, Mrs Coverton, I'm saying that Miss Barnett is making no claim against you for damages over what you have said and done to her in your attempt to promote that paper as a legal will. She also seems to be refusing to take her suspicions to the Fraud Squad, where a warrant might very well be issued on the evidence that could be collected. All in all, I hope you'll withdraw from your adversarial position, apologize, and allow us to leave as soon as possible.'

'Why, you – you— A warrant? Against *me*? How dare you!'

'Oh, give it a rest, Mother,' sighed Martin. 'Your financial genius of a son has landed you right in the soup. Well, I for one have had enough. I'm going. Are you coming, Lorette?'

'Yes, yes, wait for me.'

'Lorette!' shouted her mother. 'Don't you dare walk out without my permission.'

'I'm going, Mummy. I should have done it a long time ago.' With that Lorette hurried after her brother. The door closed on them.

Diana, aghast, stared at the closed door. Antony clambered to his feet. 'Come on,' he said.

'But – but—'

'Come on. It's over.'

'I don't understand you. The will . . . the Worlands witnessed it . . .'

'No, they didn't. Come on.'

'But, Antony . . .'

'Your son will explain it to you later,' Niall said, opening the door again to usher them out. And under his breath added, 'And I don't envy him the job.'

Mr Romstock had risen and was gathering up his documents. Ruth saw the oil-stained piece of paper about to be closed up in the folder. 'What are you going to do with the note?' she inquired.

'What?' He reopened the folder. 'Oh, return it to Mr Epps, if it really is his property. Have you his address?' He felt in his waistcoat pocket for his fountain pen.

'I'll give it to him, if you like,' said Ruth.

Niall made a little sound of dissent and shook his head. 'Don't handle that note, Ruth. If Mrs Coverton got to hear of it she'd make it sound like collusion or something of the kind.'

'Very well, then, you take it.'

'But Mr Romstock could just as easily return it—'

'Niall, are you my solicitor or not? I want you to take that note and return it to Dave Epps at the address I'll give you, and at the same time make an appointment to see him.'

'You want me to see Dave Epps?' Niall said, frowning in perplexity.

'A contract is a contract. Ethan promised to underwrite the racing-engine project and I intend to carry out his promise. See him and get some figures from him.'

'My dear young lady,' Mr Tadsley said, shaking his head at her, 'there's no need for you to carry out every jot and tittle of Ethan's undertakings.'

'But I want to.'

Mr Romstock was smiling as he unfastened the oil-stained paper and handed it to Niall. 'Now I understand why Ethan thought so highly of you, my dear,' he said, and made for the door.

Tadsley made a point of shaking hands warmly with him. 'Don't take it to heart, my friend,' he murmured. 'All of us have a few fools and a few villains among our clients.'

'But usually not both in the same body,' Romstock sighed. 'Well, let us hope that if we meet again it may be in pleasanter circumstances.'

'Indeed, indeed.' Murmuring jovially, Tadsley escorted Romstock out of the room and down to the hall for his coat.

Ruth remained standing in the conference room. Niall went round switching on lamps against the onset of the November evening. Miss Payling gathered up pencils and shorthand notebooks and then with a smile at Ruth left for her own little office.

'What next?' Niall inquired.

'About Antony?' said Ruth. 'I shall write to him telling him his services are no longer required and offering him a decent severance settlement.'

'I didn't mean that. I meant, what are you doing this evening?'

'Going home.'

'And after that? Don't say having dinner!'

'Well, I am.' She was smiling a little.

'Alone? Don't you think you ought to go out and celebrate?'

She shook her head, half amused at his outlook and half caught by the drama that had just ended. 'I don't know if it's much to celebrate, finding out that Antony was ready to do something totally crooked.'

'Look, Antony isn't your responsibility. His mother and his own silly ambitions have made him what he is.'

'But he was pushed to being underhanded because of me.'

'Oh, all right, spend the rest of your life feeling guilty about it, if you must. But at least come out and have dinner with me tonight first.'

This time she laughed outright. 'You're such a cracker-jack!' she said. 'Nothing ever gets you down!'

'Not if I can help it. My view is, every silver lining is in the cloud for a reason, so why not use it? And once nasty things have been put behind us, why go on letting them upset you?'

'True enough.'

'So will you come out to dinner this evening?'

'I don't think so, Niall.'

'Why not?'

'I'm tired.'

He couldn't argue against that. She had every right to be tired after the gruelling afternoon they had just gone through.

'Tomorrow night, then,' he said.

'Tomorrow night there's a party of buyers from Spain to entertain.'

'The next night, then.'

'The next night's Sunday.'

'Don't you eat dinner on Sunday?'

'Well – yes, I suppose I do.'

'Sunday evening then. About seven thirty?'

'No, really.'

'Why not?'

'I don't know why not. I just don't feel . . . I don't know.'

'Righto, then,' he agreed. 'Not tonight or tomorrow or Sunday. One night next week? Next month? Leap Year? Just say when.'

She laughed and headed out the door.

Niall sighed to himself.

Ruth went straight home from the solicitors' offices. Once she had had her bath and changed she began to feel less wound up. She was eager to speak to her grandmother when she rang at about seven.

'Will you accept a reverse-charge call from Freshton in Surrey?' the operator inquired.

'Yes, certainly.' There was the usual clunking and clicking then the operator's voice saying, 'You're thr-r-rough, caller.'

'Is that you, Ruthie?' Mrs Barnett cried. 'How'd it go?'

'It went fine, grandma. Antony and his mother withdrew all claims and the whole thing's over.'

'Just like that?'

'Well, no – it took us all afternoon. But it was more or less proved they'd been up to no good, and they had to admit defeat.'

'Well done, girl!'

'Oh, it wasn't me, Grandma. It was Niall Gillis who did most of it.'

'A clever young man, he seems.'

'Oh, yes, marvellously clever. I can't understand why he sticks in an office doing family law – he ought to be a barrister.'

'Mebbe he doesn't want to pootle about in a wig and a gown. Always look silly to me, they do.'

'Oh, I don't know,' mused Ruth, 'Niall might look quite good in a wig and gown.'

Oh, might he? thought Mrs Barnett. 'I suppose you won't be seeing much of him now all this problem's been solved.'

'What?' There was surprise and perhaps distress in her granddaughter's voice. 'I hadn't thought of that.'

'Lucky you happened on him, to sort out all this Worland business.'

'Oh, I didn't just happen on him,' said Ruth. And then in a more cheerful tone, 'Of course! He'll be handling the contract for Dave's new firm, and then, you see, Tadsley and Gower have always done all the legal work for Covelco.'

'So you could be seeing him again.'

'I suppose I could.'

Mrs Barnett thought it was time to take another tack. 'Your Granddad says to tell you if you feel like a breath of country air, the trees are still a picture in Homestead Wood.'

'That might be nice,' said Ruth. 'I could drive down on Sunday.'

'Yes, why don't you? I'll do a picnic basket – we could have our sandwiches by the brook.'

'That would be lovely. I wouldn't stay too long, though.'

'No, of course, you want to be back for a good night's

sleep 'cos of getting to the office in the morning.'

'Ye-es.'

'What?'

'Niall asked me out to dinner on Sunday night.'

'Oh, I see, you want to be back in time for that.'

'Well, no. I refused the invitation.'

'Why did you do that?' her grandmother said, although she knew the reason.

'It's too soon, Grandma,' Ruth said, in a low voice.

'Yes, I understand. "For everything there is a season . . ." that's it, isn't it? "A time to weep and a time to laugh, a time to mourn and a time to dance." '

'That's it, Grandma.'

'But, Ruthie, you see, the Good Book is telling us there that we should be as ready for happiness as for grief.'

'I understand that, Grandma. It just isn't my time yet.'

'All right, dear, you know best.' Mrs Barnett, who had lived with a difficult man all her life, knew when to shift her ground. 'By the way, remember Peter Graystock that has those funny pale brown cats? Hanged if someone hasn't told him they're a special breed and he's putting 'em in the Cat Show!'

'He isn't!'

'Yes, he is. And little Muriel Simpson's passed the qualifying exam for Bledstowe School.'

'That's splendid.'

'If you come down on Sunday, you could give Mrs Simpson some tips about where to buy the school uniform – it's some special London syop.'

'I'd be glad to.'

'I say,' said Grandma, as if it had just occurred to her, 'how about asking that Mr Gillis to come down with you? Seeing as he asked you out and you've said no, this would be a sort of family thank you for all he did at the office conference.'

'Ask him to Freshton?'

'He might like a breath of country air. And it's not like going out with him of an evening – more informal, if you get my meaning.'

'I don't know if he'd like it.'

'You could always ring and ask.'

'He probably wouldn't want to.'

'I suppose not. Still, no harm in asking. And I'd really like to say a word of thanks to him myself for all he's done for you. Or,' said Grandma, 'if you'll give me his address I could write to him. But it's not so friendly, is it?'

'Well . . . All right . . . I might ring him later.'

They passed the time in small talk until Mrs Monash put her head in the door to say she was about to serve the meal. Then Ruth and her grandmother said goodbye.

Mrs Barnett replaced the receiver in the phone box, pulled her wool coat around her, and set off down the lane to her home. Nights getting chilly, time to get out my winter coat, she thought.

Niall Gillis. A nice lad. It was easy to tell that he thought the world of Ruthie.

And there seemed more than a hint that Ruth thought something of him, too. Marvellously clever. Ought to be a barrister.

If only it could be, thought her grandmother as she trudged along the leaf-spattered lane. If only the child could find someone to fill the terrible space left in her life by Ethan Coverton.

Ah, for all he had loved her – and Mrs Barnett had no doubt now that it was so – he'd been no friend to little Ruth Barnett. Filling her heart and mind with a passion that still possessed her even though he was gone.

What the child needed was a simpler love, a more normal man-and-woman attraction.

This Niall Gillis, for instance. He had proved a staunch friend. And you could tell he was trying to become something more.

He was clever, Ruth said. But even the cleverest man might need a little help.

Mrs Barnett thought to herself that she might find the chance for a quiet word with Niall Gillis if he came on Sunday. She would say that she appreciated all he'd done for her granddaughter and hoped the two of them might go on being friends.

And somehow she might manage to let him know that time had to pass, that Ruth's grieving had to wear itself away gradually like a leaf turning brown in the autumn or an echo dying in the folds of the hill. A difficult thing to explain to an impatient young man, yet Mrs Barnett sensed that Niall Gillis would harken to her words.

Ah, young folk, young folk . . . You saw them rush headlong into life and you longed to cry, 'Wait, wait, that's not the way!' But sometimes in the end those eager, flying feet found the right path. And if she had anything to do with it, she would gently urge Ruth along that road, a road leading at last to fulfilment and joy.

As usual, she walked round to the back of the cottage and stepped into the cosy kitchen.

'Our girl all right then?' her husband inquired.

'Yes, Roger, I think she's going to be all right,' said Mrs Barnett, smiling.

504

HER FATHER'S CHILD

Tessa Barclay

Erica has had an idyllic girlhood as the daughter of a successful shipping magnate, Lindon Tregarvon; launched into society as a debutante, she has made a glittering catch, a Foreign Office high flyer.

But even at twenty, one's golden years can be shortlived. A visit from the Fraud Squad sends the Tregarvon empire and Erica's life spiralling out of control.

Yet Erica is her father's child. She is determined to make new lives for herself and her mother using their talent for bridge, which leads to the offer of work on a luxury liner. But, despite her success, Erica knows she must reveal the truth about the Tregarvon scandal and discovers a secret that lies murderously close to home . . .

FICTION / SAGA 0 7472 4577 0

A selection of bestsellers from Headline

LAND OF YOUR POSSESSION	Wendy Robertson	£5.99	☐
TRADERS	Andrew MacAllen	£5.99	☐
SEASONS OF HER LIFE	Fern Michaels	£5.99	☐
CHILD OF SHADOWS	Elizabeth Walker	£5.99	☐
A RAGE TO LIVE	Roberta Latow	£5.99	☐
GOING TOO FAR	Catherine Alliott	£5.99	☐
HANNAH OF HOPE STREET	Dee Williams	£4.99	☐
THE WILLOW GIRLS	Pamela Evans	£5.99	☐
MORE THAN RICHES	Josephine Cox	£5.99	☐
FOR MY DAUGHTERS	Barbara Delinsky	£4.99	☐
BLISS	Claudia Crawford	£5.99	☐
PLEASANT VICES	Laura Daniels	£5.99	☐
QUEENIE	Harry Cole	£5.99	☐

All Headline books are available at your local bookshop or newsagent, or can be ordered direct from the publisher. Just tick the titles you want and fill in the form below. Prices and availability subject to change without notice.

Headline Book Publishing, Cash Sales Department, Bookpoint, 39 Milton Park, Abingdon, OXON, OX14 4TD, UK. If you have a credit card you may order by telephone – 01235 400400.

Please enclose a cheque or postal order made payable to Bookpoint Ltd to the value of the cover price and allow the following for postage and packing:

UK & BFPO: £1.00 for the first book, 50p for the second book and 30p for each additional book ordered up to a maximum charge of £3.00.

OVERSEAS & EIRE: £2.00 for the first book, £1.00 for the second book and 50p for each additional book.

Name ....

Address ....

....

....

If you would prefer to pay by credit card, please complete:
Please debit my Visa/Access/Diner's Card/American Express (delete as applicable) card no:

Signature .... Expiry Date ....